THE SOL SAGA: BOOK TWO

RETALIATION

JAMES FOX

RETALIATION

www.dawnrunnerpress.com

Published by Dawnrunner Press
Cover by Vivid Covers

Edited by Kaitlin Ens & COLProofreading Service

ISBN-10: 1954344244
ISBN-13: 978-1954344242

0 9 8 7 6 5 4 3 2 1

Produced in the United States of America

CONTENTS

CHAPTER 1

LISA COLT FELT that familiar lurch in her stomach as the atmospheric vessel arched its way toward the Martian surface. Unfortunately, she couldn't blame her discomfort on a rough flight. It was nerves.

Not only was this her first *actual* assignment as a pilot in the Protectorate, but it was her first *command*. Her first real mission. Aside from that, she couldn't shake the feeling that something *bigger* was going on around her. The entire trip to Mars had been full of unsettled feelings about what had happened to Spalding.

Nothing about that situation made any sense. That just wasn't the person she had come to idolize. If there was one person in the system who knew that Spalding was incapable of doing what he had been accused of, summarily tried and excommunicated for, it was Lisa.

That didn't amount to much when it all boiled down to it.

There just wasn't much she could do to help. Here she was on her first fully activated deployment, a direct assignment no less. She should be over the moon ecstatic! So then, why was she so somber and anxious?

Of course, she should be nervous. Anyone in her position should be. She hadn't the foggiest idea what that command even was yet. Which was abnormal, right? Shouldn't she have been clued in before being deployed?

The craft lurched so hard that it jarred her neck a bit. That snapped her out of her head enough to take in her surroundings. Thoughts of Spalding could wait.

Pilots, marines, and support personnel littered the three rows of three seats in little clutches of units. Everyone with a window seat had their faces glued to what was happening outside. Being in the aisle, Lisa couldn't see anything. Especially not with Marconi's prominent figure blocking her best vantage.

"What a shitshow!" Leave it to Marconi to summarize the room's mood in the crassest and most obnoxious way possible. He cleared his throat loudly, chuckled, and glanced around the shuttle at the other occupants.

"What's going on out there?" Lisa asked as loudly as she dared. The wind screeching around them provided some ambient noise, but she preferred to be careful with the pressure changes wreaking havoc on her hearing.

Still chuckling, Marconi called over his shoulder, "Craft all over the place, no organization or proximity protocols being followed. It's a mess."

That didn't sound good.

One of the other pilots they had met while boarding had said that citizens were fleeing Mars by the thousands. The trip from Luna to Mars was relatively short by usual standards; it just so happened they were not in an advantageous orbital cycle when they launched. So, unfortunately, this trip had taken almost three times as long as it should've. Who knew what had happened during those three weeks?

As the pilot engaged the retro engines, slowing their descent, everyone's head suddenly jerked back sharply into their chairbacks. It was simultaneously invigorating and nauseating.

Lisa hoped it was never something she took for granted. She loved flying, more than anything, and wanted it to keep that same *thrill* it had her first time locking into a cockpit.

Amber light flashed, two quick pulses, and everyone began readying their gear to disembark. This was something they had trained repeatedly. Freshly landed troop carriers made excellent prone targets. It was essential to get the hell off the shuttle as fast and orderly as possible. Well, that's what they had screamed at them in training, at least.

A sudden feeling of weightlessness pushed her heart up into her throat as the thrusters overcame gravity briefly, then a soft *thud* reverberated through the hull.

"Touchdown," Azarov chirped. "Welcome to Mars."

Marconi just rolled his eyes.

When Lisa didn't respond, Azarov leaned over and asked quietly, "Hey, you okay?"

"Sure. Why?" Lisa did her best to sound nonchalant.

Azarvos studied her a moment, then shrugged, leaning back. "I don't know, you've just been extra quiet this trip. I figured you'd be pissing your tights by now."

The amber light came on and then flashed to green. Everyone stood and began an orderly march out the lowering rear ramp.

Even Azarov recognized something was up with her. She must really be wearing it on her sleeve! Try as she might, she just couldn't shake the feeling like she was missing something important. Round and round, her thoughts spiraled back to Spalding and what had happened to the Legion.

Of course, it wasn't fair for her to dwell so much on them. Not like she had been a member of the legendary squad. Why should she care so much that it kept her upset *for this long?* Immediately her mind began to list off the reasons. For starters, they were good people. An insanely talented group of pilots. And, probably most importantly, their deaths had left a lot of questions lingering. Not all of them about their de facto leader, Jonathan Spalding. Aldis may have held the rank, but Spalding held their hearts.

Now he was being blamed for their deaths.

Nothing added up.

At the top of the ramp, a marine was rapidly checking respirators. While the air on Mars was *mostly* breathable, it lost much of its atmosphere to space. The process had been slowed with some fancy chemistry, a kind of gas suspension mixture that acted as a "cap" on the lower atmosphere. Unfortunately, with current technology, it could not be completed. The lower pressure made exertion challenging. Even walking at a brisk pace without properly balanced gases could be dangerous.

Once hers had been given the thumbs up to proceed, Lisa got her first look at the docks of Hellas. Built into the rim of an impact crater, the outer ring hosted a variety of massive large-scale transport ships, while the inner ring had clusters of small platforms. The shuttle had landed on one of those small, suspended platforms.

The roar and screeching of the incoming craft were painfully loud. The soldiers were all hustling toward doors at a small building directly across from where the shuttle was positioned. If nothing else, she hoped it shielded her from the noise.

Marconi and Azarov flanked her as they entered the building amid a healthy stream of Protectorate soldiers. Thankfully, when the door closed behind her, it shut out most of the noise. The air had a heavier feeling to it, and from the looks of it, she assumed it safe to remove her mask.

The gate was a chaotic mess. Not at the military precision she had anticipated from years of training at the Academy. The three of them broke off from the steady stream of passing soldiers in an attempt to get their bearings.

"This had better not be some bullshit assignment." Marconi glared at her.

It took everything she had to not sigh right in his face.

Rather than make a scene arguing with her wingman within

minutes of arriving at their first official deployment, she clamped her teeth together and refused to take the bait.

Nothing had been the same between them since the encounter in her room. That night he had stormed into her room, obviously drunk, and looking for a fight. That had been the only time she had truly been scared of his grumpy tantrums. That had been something else entirely. Something far more dangerous. Lisa had been too stunned to put up any defense for herself against his claims of preferential treatment. Everything she had was from hard work *despite* being an Admiral's daughter, not because of that fact. Her imagination ran wild with what might've happened if she *had* put up a fight that night, in bed naked as she was with him inebriated and belligerent.

Sure, Marconi had always been an asshole. Hell, it was something he was proud of. Egotistical, a real prima-donna, and cranky as a bear with hemorrhoids, but at least he had been definitively *on her side.* Lisa wasn't entirely sure that was true any longer, or maybe it never had been. There was no reason to suspect he didn't have her back when it mattered, in combat, but it seemed like he wanted nothing to do with her in any other capacity. He'd do his duty; that was it.

Azarov glanced between them dubiously. To the best of her knowledge, Marconi hadn't divulged the cause of the tension between them. She sure as hell wasn't about to! So, it was just this awkward thing they had to deal with.

The really shitty thing was, she knew it didn't really matter. It bothered her that someone in her squad effectively hated her. But did it change anything for her? No, in fact, it probably made her life easier. At least he wasn't trying to get into her pants every thirty seconds anymore. A blessing in disguise, maybe?

Odds were it *would,* in fact, be another bullshit assignment. Regrettably, that's what her life had devolved into: chasing one bullshit pipe dream to the other.

Hopefully, whatever the assignment turned out to be, it

would allow her enough time to do some snooping about what had happened to Spalding. There was no way she was going to be an efficient pilot with this constant distraction.

"Well, let's find out where we're supposed to check-in." She hefted her pack on her shoulder and wound her way back into the stream of people.

"I swear to God if this…"

Whatever other vitriolic statement was going to be said was lost in a sudden flash of searing hot white light. A gust of hot air and stinging bits of debris peppered her face and threw her to the ground. Right on its heels was a sound so loud it tore away her ability to hear, replaced with a high-pitched keening.

Lisa gagged, her vision swam wildly, the world tilting and blurring.

Something clutched at her ankle; she kicked at it, blindly lashing out.

Sounds started to return thickly, like they were in the room a few doors down, not right in front of her face.

A dark smear appeared in her vision.

Then pain flashed across her cheek.

It was only then she realized her mouth had been open. Had she been screaming?

"Lisa!" It sounded so strange.

Reality came crashing back. Her vision cleared enough to make out Azarov and Marconi trying to pick her up from the ground. The former had several small cuts on his face. The latter had a gash across his lips that was absolutely gushing blood. The sounds were still muffled, but they were somewhat intelligible now.

"What happened?" Her voice sounded weird, even in her own head.

"Bomb!" Marconi shouted not two feet from her face and pointed off to his right.

Lisa followed his finger, and the dark smear she had seen

resolved into a roiling column of ink-black smoke arcing away from them.

The column was massive. The damage to the docks had to be substantial.

All around her, men and women were tending to small injuries or watching that visceral reminder they were here for a reason, not just sightseeing.

"Shit." It was all she could manage.

Azarov nodded. "Shit."

Marconi shouldered his pack from the ground and walked away, rubbing his hand and wincing.

—

The briefing room was empty, except for her squad. While Marconi and Azarov had been with her unit at the Academy, the other two pilots were new to her. Pleasantries were few and far between, but Lisa did notice they eyed her with a familiar speculative intensity. She could almost read their thoughts. *How old is she? Who does she know or blow to get this kind of promotion so quick?*

Lisa had been getting those looks her entire life. One of the perks of being the daughter of a high-ranking military official. It pissed her off. Of course, it couldn't be that she was the best-damned pilot currently in the Protectorate Fleet. Nope, it had to be because of Mommy.

Every step along the way had to be proven. It was fine; she was used to it.

Something caught her eye out of her peripheral vision, and she extracted a clump of insulation twisted up in her light copper hair. Even though it had been hours since the explosion had welcomed them to the Martian docks, her body still ached from the force of it.

In the three weeks they had traveled, the situation on Mars

had deteriorated to almost daily violence. Some events, like the bombing of the docks, were more significant than others. Lisa had overheard a few members of the deck crew talking down a hallway, sharing information about the 'Redarms.' What the Protectorate were calling the Rebels. Since Mars was not officially in a state of open rebellion, they were not supposed to refer to the criminals as rebels. It made sense, in an odd kind of way. Calling them rebels lent a certain gravity to their actions, whereas Redarms had almost a derogatory connotation.

The door thundered open with the slap of metal on metal, and it caused Lisa to just about jump out of her skin. Thankfully, hers wasn't the only ass to leave a seat. She even caught Marconi muttering under his breath something about "archaic technology and swinging doors." Not that she had seen him jump. It would've been worth it, then.

Everyone stood at attention as their unit's command structure marched in. Lisa knew just about everyone who was anyone in the Fleet, thanks to her family history, but nobody here rang any bells.

The Captain marched right up to the front, with no preamble whatsoever.

"All right, sit down. We've got a lot to cover."

They did so in unison. The lights lowered and a tactical map of Hellas City illuminated the wall behind and to his left, and on the adjacent wall was a slowly rotating globe of Mars.

"It's an absolute clusterfuck out there. We have some major catastrophe every day. MARCOM seems to think these are isolated, unrelated, random acts of violence. It certainly feels related to me."

A few pilots unfamiliar to Lisa exchanged some glances in the gallery, and there was some uncomfortable shifting in seats before he continued.

"The orders coming down the pipe for us are as follows." While he spoke, he began to indicate different areas on the flattened map. Designations for the various deployments sprang to life where he tapped. "There doesn't appear to be any centralized point of attack. Infrastructure appears to be the largest concentration of targets, but they've also hit hospitals, agricultural production decks, and a few residential neighborhoods. CENTCOM is compiling data to try to determine a point of origin. We're going to increase our ground-level protection of critical infrastructure. The docks being hit today was a major blow."

Several areas of interest were illuminated on the Hellas tactical map. Then he moved over to the global map.

"The main focus of our suppression will be in orbit by way of a blockade. Nothing comes in or out of Mars airspace without our inspection, permission, and escort." A multitude of illuminated shapes sprang to life in orbit around the globe.

Lisa pursed her lips thoughtfully.

A blockade was a good idea at first glance from a strategic standpoint. Reduce or completely eliminate the resources on the ground, and eventually, the steam would come out of the militants. Hard to put a fight when you were starving to death or lacking proper oxygen levels. It was a long-game solution. In the short term, however, it was much more likely to drive sympathy to their enemies. That, in turn, could make the blockade or ground-level efforts significantly more complicated.

It was a calculated long-vision plan which focused entirely on the desired outcome, with a callous disregard for the human life component.

The plan had the stink of her mother all over it.

It was mildly infuriating that she couldn't seem to escape Admiral Maureen Colt. Only mildly because, well, she *was* in the Protectorate and her mother just happened to be in charge of the Fleet. So, it stood to reason they'd cross paths relatively often. Still, she could be frustrated about it, couldn't she?

There had been no direct communication between them

since that last moment in her bunkroom on Luna. For which Lisa was surprisingly grateful. This is what she had been hoping for all along. A deployment that got her away from the long sinister shadow of the Admiral.

Except she was finding it to be quite a bit longer than she had anticipated.

The problem with her mother's way of thinking, and ultimately with this blockade plan, was that it was unlikely to have the desired outcome. Mars was almost entirely self-sufficient at this point, thus their bid for independence. They exported way more than they imported. With a bit of strategic planning, they could hold out for years. Indefinitely even! A blockade was only successful if it reduced resources. There was no guarantee that could be achieved.

Not to mention space was a big place. Even the orbit around a planet was a lot of area to cover. Setting up a functional blockade was going to be tricky with the Fleet components they had to work with. Mostly large carrier ships, long-range gunships, and close-air-support fighters. Historically, the best blockades were implemented by the mid-sized ships, balancing weapon range and speed.

She got the distinct impression that the CCF fighters were going to be shouldering most of the patrol work. Her ass hurt just thinking about it.

Did that mean she was going to be shooting down civilian ships?

That thought made her fidget uncomfortably in her seat a little bit.

"Any immediate questions can be directed to your wing leaders." The Captain wrapped up his tactical briefing, and the maps winked out as the lights came up to full. Without another word, he strode toward the door.

Everyone snapped to attention as he exited.

When the door slammed shut, the room erupted in hushed conversations.

Azarov whistled through his teeth quietly. "That's a whole lot of space."

"No shit," Marconi grumbled. His eyes shot a dangerous glare in her direction, but Lisa pretended to not notice.

"Let's get settled in and meet up with the rest of the wing." She was hoping they would take it as an order, but it sure sounded like a suggestion as it hung in the air between them.

Marconi just scoffed, scooped up his datapad, and then made for the exit.

Azarov held back a minute, then turned to her. "You two ever going to sort this out?"

"Who knows." She breathed out with a shrug.

She wanted to have it out with Marconi. Part of her was worried about what he would say. Nothing she did was ever good enough for him, and from most people, she could care less. From someone in her own unit and a subordinate at that, it just felt wrong. Unfortunately for her, that internal strife eroded her self-confidence.

A confrontation with him was inevitable at this point. That much was certain. If she didn't take care of it soon, there was a very real possibility it would get someone killed.

As she followed them out the door, her guts twisted up with anxiety. So much was happening so quickly, and she wasn't sure if she was up to the task. How much of that was Marconi's bullshit, and how much of it was legitimate?

She didn't know the answer but she was determined to figure it out.

CHAPTER 2

IF THERE WAS one thing Ed had not expected about running a revolution, it was just how damned expensive the whole thing was. Everyone needed credits for something. It felt like he couldn't take a shit without having to pay fifteen people for the privilege.

The reports displayed on his datapad were disheartening. His father had amassed an impressive fortune in his lifetime, but at the rate with which it was flowing out, it wouldn't even make it a full year. Given how the last month had gone, he wasn't sure that was enough time to achieve much more than being a minor annoyance to the system.

There was a robust pounding on the door, which broke his brooding over the budget.

"Yeah?" He barked as he closed the screen with a swipe.

The door swung inward on old-style hinges. It was something that always reminded him of his dad, who'd loved to slam doors when he wanted to emphasize a point.

Des entered and immediately walked to a digital wallscreen.

"What's going on?" Ed didn't like the way the older man had his shoulders hunched and his back tight.

"You're not going to like it." Des tapped the power to the

screen, and a mediacast illuminated the room.

A cold fist suddenly clenched Ed's guts into a knot.

On the screen was a massive billowing black column of smoke rising from a good half of the Hellas docks. The drone footage was pretty high up, but you could just make out tiny ant-like specks of color moving around the rubble, putting out fires, and looking for survivors.

It was several minutes before Ed found the ability to speak. "Was this us?"

Des continued to watch the screen. "Yes, I'm afraid Ballor and Cole decided it was a good 'strategic move' to try to blow up the docks."

Those two had caused nothing but trouble since their arrival. Hot-headed, brash, and dumb as a sack of bricks, the two were opportunistic sociopaths. They wanted to sow chaos and bring the planet to its knees. Casualties and destruction were acceptable collateral damage in their minds.

"Idiots!" Ed fumed, clenching and unclenching his fists at his sides. "They realize that we have to *live* here when this is all said and done, right?"

"They don't care. They intend to burn it all down and start over." Des flipped through the various news broadcasts; each one was showing the same feed. Not unexpected, the UNIC controlled the vast satellite arrays that bounced the signals around through space. They only showed what they wanted to be seen. Which ultimately meant a whole lot of this and not a lot of the atrocities the Protectorate were committing.

His dreams were haunted by the images from the Red Square Massacre. That was totally on him. It had been his plan to send people out into the streets. They had done absolutely nothing wrong. Ed still struggled to see what objective the Protectorate had with the wonton slaughter of women and children.

More than anything else, that event had solidified in his mind that the Protectorate needed to go. Anyone who was capable of something that vile should not be allowed to remain in power. He wouldn't rest until they were purged from his planet. Hell, he'd take the fight all the way to the top if he could figure out a way to pay for the effort. He wasn't sure there was enough money to be had on the whole of Mars to fund that level of the campaign.

"You're going to have to do something with those two," Des said, glancing over at him.

Ed scrubbed his face with his hands vigorously. He needed a good shave. The stubble forming on his face was coalescing into a proper beard at this point. Come to think of it, he needed a shower too. He couldn't even recall the last time he'd had one.

"I know." He sighed heavily. "But damn if I didn't wish they had blown themselves up in that blast. Come to think of it, where did they get that much boom?"

Des raised an eyebrow.

"You've got to me fucking kidding me? We *just* got all of that!" Ed groaned.

It was one thing to step out of line and do something you felt would be helpful, despite being told not to, repeatedly. It was quite another thing to steal a couple million credits worth of newly acquired explosives. A feat that had burned quite a few bridges to his more notable underworld friends, he might add. There would be no replacing what had been used.

"What are you going to do about the General?" Despite being alone in the room, the older man dropped his voice to just above a whisper.

"So, we're just going to go with bad news today, is that it?"

Des frowned. "You knew the risks when you went for him. People are watching to see what you do next. I hate to say it this way, but what you do—or don't do—with 'Red' Brennan is going to define what your leadership means to the rebellion."

Sure, that sounded simple enough.

Brennan was a risk, but it was one Ed thought was worth taking. Not only was he intimately aware of all the Protectorate protocols, but by all accounts, he was an honorable and sympathetic leader. If the way he was responding to his role in the massacre was any indicator, that information was accurate. Unfortunately, he had yet to come to grips with what had been done. What they had found in that Protectorate safehouse was a broken shell of a man. Not the feared brilliant soldier they all needed.

"I'm not a soldier Des, we've talked about this." White-knuckled still, Ed made his way back around his desk and sat heavily in his chair. "I need someone to lead the charge. That's not something you or I can do. We can run the business of the rebellion, but we don't know the first thing about fighting trained soldiers."

There was another knock at the door, this one far less robust than the previous.

Ed held back another sigh.

"Come in."

The door swung open to reveal an intelligence tech. He was one of the lower-level members working to decrypt the massive data dump they had collected on the day of the massacre. So far, nothing they had untangled was really useful.

"What have you got for me?" Ed said, trying to keep the anxiety and anticipation out of his voice.

"Sir, I think you need to come see this for yourself." There was something in his tone, subdued excitement, maybe? It made the tiny hairs on Ed's neck stand straight up.

Yes! Finally!

With a glance toward Des, Ed rose and followed the youth out into the hallway.

The offices of his late father were perched above and off into the corner of the Vulcan facility. Had it been Ed's office, he would've preferred to have been off-site, at a nearby location that was less a giant sandy pit in the ground and more picturesque. Maybe a coastal business office? That wasn't his dad's style, though. He wanted to be in the mix, sleeves rolled up, overseeing the day-to-day. That's why everyone had loved him so much.

That granular level of oversight was the exact opposite of his instinct. Which was to say, he preferred a more laissez-faire approach. Hire the right people, share the big picture, and let them carve their own roads toward it. Autonomy was important to him. It wasn't because he was lazy. Although, he would admit to enjoying freedom from responsibility and a propensity to strive in that direction if given the opportunity. It was mostly because he refused to allow himself to become a lynchpin. If any one person became too important, they just became a target.

Not being a target was core to his central philosophy as a person.

It was also a shitty way to run any business. Given his extensive experience with the criminal underground, he had seen how rival crime bosses had completely unraveled their competition with a single shot. Ed thought it boiled down to ego. They were "the boss" because their fragile egos would not allow anyone else to share in their power or glory. That wasn't him. Hell, he'd rather fade into the background and run this effort from the shadows. He was a lot more likely to survive it that way. Being out front, there was a much greater chance of catching a stray bullet.

The youth strode ahead of him at a brisk walk, a little faster than Ed would've preferred. Seeing a superior hurrying around usually meant bad news, and morale was already being an issue. At least attrition wasn't widespread yet. That would come next unless he could figure out how to get things locked down.

More and more people had flooded to the Vulcan complex. It was frustrating. The Protectorate was sure to discover their location sooner rather than later. They had been incredibly lucky that they hadn't already been wiped off the Martian surface. Sure, everyone was acting as carefully as they could—using the equipment and ore haulers to smuggle themselves out of Hellas proper and into the mining complex. It was just a numbers game at this point. Eventually, someone would screw up, then they were all dead.

Ed *hated* relying on people. The odds of being let down were far too great. Better to rely on yourself.

Besides, for this rebellion to have any chance whatsoever, they had to spread out. It couldn't be a single city. That would allow the Protectorate to focus. And that would be incredibly bad.

They approached the intelligence wing, a converted mess hall, which had two armed guards standing at relaxed attention outside the door. They both saluted as he came into view.

"Stop that," he snapped.

The two shared a look.

As the tech opened the door, Ed leaned in close to the older of the two. "I'm no soldier, and you need to remember that."

The man screwed up his weather-worn face in a tight frown.

But Ed continued through the door, letting it whisk shut behind him.

Technology! Far superior to the swinging old-style hinged doors.

The room was a disaster. Workstations dotted every available flat space with enough room to hold it somewhat steadily. Cables were draped over everything; some even being suspended from the ceiling by seismic strapping. People milled about everywhere or sat at workstations pouring over the mountains of data they had stolen. At least that much had been successful. Too bad the encryption was far more complex than they had been led to believe it would be.

As they wound their way through the labyrinth of cobbled-together clumps of digital warfare, the youth turned and spoke quietly so as not to disturb anyone. "Nobody except my pod has seen this yet. We felt you should get eyes on it first."

They approached an empty workstation, despite three other techs sitting clustered nearby. One was eating some kind of noodle-laden soup while the other two whispered with their heads close together. All three stood when they saw them getting close.

"Have a seat. I'll turn on the privacy screen."

Ed complied and grabbed the nearby headset.

The screen darkened slightly, indicating the privacy view had been set. No one more than three feet away from the screen would be able to see what they were doing. An interesting and handy combination of thermochromic and electrochromic technologies that had been developed by the banking institutions, of course.

Once he had settled the headset on his head, one of the techs leaned over, and she pressed a button on the keypad. A video file began to play; the time stamp said it was mere minutes before the slaughter on the steps. It was a helmet camera assigned to a Marak, Jared. It scanned across the assembled crowd.

A pang of guilt ripped its way through Ed's chest. All of those people would be dead in a few minutes, and none of them knew it.

"What am I looking at?" Ed asked briskly.

"Just wait for it," said the girl to his right. She had leaned down so far to watch that her cheek was close enough to his ear he could feel the heat radiate off of her.

Ed didn't feel exactly comfortable with the proximity, but he let it slide for now.

A radio broadcast suddenly filled the headset, a click preceding it indicating it was a private channel, "Operation is a go."

Then the feed turned, showing a line of Protectorate soldiers standing on the steps of the administrative building. Running up to them from behind the building was Brennan.

The feed shook a bit, and Brennan could be seen pointing to the side of his helmet and then used some hand signals.

A beep, then, "Jesus, Keith. I don't like this."

The voice wasn't Brennan's. Ed assumed it must be this Marak person they were watching.

Brennan looked tired, and worry stretched his face visibly

through the visor of the helmet as he looked around at the assembled masses of people. He certainly didn't look like a person about to order the slaughter of innocents.

Beep. "Stay sharp, Colonel." There was a pause, then, "And Colonel…"

Another long pause before Marak replied, "Yes, General?"

Beep. "Keep the men calm, weapons off. Do not flinch."

Ed felt his eyebrows raise. This was definitely *not* the conversation he had seen repeated half a hundred times on mediacasts. That one painted Brennan as a terrified, overwhelmed, and callous mess. If anyone sounded nervous here, it was definitely Marak.

They all watched as Marak reached out and lightly punched Brennan in the chest, then moved away.

As soon as Brennan had turned away, a double-beep sounded, then Marak said, "All right, let's get this done."

A crackle sounded, then, "Aegis, CENTCOM, be advised: drone reports weapons spotted in your AOR."

A quick conversation followed, between Brennan and Central Command, appraising them of weapons being in the crowd. Which, of course, was bullshit. Ed had made it clear that he'd kill anyone he found that had brought a weapon to the assembly himself. Everyone had been checked beforehand. Unless some random person had joined up from within the Square, who had already been armed, there was no way any weapons had been present.

Marak's voice suddenly came back across, louder than the others, "General, recommend we go weapons hot."

There was no response.

A silent channel sat open.

"General, do you copy?" Marak again.

Nothing.

"Bravo 2, this is Bravo Actual. Weapons hot!"

All up and down the line, weapons were raised. Ed watched

in horror as Marak leveled his rifle on the crowd. A voice sounded dully through the noise and helmet, someone shouting one word "Marak!" While it was audible, even to the helmet camera and obviously to Marak himself, he did not seem to react.

Motion to the side caught Marak's attention, and the feed spun to see Brennan dashing up to him, then ripping off his helmet and throwing it to the ground. The whole time Brennan was shouting and shaking his head in the negative. Then the video feed shuddered and tilted violently as the helmet was removed.

The external noise was so overwhelming that the conversation the two had could not be overheard clearly.

"What are they saying here?" Ed asked the techs.

"We're trying to clean it up, but it's a mess. Isolating their voices is going to take some time if it's even possible—which it might not be," said the tech who had come and gotten him from his room. Simon, he thought his name was.

The titled angle of the helmet camera made it difficult to see the crowd, but suddenly Brennan, Marak, and the other soldiers they could see reacted to some unseen threat and leveled their rifles once again at the crowd.

"Aegis Two, the target is twenty meters out." A voice crackled over the comms.

"Wait, I thought they wore earpieces? The comms units are in the helmets?" Ed looked at everyone, confused.

"They wear earpieces," said the other tech around a mouthful of noodles, "this is something else that was in the helmet itself."

Ed's frown deepened as his gaze returned to the feed.

Rifle shots lit up the screen; the sounds clipped the boundary of the microphone, creating an awful screeching sound as people screamed, rifles fired, and his people died.

"Aegis Two, great work, leave no one standing. Avoid the King at all costs after this. Acknowledge Aegis Two." A pause. "Aegis Six, we've lost comms with Aegis Two. Going to backup comms protocol."

There was a high-pitched sound that overpowered the sounds of the slaughter, then the feed cut off.

"What? That's it?" Ed couldn't keep the disappointment from his voice.

The three young techs shared a look.

"Sir, Marak was playing for another side. Brennan was a fall guy. He could *hear* Brennan's orders, and Brennan's comms were blocked to the rest of the unit—but not to Marak's private channel." The tech made a motion, both hands coming together and index fingers touching.

"I don't get it." A touch of anger was creeping into his voice. Nothing pissed him off more than being made to feel stupid. Whatever these three saw, he hadn't. "Just tell me what I'm missing."

"It was a setup from the beginning. Colonel Marak was in on it. They *caused* the slaughter. Brennan didn't. Someone high up wanted it to happen, and they intended for Brennan to take the blame for it."

It suddenly clicked for Ed. They were right. That was why the conversation was so confusing. Whoever Marak was talking to was sending a "target" to the front. But that didn't make sense. This was before they knew there even *was* a target? This sounded like he was under orders from the Protectorate to move forward in the crowd.

That's what Brennan had said when they had rescued him. That drone footage had targeted weapons and potential explosives charging the line of soldiers and the front of the administrative building. But if that person was working with the Protectorate…

Ballor and Cole's antics would have to wait. This was a much higher priority.

"Someone go find me, Brennan."

CHAPTER 3

A SUBTLE CHIME sounded from the other room. She ignored it again. The heavy drapes had been closed for days. She wasn't even sure what time of day it was.

The chime sounded again, somehow more insistent this time.

Helena Chu cracked open one of her eyes. It still hurt, dried tears caking the lengths of her lashes, turning them into a tangled web. Despite the time that had passed from the *lesson* she had been taught, the pain still lingered. When it hurt to open your eyes, well, it made getting out of bed seem like an impossible task to overcome.

She did it anyway.

Clawing her way into a seated position, she activated the wallscreen with a gesture and checked the exterior camera feed. As expected, it was two Protectorate Peace Officers and her daily meal.

She activated the intercom. "I'm not hungry."

The response was immediate; they had done this little dance before. "Governor, you're required to eat. Please let us in, and eat, or we will be forced to make you do so."

That, as it turns out, could be much more unpleasant than it sounded. Especially as one was recovering from as intense of a beating as she had endured.

Fine.

With as much haste as she was able, she flipped the luxurious, now blood-stained, synthetic down comforter off of her and strode to the door. She was in her underwear because it had hurt too much to change her clothes, but she didn't even flinch when the doors opened, and the two guards surveyed her and the room. What did she have left to hide of her body? Nothing.

They entered the room with the pipsqueak of a girl, Natasha Everly, who was carrying her platter of food. It was a meal fit for a king, various meats and cheeses, fruits and vegetables, along with a carafe of some kind of sparkling juice beverage. The smell of it passing by made her stomach twist in on itself. She knew she had lost a considerable amount of weight; not even her underwear was fitting snuggly any longer. The food smelled divine, but the thought of giving in and accepting *anything* from these monsters spoiled the effects.

The two guards took up a position near the door, avoiding the russet-brown bloodstain in the otherwise white carpets between the door and the bedroom. It made the room appear like a giant Guernsey cow hide. She wasn't sure if these two guards had been there at her beating. It was possible, but the way they avoided the massive stain told her they were at least somewhat aware of what had happened there.

As Natasha arrayed the various small plates of food on the table and removed the coverings from the carafe, and poured a glass, she kept glancing at Helena. When her eyes passed over the bloodstain, they grew wide, and she hurriedly looked away. This is how it went, every single time. It made Helena's blood boil. How could people just stand by knowing what had happened to her?

The worst part was she knew it wouldn't be the last beating she'd receive while in the custody of the new Martian government. It was all just a matter of time before Bruce discovered another reason to teach her a lesson. She wouldn't be the least bit shocked if Minnie were the mastermind behind the beating. The old crone was a sociopath.

"Would you like your daily digest, Governor?" Natasha asked, finishing with the arrangement and pulling out her small datapad from a deep trouser pocket.

It had been fifteen days since the beating. Every day she had refused the condensed news report from Natasha. Part of her ached to know what was going on. The more resolute part of her refused to allow a return to normalcy.

Instead of answering, she just turned and limped her way back to the bedroom.

Natasha sighed delicately behind her.

Then she eased herself back into the soft bed.

The door opened, there were some rustles and footfalls, and then the door clicked shut.

If she were lucky, they wouldn't bother her again until this evening when they came back for the dishes.

This was the routine.

Helena knew her health was failing. Without proper nourishment, her body wasn't healing as quickly as it should have. The beatings had disrupted her vision, which was not returning to normal. Her left eye was consistently blurry now, creating a world that was reminiscent of a bad watercolor painting. Several ribs had been broken, and without being properly set, they had healed in a way that had created some substantial back discomfort.

Not that she had any right to complain. At least she hadn't been murdered in cold blood outside the building that was a supposed symbol of justice for the people.

She couldn't even bring herself to look at the reports of what had happened. During that beating, she had heard the rifle fire through the broken window. She had heard the screams of pain and panic.

There was nothing she could do.

Everything in her that wanted to die *was* already dead. Failure was a kind descriptor for what her life had amounted to. How could it have all gone so terribly wrong, so fast? How had she not noticed? What had she ever done to deserve this?

She screamed her frustration into the pillow, not wanting the guards outside to hear her moment of weakness. It hurt, the muscles in her face stretching around the scream irritating the healing bruises.

"Helena?" A soft voice whispered tentatively from the door.

She froze, her eyes widening with shock.

A soft knock at her open door sounded in the room. "Helena, it's Natasha."

Tears suddenly sprang to her eyes. The one moment of weakness she had allowed herself during these hellish few weeks, and it had been seen. Natasha would go and gleefully report to Bruce that their torment of her was working, that she was breaking. The realization made her want to give up, to use the down comforter to smother her life out.

No, she wouldn't give up. She *couldn't* give up. Not now. There were too many souls screaming at her from the other side, haunting her dreams, begging her for revenge. She *would* give it to them. If it was the last thing, she did.

Rather than try to explain anything, she just turned and slowly sat up.

Natasha stood halfway through the threshold. Her young eyes were wide with fear, her lips twisted with concern. "Are you okay, Helena?"

Helena should've laughed. The absurdity and naivety of the question galled her.

"I'm afraid it's been a very rough month, Natasha." The first admission that things were bad, she had spoken since that awful day.

Natasha looked down at her feet, shame staining her face red, the flush giving her a cuteness that emphasized her young age. She had to be what, nineteen? Maybe twenty?

"I'm sorry, Helena. I wish there was something I could do to help." Natasha twisted her feet into the carpet in discomfort. Not even having the courage to glance up.

Of course, Helena had brainstormed at least fifty different ways to make an escape attempt. Unfortunately, every single one of those ideas required some kind of outside assistance. There was just no easy way to overcome her current obstacles. She wasn't strong enough to overpower the guards. The apartment she was in was as effective as a jail cell in keeping her contained. Everything that had any chance of success required someone on the inside.

Could Natasha be that person?

Helena hadn't considered it before this moment. The girl was young, somewhat stupid, and incredibly naive. But, could her guilt be enough to offer some assistance? What would the repercussions be if it didn't work? Could it get any worse than it already was? She knew it could always get worse. She had learned that the hard way, it seemed.

All those souls screaming for revenge rang in her heart. Ultimately, she decided, it was worth a shot.

Testing the waters, she told the youth, "I wish you could too, Natasha. I'm just in so much pain I am not sleeping well. I can't even eat the food you bring me." Helena smiled sadly for emphasis.

Natasha looked up finally, a little surprised that Helena was talking to her. It was perhaps the longest sentence Helena had strung together since that afternoon with Bruce and his cronies. To be perfectly honest, it hurt somewhat to talk that much at once.

Helena pressed the moment. "If I could only get out of pain for a few days, I might be able to get some strength back. I just don't think that's possible." She let her head hang down and picked at the comforter draped across her lap.

"Maybe I could get you some painkillers?" Natasha sounded hopeful.

Helena had to hide her smile.

Bruce had explicitly denied her the use of any painkillers or stims. He had told the guards, "Make sure she feels every bruise, every broken bone, for as long as possible. I want this lesson to sink in *deep.*"

Oh, it has Bruce, but it's not the lesson you wanted me to learn, I guarantee that.

Certainly, this had been communicated to Natasha. So, if she were willing to break with the very explicit instructions to help Helena in this way, perhaps she could be convinced to help her in more meaningful ways?

"Oh, Natasha, that would be so nice of you! Are you sure you can do that?" It was a delicate dance to be had, acknowledging that there was some inherent risk but not scaring her too much from the ask.

Natasha bit her lip, thinking. Then, she nodded. "I won't be able to get any stims. Those are under constant guard. But I can probably fake a headache and get some painkillers. They won't be anything grand, but maybe they will help a little bit?" She sounded hopeful. "Just until you get your strength back."

Perfect.

Helena just smiled and nodded. Both actions hurt, but it was worth the discomfort.

The girl smiled back, then spun and strode from the room.

When the door clicked shut, Helena checked the exterior camera to make sure Natasha had indeed left. She caught a glimpse of the girl's back swaying down the corridor. The guard standing outside her door watching her with a wry grin on his face.

Another idea occurred to her. Natasha was a pretty thing, not in a mature, sophisticated, or beautiful kind of way—but she had that cuteness of youth. Something men seemed to be drawn to like moths to a flame. The guard sure seemed distracted by those flimsy trousers as they faded into the distance. Was that something she could use?

The old Helena would have balked at the idea of entangling someone like Natasha into her schemes. Luckily for her, that weaker Helena had bled out on the floor in the next room. She didn't hope that Natasha was hurt—she just didn't care. What was one girl's safety weighed against her chances of escape?

Something about the last thought troubled Helena. It sounded too close to something Bruce might say. It made her stomach twist up into knots.

All she could do now was wait and see.

It didn't take her long to fall asleep.

— — —

Helena was startled awake.

She wasn't sure what had roused her, but the sudden movement caused a cascade of pain throughout her body. It was a dull pain now, not the sharp, intense version it had been in previous weeks. She could manage this physical pain. The emotional pain was a different monster altogether.

Not hearing or seeing anything, she did her best to settle back into a comfortable position and drew the comforter up to her chin.

Click.

The sound of the door closing was barely audible. Someone was taking great care to keep the automatic door from making too much noise.

Panic clawed its way up her chest. Her face went cold with fear and anxiety. The door to the outer room was still open partially. Natasha had not closed it when she had left. Helena strained her hearing as much as she could, trying to detect any movement from the other room.

There was nothing.

Had they left?

She wasn't sure what the best play here was. Whoever it was could be just on the other side of the door, waiting to ambush her. Or, they could've already done whatever nefarious task had brought them unannounced into her room and left.

With her muscles screaming at her to act and fight or flight instincts fully taking over, she stealthily eased the comforter off of her and carefully eased herself to the edge of the bed. There was nothing she could use as an improvised weapon remaining in her rooms. Those had all been cleared out before she had been escorted there, evidently. So, she stood and drew her fists up into a defensive position across her chest.

It had been years since her last self-defense training course, but she knew enough to at least give herself some confidence as she tiptoed toward the door.

Without touching the door itself, she utilized the angles to try to peer around the doorway. Not seeing anyone in the dark room, she used a toe to slowly ease the door open. It eased into the pocket in the wall silently on its mechanical track. A quick glance left, retreat, and quick glance right. The room was empty as near as she could tell.

Cautiously, she stepped into the room. Her heart thundered in her chest. She could feel the pulse on her neck leaping out like a caged animal. The beating echoed in her ears like timpani drums. While she didn't relish the idea of enduring another beating, she'd be damned if she just invited it as she lay in bed. No, she'd put up a fight. She'd rather die fighting than accept defeat.

Movement caught her attention. She whipped her head around to see a shadowy figure detaching from the wall nearest the dining table. The person must have been so still that she hadn't noticed them standing there until they had moved.

The person was gliding silently across the room toward the door. They'd cross within a meter of her current position. The room was so dark that up against the dark wood paneling of the bedroom doorway, she must've been almost invisible.

As the person crossed in front of her, she lept. Tackling the person to the floor with a flurry of haphazard blows to the back of the head, neck, and upper back. The person grunted with pain, then slammed into the ground with the full weight of Helena riding them down.

The moment overwhelmed Helena, and she rained down blows furiously. Everything she had been taught left her, and some kind of animalistic instinct took over. She clenched her fists together and continued to drop ferocious strikes. It wasn't long until her fists came back sticky and warm.

Reality slammed her back. Helena was breathing hard from the exertion and lack of calories. Stars dotted her vision, and she worried she might pass out. She stumbled to her feet, dizzily, and fumbled around for a light panel.

When the lights flipped on, she gasped. Cute blue eyes stared across the ground dully, the life beaten from them. The girl's brassy blonde hair was stained crimson, her head sitting at an odd angle from the break in the neck.

Natasha clutched a half-empty bottle of painkillers in her lifeless hand.

Helena retched violently, nothing but a small glob of bile hitting the floor. What she had just done in a blind panic nearly overwhelmed her.

Use this! Now!

She bent down and began searching the girl for her passkey. Obviously, she had a way in and out of the room. This could be Helena's one and only chance at escape. She dreaded to think what would happen when they found the girl's body.

In the same pocket she kept her datapad, which Helena also took, she found the passkey. A simple government identification card with all the authorization she needed to escape.

Suddenly realizing she was mostly naked and blood-splattered, Helena froze. Did she dare take the time to dress?

She glanced at the table where her food from earlier still sat arranged as it had been by the girl she had just murdered.

Shit!

That meant it wasn't yet night. The room was just dark because that was the way she kept it. She glanced down at the datapad in her hand; the time read 16:40. Almost time for shift change at 17:00. If things were still running the way they were supposed to be.

Not that she had been keeping track of any of these details, damn her for being so foolish, but she'd expect the cleanup would happen around the same time as shift changes. That's what made the most sense to her, anyway.

That meant she had to act, and *now.*

As she shoved the passkey into her bra strap, she clutched the datapad tightly. It was the best she could do.

She ran to the door and spared a look behind her at the dark shape lying on the ground. Whoever came in to clean up would immediately call the guards. That could be mere minutes away. It was a bad idea to just leave the girl lying there.

Cursing under her breath in a constant stream, she set the datapad down near the door and ran back to the corpse. She awkwardly heaved the girl into a sitting position and then put her shoulder into the girl's stomach and heaved her into the air. Despite Natasha having been a tiny thing, Helena was weak and still healing from being broken. It took a lot of huffing and puffing, but she eventually slung the girl like a sack of potatoes onto her bed.

After steadying herself and catching a few quick breaths, Helena slung the comforter over the body. Hopefully, anyone who showed up would mistake it for her and ignore her as they had so many times before.

On her way back through the bedroom door, she snagged a bathrobe off a hook nearest the door. A luxury she mainly had ignored since her beating, but at least she might not attract immediate attention.

As she slung it around her body and drew her arms in, she glanced toward the exterior camera feed to check and see if the guards were there.

Blessedly, they were not. Shift change was already working in her favor.

A plan was forming in her head as she dashed from her bedroom back to the exit. She'd make her way to the lower levels of the building, which housed the engineering and environmental systems, to hide for a day or two. Once it was discovered that she had escaped, they'd assume she'd make straight for the streets and freedom. No one would expect her to remain in the building.

She'd find a way to get word to Brennan.

He would come for her.

Her stomach twisted and growled loudly. She ran to the platter of food and shoved whatever she could in her mouth, and filled her pockets. Before leaving, she grabbed the bottled water in one hand, then scooped up the datapad with the other.

Feeling suddenly giddy, she stepped up to the door and awkwardly pressed her chest, and the passkey, up against the control box. The door opened with a soft *whoosh.*

This was it. She was free.

She dashed out of the room, robe fluttering around her, all the pain suddenly a distant memory.

The hallway stretched out to either side of her, not unlike an apartment complex. She instinctually turned right and raced toward the stairwell, knowing the elevators would be swarming with activity during this time of day. Hopefully, the stairwell, and being so high up, would allow her more opportunity to avoid bumping into anyone.

As she raced down the hallway, the datapad buzzed in her hands suddenly. She ignored it. Nothing was going to stop her from reaching the stairs. Moments were everything right now.

Before she had sprinted no more than half the distance, her body began to fail. Her chest was heaving against the newly knitted ribs, sending a shock of pain through her with each ragged breath. The hallway spun, and her vision fogged.

Suddenly her hunger strike seemed not only pathetic but counterproductive. She should've been storing up all the strength and healing she could have. What a silly proposition to refuse nourishment and compromise her health. It's not as if the ones who had beat her within an inch of her life, and much worse, would actually care about her well-being. Certainly, they wouldn't be the slightest bit perturbed by her slowly wasting away in bed.

Frankly, she was probably doing them a favor by quietly committing slow suicide. Minnie Farina would have loved to write that mediacast, of that she had no doubt. The snake would milk every drop of sympathy from it she could to try to save face for this visibly corrupt administration. The sad part is it conceivably worked on more citizens than she'd care to admit.

Stumbling, panting, and dizzy from the sudden expenditure of energy, she finally made it to the stairwell. Freedom waiting just on the other side. She repeated her chest-bump trick with the passkey, only to have it beep and illuminate red.

No, no! No, no, no, no, no!

She tried again.

Red.

The staircases were locked down!

That was a building fire safety violation!

Damn it!

Bruce wouldn't give two shits about fire safety; she should've anticipated that he would have cut off escape routes.

She spun and started running back the way she had come.

How stupid of her! It was way past time that she started thinking like something other than a city administrator. She needed to start thinking like a soldier, a survivor. Bruce was cold, calculating, and devious. Nothing would be easy, no protocols reliably followed. He was in this for himself and whoever he reported to. That was it. Something as fatuous as *fire codes* wouldn't trouble his sleep a wink.

A figure stepped out of the elevator down the long corridor. Too far away to hear the beeps of the elevator.

Helena slammed to the side, ducking into a doorway, sucking air.

She tried the door behind her with the passkey, this time staying pressed against the wall and using her hand to swipe behind her. She heard the telltale beep of a locked door.

Likely she could've checked all sixty-seven doors other than hers, and they'd be the same. Bruce would take no chances with his favorite prize. Odds were slim that there was anyone other than her on the entire floor.

Distant talking could be heard, not nearly loud enough to make out the words, but she knew they would be getting to her room any moment. She drew out the datapad, swiped away the five missed calls notification without so much as a second glance, and checked the time. 16:58.

This would be the shift change then. She had failed. They were going to find the body of Natasha or find her cowering in the hallway, probably both. This attempt was over. Likely she'd get beaten again, just for the sport of it. Her escape attempt being nothing more than a flimsy excuse for the spectacle.

A sob wracked her body, and she covered her mouth to hold back any noise.

Scenarios raced through her brain.

Maybe she could find a way to disguise herself? Right, one of the most recognizable faces on the entire planet.

Maybe she could hack into one of the adjacent rooms and wait out the search? Like she knew the first thing about hacking, *and* moreover, the search would likely *start* on this level.

Maybe she could charge the guards and overwhelm them before they shot her? Even in the best shape of her life, there'd be no way to cover the thirty or more meters fast enough to avoid a rifle blast.

Maybe.

Maybe!

No. This was it. She'd die for this.

And well, she should.

She looked down at the blood on her hands, partially dry in places. Still tacky where it had been thickest. The coppery smell wafted up to her. That, and the running, and the first meal in weeks, all culminated into a wave of nausea.

There was nothing she could do, she held her hands to her mouth, but all that did was create a spray of vomit. At least she was quiet about it. Maybe the guard wouldn't have noticed.

A moment later, those hopes were dashed as a rifle barrel preceded a guard's form coming around the corner.

His eyes went wide when he saw her. And why shouldn't he be shocked?

There she was, standing in her now ill-fitting bra and panties, robe pulled down to her sides burdened as it was with the stolen datapad in one of the pockets, and soaked with her vomit all down the front. She had blood up to her wrists and splattered across her chest and face. Her body was extremely emaciated from lack of food and was a colorful tapestry of partially healed cuts and yellowed-purple bruises. Sweat poured from her forehead to mix with the vomit now dribbling down her chin and neck to splatter onto the floor.

If she could catch her breath, she'd probably laugh at how she must look. Some kind of ghoul from ancient myths brought to life.

"Holy hell," the guard breathed. He brought his rifle down to his side, then glanced back the way he had come. So, there were two guards then. Great. This day just kept getting better.

"Help me," she breathed out the faintest of whispers.

He turned back toward her. His brows knit in consternation.

A sudden ember of hope blossomed in her chest. It looked

like he might actually be *considering helping her!*

She didn't dare move, speak, or even breathe. He *needed* to help her.

He brought his gun back up, suddenly, and pointed it down the hallway. His posture returned to threatening. The muzzle of the rifle tilted and panned as he scanned the hallway beyond.

"Okay, I'll help you. But just this once," he whispered the words, but they exploded with hope and light inside her mind. "I'm going to go distract the other guard, and however you got out, I want you to get back in. Can you do that?"

He watched her nod vigorously out of the corner of his eye as he took another step down the hallway, making an overly dramatic show of checking around the corners.

"Don't make me regret this, okay?" he said as he turned back toward her room. "Or we'll both get it. Understand? You have three minutes after we enter the elevator."

He started to walk back.

"Wait," she whispered, "What's your name?"

"Osion. Osion Quinn." He didn't stop or turn around.

"Thank you, Osion!"

After a moment, she heard some laughing fading down the hallway.

She counted to sixty, then dared a peek around the corner.

The hallway was empty.

With what little energy she had left, she raced to the door and keyed herself in. She collapsed against the door.

Now she'd have to figure out how to dispose of a body without leaving her rooms.

A pulse drew her attention back to the clutched datapad in her hand.

At least this effort wasn't completely in vain. She now had a way to communicate with the outside world.

If she were smart about it, that could be even better than her freedom.

CHAPTER 4

"WHAT THE FUCK, Sebastian?" Jonathan Spalding stood outside Foster's, an establishment he had practically funded over the years. Now he was being denied entrance.

Sebastian had been a longtime friend, hell, closer to a distant cousin than just a mere friend. Now, the weasel-faced little shit just stood there with his arms folded.

"Look, Jon," Sebastian began.

"No, you look, Seb," Spalding drunkenly shouted over him. Then realized he didn't have anything he could say. What was there to say? He *deserved* to be let in? That if he didn't get another drink in him soon, he'd lose his stupor? Then he'd have to think about how his life had been taken from him.

No, he'd get good and drunk *somewhere*, even if it wasn't his favorite haunt.

He blew a raspberry at Seb instead and waved him off.

"Whatever, man."

For what it was worth, the fuckhead at least had the decency to look embarrassed. Maybe even a little sympathetic.

Spalding stumbled into the street. It was nearing midnight, but he wasn't exactly sure how long he had been shambling from bar to bar. He wasn't sure which hurt more, his fists from throwing punches or his face from catching them.

Every single bar he had stopped at had eventually been overrun with off-duty Fleet soldiers. And every single one of them had a score to settle with him, it seemed like. He had been in more fights in the last few days than he had been in the sum total of his career. Granted, he may have picked a few of tonight's events himself, but for the most part, he was just trying to drink away his woes. Couldn't a man just drink in peace?

There were no shortages of bars on Luna.

There were also no shortages of off-duty Fleet fuckers.

Even just walking down the street, he'd have to cross over to the other side of the walkway to avoid large cadres of cadets or seasoned squads meandering leisurely down the walks. Each and every one of the uniformed brats was like a railgun blast through his heart.

Unfortunately, as he walked, he began to sober up enough to really wallow in his predicament. Summarily dishonorably discharged from the Protectorate, his very *existence* struck from their records. It was as if Jonathan Spalding had never existed in the first place. Everything he had ever worked for gone like a fart in a hurricane.

"I need a drink," he mumbled to no one in particular.

A few young kids looked at him nervously, then scampered off.

He wrinkled his nose. Something stank to high heaven.

With a whiff under his arm, he realized it was him.

This is bullshit!

Nothing he could think of would help. The Protectorate Affairs Offices wouldn't even acknowledge his name, let alone the fact he had served most of his life with them. They were the path to help when a soldier was in need. If they wouldn't even verify his damned name, how could he expect anything from them at all?

No food.

No home.

No alcohol.

What was he even doing being alive?

That's when his brain decided to flash a particularly pleasant memory of Amanda into his drunken consciousness. It staggered him worse than any physical blow ever had. He slammed into a nearby wall, hard enough to leave a bruise on his shoulder. Sobs spluttered out of him wetly.

Memories of the Legion played over and over, all the laughing and camaraderie they had shared. The countless pranks, both the fun and tense situations shared. They were all dead. And more importantly, it had all been *his* fault!

At least that was what everyone thought.

Perception, in this case, was all that mattered.

"It wasn't my fault." He whined to his knees, drawing them up to his chest, with his back pressed against the wall. "It wasn't my fault."

He wasn't sure how long he sat there sobbing like a child. Eventually, the flashbacks faded, and he stood. There was a mission to complete. Find and consume as much alcohol as possible.

Yawning but walking somewhat straighter than he had before, he pushed off the wall and waded his way back into the stream of humanity. It must be nearing daybreak because the streets were filled with people rushing to and fro in work attire. Finding bars open during daylight hours was somewhat tricky. If he didn't find a place to get a good buzz on soon, he'd likely have to spend the day sober. That didn't sound fun at all.

Pain suddenly flared across his back, and something soft and black was pulled over his face.

"HEY, WHAT THE—" A punch in the kidneys knocked the wind spluttering from him.

Kicks and punches rained down on him as he was bodily

dragged off somewhere.

He was too stunned from the sudden ferocity of the attack to mount any kind of proper counterattack. The initial blow to the back of his head had sent the world careening. Even more, than it already had been, which was no small amount.

He struggled with his assailants to the best of his ability. The years of combat training overrode his sloppy inebriated state enough to absorb some of the more brutal unseen blows. The sounds of the street grew distant as he was partially dragged, partially rolled across the sidewalk.

"Do it," came a hoarse grunt from the man holding his arms pinned up around his head.

Whatever it was they intended to do, Spalding wanted no part of it. He found purchase with his feet suddenly, as the other assailant released him to do whatever *it* was. With as much of a burst of power as he could muster, he planted his feet and leaped backward into the one still holding him.

The gambit paid off as the man lost his footing, and the two crashed to the ground. He was rewarded with the soft hollow thud of a head striking the ground, followed by a grunt of pain.

Spalding ripped the hood off his head and quickly surveyed his surroundings. They had forced him into a narrow gap between buildings. Trash receptacles and utility boxes were speckled throughout, but otherwise, there was nothing advantageous to be had.

In the second it took to scan the area, the partner managed to grab at his feet. Spalding scrambled, kicking and thrashing about as he tried to regain his feet.

Thankfully the one he had overpowered still lay stunned on the ground, holding the back of his head and groaning softly.

A kick landed hard in his ribs, and it doubled him over sucking air. The pain made his gorge rise. That or all the sudden movement.

The man was not overly big or menacing; frankly, Spalding

was somewhat disappointed at how *normal* he looked. No uniform or distinguishing military marks, although his clothing would be considered on the slightly higher end.

Staggering backward a few steps, Spalding fought to regain some wind. Hard to put up a decent fight if you couldn't breathe right.

The man pressed his advantage and came in aggressively, launching an onslaught of hard punches. Luckily for Spalding, only about half landed. Unfortunately, the half that did land hurt like hell and mainly were taken to his face and neck. The ferocity of the attacks sent him staggering back, deeper into the narrow alley.

Sparing a quick glance at the now motionless man on the ground, Spalding decided to attempt some offense himself. The attacks were sloppy, and what hits he did land were glancing slaps more than anything.

A flash of metal in the dim artificial light glimmered in his assailant's hands.

"Ah, the fun's over then, I guess?" Spalding croaked.

Spalding lunged as the pistol was drawn on him. If he was going to die, he was at least going to go down fighting. The move caught the gunman by surprise, and they wrestled for control of the weapon. Now, as they grappled, Spalding let his training take over. He was all headbutts and tightly thrown elbows. One particular elbow caught the man under the chin, and it rattled him enough that he lost his grip on the pistol.

The two disengaged with a violent shove. Spalding's feet got tangled, and he fell to the ground. He drew himself up, fully expecting another round of beatings. He pointed the weapon down the alley. It was empty. Rapid clicks of footsteps echoed dimly from the mouth which led out to the main street.

Spalding hauled himself to his feet, the pistol held in front of him. The one who had struck his head was still prone, but he wasn't going to take any chances.

He coughed into his elbow, blood stained his sleeve. This hadn't been the worst beating he had ever sustained, but he was certainly glad it was over. At least for the moment.

"Hey, your buddy is gone." Spalding edged his way carefully over to the prone figure.

There was no movement at all.

With the edge of his foot, he reached out and nudged the man.

The response, or lack of one, was not a good sign.

He leaned down and checked for a pulse.

That was when he noticed the pool of blood.

Evidently, he had fallen harder than Spalding had initially thought. Blood leaked slowly from the crack in the back of his head.

Regret swelled in Spalding's chest. He was a soldier and no stranger to death, but this just seemed like such a waste. Hopefully, these men weren't stupid Fleet cadets jumping him to somehow prove how macho they were.

If they were cadets, he should report what happened.

Thinking a little more clearly now, he reached into the man's pockets, hoping to find some form of identification. All while keeping a wary eye toward the main street, just in case his buddy decided to come back with more help.

After emptying a few odds and ends out of various pockets, Spalding withdrew a small knife, a pistol that matched the make and model he currently held, and a datapad. Nothing really stood out as out of the ordinary, well, except for the weapons, obviously.

There were also no clues as to who this person was, or more importantly, why they had just tried to execute Spalding. Well, except for the obvious reasons, he supposed.

Fuck Admiral Colt right square up her…

A sound from the street disrupted his thoughts.

Better to just keep out of the area and find a place to lay low for a while.

Something about this whole encounter felt different to him.

This wasn't some random act of violence from some headstrong cadets looking to prove how tough they were. This was something else entirely. It had felt like there had been a *plan* of some kind in play.

He decided it was time to get far away from this alley. He cautiously made his way to the main street and pressed his back against the far wall, peeking around the corner to avoid blundering into an ambush. Slightly more people walked up and down the road now, as daylight was rapidly approaching. There was no sign of the man who had gotten away. For that, he was grateful. There was little fight left in him.

As he slunk out from the alleyway, he kept one shoulder as close to the building as possible, so there was only one angle to watch. He'd spare quick glances behind him at random intervals to avoid picking up a tail.

Mostly sober now, the pain of the night's events was beginning to throb all across his body. Burning sharp pain in his chest warned him of a potentially broken rib. While he should probably visit a hospital, first he had to try to get to the bottom of who had attacked him. And, hopefully, why?

Streets blurred by as he limped and shuffled as quickly as he was able. Without having any real clear idea of where to go, he just took streets at random. Sometimes spontaneously doubling back. It didn't appear he was being followed. That was good, at least. Best news of the night so far.

The area of Luna he was in was a rough part of town, speckled with bars, clubs, and so-called "houses of pleasure." Eateries and small convenience stores also were intermingled in, around, and between the various recreational establishments.

A sign caught his eye, an electronics repair shop. It was nestled in tightly between a bar called simply "Jims" and a cafeteria which claimed to have "Old-World-Fare." As Spalding approached the locked and gated doors of the shop, he could smell the warm earthy aroma of baking bread wafting from the neighboring building. His stomach growled. It smelled of yeast and molasses, with a warm undertone of caramelizing sugar. It made his mouth water.

The lock which connected the two ends of the gate in the middle of the door was of usual make, a digital pin that utilized a tiny bit of high-thread carbon fiber to lock the two together. There was no way he was going to guess the twelve-digit pin. Nor could he break the strong bar.

He gave up on the lock and instead examined the connections of the gate. The building was a bit rundown, and the fastenings of the gates were loose from years of use and little maintenance. Using his newly acquired knife, he pried at one of the plates which moored the entrance to the threshold. It wiggled a bit but refused to yield to the applied pressure.

"Can I help you?" said a voice behind him.

Spalding spun, gun leveled, and the knife held out defensively in front of him.

An older gentleman stumbled back a step, his hands quickly coming up in a placating gesture.

"Woah there, buddy," he said quickly. "Looks like you've had quite the night!"

Chancing a glance up and down the street for other potential threats and seeing none, Spalding whispered, "This your place?"

The older man nodded slowly, his hands still raised in front of him.

"Open the door," Spalding demanded quietly and then stepped aside to allow access to the locked gate.

"I can do that," the man said slowly, "but I'll need to reach into my pocket to get my datapad."

"Why?" Spalding said, tightening his grip on the pistol reflexively.

The man shrugged and looked somewhat sheepish as he chuckled. "I'm old and can't remember my pin very well."

Spalding felt his face flush with shame. What the hell was he doing? Tormenting an old man like this.

"Go ahead," Spalding said, refusing to let his guard down.

The man slowly lowered his right hand and fished into his baggy trousers. He was well dressed, if in a far outdated style. The man himself had gray hair that sat atop his head in a slightly stringy mess, a gray goatee, and large watery eyes. Everything you'd expect from a grandfather type, down to the baggy but comfortable-looking clothes.

After a moment, he withdrew a datapad and motioned to the door.

"May I?" His voice was quiet but confident. There wasn't any real fear in his voice. That fact set Spalding's nerves to twitching. Being held at gunpoint by someone who had obviously been in at least a couple fights recently. Who in their right mind wouldn't be feeling a little trepidation?

"Sure, but move slow." Spalding circled around behind him. Looking up and down the street, which was becoming slowly more populated. No one had noticed them yet, but it wouldn't be long before someone saw the two.

After a moment, the lock clicked open, and the gates rattled back into their housings.

Then, the door opened with a soft chime.

Grandpa turned around and motioned for Spalding to go inside.

"You first," Spalding said.

With a grimace and a shrug, the other man stepped inside the building.

Spalding spared one last glance around and then followed him inside.

A blow to his stomach almost dropped him to his knees.

Rough hands grabbed his, twisted, pulled.

Then a cold barrel was being pressed against his temple.

What the hell just happened?

"Now, son, I'm only going to ask you this one time." Grandpa took a few steps back, the gun held steady as a stone in one hand

and aimed precisely at his head. "Is it your intention to rob me or cause me harm?"

"No," he coughed, still trying to catch his breath. He was getting really tired of having the wind knocked out of him tonight.

With a few deft movements, Grandpa unloaded the weapon and disassembled it. The three pieces clattered to the floor along with the unspent ballistic shell.

"Who," Spalding croaked, "Who, *are* you?"

Grandpa didn't respond, still assessing the threat Spalding represented.

"Is that your blood or someone else's?"

"I think it's mostly mine," Spalding replied, finally able to string together a proper sentence. He straightened to his full height. "But I gave as good as I got."

The elderly man smirked.

There was a tense silence as the two weighed what to do next.

Finally, the stranger broke the silence. "Coffee?"

Spalding furrowed his brows. Then, his stomach growled again. "Actually, that'd be great."

He directed Spalding to a stool nestled against a countertop with various bits of electronics scattered across it. "Have a seat. Oh," he said, raising something pinched between his thumb and index finger, "and if you were thinking about putting your pistol back together, don't. It won't be much use to you without the firing pin."

Despite a concentrated effort to *not* be impressed, Spalding felt his jaw go slack.

Grandpa smiled and practically waddled into a back room.

Well, this night just kept getting stranger and stranger. As instructed, Spalding felt his ass hit the stool. He hated to admit it, but it hurt. All the brutalization of his body over the last few weeks was beginning to pile up. Tonight had not been awful by itself, but injuries were starting to stack up in a way that he didn't much appreciate.

A rattle at the door caused him to jerk off his stool.

The door opened and revealed a young girl, maybe early twenties, perhaps even a bit younger. She stopped when she saw Spalding, half in-half out of the door.

"It's okay Rylan, he just needs some help." Grandpa peeked around the corner from the back room.

The girl nodded, her brassy curls swaying slightly. Spalding noticed she watched him out of the corner of her eye, despite the assurances from the other man.

She sat down a bag on the other side of the counter from him and flipped a switch. Some digital signage sprang to life in the front of the store, facing out toward the street.

That's when she looked up and noticed how rough Spalding looked. Her brows furrowed with worry.

"It's not as bad as it looks," he said, trying to keep an edge out of his voice, with little success.

"Well, it looks pretty bad," she said, apprehension creeping into her voice. "Can I get you a medical kit?"

"That'd be much appreciated." And he wasn't even remotely kidding.

"Okay, one minute." Then she, too, disappeared into the back room.

Despite the beating and the years of sustained damage in the military, his hearing was still reasonably good. He could hear hushed whispers coming from the back, but not well enough to make out what they were saying.

Spalding sincerely hoped he wouldn't have to hurt these people.

Although the prospect of trying to fight this superhero old man was somewhat daunting.

Before he could consider his options too profoundly, the curtain was pulled back, and Grandpa stepped out holding two steaming mugs of delicious smelling coffee. Just the thought of a nice hot cup of coffee just about sent his knees trembling.

"Here you go," he said, offering Spalding a mug. "Careful, it's hot. Hope you don't mind that."

"No," he said, accepting it. "I prefer hot coffee."

"You former Protectorate?" Grandpa asked around a careful sip.

Spalding just held the mug and inhaled the aroma for a second, eyes closed. Then said, "Fleet."

"Ahh! I thought I recognized your face." The old man smiled and snapped his fingers, "Spalding, right? The Face of the Fleet!"

Spalding paused, bringing the mug to his lips. *Damn it*! He was going to have to be more careful about what he revealed about himself. Knowing it was too late, he still considered trying to lie his way out of it. It'd do no good, so instead, he just nodded.

The girl, Rylan, came out from the back carrying a red zip-pack. She paused, looking at the older man for approval. He nodded and took another sip of coffee as he eased himself onto the stool opposite Spalding.

Rylan put the pack on the counter and began withdrawing sterilizing spray, bandages, and even a couple painkillers.

"I won't be needing those," Spalding said, indicating the later additions.

"No?" Rylan said curiously.

"I avoid them as much as possible." Then, finally, he took a sip of coffee. It burned his lips and stung his tongue but tasted delicious. A medium roast, a hint of sugar, no cream. The same way they made it at the barracks.

"You were Fleet, weren't you?" Spalding asked the old man.

He nodded. "Colonel Jorge Dillard, retired."

Spalding felt his tongue stick to the roof of his mouth as it suddenly went bone dry. The name wasn't familiar to him, but a retired Colonel was not the type of person Spalding had ever wanted to hold at gunpoint.

His emotions must've been visible on his face because Jorge smiled broadly over his mug, his mustaches twisting up into a gray crescent.

"Now, about what happened to you?" Jorge inquired. It was a polite question, but it was laced with a strength that didn't allow him to avoid answering.

Spalding spared a glance for Rylan, then back at Jorge, who answered the unasked question with a slight nod. It was okay to talk openly.

"Well, you've surely heard about my discharge?" Spalding began tentatively.

"It was heavily televised. I'd be surprised if the whole system wasn't aware of what happened to you."

Well. There it was. His reputation was ruined. Forever.

Suddenly, there really didn't seem to be any point in continuing the story.

He shrugged, defeated. "Guess you've heard everything you need to, then."

Jorge's brows lowered into a scowl. "I'd not discount my opinion so quickly."

It was Spalding's turn to scowl. *What's this guy's deal? Is he just toying with me, or does he actually care?*

With nothing else coming to mind, he began his story while Rylan reached over and began picking bits of dirt and debris out of his scrapes and bandaging the wounds. Her touch was simultaneously confident and gentle.

CHAPTER 5

"WHY?" THE LITTLE girl's voice echoed across the misty marbled expanse; it had an odd quality to it, Brennan thought. Sounds fading in and out spontaneously, unnaturally. Light came from everywhere and nowhere at once. The soft plea rebounded off unknown sources lost in the encroaching fog. Despite the distance, Brennan could see the terror in her wide eyes.

Then the gunfire ripped into her stomach. The wet squelching sounds punctuated with subtle *thumps*. The smells of iron mingled with piss, strong enough to burn his nose. The girl dropped her stuffed animal, with half its face blown to torn-puffy bits.

Her eyes dulled, then her knees buckled, and she collapsed to the ground as delicate as a flower knocked from its stem.

Darkness.

Brennan felt his eyes open, but the room was so utterly black it felt as if he had lost his power of vision. Part of him was glad. Some cosmic price had to be paid for what he had done. Seems like his vision was a paltry recompense for all the lives lost.

The other part of him quailed in fear. Fear of what images would fill his mind without the distractions actual sight would offer. A memory of the girl flashed through his mind: her eyes were round, brimming with fear and confusion.

Cursed with a soldier's ability to wake fully within moments, reality didn't so much *crash* down as ease back into standard operating procedure. Brennan eased himself into an upright position, swinging his legs over the side of his bed. More comfortable than a bunk, by far, but quite a margin removed from anything one might consider luxurious. For being set up in a mining platform rig conference room, far removed from civilization, he certainly couldn't complain.

Not about the bed, at least.

More out of habit than desire, he dropped gingerly to the floor and began his new morning ritual. It was impressive how quickly his body had reacted to the lack of genetically enhanced food and gene therapy. His alcohol consumption had been partially to blame, most likely. At this point, he'd rather do a few hundred extra sit-ups as give it up. In fact, he now wondered why he had been so adamantly opposed to it in the first place. He eagerly anticipated ending his exercises so he could ferret out the bottle he had just opened last night.

Halfway through his leg routine, a knock sounded from the door.

The room wasn't overly large, so the sound was easily heard.

Brennan ignored it anyway.

It sounded again, a bit louder this time.

Then a chime sounded, and it opened.

Brennan sighed from the floor. Sweat rolled down his forehead and fell off the bridge of his nose. He hadn't remembered sweating as much while in the Protectorate. Maybe that was a side-effect of the gene therapy too?

"I knocked," Ed McAaron said, a touch on the grumpy side.

"I heard," Brennan replied, suppressing a groan with only partial success as he levered himself to his feet.

The two men stood there facing each other. McAaron in

designer shirt and trousers, hair smartly coifed into that style that seemed to simultaneously give the impression of having each hair expertly placed and a just-got-out-of-bed look. Meanwhile, Brennan stood stripped to the waist, sweating profusely in the stifling room. Nothing but his military-issued underpants on.

After the silence stretched on for longer than he would've liked, Brennan finally spoke, "Can I help you with something, sir?"

McAaron barked out a bitter laugh. "Don't patronize me, Keith." Then he eyed him and sighed. "Would you wipe off and put some clothes on. You're damaging my fragile ego."

It was Brennan's turn to laugh, but his heart was only half in it.

This trust-fund-brat was a bit of a paradox. Everything he had read about the heir-apparent to the McAaron businesses and fortune spoke of a spoiled, bored, and exceedingly bright aristocrat. What stood before him, while being admittedly well-dressed, was a shrewd and charismatic businessman. A far cry from the military genius that this whole *resistance* operation required to be a success. In a pinch, Brennan admitted he'd prefer a charismatic leader over an efficient one.

He set about gathering up the nearest clothes he could find, some casual wear he had been loaned by one of the factory employees. It seemed people got a little twitchy with him wearing Protectorate BDU's around. Come to think of it, wearing them made him a little antsy. That dove-gray he had always worn with pride felt somehow darker than it once had.

"Would you like a drink?" Brennan asked, pulling his shirt down over his head.

McAaron looked somewhat confused, then checked his wristwatch.

"It's 0600."

Brennan shrugged. "Suit yourself."

McAaron sighed and sat down in one of the two chairs in the

room. "How long are you going to keep this up?"

It galled Brennan a little. The nerve. Wasn't this how the wealthy lived their *entire lives*? Steeped in sex, drugs, and alcohol on a daily basis? How dare he judge him!

Then, as if the big bag of hot air that had been swelling inside of him was suddenly pricked, the fight drained from him.

"At least for today," he said in a half-whispered rush.

McAaron frowned but said nothing further on the subject. He just sat there, watching Brennan change and wipe his sweat-soaked forehead down with a hand towel he found on the floor.

"Intel found something I think you should see." McAaron finally said as Brennan took a seat across the small table from him. "I have to warn you though, it's footage from the... *event*."

There was no reason to elaborate. Brennan knew.

"Not interested," Brennan said, grabbing the bottle of cheap rice liquor.

McAaron snatched the bottle from him, quick as a viper.

"I think you will be."

Something about McAaron's tone prompted a fight-or-flight response in his body. He could feel his muscles relax into battle-readiness. Coiled, like whips ready to lash out and draw blood. His eyes opened a bit wider, eyes dilating to expand his focus and take in more detail. Both his breathing and his heart rate slowed.

Although it was a subtle shift, McAaron caught it. He raised a hand between them, then spoke slowly, "Look, I don't want to poke you. If you want to lay around here, mope, and drink yourself stupid every day, that's on you. But, what I have here," he rested his datapad on the table, "might change your mind on how you want to spend your days."

I sincerely doubt it.

"Fine, show me," he snapped.

McAaron began playing helmet-cam video from that fateful day on the steps with a few deft swipes and taps. It was Marek's footage.

"What is..." Brennan started.

"Just watch," McAaron said. Then, he uncorked the bottle and poured an overly cavalier amount of the pungent semi-opaque liquid into the glass.

Brennan eyed the glass, his mouth suddenly exceedingly dry.

Then something in the video jerked his notice back to it.

Stunned, he watched the video to the very end.

He wasn't sure he had blinked or even drawn a breath while he had watched.

Minutes passed.

It couldn't be real. Could it?

"I think..." McAaron started, but it was Brennan's turn to interrupt.

"Play it again," he said, with a bit of his General's tone returning.

McAaron complied.

Again, he watched it without comment or movement.

When it finished, he simply looked at McAaron and said, "Again."

This time, McAaron sighed and grumbled something under his breath before acquiescing.

The full video played. When it finished, he closed his eyes and replayed it in his mind.

"I'd be curious what you make of this?" McAaron asked after a few moments.

Brennan grunted, then stood so quickly he knocked the chair to the ground. McAaron half-rose reflexively from his chair. What? Was he expecting an attack?

That's when he realized his fists were clenched so hard his knuckles were standing out bright white against his dark skin.

"If ever you become an adversary, McAaron," Brennan said slowly, in a dangerous, threatening tone, "you can rest assured you'll know about it beforehand. Sneak attacks are not my style."

Somewhere halfway between seated and standing, McAaron

rose fully and chuckled. "Yeah, I'd imagine that's true."

Then he did something unexpected. He slid the overly full glass of liquor across the table toward him. It sloshed a bit, and Brennan felt a lurch at the frivolous waste. But, he noticed with some confusion he had not rushed to pick it up. Instead, he looked at McAaron coldly.

"There'll be time for that later."

McAaron grinned broadly.

— — —

Sometime later, Brennan wasn't sure how long precisely, when he finally brought his body under some semblance of self-control. He had let his beard grow out, unkempt and wild—also a new repercussion of discontinuing gene therapy—and his normally close-cropped hair had become a black bramble briar perched atop his head.

The ritual of hygiene brought back some of the military attention to detail. With it came self-reflection. There was a boiling riptide of shame curling up beneath his stony resolve. The man he had allowed himself to become was a disgusting mockery of everything he stood for. No longer. Now was the time to make those who were accountable pay. Now was the time for retaliation.

Leaving the stuffy little office felt good. Immediately upon entering the hallway, a weight was lifted from his shoulders. The air felt calmer, lighter, and more pleasant. Even his posture felt different. Head back, shoulders drawn back, core coiled tightly. This felt right. This was who *he* was. Funny how quickly he had been pulled back from the darkness.

He would be eternally grateful to McAaron for that. More than anyone else ever had in battle, Ed had saved his life. Maybe even his very soul.

After exiting the office wing of the complex, the small hallways gave way to large corridors, wide enough to drive machinery through. The building was a massive tangle of cranes, conveyances, wires, and machinery. It was confusing to navigate, each passageway looking eerily similar to the last. The hallway designations had been removed shortly after Brennan had arrived in an effort to confound any would-be invaders. That had been a frustratingly intelligent tactic, it seemed.

The sounds of the central bore room greeted him several minutes before he cleared the archway and into the gigantic circular chamber. A gaping maw stretched out below him, miles into the ground. A combination of catwalks, cranes, and earthsaws crisscrossed the cavity. All were dormant now. For there was far more significant work to be undertaken these days.

"General Brennan, sir," said a young man, who had just moments prior been leaning casually against the railing. Now, he stood back rigid, eyes straight ahead, in a poor semblance of military attention.

"What's your name, soldier?" Brennan barked.

The youth blanched white as a sheet, then squeaked out, "Tim, Tim Parson," then followed with a hurried, "sir!"

Brennan eyed him critically. Letting all the suppressed anger he had carefully cultivated over the years bubble up to affect his body.

Then, right before he thought the young man might pass out from anxiety, he said, "Where can I find the mess?"

Confusion, then relief came over him in a rush alongside his returning color. "Two floors up, two rights, and at the end of the hall."

Brennan committed it to memory, then nodded. "Keep up the good work, Parson."

The revolutionary beamed and snapped out a halfway decent salute before returning to his, now more vigilant, guard duty.

That was one of his strengths. Encouraging soldiers to be *better.* He thought that was one of the qualities that made him such a successful leader in the first place. His ability to inspire greatness out of the troops under his command. Some leaders yelled, screamed, and demanded. That wasn't his style. His soldiers needed to want to be better *all the time.* Not just when he was around. That was something that went deeper than a surface change.

Parson's directions were precise, and he soon was walking through the threshold of the mess hall. It was a large room by any standard, but it was so packed with people it felt cramped. Hundreds of people sat and ate or stood in tight clumps and conversed quietly.

As he strode purposefully into the room, he noticed the volume level in the room drop as he passed. Leaving a wake of hushed whispers and vengeful faces. Not that he could blame them at all. Their response was perfectly reasonable. Justified, even. Except, now he knew the truth. It hadn't been him at all. Instead, it had been an elaborate setup to make him… Well, he knew what he did. No sense in rehashing it any more than he already had.

When he grabbed a metal tray at the far end of the line, one particularly muscular young man made a show of standing his ground between Brennan and the queue. Arms like long-hauler steel bulkheads were crossed tightly against an expansive chest. It was evident to anyone with only one good eye that the boy had himself all worked into a lather and looking for a fight.

Brennan stood quiet. Not passive, but stoic. Resolute.

The boy smirked. "Can I help you with something there, Red?"

The nickname stung. McAaron had warned him about it, but it still was a cheap shot. He refused to let the kid rile him up and instead just continued appraising him calmly.

A few other men of varied ages that had been loitering nearby perked up at the exchange.

So, the young alpha has friends.

Brennan didn't spare them a second glance. He only had eyes for what was in front of him. Which was more than he technically wanted to handle at the moment. His face still hurt from the multitude of beatings he had endured while in captivity. Some of those beatings had been rather inspired.

Without an active participant, some of the bluster had begun to wane from his opponent. The group shrugged at each other; some went so far as to call out half-hearted attempts at insults. Something, *anything*, to provoke a response.

Like moths to the flame, onlookers gathered around tightly. Some craned their necks around others to get a glimpse at what was happening. Simultaneously, the group's immediate area was cleared of any objects that one might be remiss about being broken by the impending scuffle. Brennan could feel the certainty of it. Like the hair on his arms standing on end the moment before a nearby lightning strike.

He'd be damned if he was the one to start it, however.

The two squared off; they couldn't have been more opposite if you had scripted it. One wore an eager grin, obviously to cover up any signs of nervousness. The other was loose, calm, and ready for violence.

With a chuckle, the boy darted forward with a haphazard strike to the face.

Brennan took it wholly on his left cheekbone.

A loud crack echoed in his head.

Then a surprised shriek of pain.

The boy jumped back, clutching the wrist of the hand he had struck with. The weird approach angle and lack of fighting skill had compounded into an awkward punch. Against the rigid protuberance of his cheekbone and the well-balanced stance, there was never a chance of it causing any real damage except to itself.

It still hurt his face, though. Damn it, but he'd had the shit beat out of him enough lately. Seemed like he couldn't heal fast enough to not be sore before the subsequent injuries piled on.

The group took a collective step back as Brennan stepped

forward and grabbed the youth's wrist in a vise-like grip.

His cadre melted back into the crowd, wide-eyed. Leaving their friend to his fate.

Brennan brought the kid's wrist up to his face. Docile as a pet bunny, he complied with only a half-gurgled protest of pain.

"What's your name, son?" Brennan asked as he examined the wrist. Definitely fractured. It was already beginning to yellow.

"Fuck you!" It was half spat through snot bubbles and tears, which made it lose some of its ferocity.

Brennan squeezed the wrist a little bit harder than was absolutely necessary.

The boy wailed.

"Your parents must not like you very much," he quipped, "with a name like that."

"Wha-what?"

Brennan sighed and released the wrist.

Try a different tactic.

"Who taught you how to punch?" Brennan asked.

The crowd mumbled, and everyone exchanged confused or disgruntled looks. Was there going to be a fight, or not?

The youth noticed from his hunched-over position. He was losing his audience.

So, instead of being bright, the hilarity continued.

Brennan watched the boy's leg muscles tense, saw the quick inhalation that preceded the incoming lunge. It was sloppy and telegraphed. When Brennan side-stepped it smoothly, it may have looked like magic. It was just training.

A wet *SLAP* sounded behind him, followed by a groan of disoriented pain. A collective wince from the crowd around them filled the silence.

Slowly, Brennan turned around, taking in the crowd. Most eyes refused to meet his. Although, here and there were some burning embers of hatred. He'd have to deal with all of that eventually. He knew that. Not here. Not this time.

Instead, he addressed the crowd and pointed at the kid lying on the floor. His headlong lunge had evidently ended face-first on the hard floor. Now, snot, tears, and blood were smeared across his face, the floor, and his shirt. Not a good look.

"I know most of you hate me, and none of you trust me. That's fair. I get it." He slowly rotated, trying to catch as many eyes as he could. "What you fail to realize is, you need me."

A rumble of murmurs rolled through the crowd like angry thunder.

Time to drive the point home.

He pointed to the whimpering youth holding his bleeding nose. "You can follow *that* into battle and die." It was a simple statement of fact. "Or, you can use the resources you have available—you can use *me*, and maybe, just maybe, get some retribution for those you lost."

More angry murmurs, some curses were hurled his way.

Then a louder sound, gasps, excited noises, and the crowd parted, revealing McAaron and a few of his usual entourage.

McAaron took in the scene. It couldn't have looked good. The youth mewling and half-dazed sprawled out on the ground. Brennan looming like some kind of dark, vengeful god.

Well, which way is this going to go? The thought wasn't one he relished. He typically tried to avoid fifty-fifty fights.

"Well," the younger man said after a moment, "I'm assuming this was all started by you, Peter." The boy babbled something unintelligible from the ground but pointed at Brennan.

McAaron laughed, bitterness making it an ominous sound.

"General Brennan wouldn't start something and leave it unfinished," he said. "And more importantly, if *he* had started it, I'd expect everyone in this room to be hacking him to pieces by now. Instead, you're all just standing around with your dicks in your hands."

Eyes which were just mere moments prior alight with fury were suddenly downcast and softened with shame.

McAaron looked around the silent room. "Yeah, that's what I thought."

Much to Brennan's surprise, McAaron casually walked over and kicked Peter square in the face. His head rocked back awkwardly with the force of the blow, and the boy went limp. He wasn't dead, but he was undoubtedly unconscious.

Brennan's battlefield instincts kicked in, and he dropped to his knees at the boy's side. He checked the spine, pulse, and breath. Just knocked out. His nose was broken, maybe some damage to his jaw. He'd live, but he'd probably wish he hadn't for a few days.

When Brennan stood, he found McAaron in his face, a finger shoved up under his chin.

"If I ever find out you've laid a hand on any of mine," he smiled darkly, "I'll kill you myself. Are we clear?"

Nobody likes being threatened. That was particularly true for Brennan. Too long being a General made his back come up instantly. There was no way this pompous rich asshole could take him in a fair fight. Hell, he probably couldn't take him even in an unfair one.

Chain of command.

It had been drilled into him from a young boy.

Instead of reaching out and crushing his windpipe, Brennan stepped back and snapped to attention with a smart salute. "Yes, sir!"

As McAaron walked away, so did the crowd. Thankfully, Peter's friends leaped out of the group to scoop up their limp pal. No one so much as spared a glance at Brennan.

The crowd resumed its regular activities as if nothing had happened.

Instead of death glares, everyone pointedly ignored the area Brennan was in. He had gone from the shiny thing you couldn't look away from in the room to a black hole. Funny how crowd dynamics worked.

Suddenly finding himself no longer hungry, Brennan made his way out of the mess hall, where he found McAaron and his lawyer advisor, Des, leaning against the threshold.

"Walk with me," was all that McAaron said before turning to start walking briskly down the corridor.

Brennan fell into step next to him.

They walked for a time in silence, and although he had no idea where they were going, he quickly noticed the number of others in the halls began to thin out. Until they rounded a corner, and Des remained at the intersection. The long corridor before them was devoid of human life. Some steam wisped up through the metal grates below them.

"That was well done. I wasn't certain how'd you'd play that out, but you did surprisingly well. Did you know what was happening?" McAaron's keen eyes peered at him quizzically.

So, this had been a staged test. Brennan found his respect for the younger man grow considerably. It was a shrewd move, not one he would have been comfortable deploying, but it was as efficient as it was brutal.

"Something had seemed off," Brennan admitted openly. "Besides, I won't strike my own men. It goes against my duty. The kid was no real threat."

McAaron laughed. "He's one of our best fighters."

"Well, I'll look into that, sir," Brennan smirked.

"You can dispense with that 'sir' shit," McAaron said, a sour twist to his mouth. "Makes me miss my dad."

A sudden flush rose to the other man's cheeks, Brennan noticed. It was obviously a tender topic. Most assuredly one to avoid in the future.

"Of course," Brennan almost stumbled and called him 'sir' again. Some habits were hard to break. "But only in private, I'm afraid I must insist on the honorific when around others."

McAaron waved it off.

"Do you think that little stunt will work, then?" Brennan

asked, genuinely curious.

"Look, Keith," McAaron hesitated. "You don't mind that I call you Keith, do you?"

Brennan shook his head.

"Again, only in private." McAaron leaned against the wall. "I'm not going to sugarcoat it. Half the people here are scared to death of you like you're some kind of demon straight from hell. The other half wants to murder you in your sleep. I'm not sure which to be more worried about, frankly."

It hurt to have those things said to him. Especially knowing now that he wasn't responsible for the deaths of so many innocents. His self-loathing had subsided somewhat. Ultimately, he felt responsible. Still, it had happened under his nose; that much was a simple fact. However, he had been misled. People he had trusted had betrayed him and the people they had sworn to protect. It was slightly more complicated than he had been led to believe.

McAaron continued, "I think we may have circumvented some of the violence against you for now, with your reluctance to fight back and my support. But, I think it may have generated even more fear of you. I'm not sure how that's going to play out yet, but at least I don't have to worry about our own men jumping you on the shitter."

The two stood there for a moment in contemplative silence.

A slight clang sounded back the way they had come. Des rapped a heavy gold ring on one of the three-inch metal pipes that ran the length of the corridor.

McAaron clasped him on the shoulder. "You okay?"

He nodded.

"Good. There's work to be done." McAaron started walking toward Des, calling over his shoulder as he did, "my office, 1600."

Brennan watched the intersection that they disappeared around. It wasn't long until a group passed by, murmuring.

McAaron was proving to be a much more cunning leader

than he had initially thought. The test today had taken Brennan totally by surprise. Not the fight in and of itself, but that McAaron was shrewd enough to read his people and stage what was needed. He wasn't sure he had thought McAaron was up to it. It was probably way past time to get up to speed on precisely what the potential was there.

There might actually be a pathway to success for this endeavor.

One he might even manage to live through.

However unlikely that was, he would grasp with any chance.

Feeling somewhat better than he had this morning, he decided he'd jog back to his rooms.

As he flashed by people, he noticed widening eyes and heard hushed whispers trailing him. It hadn't been very long, but events like that tended to spread quickly as a wildfire with the wind at its back.

Time to play the game.

Or die trying.

CHAPTER 6

NOTHING PISSED HER off more than inefficient information gathering. There was no more remarkable example of that in the system than the *headquarters* of the revolution. She struggled to even call it a headquarters; that title implied that someone here knew what the fuck they were doing.

Frankie Zoya had spent a lot of time pissed off lately.

A large part of her regretted not using her alias and fleeing this shitshow.

The other part of her had checked the status of the craft she had registered that alias on and found that it was lost in space—with all twelve-hundred passengers presumed dead.

So, not really much choice at all, as it turned out.

Still, she wanted to complain despite it being irrational.

What was happening at the Vulcan Complex was little more than collective dick-jerking and jaw-flapping. Nobody here had any clue what to do; next, that much was obvious. Their intelligence department lacked enough of its namesake to qualify for the title. For almost a month, she had been sneaking good data onto the desks of her superiors. Not wanting to attract too much attention lest she blow her cover. Not that she had any faith in any of these idiots to actually do a job decent enough to find out her true identity. It just wasn't worth the risk.

Instead, she floated the information without leaving a trail back to herself and watched as it got misinterpreted or flat-out ignored. It was all good data. Just over the heads of her fellow analysts. If you could even call them that.

It had been her research that had wrestled the footage from Marak's helmet-mounted camera away from the Protectorate's digital vault. She had burned one of her few remaining backdoors in the effort, too, which stung deeply. If this war effort stood any chance whatsoever, it needed the insight and leadership of Keith Brennan. All of this posturing was juvenile and wasted the resource they lacked the most: Time.

Idiots!

She had had every intention of staying outside the complex itself and operating independently. Much safer that way for everyone involved. The last thing she needed on her mind was whether or not her own baggage was going to bring the Protectorate crashing down on the complex and ruining any chances of it eking out what small success it was able to.

Moreover, she had nightmares enough to contend with.

On reflex, she reached into her coat pocket and ran her fingers across the cold grip of the knife she had used to stab her once friend.

The friend that had betrayed her.

Tried to kill her.

She wouldn't even use her name.

If that was even her *real* name.

It was the right move; she knew that. Still, she felt the guilt of taking another person's life. She could still feel the warm stickiness of blood on her hands. Interesting, that. Maybe it wasn't just an old saying for no reason—having blood on one's hands.

Frankie suppressed a shudder.

In the almost month she had been there, her hair dye had

worn out, without hope of it being replenished. That was unlucky. She was still utilizing prosthetic implants to alter her facial structure slightly to hide from any facial recognition being deployed within the complex. Their rudimentary central intel division had disconnected and dismantled the interior camera system to reduce the Protectorate's ability to hack into it and gather intelligence. But who knew how good of a job they did? The problem with technology was that it was so prevalent, you could never be sure where it had spread.

That wasn't even her biggest worry for a leak.

The complex was now home to almost twelve thousand citizens. Of that, only twelve hundred were previous employees with any semblance of prior vetting. That meant they had over ten thousand potential moles, leaks, or opportunists. That was far too many.

Watching the screen as her fingers flashed across her keypad, she ran scenarios for a distribution operation to spread the revolution across the Hellas metro area. The city itself, nestled in the canyons of Noctis Labyrinthus, was a sprawling network that comprised only half of the near thirteen thousand square kilometers of the greater metro area. Most of which consisted of above-ground infrastructures like farming platforms, solar arrays, power plants, research, and manufacturing plants. And, of course, resource platforms like the Vulcan Complex.

The scenarios she was running would create a nasty network of smaller cells, with several close enough to each other to provide assistance if necessary. Their numbers were nowhere near high enough to withstand the full might of a Protectorate assault, so being hidden was their best option for staying viable. The fact that no one had distributed their force already was absolutely beyond moronic to her. In her opinion, every second they were all crammed into one space, they were an irresistible target. One air attack could end it all before it even got started.

What a waste that would be.

So, she endeavored to put together all the data, run the scenarios, and gently push the powers-that-be into the right course of action. Credit wasn't necessary for her, not when lives were on the line, but bloody hell—some acknowledgment of her hard work would be a welcome difference in her life. Just once! Was that too much to fucking ask?

She scrubbed her face with her hands vigorously.

Exhaustion was making her more emotional than she usually allowed herself to get. Between the nightmares and all the work she was trying to do, she wasn't sleeping much. That deprivation was fraying her usually steadfast resolve.

A chime sounded from her workstation, and she glanced at the monitor distractedly.

What the hell is that?

The signal-floor across an insanely vast frequency range had suddenly spiked. A *massive* spike! More extensive than she thought was possible.

Solar flare?

That didn't make any sense, there were warning systems for that, and those were totally silent at the moment. It was a strange frequency range for that kind of natural event too. This was definitively in the *created* spectrum. It was some kind of communication; she just had no idea what.

It had to be an attack of some kind. Something to this scale, some new type of electronic warfare tactic? Playing off that hunch, she brought up monitoring station data from several observatories and datacenters across the globe. *All* of them were reporting this spike.

As quickly as it had appeared, it was gone.

Frankie just sat there stunned, with her mind spinning circles around itself. Every scenario she thought of to explain it away came up short. It *had* to be a natural occurrence, then. Right?

She reached out to open a secure line to the dipshit running the intelligence center for the rebels. Her fingers hesitated above the switch. Chief Ninlil Aslan was the last person *anyone* should want running their intelligence department. Evidently, she had previously been responsible for all the complex's electrical infrastructure and that of the McAaron household. Originally from a small outpost town outside of Jezero, on the edge of the northern crater.

Naturally, Frankie had pulled her dossier. Tall, freakishly thin, and a twitchy chain-smoker, she had studied Electro-Combat Defense Strategies from some unknown Protectorate professor in recent years.

Chief Ninlil Aslan strode through the crowd toward her station. Her long black hair done up in a braid that hung straight as an arrow down along her spine. Her skin reminded Frankie of polished sandstone, the rose-gold and brown shades somewhat luminous in the artificial lighting. She was stunningly beautiful by any standard.

It pissed Frankie off somewhat the way men reacted to her presence and hung on every word. Frankie ranked her slightly less worthless than her previous boss.

If she took a moment to self-reflect, she'd realize that she had never appreciated any of her superiors. What did that say about her? Best not to overanalyze that.

There was no way she was going to escalate this to Aslan. Not in a million years.

Instead, she isolated the data from the signal, stored it on her personal drive, encrypted it, and buried all the tracking markers within the systems that had registered her activity. Not only did it no longer exist within their systems, but neither did her interactions with it. On a whim, she wiped her activity for the entire day and logged herself as "ill" within the note field. Only a few people had seen her that morning, not that she had spoken to any of them. Or anyone at all for days, for that matter.

With a swipe, she powered off her workstation, placed an extra-fine filament wire on the far edge of the keypad as her usual tamper-detection, and fled the intelligence room. Which, if she wasn't mistaken, had once been the security room for the complex. Now, repurposed as the hub of military intelligence.

Her derisive snort caused a few heads to whip in her direction.

It wasn't fair to everyone, and she was projecting her own frustrations with her situation. She fully realized this. That didn't make her want to change, however. Yes, she was pissed off that she couldn't be *herself.* She was highly pissed off that her considerable skills were being completely, *totally,* underutilized.

But, what was she supposed to do?

There was no clear path to success here.

If she came out and told them she was a Homeland runaway, they'd immediately isolate her and mistrust her.

Far worse would be to give them her name. If they looked her up, who knew what they'd find. Besides the fact that Homeland would be watching her files and would immediately trace any outside access of it. It would lead Brillian right to their front door. She had resisted the urge to look herself up on many occasions. So far.

As she stalked out of the hallway, grinding her teeth furiously, she let the bustling activity in the corridors wash over her. Usually, she would consider herself a keen observer. Eyes constantly darting about, gathering information on everyone and everything. Exhaustion really was taking its toll on her.

Sleep. She needed rest, but that strange signal had her dander up. There was something weird about it. Maybe she'd go back to her room and backdoor into the intel systems and continue her analysis from there. At least it hadn't been directed at the Vulcan Complex. Then she'd know for sure it was an attack, and they had been found out before she could convince the leadership to vacate.

Another thing weighing heavily on her was how the hell had the Protectorate not thought to look here? Tracking down the hub of rebel activity had taken Frankie less than six hours. Hell, the autonomous cab ride out to the outskirts of the metro region had taken longer.

Someone hurrying by bumped into her shoulder. Being as small as she was, the blow staggered her. She whipped around furious, only to find the man's back retreating hurriedly around a corner. The curses and insults died on her tongue. They had been colorful too, damn it! Spending time around all these platform workers had introduced her to some very interesting slang, where foul language was concerned. A few she had been eager to deploy at the earliest possible convenience. Was it silly that she felt disappointed about not being able to use them?

Literally shaken from her thoughts, she realized she was adrift and lost. She had always had a focus. Her entire life had been focused on protecting the world. The whole system, really. But, Mars in particular. But now? All of that had been stripped from her. She felt naked, exposed, and worthless. Of the three, she'd prefer to be naked and exposed but with a job to do.

The issue with the emerging rebel army was that it hadn't decided it wanted to actually *become* an army yet. It was still playing at the idea. Nobody had stepped up to take charge and DO something! Which, in her opinion, was an infuriating waste of time and opportunity. The Protectorate was weak on Mars right now, but that would change quickly. It was somewhat surprising that it hadn't already. Had she still been with Homeland, she'd have this whole Hellas region swarming with ground soldiers.

So far, though, no significant response from the Protectorate. Little more than policing efforts.

But why?!

Why go to all the trouble to disrupt the planet, only to sit back on your heels *now?*

There was zero tactical advantage to waiting.

Someone had better do something soon, or she was going to scream.

Shit, or get off the pot already!

Was she actually *hoping* for war? Hoping for an uprising? Possibly. A small part of her railed against the notion; would give anything for a peaceful resolution to their predicament. The logical part of her knew that they had gone too far for a favorable outcome, beyond a doubt. That day in Founder's Square had sealed the deal on that. There would be more blood before this was all said and done. A *lot* more of it.

When the door hissed open to her room, all she wanted to do was take a nap. The tight quarters consisted of a foldable bed that was more cot than a bed, a lavatory drawer and sink, a small closet for her personal belongings, and a bit of corner shelving which served as a low-duty workstation. Not nearly so powerful or connected as the systems in the intel room, but serviceable for her needs. A thin wall-mounted mirror and an empty digital picture frame completed the furnishings. It wasn't much, but it was hers.

Images of a blood-spattered lavish apartment flashed through her mind. The corpse of someone once considered a friend bleeding into the plush carpets.

That was always the type of living environment Frankie had wanted. Something minimalist, clean, but tasteful. Something she could revel in as an outward expression of her internal style. What that style was, she had no idea. It sure would be nice to figure it out one day, though.

The complex was hot, humid, and a thin sheen of sweat had covered her body from the brisk pace she had set. As the workstation began to load her personal files, she stripped to her undergarments and locked the door to her quarters. She drew some cold water from the sink with her hands and splashed her face and chest. The sudden cold sent a shiver of exhilaration through her. Which helped to calm her racing thoughts. She was all over the place today. Maybe she really was getting sick?

A chime sounded from her workstation, and she eased onto the small stool that was part of the little desk setup. It was hard and uncomfortable on her ass; neither had much padding to speak of, so she slouched on it.

"Let's see what exactly you are." She often spoke to herself when she was engrossed in a task. It didn't even feel weird to her anymore. When she had been younger, her parents had tried to get her to stop the embarrassing habit. Their insistence had worked for a time. But as soon as she had struck out on her own, the practice reasserted itself.

Fingers flying across the limited keypad, she began analyzing the signal. Whatever it was, it was huge. Anything she applied to it immediately bogged the system down to the point of being almost entirely worthless.

Sighing, she set up several processes to run back-to-back and then hopped up from the stool. There'd be no multitasking on this one.

Instead, she flopped down on the bed and stared at the ceiling.

She loathed feeling like this. So much angst. Was it really that critical that she contribute? Realistically, she should be counting her blessings that she was still breathing. The thought gave her little comfort, but she managed to drift off to sleep as her processes ran the data.

Problems for tomorrow.

CHAPTER 7

THE EARTHENWARE DISH smashed against the wall of the conference room. Bruce watched with no small amount of satisfaction as the fragments skittered and spun across the room. A gratifying white pattern of dust clung to the wall where it had impacted.

The administrative aide stood in stunned silence, eyes as wide as the plate had once been and twice as white.

"Out!" The word was forced between angry gasps of air and clenched teeth.

The aide complied promptly.

Once alone, he collapsed into the unreasonably comfortable high-backed synthetic leather chair. It galled him that proper leather had gone out of fashion so thoroughly. In his mind, there was nothing more pleasing than the feeling of adequately maintained animal skin. Pity they were so hard to come by these days.

Nothing was going right. Absolutely nothing. With the escape of Brennan, one of the most critical pieces he had to play had been lost to him. He maintained control of Helena, but she was rapidly wearing out her worth. Something would have to be done about her, and soon. The question was, how to turn that loss into an advantage?

Bruce pinched the bridge of his nose with his thumb and forefinger. A technique to relieve some of the pressure building up behind his eyes. Running things on Mars had been a touch more daunting than he had initially planned. Yes, everything had, for the most part anyway, gone according to his designs. Still, the few bumps thus far had been considerable.

A delicate chime sounded from the breast pocket of his coat.

What now?

He reached in and withdrew his mobile datapad and almost dropped it.

The screen read, in all capital letters: SECURE TRANSMISSION.

There was only one person this could be.

Suppressing his gag reflex as best he could, he fumbled the ACCEPT button. The decorative diamond stud set into the space behind his right ear was a bone conduction speaker, one of the few technologies preventing digital eavesdropping. Given his line of work, a handy thing if you could stomach having someone shout *inside* your head.

"Hold, please," the person on the other line said. A sweet voice, like threads of silk in a summer breeze. Pleasant to hear. Probably why she got the job.

"Bruce." This voice, however, was dark and commanding. Full of confidence and male vigor. It had that tonal quality that every man aspired to. Resonate, rich, and virile.

"President Trent, how wonderful to hear from you." It was far, far the opposite. But, what was one supposed to say to the most powerful man in the solar system? The most powerful *human* alive today? "How are you?"

There was a grunt from the other side. There were no delusions of friendship shared between them, for either party, it seemed.

"I'd be better if you told me you had recaptured our mutual

friend?" It was most certainly a question, not a statement.

"Afraid he's still in the wind," he replied and quickly followed up with, "but we will get him. There's nowhere he has to go. He may have died in the safe house attack for all we know."

It was true. His troops abandoned the safehouse in preparation for a tragic 'accident' or 'terrorist attack' that would rid him of the nuisance. Unfortunately, in that small window of time, the General had somehow managed to be rescued. At least, that was the assumption they were operating under. Who had done the deed was a question that kept him up at night. There was no way anyone could trust him after what had been arranged at Founders Square. Was there?

Bruce realized Trent had been talking, but he hadn't paid attention.

"I'll get right on that." He hedged a response. Affirmation was always appropriate, right?

"I bet you will," came a slow, dangerous response. "Bruce, need I remind you that the point to all of this was a quick transition of power? Disruption, *not* destruction!"

Incorrect. The thought made him smile. The point to all of this was *money*. The power was just the way to achieve that goal. This was about setting up a dynasty that would last centuries. With the kind of power he was seeking, it would flow for generations. And, of course, everyone else involved that helped him achieve that if he must. Again, however, how do you correct someone like President Trent?

You didn't.

"Understood, sir. If I may, we still have Governor Chu. She has proven to be most valuable with domestic matters here, naturally." It galled him to admit it, even to himself, but they would have faced an outright rebellion from day one if anything had happened to the stately woman. *Well, anything the public had been made aware of!*

The thought sent a little shock through his body. A quick

tingle that began in his spine and radiated both up and down through his body. He could still smell the blood in the air, feel the burn of impact abrasions on his knuckles. That kind of power was seductive. Being able to revel in that delicious moment, for all the indignities he had suffered under her yoke... It had been immensely satisfying. An epic thrill ride he'd love to savor one more time before her tragic end.

Something about the knowledge he'd be the last to enjoy that intimate moment with the Governor was empowering. He couldn't wait.

Alas, he must.

She was still marginally valuable for their efforts, and he wasn't confident that losing another key player would be tolerated.

"There are several of us that are concerned you're losing control of the situation there, Bruce." It was a low growl, as menacing as a mountain cat stalking prey in the darkness. The previous warm thrill was replaced with a shock of cold ice in his veins.

"I assure you, Sir, your trust is not misplaced. Everything is going according to plan here. We are, even now, drawing up plans to use Governor Chu to draw out whatever organized insurgents still remain in Hellas. If the General is with them, he will come for her. And we will be ready if he does."

Bold. Confident. Decisive.

That's who Bruce Afolabi was.

It felt good to hear it in his voice.

"You had better be."

The only indication the line had terminated was the telltale click.

He sat there, idly twirling side to side in the chair. The long highly-polished conference table glistened brightly under the daylight-balanced lights illuminating the room. Not as glorious as the council room table, but still thick and sturdy wood, it was beauty and function rolled into one.

Much like himself, as it happened.

Sighing, he stood and made his way out into the hallway.

Much of the Administration Building had been locked up; the rest had been repurposed by Protectorate officials. Now it was more of a military hub than any kind of civic government operation. Everyone around him was dressed in the dove-grey of Protectorate field uniforms, the subtle differences he refused to acknowledge or understand. In contrast, he was dressed in a dark navy mock-velvet long coat with silk pipings in golden silk. His vanilla white dress shirt was accented with a hex patterned textured necktie of the current oversized fashion and calf-high polished carbon fiber boots. It was one of his favorite ensembles. The one he wore when was feeling especially powerful.

Everyone looked at him as he passed. The attention felt lovely.

Trent may be the most powerful man in the system, but Bruce Afolabi was the most powerful man currently on Martian soil.

Truth be told, it made him desire *more.*

First, he needed to find Brennan. If the little fucker was still alive.

Then, he'd have the opportunity to deal with Helena, once and for all.

That would be two glorious victories.

As he approached the elevators to the private apartment wing, he slowed his brisk pace somewhat. He could pop up and pay the captive Governor a quick visit. His handiwork was almost completely faded now, which was mildly disappointing. He had rather enjoyed surveying the swirls of purple, yellow, and green.

Two guards stood at the elevator, neither so much as twitched in his direction.

That reminded him of the missing girl. Natalie? Nadine? Whatever her name was. She had gone missing a couple days ago. It was somewhat alarming, but nothing seemed to be amiss. The guards on duty reported nothing out of the ordinary, and her datapad had not been online since she had left the building the night of her disappearance.

It was probably nothing, but it made his hair stand on end.

Dismissing the idea of visiting Helena, he continued past the bank of elevators.

There was more important work to be done, sadly.

He could hear the buzz of the central council chamber before he even turned the corner near it. The amphitheater-style room sloped gently to the low floor with aisle after aisle of the flip-bottom chairs. The red fabric and black-swirled orange wood shone like the surface hills during a Martian sunrise. The circular room gave it the feel of the famous Red Planet. All intentional design, of course. Beautiful, if lacking some subtlety, in his opinion.

The room was an absolute hive of activity. Gray figures were seated at every makeshift workstation, others darting all around. It all felt like some macabre choreographed dance. The lives of millions of Martian citizens hanging by a delicate thread tossed amid the sea of gray.

Bruce scowled deeply.

There was nothing worse than being distracted by beautiful things. He had a sharp mind and vast intelligence. He probably would've been a playwright or storyteller if he hadn't been so drawn to civic duty. Seeing the world's beauty was a gift unto itself, but being able to viscerally describe such beauty; well, that was next to godliness.

As he walked through, many of the intelligence officers saluted. These were the brains of the entire military operation. They respected him. The realization never ceased to brighten his spirits.

"Good evening Mr. Afolabi, sir."

Soon you'll be calling me President, so don't get used too used to using that honorific.

"We need to find Keith Brennan," he said, flicking a speck of dust he had somehow managed to pick up on the walk there from his shoulder. "Immediately."

The officers all exchanged weary looks. The one who had greeted him finally said, "We understand sir, we have every available resource scouring the city as we speak."

There it was then. Every available resource. All one could do is wait for the rabbit to be flushed out of the brush.

"Excellent!" he chirped cheerfully.

He sat in a chair and motioned to a passing gray-coated woman no older than her mid-twenties. "Could you have some food brought in? I find all this hunting stirs up an appetite!"

The woman looked mildly confused, but he didn't pay her any further attention.

The group he sat near eyed him askew, but then they wisely got back to work.

None of what they were doing made any real sense to Bruce. His talents were not even ancillary to technology. He did pick up on the fact they were using facial recognition from drone swarms throughout the underground city and the surface structures.

If Brennan were alive, they would find him.

Of that, Bruce had little doubt.

Instead of wasting his energy watching the work being done, he set his mind to task on how to spin the current challenges to his advantage. Brennan would work itself out, one way or the other. His plan to turn the city against him had been executed brilliantly. Marak had done an excellent job there. That was another loose end he'd have to deal with before too much longer. There was nowhere that Brennan could turn to for succor. He'd go down as one of the most loathed people in history, and Bruce was going to do everything in his power to amplify that narrative.

Helena presented a much more unique problem. Just killing her would be fun, but he couldn't shake the feeling that it would be a waste of a quality resource.

In an ideal world, he'd find a way to make her death elevate his status. Despite what he had shared with Trent, Mars was an absolute mess at present. Lawlessness was at an all-time high. Protectorate outposts were being attacked at random, bombings and lootings happening all over Hellas city. From the inside, it looked like a proper rebellion. Of course, he made sure to filter everything to fit the 'terrorist threat' angle they had established shortly after the assassination of that prick Motwani.

The world was far better off without that piece of shit skulking about. With all his talks of enduring independence and "strong separations deepening systemic resilience." Bullshit. His version of the world lacked one critical thing—a bottom line worthy of the effort. What good was it for Bruce to have the world lifted up around him? That just meant less money for him.

No, Helena needed to take the fall for the failings of the Martian people to properly transition. She obviously had to die, of that he was sure. She was too headstrong and had nothing left to lose. He didn't need that kind of wildcard in his deck. Now, if there was a chance he could brand her as the scapegoat for all of this. Well, that would be a meaningful use of her life. At least she would not die lacking value.

The thought made him smile.

See? he thought to himself. *And they said I couldn't be kind.*

CHAPTER 8

THERE JUST WASN'T enough room in his large duffle for *both* the bottles of Sedona Bourbon. It was fucking unfortunate at best, an epic tragedy at worst.

Spalding considered his options. A bulk of his belongings had already been sold off to random buyers. None of his *friends* would even return his messages. And several had blocked any contact from him. Some friends.

Resisting the urge to question his life choices, he tossed the older bottle of amber liquid into his pack, where it clattered with the other vintages.

"What about this?" Rylan asked, poking her head in from the other room.

Spalding was a bit bashful about his old personal apartment. It was smaller than he would've liked. With his staying on base, this had more or less become something of an investment property than a proper home. Rendered to little more than an overpriced storage unit, given he hadn't *actually* rented it out. But, the price had been reasonable when he had purchased it. In an up-and-coming area, or so he had been told. Whether or not that was going to ever pan out was no longer an issue. That life, those dreams, were a thing of the past now.

The young girl had insisted on helping him, however. So, here they were.

She held up a rolled-up bit of parchment, old-looking by its tattered edges. He instantly recognized it as one of several commissioned art pieces he had done. Everything was a digital recreation these days, and it was a challenge to find actual painters. It had cost a fortune, but the set of three landscapes were of birds of prey in various environments. He had always felt a certain kinship with the birds, lords of the sky. Not that any existed on Mars, or many remained on Earth for that matter. Still, he liked them.

"Sell," that was all that he said, then turned back to the bag on his bed.

Purging his life was mildly depressing, he was finding. Here he had collected all of the *stuff* that he was going to build a life with. Maybe even one day a wife, kids, grandkids. Someone he could tell his stories to, the actual and the fabricated.

Sure, he could still have those things, possibly. The thing that had him down was that the life he had been building had been torn away from him. Politics, as best he could tell, was the reason. He wondered bitterly how many other failures he had heard of or seen were the same political sabotage.

He glanced at the bottle of Sedona. It was an old vintage, having sat in the bottle for a hundred years or so by the imprinted date. The amber liquid bordered on burnt orange, which is probably what gave this straight bourbon its unique name, "Louisville Sunrise." It had a nice ring to it, and by all accounts, was smooth as a summer breeze back on Earth.

His mouth, suddenly drier than it was a moment ago, ached for a splash of the burning liquid. How long had it been since his last drink? Well, there wasn't a drink in his hand, so, far too long. Just one drink wouldn't ruin the bottle, right?

"What about this one?" Rylan poked her head back in again,

holding up a box of what appeared to be odds and ends.

"Look, just box it all up and sell it all, okay?" He had been a bit snippy with her all morning, but it had finally been enough.

With a sigh, he hefted the bottle and tossed it underhand to her. Juggling the box and catching the bottle put her a bit off-balance, but she managed.

"Sell that too," he choked out.

Rylan studied the bottle for a minute, her eyes wide with surprise. "Is this the real deal?"

He ignored the question and instead emptied his bedside closet and began rolling up articles of clothing to shove into his duffle.

"Look, Jonathan," she started softly but picked up steam as she spoke, "this is likely for the best. If you leave this here, eventually someone will find out you're gone and come to take it all anyway."

He nodded angrily as he shoved rolled-up pants into the bag.

Without getting further acknowledgment, Rylan exhaled softly and went back into the other room. He could hear the bottle clanking around as she packed it away to be sold.

It was difficult to not be bitter. He had never done anything but his duty. Sacrificed everything he could to serve. Sure, he had had other options along the way. Some had even been tempting. All he had ever wanted was to be the best pilot in the system. To be remembered as having *done* something with his talents that was meaningful.

Instead, his name had been struck from the records of the Fleet. It had all been for nothing and no one. His accounts had been seized, his personal property on base had been taken as 'evidence' during his Admiral's Mast. Everything, gone in a flash.

The worst part was, he still wasn't even sure *why!*

They blamed him for the deaths of the Legion. Called him derelict in his command. Obviously, that wasn't true… Was it? He had trouble remembering the precise details of that encounter.

The recent binge drinking might have something to do with that.

No, it was much better to call this a total loss and flee to the belt. Start over. He wasn't without talent, and those talents could be put to good use for a pittance of what they were worth. And, he'd be grateful for the opportunity.

"Fuckers!" the word grated out between clenched teeth.

Get him alone in a room with Admiral Maureen Colt for two minutes, just *two fucking* minutes! That would set the universe right again.

A chime sounded from the other room.

The front door.

Rylan ducked her head in with a questioning look on her face.

Spalding shook his head slowly and pressed a finger to his lips to indicate she should be silent. The girl nodded and looked anxiously into the other room toward the exit.

The chime sounded again.

Spalding crept over to the wall panel in the bedroom and activated the exterior camera. The hallway showed a group of Protectorate youths. Pilots by their uniforms.

Swearing silently to himself, Spalding glanced around the room.

He had been hoping it would take them a little longer to discover this place in his records. There had been some extra steps and extra fees involved to keep this out of the city registry. Someone would've had to have gone to a lot of work to track this down. But, when you were one of the highest-ranking members of the Protectorate and wanted to burn a bridge—why not be thorough.

The chime sounded again, several more times in rapid succession.

Spalding wanted to activate the external mic to eavesdrop on the conversation, but he knew it would turn on a blinking indicator to let people know they could be overheard. An annoying feature in this particular circumstance.

A loud thud drew his attention back to the monitor.

The group had taken to shouldering the door. A fat lot of good that was going to do.

Rylan waved at him to get his attention, then shrugged dramatically. Her question was straightforward enough to understand, "What are we going to do?"

If she wasn't with him, likely he'd open the door and beat their faces in.

It was not likely that he'd win the encounter, but he'd rather fight as run.

Another reason why abandoning his life here hurt so badly.

With her safety in question, that wasn't even an option.

Thinking on his feet and adapting to situations was one of the things he was known for. Hard to be the Fleet's best pilot without being mentally agile. Former best pilot.

His apartment was only three stories off the ground, with several windows. None of which opened quite enough to squeeze his bulky frame through, but Rylan could maybe manage it. Falling the ten meters to the ground, however, might be tricky. Not to mention the entire point for being there was to gather up anything he could sell quickly on the black market and book a one-way ticket out to the belt and hopefully a fresh start.

What a fucking cliché I've turned into.

The windows were a bad idea. Now that he thought about it, there was some kind of fire-escape mechanism to the side of the bedroom. The agent he had purchased it from had pointed it out during their technical walkthrough post-purchase.

He pointed to the window and shoved a few more things into his duffle before sealing it shut and slinging it over his shoulder. The dozen or so bottles of rare liquor sloshed and clanked around, graciously muffled by the clothes and bag. Just the bottles alone should earn him enough to flee. It infuriated him that someone else would benefit from his years of saving and collecting, though. It really, *really* hurt.

The pounding at the door began to increase in frequency and volume as the young pilots tried to force their way in. Spalding examined the window, and in short order found a small emergency release latch. Not knowing exactly what would happen when pulled, he motioned for Rylan to step back.

When she was a reasonably safe distance away, he stood to the side—in case the window fell inwards, which would be ridiculous, but you never know—and jerked the small switch down. Immediately sirens blared.

Damn it!

He hadn't even considered they'd be tied to some building-wide system.

The good news was that the whole floor-to-ceiling glass panel didn't plummet to the city streets below. Instead, it swung out on hidden hinges allowing access to the now fully-deployed emergency ladder.

A wide-eyed Rylan looked over the edge down at the street below.

"Don't look down," Spalding told her as he slung the pack and maneuvered her into going down the ladder first.

"Too late," she said as she grasped the first rung and gulped.

"HEY!" shouted a voice from the bedroom doorway.

Spalding jerked around to find the first of four young men in dove-gray uniforms walking into the room. All were smirking.

Evidently, triggering the fire alarm also unlocks all the doors. Makes sense, but damn it if it wasn't incredibly inconvenient at present.

"Oh, hey guys," he cooed mockingly, glancing quickly to see Rylan's progress. It was painfully slow. She only just now fully clambered onto the ladder. "Careful, there appears to be a fire in the building."

A rather large youth in the back chuckled while the others just looked on eagerly. Everyone knew what was coming. Spalding had seen this look a lot in the last few weeks.

That's when they rushed him, and he realized he was standing with his back to a ten-meter drop to the plasticized pavement. He spun, drawing the duffel around his body with all the strength he could put into it. The heavy bag gained quite a bit of momentum and slammed into the first two solidly. They lost their footing and were slung against the wall nearest the bed.

The back two had enough time to dodge out of the way.

That gave Spalding enough time to drop the duffel and step into their defenses.

The fight wasn't pretty, but it was over quick enough.

Everything happened in a blur of violence. The bleachy smell of sweaty bodies comingled with the pungent iron smell of fresh blood.

By the end, three of the four youths lay sprawled out unconscious or dazed on the ground. The fourth hopped around grasping at an elbow that had been forced in the wrong direction; it flopped around disgustingly. The pain should keep that one busy for long enough that he could make his escape.

Spalding slung his bag over a shoulder and only then realized that one of his hands wasn't responding correctly. Unfortunately, it looked like he had broken some of the smaller bones and maybe damaged his wrist. The problem with hitting things is that they were often pretty hard.

He looked at the ladder.

That was going to make his escape plan somewhat more interesting.

With a quick glance at the room, he knew he was running out of time. The young pilots were beginning to get their wind back. There was no way he'd be able to take the group a second time, so he had to get out now.

Cursing under his breath, he looked down to see Rylan just reaching the bottom of the ladder. With her mostly out of the way, he swung a leg out. Reaching across with his good hand, he grasped a rung. The extra momentum from the heavy bag propelled him out the window and onto the side of the building. He smacked his face against the metal ladder harder than he would've liked.

"Don't hurt the moneymaker, might need that soon," he grunted to no one in particular.

Now comes the painful part.

There was no way to safely and effectively descend the ladder as intended. So, he reached around with his damaged right hand, encircling the outer edge of the ladder. Then, he quickly reached around the opposite edge with his left hand and grasped his right tightly. It hurt; he may have screamed. He couldn't tell from the adrenaline pumping in his ears.

"Hey, grab him!" Came a voice from inside the room.

Time to go.

He hopped a little and placed the arches of his booted feet on either side of the ladder. He slid down the rail. As best he could, he used his elbows along the rail to control the speed of his descent. It didn't quite work as he intended, and he slammed into the ground hard enough to lose his breath.

Luckily, nothing further appeared to be broken. The first win of the day!

Rylan helped him to his feet, and the two sped off down the alleyway.

Drones were just beginning to screech into the area to investigate the fire alarm.

Another good reason to get the hell out of the district.

"Well," Rylan puffed next to him as they ran, "that was fun! Can we do it again?"

He couldn't help himself; he laughed like a lunatic as they both ran down the street. Blood and snot frothing out of his nose in great bubbly gouts. It felt good to laugh again. The combination of a high-stress situation and levity reminded him of the Legion. Damn, but he missed their faces.

Rylan laughed just as wildly beside him.

She was cute. He liked her style. She might be the only person he would miss once he left this damned rock.

— — —

"Thank you, Colonel," Spalding said as he reached out to grasp the older man's hand.

His grip was painfully tight, his hands gritty like sandpaper from overuse.

"It's just Jorge now," he squeezed thoughtfully, "as I'm sure you'll come to understand in the months to come."

Spalding couldn't help but flex the life back into his hand once he had it back. He caught the sad smile on Jorge's face.

There was a story here, but not one he had the luxury of time to dig into.

Rylan handed him a small pack. When he looked at it quizzically, she just shrugged.

Inside he found some meal bars and a few snacks of various makes.

"Are these the ones made from bugs?" Insect protein was disgusting. He much preferred the kelp products.

"Mostly plant," she said, making a face. "But we had one beef bar I gave you."

It wasn't so much that animal proteins were rare, just expensive. The economics of it drove the price through the roof. He was no stranger to animal proteins, as they were the preferred military diet staple. Still, it was quite a sacrifice for these two to share with him.

It made his chest ache. He didn't deserve their kindness.

"I can't," he started.

"You can, and you will," Jorge said firmly, clapping him on the back and turning him toward the waiting shuttle. "Pay us back someday. I'm sure you'll find a way."

Spalding smiled. It wasn't likely. The old man was letting him off the hook, and they both knew it.

He turned to leave Luna, possibly forever, and began walking toward the shuttle.

Before he had made it halfway, he had a thought and turned back.

"Will you be comfortable with me reaching out every now and then?" A disgraced pilot, on the run, just about worthless as a person could be. Who would want that?

The two shared a long look, then Rylan smiled and called out, "We'd be offended if you didn't."

Spalding smiled and nodded.

Minutes later, the engines roared to life, and the shuttle took off. It's VTOL engines punching it straight out from the smaller municipal spaceport. More expensive by far, but equally more discrete. Spalding and Jorge had both agreed that the Protectorate Fleet home port was the *last* place he should try to hitch a ride.

He couldn't help but feel a thrill as the moon drifted away. Flying was what he loved. This is who he was. Closing his eyes, he leaned back into his seat and let his mind wander. Thoughts of the Legion, of the laughter and camaraderie, and of Aldis. He missed her terribly. There was something about Rylan that reminded him of her. It hurt to think about.

Jorge had refused payment of any kind outright. But, Spalding had snuck one of the rarest bottles of liquor he had into their cupboard when they hadn't been watching. It should settle any kind of debt they had.

The best way to repay their kindness was to never contact them again.

He had enough blood on his hands.

CHAPTER 9

WHAT WAS IT his dad had always said? "There's much to be said about home-field advantage."

No shit!

Ed stood inside the landing platform's observation tower, watching the tiny two-person shuttle arc in low from the north, scooting by the white-peaked Olympus Mons. The towering ancient volcano has a rather unique look to its peak, almost like a castle parapet. The atmosphere on Mars was a very fragile thing. One of the biggest struggles they had in their terraforming efforts was the rapid decay of the atmosphere. However, as moisture had been released, the peaks had quickly been coated in white snow. Climate Engineers believed that at twenty-one kilometers high and perpetually frigid, the snowpack would eventually condense into glacial ice.

There seemed to be quite a bit of excitement in the scientific community about watching the birth of a glacier.

Ed wondered if they got their rocks off watching water boil too.

Scientists. Such an odd bunch.

The high-pitched whine of the engines approaching broke

him from his curiosity about what scientists thought about during intimate moments and back to reality.

The landing platform of Vulcan Complex was a small thing. Not a freighter dock by any stretch. Unlike most of his competitors, Martin McAaron had decided not to invest in off-world hauling and instead focused on acquiring and refining materials. "Collect, and they will come." He had often said about the decision. It had proved to be a genius move. They had saved countless sums of money on not building that level of infrastructure, and their clients had gladly paid third-party freight haulers to get their goods at market price.

The shuttle touched down gently and began powering down.

Ed turned to exit the little tower, but Des grabbed his arm.

"Be careful, Ed. This is dangerous. *Dangerous.* He is a *dangerous*, man." The words came out quietly, even though the only other person in the small room was an armed guard. Thomas, he thought his name was.

I really need to get better at remembering people's names if I lead this thing.

Des squeezed Ed's bicep before letting go.

"Don't worry," Ed said with a twinkle in his eye. "Gregório and I go way back."

It was a lie. He had never had any direct interaction with the self-proclaimed King of the Pirates. And, by all accounts, Gregório Helier was an absolute sociopath. Several of Ed's contacts dealt with various connections to the pirates that roamed the belts. No one ever said anything even remotely positive about the man. Except that he always delivered, if you could pay the price.

As he exited the small room, he fastened a rebreather to his face. Made of transparent silicone, it securely covered his mouth and nose. The weak atmosphere, especially in the higher altitudes of Arsia Mons, was dangerous for long periods. So was the weak pressure, but that was bearable for hours. Not minutes, like the low oxygen. An extra layer of thin positive-pressure protection was all he wore, besides a long thick coat and his everyday smart business attire.

Gregório, as it happened, hopped out of the shuttle bare-chested. His caramel-brown skin was riddled with tattoos, some of which appeared to be created with color-changing ink, which gave the three-dimensional art an unsettling degree of *motion*. The blazingly colored patterns depicted a dense jungle scene, with brightly colored plumed birds of various species and a sizeable yellow-eyed jaguar, all of which were framed by geometric serpents. The chaos of the man's decorated body paired nicely with the rainbow-dyed dreadlocked hair that swept from the top of his head down the shaved sides in an almost wave-like pattern.

Ed could appreciate the man's style.

Wish I could get away with being done up like that!

It was simultaneously attractive and off-putting.

Which was undoubtedly the point.

"Olá! Bom dia!" he said, swaggering up to Ed.

Ed noticed the pilot had not exited the shuttle, nor had the shuttle been appropriately powered down. That was slightly alarming.

"Thank you for coming on such short notice." Ed reached out to shake the man's hand, but instead, Gregório reached for his shoulder and, like a pouncing predator, pulled him in for a tight bear hug.

"It is my distinct honor to be invited to such a noble facility!" He had a way of talking that was very unique. It had a sing-song quality that was enjoyable to listen to, even if his accent was so heavy that comprehension suffered slightly.

"Would you like to go inside," Ed asked, looking at the man's bare chest. He noticed that the two jaguars inked across his breasts had what appeared to be topaz piercings for eyes set into his nipples.

When Ed jerked his eyes away from the man's bare nipples,

he found Gregório smiling broadly at him. "You approve of my art?"

"Lovely," Ed choked out.

Great job at not making it awkward! He internally chided himself for allowing this guy to unsettle him. They were just nipples, for God's sake!

As if relishing the attention, the Pirate King raised his arms over his head and stretched, yawning. "No, I enjoy the brisk air of your mountain!"

At least he's wearing a breather.

The last thing Ed wanted was this man to meet some untimely doom on his watch. He needed his help and the support of his vast network.

"Okay," Ed began slowly. "Well, I like to do business frankly. So, if you'll excuse my bluntness, I'd like to get right to it."

Gregório motioned for him to continue, still admiring the view from the platform.

"We're fighting for our lives here. We need weapons, armor, food, medical supplies."

"Easy."

Ed stopped, somewhat startled.

The pause stretched long enough that Gregório raised an eyebrow as if to ask, "Is that all?"

Ed cleared his throat then continued, "Gunships, transports, ground vehicles, armaments for them all, along with spare parts."

Again, Ed paused, but Gregório just smiled winningly.

All right, then...

"We need ECM deployables, explosive payloads, and...." Here was the kicker. Ed drew in a deep breath, "And, we need you to take control of the belt and block all supplies from the outer planets to Mars."

Still, the man smiled, his face unchanging from its affable expression.

The pause lingered again until finally, Ed said, "I think that's it."

Gregório clapped suddenly, almost making Ed jump. Then he rubbed his hands together briskly, his smile growing to show teeth. Somehow, it looked less friendly and more like the expression worn by his nipple-eyed pet cats.

"Now," he said, his accent giving the short word a musical cadence, "let us discuss the price for such a handsome list, yes?"

"I'm prepared to deal at market value, plus ten percent. Running a war is expensive, and I can't afford to bankrupt us on this deal." It was sad but true.

"Fifty percent over market value."

Ed choked, "*Fifty?* You're insane."

The smile fell from his face instantly. That, evidently, struck a nerve.

After a tense moment, Gregório pointed to the sky with one finger. Then, as if mockingly, he flicked the finger at the sky and waggled his eyebrows across the distance toward Ed.

"Do you know what's happening up there?" Gregório asked, a sly tone matching his mocking expression.

"No," Ed stated flatly. He didn't like this man, he decided. But he would use him if he had to.

"The silverbacks are, even now, beginning a blockade of Mars."

Ed resisted the urge to inhale sharply. Instead, he kept his expression neutral.

A blockade!? Fuck! His thoughts tumbled around on top of one another, reassessing his plan.

"Well," he started, thinking as he spoke, "can we even make this deal happen, then?"

Gregório smiled and nodded. "I think yes, but time is short. Makes the price more expensive, you see?"

Bugger me up the... That's how he was asking for the extra cost. This would likely be the only delivery the rebellion would be getting from the outside.

His mind raced, running various scenarios. All the equipment they could ever possibly need was already *on* Mars. It just so happened to be in the hands of the people they were trying to wage war against. The point of this was to arm themselves enough they stood a snowball's chance in hell of seizing some of that equipment and gain a foothold on the planet. Remove it from the hands of the enemy and put it in the hands of their allies. Without that initial stockpile, they were doomed.

"Okay, I guess we…." Ed started, but Gregório began to chuckle quietly. "What's so funny?"

"Too long," he sneered. "The price is now sixty percent over the market." He tapped his bare wrist where a watch would've been. "Economics travel quickly during times like this, no?"

"Fine," Ed said tensely. "Market plus sixty."

Gregório clapped again, loudly, and nodded.

"Initiate the transfer. I will transmit routing details on my way out."

Then, much to Ed's surprise, he turned to walk back toward his waiting shuttle.

"Wait, what about the equipment? I'm not just going to pay you a fortune on your *word* that you'll get us what we've paid for *at some point?*" The audacity! Ed certainly was over a barrel, but he wasn't just going to transfer basically all the funds he had left without some kind of assurances. Hell, at the very least, a conversation about what to expect would be nice!

"You have my word that the equipment will be here in a timely fashion." Then, as if satisfied with the concession, the King of the Pirates sauntered off and boarded the shuttle.

Ed stood in stunned silence as Gregório waggled a pinky at him and ascended from the platform. The scorching blast of air drove him from the platform and back into the observation tower in a rush. Before he could even shut the door, his body had burst into a thick sheen of sweat from the intense heat.

"How'd it go?" Des asked immediately.

Ed dusted himself off and ripped the mask from his face. "I

think the next time I see that man, there's going to be bullets involved."

Des scowled.

Not feeling up to going into details, Ed turned to his guard. "Call down to Murray and have them initiate a transfer once they get account details from the shuttle. Make damned sure it's secure."

"Wait, I thought you said it went poorly?" Des asked, confusion tinging his voice.

"Oh, it did. But we got some promises we'd get what we need."

A promise was such a strong word for how the conversation had actually gone. No reason to mince words about it now.

"Sir," Thomas said abruptly, "transmission information has been received. Murray is requesting confirmation on the amount. He, uh… Said it's rather large."

"If by 'large' he means every fucking credit we have, he's rather astute." Ed sighed heavily and scrubbed at his face. "Yes, send it."

Thomas muttered into his mic, an edge to his voice.

Everyone knew that if Gregório failed to deliver, they were on borrowed time anyway.

It was quite the frustrating pickle they found themselves in. How much of it was his fault, Ed wasn't exactly sure, but it felt like a lot of it. Most of it, in fact.

"Sir," Thomas said abruptly. "Thomas says we have incoming freight haulers."

"Who?"

A pause. "Unknown origin, sir, they have their transponders off."

Could it be Protectorate already? If that were the case, at least Gregório would likely use the McAaron legacy fortune to hopefully cause the Protectorate shitheads a few headaches. Ed could die knowing someone had caused them some pain.

Thomas had that far-off look in his eyes that meant he was listening to someone else talking through comms. His head jerked up, and his eyes focused on Ed. "You need to get down to Ops immediately."

So this is it, then.

Ed nodded and followed Thomas, Des bringing up the rear.

There was so much *more* he wanted to do. Yes, sure, most of it was fulfilling this petty grudge he had with the Protectorate; but something had been stirring in him lately. He felt like he could actually do some good for the planet. His Dad had left him with a fortune, and circumstances had positioned him to use that boon to the improvement of an *entire* world! How many people have ever had the opportunity to make that claim?

Politics aside, Ed had always hated the way the Protectorate ran Mars. He had watched on from a young age as the Martian people were screwed over in every dealing. Corruption was rampant, but nobody seemed to care. Just the cost of doing business. If you could squeak out a margin and stay afloat, well, then you were winning one over on the Protectorate. Winning one for the home team.

The Protectorate relied on the corporations to survive. All the technology they boasted, all the wealth too for that matter; it all flowed from the corporations. Most of the massive corps were located on the resource-abundant outer worlds. Some of the oldest and most stable were on Mars, however. The Martian industrial complex was the backbone of the Protectorate.

Or maybe they didn't think that was true anymore. Perhaps they felt it was time to break that backbone once and forever.

The walk felt like it took an eternity. Something about knowing your death was imminent made time slow down, your mind grasping at every detail like a starving man clutches at food. Trying to pack away a lifetime's worth of data in minutes. Funny that we spend the bulk of our lives ignoring the details, being "too busy" for them to matter. Then, when death was knocking, all we wanted was one more smell, one more taste, a final touch.

Humans were idiots, Ed finally decided.

The door to the converted mass hall, which served as their central operations room, or CENOPS as the former soldiers had advised him to call it, swung open to reveal a cacophony of activity. People dodged each other as they scrambled around while others yelled across the room at each other. There was far too much going on simultaneously for Ed to make out anything.

The chaos further darkened his mood. Dread filled his gut like a lump of molten lead.

Des mumbled something that was lost in the clamor and darted off, grabbing the nearest Analyst by the arm and leaning down to listen to what she had to say.

The large screens at the end of the room showed at least a dozen large-sized unidentified incoming spacecraft. They were coming in hot too! They were descending at a breakneck pace, then arcing hard against the level ground of the Tharsis Plateau and using that velocity to close the distance to the Vulcan Complex rapidly. They had mere minutes before the vanguard flew over the facility. It looked like a bombing run to Ed's untrained eyes.

An unnatural hush fell over the room. Everyone knew what was coming, but no one had expected it all to end so soon.

That intel recommendation that had slid across his desk about dispersing the rebellion now made a lot more sense to him. One bombing run and the uprising was over before it started. Maybe he wasn't the brilliant leader of the free world he thought he was?

Ed closed his eyes and let his mind wander.

There was still so much he wanted to do.

"Sir," said a woman's voice close to him.

His eyes popped open, and a young blonde-haired, green-eyed woman stood in front of him. A huge grin splitting her pale cheeks, pearly teeth shimmering in the artificial light.

"What?" he asked, confused by her expression. *Maybe she's nuts?*

"Someone would like to speak to you," she said, taking off her headset and handing it over to him.

He took the proffered device and looked at it apprehensively. Would he want to hear the Protectorate gloat over their impending victory? Part of him wanted to drop the headset and grind it under his boot heel. Never let the villain have the last word.

Instead, he affixed it to his head and adjusted the mic.

"This is Edward McAaron." He let his voice take on a deep, resonate, tone. It sounded stronger to his ears than it did in his mind. That was good. He'd want to sound strong, if for no other reason than his own ego.

"Que gostoso!"

The distinct voice rang sing-song in his head.

The relief was so overwhelming that Ed felt his face go cold and his knees almost buckled.

Gregório laughed wildly over the open mic. "You pay extra for the rush, yes? Adoro!"

Ed found himself laughing while moisture threatened to spill from his eyes.

"How.." He was unable to finish the question as Gregorio's laughter grew even louder. I make anything happen. And for someone who throws sand in the silverback's eyes? I plan ahead!" The line terminated and Gregorio was gone.

Ed swore happily. The damned pirate must have planned on Ed agreeing to whatever price was named. That's the only way the supplies could be here this fast, they had already been in low orbit waiting for the delivery confirmation. As the first of the freighters flew over the complex, active tracking picked up several hundred smaller and much slower-moving airborne targets.

"What is that? Those small things?" Ed asked, pointing at the screen.

"Airdrops, sir," said someone from across the room.

As more and more of the tiny dots filled the screen over the complex, Ed felt his heart swell. With equipment, they stood a chance. Mere minutes ago he was expecting to catch a bomb with his face. Now... Well, now he knew he could still make a difference.

"Let's go see what Santa brought us, shall we?" Ed said, smiling so wide it hurt his face.

— — —

The last of the freight haulers had already arced back into the sky. They weren't made for atmospheric flight. Oh, sure, they could do it with enough velocity; but it would be one hell of a bumpy ride. As Ed stood clutching the handhold on the outside of the truck, the wind whipping at his coat and hair, he felt more alive than he had in a long time. Maybe ever. He couldn't stop grinning.

The convoy of trucks crested a small hill and revealed a field absolutely littered with steel cases. Hundreds, perhaps thousands of them glittered like treasure in the sand. It took his breath away.

Ed shared a look of pure delight with the driver.

"Fuck yes!" he hooted, more to himself than anyone else.

The driver continued beyond the first few cases, which stood a few meters high on average. Some were shorter, or wider, but they were all reasonably large.

Let's hope it's not all stuffing!

Other trucks began to peel off. Loading crews falling off the sides where they had been similarly clutching to the trucks. Miniloaders were affixed to the rear of each truck, and teams began to deploy those to gather up the crates.

When his truck pulled to a stop, Ed hopped off alongside the loading team. Though, he was out of his element and had no idea how to help. He had just wanted to come and enjoy the moment with his people.

"Sir, you're going to want to come see this." A voice crackled across the comms in the truck. "Someone bring McAaron to sector 6, truck 3-5-2-0."

One of the loaders raised a hand to block out the sun and scanned the horizon to the northwest. Then he pointed. "That one right there, sir."

Ed followed his finger to the truck, thanked the man, and started jogging that direction.

All around him were whooping and joyous yelling of people who stood a fighting chance. He grinned like an idiot as he jogged. When people saw him, they raised up rifles, rocket launchers, packs of explosives, or helmets and cheered his name. Holy hell it felt good!

As he ran up to a truck with a digital indicator reading 3520, he slowed. His cheeks puffing in as he sucked for breath. It had been a while since he had run that much, and the lower pressure made you tire much faster.

"What," he started but had to pause before he could get the rest out, "have you got for me?"

A pair of women stood at an opened case and pointed inside it.

Ed moved over to stand with them and peered into it as well.

Inside was a carved wooden box, painted brilliant jade, navy blue, and canary yellow. The colors were faded, flaking off and scuffed. It appeared to be some kind of flag design, one he wasn't familiar with. Of course, history was not one of his strong subjects.

A hastily scribbled note was affixed to the top of the box.

ED, A LEADER SHOULD HAVE SOMETHING NICE, NO?

The three stood there looking at it with various expressions.

"What is it?" one of the women asked.

Ed reached out to finger the edge of the lid. "I have no idea."

Let's hope it's not a bomb.

With more than his fair share of trepidation he gently eased the lid open.

His breath caught.

Inside, nestled in a fitted black velvet liner, was a matched pair of the most beautiful handguns Ed had ever seen. Not that he had seen many, mind you. The guns were a black powder-coated metal, with rose-gold accents, and a worked floral pattern along the bottom side of the barrel and down the middle of the grip. Gemstones were set in the center of each of the tiny flowers, just little chips of ruby, sapphire, topaz, even the occasional diamond here and there. The hazy crimson sunlight of Mars made it sparkle like a flame.

"Now those are guns!" said one of the women standing next to him, the other whistled her appreciation.

Damn, but he liked that man's style.

As he reached in and withdrew one of the handguns, he sincerely hoped his earlier prediction about getting into a fight with the Pirate King wasn't prophetic.

He'd hate to have to try to kill the man with his own gorgeous gifts.

CHAPTER 10

SWEAT SPLATTERED ONTO the ground beneath him as he finished his floor exercises for the morning. Thankfully, his body was responding to the routine much better than he had anticipated. Brennan felt like he had somewhat undervalued the gene therapies provided by the Protectorate. What he would give for a few quick treatments now, to get him back in top shape.

Ah well, he'd have to do it the old-fashioned way. Hard work and eating healthy.

Not that his diet was awful.

Not since giving up the alcohol, at least.

He grabbed a towel from his bed and toweled off his face and bare chest. The room had a slight humid quality from the atmospheric condensers. Being a surface building required more *substance* to the air to avoid rapid depletion of the oxygen. The building was not normally open to the lower pressure outdoors. However, each time a truck came in and out. Hauling the pirate spoils from the plateau almost nonstop; every little bit helped.

There wasn't time for a shower, which was rather unfortunate. Between the exertion and the humidity, the sweat he had toweled off had almost immediately sprung back. So, when he pulled his shirt over his head, it clung to his back and was almost immediately damp with sweat.

No matter, he'd been in worse situations, without a doubt.

It seemed a bit silly to be complaining about a sweaty back.

Maybe he really was getting too soft for this job.

This job.

He wasn't even sure what that was. The rebellion, such that it was, could barely tell its own asshole from its elbow. McAaron was bright but lacked the gumption to do what was necessary to see this through. And Brennan couldn't be *that guy* for him, at least not the Brennan he had been. People still considered him a threat despite the little charade that McAaron had put on. Despite knowing it had not been his fault, they still blamed him. Everyone needs a scapegoat. They had begun calling him Brennan The Red, or just Red Brennan.

That stung a bit. He hated to admit that, but there it was.

And there was nothing at all he could do about it. Simple as that.

Which ultimately served his purposes just fine. He didn't care what people thought of him. He did, but not really. Not to the level that he figured was expected of him.

At this point, what he wanted was simple enough. To rescue Helena and to make the Protectorate pay for what they had done. Not for himself, but for that young girl and her father. For all of those innocent people that had been mowed down like so much tall grass. Snuffed out in a blink. Many of them had been dead before they realized what was happening. That may have been the saddest part.

Those two things were all he was focused on. Nothing else mattered.

Let them call him whatever they wanted. It didn't matter to him one bit. Hell, if anything, it may actually give him an edge in battle. People didn't like to fight against named men. If you had earned a name, it usually meant you were good at what you did.

Brennan had a reputation as a killer and the name that went along with it.

His reinforced positive pressure undersuit was thankfully more moisture-wicking than the simple loose cotton shirt he had slept in. Deciding he'd rather look the part, he quickly changed into the military-style undersuit, and from the nearby closet, withdrew basic action combat uniform pants and jacket. Even lacking the ancillary bits, the dove gray coloring sent a pang of regret rippling through his body. That life, his life, was over. This was to be something new.

Symbols were fundamental to Brennan. Probably to everyone who spent their life in the military service. You were conditioned to respect the symbolism.

That dove gray uniform was a symbol of everything they fought against. Gray, neither all colors nor none. The happy medium to stand in defense against all.

Not when it came time to defend those who disliked the system.

He tossed the uniform onto his bed. There was no way he could wear that.

The one alternative he had was the shirt he had just tossed onto the bed, a black casual cotton tee, and navy loose-fitting cotton trousers. The clothes that they had brought from the safe house for him.

Like it or not, symbols were important.

That thought got his wheels turning. He glanced back at the ACU crumpled across his bed.

Making the decision, he pulled the black shirt over his head and grabbed the trousers from the floor. Once dressed, he gathered up the ACU and exited the room. He had a quick stop to make.

— — —

"You want to do what now?" the man said, eyebrows raised.

Brennan sighed. This was the third time he was going over it. The instructions were so simple; how stupid could this man be?

"I want you to dye it blood red. Like," he made an emphasizing gesture with his hands, "deep, *deep*, red." The man continued to stare at him blankly. "Not black, though. Red."

"But," the man glanced around the little room, and finding no one to back him up, asked, "why?"

Brennan wondered if anyone would miss this idiot. He had a quick daydream about reaching across the small counter and ripping the man's throat out with his bare hands.

That probably wouldn't earn him any respect with his new people.

Pity.

"Son," Brennan stated, a dangerous growl entering his tone.

"Katsuhito," he replied briskly.

Brennan blinked.

"What?"

"Katsuhito," the man repeated. "That's my name. Not son."

Brennan blinked again.

"Look, I don't give a rat-flying-fuck what...." He trailed off as the man's expression suddenly darkened.

What the hell is with this guy?

The other man was young, maybe mid-twenties. Short, stocky, and wore his hair long. He certainly wasn't going to win any beauty contests, but he looked sensible enough. Well dressed, well-groomed, good posture. Everything about the man's body language indicated that of a reasonable human, so...*What the fuck?*

"Okay, let's try this again." Brennan cleared his throat and took a deep breath, settling into a firm but conversational tone. "Do you know what they call me?"

After a moment of consideration, the man nodded.

"I want to nurture that symbolism. They call me *the Red*, so

I'm going to dye my uniform Red. Plus, we're the rebels on the *red* planet. You get the theme I'm going for?"

The man considered, then nodded. "Come back in an hour."

Thank all the gods!

"Great! So, can you do it?"

"Sure! I don't know why you didn't just say so to begin with." He gathered up the ACUs and walked to the back of the makeshift commissary. "Have to make it all complicated."

Brennan left Katsushito to his grumbling, eternally grateful that moment was over.

He also made a mental note to never revisit the commissary for any reason whatsoever. He'd rather go without as deal with this man again.

A quick glance at his watch indicated he had spent almost an hour arguing over something so simple as clothes dye. So, he broke out into a light jog. He had an hour before his new uniform would be ready, and he estimated that he should debut it when he met with McAaron later that evening. If they wanted a monster, he'd give them one.

He would need to visit CENOPS and review the latest intelligence from Hellas. The intelligence division was almost entirely worthless, he had been deeply disturbed to discover. They were trying, but most were previously little more than desk-workers. Accounting and deep-level intelligence were about as far apart as one could get when sitting behind a workstation. Still, it was something. What he wouldn't give for one or two of Homelands brightest working for their efforts. Now those people were brilliant.

Work with what you've got.

What they were calling CENOPS was effectively a redecorated mess hall. Instead of dining implements, there were workstations stacked haphazardly and cabling draped on every available open space. The room was in a constant state of chaos. No leadership, no direction, no accountability. Everyone was running around between the stations talking loudly, some even going so far as having to shout to be heard over the ruckus.

It made him queasy to watch it.

There was one analyst, sitting calmly at a desk, pounding away at keys like she might actually know how to manage a workstation. He decided that he'd ask her and ignore everyone else.

As he approached, he noticed her flinch. With a few lightning-fast keystrokes, whatever had been on her screen, which had been obscured to him, was suddenly gone. Replaced by the black, blank, default screen.

Well now, that was interesting. Got something to hide, do we?

"Would you like to share with me what you were just working on?" He folded his arms and let years of command training come out in his voice.

She didn't so much as twitch a muscle. "I was watching a mediacast, sir." It came out even, calm, and concise. He didn't believe it for a second.

Pressing would do no good, so instead, he let it slide and changed the subject.

"I need some intel on Hellas City," he said. "Can you pull that data for me?"

She nodded. "Yes, sir, I certainly can."

Within a few keystrokes, a wireframe of Hellas loaded onto the monitor.

She regarded him out of the corner of her eye. "What data points would you like?"

"The standard RECSEC package." He intentionally made his tone casual and watched the girl closely.

There.

It had been subtle, but he had seen it.

She glanced up at him, a look that was half embarrassment, half confusion. "I'm sorry, sir. I don't know what that means."

Yes, he thought smugly. *You most certainly do.*

There had been a flinch to his word, albeit a very slight reaction, where her muscle memory had taken over, and she had *almost* started pulling data. She absolutely knew what RECSEC was and was accustomed to that specific request. This girl was no desk worker, no accountant, or project manager. No, she was something else entirely.

The silence stretched out between them. Brennan stared into her eyes, face devoid of emotion. Even more telling than the flinch was the recognition in her eyes. Sure, she was making a show of not being able to fulfill his request; but he could see in her eyes that *she* knew that he knew.

"Sir?" she finally asked.

"Which question would you like me to answer?"

She paled somewhat.

That was all the confirmation that he needed. She was hiding something. Not only that, be now she knew that he was aware of it. The confusing wordplay about the 'unasked' question had not been missed.

"The first," she hesitated, then the embarrassed façade dropped suddenly. "The second, later, if possible?"

He grunted and motioned to the screen.

Immediately, she turned and began compiling the relevant data points for a recon-security sweep. Specifically, troop placements, both of friendly and enemy forces alike. It was an excellent general overview of any area of responsibility.

Brennan would have to follow up and find out who this person was. She was obviously either a former or current intelligence analyst. Why was she keeping it a secret? That was the problem. People usually did not lie just for the pleasure of doing so. There was a reason this information was being kept from leadership. It could be something as mundane as a lack of trust; hell he could get behind that line of thinking himself. The whole operation was a complete clusterfuck.

Or it could be something more sinister. A spy for the

Protectorate. An embedded intelligence operative would be the end to this effort. If that were the case, it was certainly already a lost cause. Which made him cautiously optimistic about the truth of the matter.

"Here you are, sir." The monitor sprang to life with gray dots of various diameters indicating troop concentrations of Protectorate soldiers, dashed lines to show previously confirmed movements, or semi-transparent solid lines to predict suspected activities. The opposing forces were shown in red. All the movement data was established for that, obviously. However, the pitifully small cluster of dots was outnumbered significantly.

"Well," he said as part of a lengthy sigh. "That's disheartening, isn't it."

She glanced up at him questioningly and then back at the map. After a few moments of consideration, she said, "No, not really."

He felt an eyebrow raise, and she cleared her throat before continuing.

"You can see from the troop movements that they're sweeping in ever-widening arcs from the city center. It's a standard search-and-capture protocol. Which tells two things. First, they have no idea where we are. And, equally good, they are encountering at least minimal resistance from the general population within the city."

"How do you figure that?" It felt a little strange to be asking this young woman the question, but he was intrigued.

The girl leaned forward in her chair to draw on the monitor. "You'll notice that troop movements here and here were stalled. They received reinforcements from here," she pointed to an adjacent location of troop concentration, then one on the other side, "and here. That tells me that something happened that made them think they had found us. Or were met with enough resistance to have to call for help. Keep in mind that most of the Protectorate divisions are not comprised of hardened soldiers.

They are analysts, medics, emergency personnel. More police than combat soldier, in most cases."

It was true, but Brennan had only ever seen the military branch. So, to be up against that force was somewhat daunting. He knew the inner workings of the Protectorate military like the backs of his own hands. Every dimple, crease, and scar.

The doors banged open behind him, and people began to clumsily stagger to their feet.

Brennan spun to see McAaron striding purposefully toward him.

Reflexes took over, and he snapped to crisp attention, a salute up before he had time to consider if that was appropriate or not.

McAaron looked at him, somewhat confused. Then gave a lazy salute as he came to a stop in front of him. He glanced at the girl sitting behind him, then shrugged. "Hope you're not busy. I need a moment of your time."

"Of course, sir," Brennan said and fell into step beside him.

The two exited the room and walked in silence for a bit.

McAaron had an unreadable face. Which most likely meant bad news. Brennan had found the man to be highly expressive. Practically wore a sign that spelled out his emotions for all to see. That was part of what made him so trustworthy. Between that and his glib charisma, he had all the makings of an excellent leader. The kind of leader an effort like this needed. Brennan could be the hammer, but McAaron was the balm.

The two climbed an extruded metal staircase that led to a catwalk surrounding the inner drill core. From there, they wound their way to an old-style swinging door tucked in the far corner of the raised catwalk. The room was detached from everything else, no adjoining rooms, and only the one approach down a long skinny catwalk that forced them to walk in single file. It was precisely the type of place Brennan would want to make a last-stand in. He was impressed that McAaron had chosen that for his personal office. Maybe he wasn't giving the man enough credit?

The door swung open to reveal a very cozy-looking office space.

McAaron sat heavily in the well-worn chair behind the desk.

Brennan came to casual attention in front of the desk.

McAaron reached under the desk and withdrew a crystal carafe of clear liquid. He chuckled mirthlessly at Brennan. "You can dispense with that formal pomp when we're in private, Keith. I am not your commander, and you're no longer a Protectorate soldier."

The comment caused an unexpected lurch in his chest. If he wasn't a soldier, then what *was* he?

"Pardon me for saying so, sir, but I have to disagree on three points," Brennan said, the words clipped, sharp, and delivered with military efficiency. "First, hierarchy is crucial. I need the men to see that I respect and follow you and that orders come from the top. They're not my orders; they are yours. That's critical for every military campaign."

McAaron pulled out two highball glasses and began filling the first cup.

Even from this distance, he could smell the warm, smoky-sweet fragrance wafting from the glass. The aroma had the slight burn of jet fuel and the subtle sweetness of saffron. It set his mouth to watering and his nose to burning.

"Second, you *are* my commander. I follow your orders. I'm here because you brought me inside to do a job. Ask yourself this; would you have rescued me if you hadn't needed someone to lead your troops?"

McAaron paused his pouring and glanced up. "That's fair, I suppose."

The acknowledgment of that felt good. Nothing about this was personal. They were not longtime friends. This was business, at best. Sure, he liked him well enough. But he wasn't about to start calling him Ed, or Eddy, or whatever friends did and invite him over for dinner.

McAaron handed him a glass.

Reluctantly, Brennan took the glass and held it as McAaron drained his in one quick slosh down the back of his throat.

Teeth clenched and inhaling from the burn, he asked, "And three?"

Keenly aware of the weight of the full glass in his hand, Brennan looked up sharply, "Sir?"

McAaron took note of his own glass hanging at his side. "You said there were three points you wanted to make. I agree with the first two, but I am curious if you're going to go three for three."

"Oh, yes." Brennan sat the glass, still enticingly full, down on the edge of the desk. It was difficult to think with that distraction in hand. The pull to drain the glass was too strong. "Third, with all due respect, sir, I am still a soldier. I may not be Protectorate, but I am and always will be a soldier. This is what I do."

McAaron nodded. Then leaned back in his chair. "Okay. Then, General Brennan, we have a severe problem that's about to make our lives absolute hell."

To business then, at last.

Brennan waited patiently.

"The Fleet is, as we speak, setting up a blockade of the planet in upper orbit. Nothing in, very little out. And not without a thorough inspection."

"This was not unexpected," Brennan began. Still, it was disappointing it was happening so quickly. That was going to make their job much more laborious. Atmospheric travel was definitely an option, just not one he would have preferred if given a choice.

"No, that's true." McAaron ran his hands over his face and breathed through his hands hard. "I was just hoping we could get a bit of a stockpile going. As it is, I just gave away my family fortune for just barely enough equipment to outfit who we have."

Well, there was that at least. Brennan had wanted to inquire about the black-market purchases. It was going to be impossible to wage war without weapons.

"What do you need from me?" Brennan asked.

"If they get this blockade in place, we're fucked." McAaron smiled broadly. "I'd like you to be my chastity belt."

The joke wasn't funny, so Brennan didn't laugh.

Instead, he considered their options.

They had no ships, nothing outside the few small transport shuttles that McAaron Senior had used to get around and inspect his various facilities. Those were already very high risk, being registered as belonging to the family. Plus, they had no weapons nor military value whatsoever. They were little more than a moving target. Any CCF pilot worth a damn wouldn't even bat an eyelash over chasing the tiny craft down and obliterating them.

A chime sounded from his datapad, and he withdrew it from his pocket. He had a message from CENOPS. The subject line indicated it was his RECSEC data. That reminded him he would need to find out who that analyst was.

Ignoring that information, for now, he focused on the task at hand.

This is where his knowledge of the Protectorate came in handy. If a Martian force was attempting to blockade the planet, what would the Protectorate do?

Well, for starters, they'd blow them out of orbit with their air-defense-artillery artillery installations. There was a full dozen in the greater Hellas region alone. The enormous cannons were mounted on the surface and easily as big as any of the surrounding buildings. Each had an attached military garrison built below the surface. They were designed for precisely this reason, stopping a blockade and controlling the orbit of the planet.

Unfortunately, all of those were under Protectorate control, and that was who was also performing the blockade.

There was only one thing to do.

"There are twelve ADA, air-defense-artillery, batteries in Hellas. If we capture those, we control the airspace from the ground. They are heavily defended, but they are also heavily provisioned bases. We can kill two birds with one stone, secure *and* further equip our soldiers."

For what it was worth, McAaron spent a few moments thinking through the implications. "If they're so heavily guarded, how do you plan on taking all twelve? Not like we can attack them one at a time."

"No, sir," he replied. "You'll need to take all twelve almost simultaneously. I'm not going to sugar-coat it; this will be a risky move. However, it is also likely our *only* move. Unless you have an abundance of armed spacecraft hidden somewhere in these caves?" Brennan tried to make it sound lighthearted, but it just came across as hopeful. Maybe it was a more serious inquiry than a joke?

"Wish I did," McAaron replied sadly.

A knock sounded from the door.

"Yes?" McAaron barked.

Brennan was happy for the distraction. What he wasn't telling McAaron was the likelihood of success for the operation. The odds were not remotely acceptable.

They were out of options. Either seize the ADA batteries or slowly starve. Despite the notion that Mars was a self-sufficient colony, the Protectorate directly controlled a large portion of that infrastructure. Or in orbit and out of their reach.

The door opened, and a young man popped his head in. He paled slightly when he saw Brennan in the room but gave his report anyway. "Hi, uh, sirs."

McAaron rolled his eyes, and Brennan had to fight back a smile.

"Out with it. We don't have all day," McAaron barked.

There were even odds the boy would either run or piss himself right there on the spot.

"Des wanted me to tell you that the operation you had him on is complete and ready for deployment." It was apparent that the youth had no further details but was just securely passing a message.

Ed certainly knew what it was about because he clapped his hands together and rubbed them vigorously. "Excellent! Tell him to get it started."

The boy was gone before Brennan could turn back around.

"This works out well," McAaron said. "I've instructed Des to work with CENTOPS to figure out the best way, and best places, to divide up the forces. Specifically, the leadership. I don't want one stray bombing run to wipe out the whole effort. This is so much bigger than just us."

"The ADA's would be solid footing to run our operations out of."

McAaron smiled. "My thoughts exactly!"

A plan had started to crystalize in his mind. If they could secure even half of the installations, they'd have an edge in the battles to come. Each base was well equipped and defensible. It certainly beats trying to operate so far outside the city. They were on borrowed time. One of these missions was going to inevitably lead the Protectorate back to their hideout. Likely Ballor and Cole, since they followed no central strategy other than chaos. That was another problem he was going to have to deal with eventually.

McAaron hopped up, twirling a heavy ring on his finger. "All right, General. Let's figured out how to make this happen."

— — —

It was sometime later when Brennan got back to his room, well beyond dark. As soon as he entered, he smelled a foreign, chlorine-type chemical smell. On the edge of his bed was a small brown-paper-wrapped bundle. He knew immediately what it contained.

It didn't take him long to get changed. Being back in uniform felt strange, that was for sure. Not something he had ever expected to wear again. Something about *this* particular uniform felt better. Somehow more personal. This was something that *he* wanted, not something he was ordered to do.

He left his quarters and made his way to the mess hall.

This time when he entered, the room fell utterly silent almost instantaneously.

That was his desired effect.

He strode to the rear of the line, the wide eyes and open mouths tracking his every movement.

The blood-red dyed uniform stood out prominently against his dark skin, as intended.

That's when the whispers started.

"Red Brennan..."

CHAPTER 11

TWO OF THE Protectorate guards conversed quietly across the room from Helena while several more continued searching the apartment. The dove gray-colored uniforms contrasted grossly with the warm white interior. She could smell the sweat from their exertion; it gave the room that musky cloying locker room scent.

"If you could tell me what you were looking for," Helena whispered, "I might be able to help you find it."

One of the guards, Quinn, standing a half step to her right, didn't immediately respond. There had been no discussion since her miserably failed escape attempt. He had covered for her. She had no idea why, but she was grateful for that tiny glimpse of humanity.

They had not spoken about it, even though it had been days since their encounter in the hallway. It made Helena nervous. There was no worse feeling than giving someone the means with which to destroy you and the trepidation you experienced, wondering if now was the moment they decided to use that power. It made her feel vulnerable. That was not something she relished in the slightest.

"The girl who was assigned to you," Quinn said unexpectedly, "she's been missing for a few days."

He thankfully didn't mention her escape attempt coinciding with that timeline. That meant it was unlikely anyone had known about the late-night visit. Otherwise, they'd have connected it all sooner. There was really only one play here.

"Natasha?" Helena kept her voice even, inquisitive. It was difficult to say her name without a constrictive feeling gripping her throat. Her eyes ached with a desire to glance at the fresh bloodstain that had been added to the carpets. "You think she's hiding in here?"

Quinn glanced at her sidelong but said nothing.

The other guards looked over at them. Helena bit her lip and remained silent.

This had obviously been expected. There was no way a member of her guard detail could just go missing without explanation, without prompting an investigation. Frankly, it showed just how disorganized this whole building was that it had taken as long as it had. If this had been her show, she would've had the building turned upside down that very next morning when Natasha failed to show up for the breakfast shift.

Good thing you're not your own captive, then!

One day, she was going to have a mental breakdown about what had happened in this room. She knew that. Unfortunately, she didn't have the luxury to process it all just now. Right now, she compartmentalized everything and plowed ahead. That was all there was to be said about it. Her first and only concern was escape.

"All right," a gruff voice said from the bedroom. "Pack it in."

The Senior Analyst strode from the other room and angled directly for Helena.

He was an older man. She had seen him around the building for years, but his name escaped her. She did remember he was thorough and reliable.

She regarded him as he came to the small table she was seated at. His keen eyes did another scan of the room, lingering on the bloodstains for longer than Helena would've liked.

"Find what you were looking for?" Helena prompted, hoping to distract from his analysis. It would be most unfortunate for him to notice the slight shade difference between the stains.

"Not yet," he remarked absently, "but we will. It's just a matter of time."

Then he turned and looked her full in the face. There was sadness in his eyes but iron in his tone. Another one who saw the injustice being done but was somehow duty-bound to continue doing the bidding of Bruce and whoever was pulling his strings. People like this made her sick. There was no way in hell she would ever stand by and watch innocent people be harmed by the people who had sworn to protect them. Even if it meant ending her career or her life.

"Listen, Ms. Chu," he said quietly, pausing, then he continued, "Governor if you had anything to do with Natasha's disappearance, you should tell me now. We will find out, trust me. I'm very good at my job."

Interesting that he call her Governor still. Was he signaling something?

Would it matter if he was?

That wasn't the biggest question, though. Was this a test? Quinn had already informed her it was Natasha they were looking for. But this man didn't know that. Did he? Were they hoping to throw her off by granting her inside information, then assuming she'd speak freely about it?

Too bad silence wasn't an option. That would certainly make her look guilty.

She decided ignorance was her best shield.

"Disappearance? I had noticed she wasn't around the last few days." She let her brow furrow with concern. The action made her feel slightly sick to her stomach. Lying about it felt somehow disrespectful to the dead, adding insult to murder.

Quinn stiffened next to her. It was subtle, but both she and the older analyst noticed.

"Yes," he said the word slowly as if distracted by some other train of thought. "We had somewhat expected to find her here, as it turns out."

"Here?" Helena blurted the word out and looked at Quinn with a half-smile on her face like it was some kind of inside joke she wasn't privy to. "Why would she be here? I'm pretty sure that woman hates me."

Both men regarded her coldly.

Finally, the analyst sniffed loudly and turned to leave.

Quinn followed silently.

All the soldiers convened at the doorway, where they had a quiet conversation. Several heads were shaken, then they gathered up their equipment and strode out into the hallway. The door shut, locked, and the room fell completely silent.

Immediately, Helena sprang to action. During their investigation, she had kept a keen eye out for them potentially planting surveillance equipment. She had to know whether or not her room had been bugged, and it would be regrettable if she took too long and forgot where to look.

After an hour of intense searching, she could not find any trace of surveillance devices, which could've meant any number of things. Either they hadn't planted any, she wasn't skilled enough at locating the devices, or they already had devices in place.

The latter was the least probable. If they had eyes and ears in the room, they would've known she had murdered Natasha. That was a recording she hoped to never hear if it existed.

That left the prior two circumstances. If situations had been reversed, she absolutely would've used the opportunity to bug the room. So, she had to operate under the assumption that they were just better at hiding the devices than she was at locating them. Which made sense. She had no clue what she was even looking for.

The best news of the day was that they had not been able to discover her hiding spot and the datapad she had stuffed there. Thankfully, they had been looking for something body-sized, foul-play-related, and not small, concealable objects like a datapad.

Exhausted from the day's stress and her overall poor health, Helena washed up and stripped down to her nightclothes. Then she crawled into bed as she always did and pulled the comforter up over her head. As she wriggled into the bed, she found the small tear she had made in the foam mattress near the head of it, under the pillows. The metal frame hid the small cut perfectly. This had been a trick of hers as a child, a way to hide datapads and books so she could stay up all night reading. The practice had driven her parents crazy, but they were never able to discover her hiding spot.

She used her body to shield the light from the datapad from illuminating the comforter. If she were being surveilled, that would definitely be something they'd notice. Thankfully modern batteries were incredibly efficient, but eventually, the datapad would run out of charge. Every single time she powered the device on, it had to be used to maximum effect.

Her immediate reaction was to message Brennan and let him know she was safe and coordinate with him on a means of escape.

That would be a huge mistake. Anyone watching would be expecting exactly that. And, more importantly, Brennan would drop everything he was doing and charge into the building like a raging bull. No, that would just get everyone killed. Everyone expected the damsel in distress to go running to the man in her life. That was one trope she refused to reinforce. She'd rescue herself, thank you very much.

Her first escape effort had been spontaneous. She'd even go so far as to say it was ill-conceived. Desperation had seized upon opportunity, and that perfect storm had birthed a half-cocked idea. In hindsight, she should've been more careful. Of course, the entire floor would be locked out. Why she had not thought of that previously boggled her mind. The next attempt would need to be flawlessly planned. She would not get a third.

There was already a tiny kernel of an escape plan blossoming in her mind. It was something that needed to be nurtured, protected from the wind, and softly worked into life, like the tiny ember of a campfire. Work it too vigorously, and you'd put it out, but similarly ignore it and lose it.

The datapad powered on and gave a silent notice that it was operating in encrypted mode. That would mask the signature of the device from anyone who was watching for it to pop up. That had been the first thing she had done upon discovering the device on the young woman. The more time she spent with the device connected to the network, the more time she allowed the Analysts to break the encryption and discover it was Natasha's. And, worse still, exactly where it was accessing the network.

Frankly, it was sloppy of Bruce to keep the network active on these upper levels. The shielded rooms would not allow outside communication without a direct internal network. She could've been completely shut off from the outside with the flip of a switch.

Bruce always had been an idiot. Had she really only kept him around because he was pretty to look at? That was the most logical answer. That, and she had enjoyed his attention and flattery. Sure, she had kept herself professionally detached, but that also egged him on even more. It had felt good. Reflecting on that now made her taste bile. One day, she was going to enjoy killing him.

But that was a thought for tomorrow, what was she going to do with herself today?

Who could she trust absolutely?

None of her media contacts, certainly. They'd turn her in just for the better story.

None of the government contacts because their loyalties would be questionable.

Not Brennan.

She needed someone she knew without a doubt was never going to side with the Protectorate.

That only left one person she knew of.

Edward McAaron.

The McAaron family was one of those local families that had been around for so long and were so involved that *everyone* recognized the name. But very few people actually knew them. Helena would certainly never consider herself a friend of any of them. Although Martin had been one of the pillars on which the community had relied. For her, he was little more than a familiar face in the halls of the building.

By all accounts, and those were very limited given her circumstances, her friend and mentor, President Motwani's assassination had been pinned squarely on Ed McAaron. She found that to be preposterous from her minimal dealings with Martin. The Protectorate seemed to want to undermine everything that had any kind of stability on Mars. A power shakeup.

The problem was how to contact McAaron. Bruce had complained openly about not being able to track him down. The few mediacasts she had been allowed to watch had implied he was a dangerous terrorist on the run, and anyone with any information was *required* by law to report it immediately.

No, unfortunately, there was just no way to reach out directly to Ed. Not only was he certainly to be in hiding, but everyone would be closely monitoring all of his known contact points. What she needed was someone ancillary to him. Connected, but by a few degrees of separation.

The question really was, who would someone like McAaron trust? If you were the heir to a legacy fortune turned suddenly criminal, who would be the first person you would call.

It hit her like a brick in the jaw.

The family attorney.

History had a funny way of repeating itself in human culture.

Throughout that collective history, the wealthy turned to trusted family advisors whenever attacked. There was a family attorney, Helena had direct dealings with him on more than a few occasions as a pass-through entity for the McAaron-run corporation, Avylyn System Enterprises.

Desmond Stuedle was his name. An older gentleman, possibly even a few years older than Martin if she recalled correctly. An assuming, taller man.

It took minimal effort to find his contact information as the principal contact point for legal dealings for ASE.

Helena typed out a message.

Her finger hesitated over the transmit button.

What if he was also being watched? How probable was it they'd connect the lawyer to the family? If this was her *one* shot at connecting to McAaron, was he her best option?

She had to try.

The datapad buzzed briefly and indicated the message had been sent. Moments later, it registered that it had been viewed.

Was that too fast? Who checked their messages *that* quickly?

Wishing she had paid more attention to her electronic warfare in-services, she racked her brain on how long it might take to triangulate where the message had originated from if the datapad were being monitored by the enemy. Frankly, she had no clue.

Just as she decided it would be best to power the device down and try another tactic later, it vibrated again.

"Not like this. Use the following information sparingly."

A moment later, a unique address appeared.

A thrill shot through her.

Could it really have been so easy? Or was she being set up?

The benefits were worth the risk, she decided. And she stashed the datapad under her pillow. She leaped out of bed with growing excitement, tossing the comforter back, and went to the entertainment center. They had disconnected the media streams, so she had no outside knowledge of what was happening except for their reports to her. They had neglected to disconnect the music streams.

She selected her favorite music stream with a few practiced motions and turned the volume up, only slightly louder than she would normally. She hoped it was enough to provide sufficient background noise to block out her voice. After her bungled escape attempt, everything from here on out was going to be meticulously planned. No more half-cocked efforts. She felt as if her luck had been spent up; now it was time to play this smart.

She crawled back into bed, mumbling to herself. It was something she had always done, even as a kid. Sometimes you had to vocalize what was on your mind. The words she spoke were mainly nonsense and served as an added layer of smokescreen if someone was listening.

Once snuggled under the comforter again, she reached out and grabbed the datapad. A click on the address, and the connection rang.

One ring.

Click.

"Is this line secure?" came a strong male voice from the other end.

She wasn't sure? She *thought* so! But espionage was not her strong suit.

"I believe so. It says encrypted on the top menu."

There was a slight pause.

"Hello?" Helena asked into the empty air.

"We will call you back momentarily."

The line went dead.

A frigid feeling settled into the pit of her stomach.

Had she just screwed up?

That had definitely not been Desmond. He had a full-bodied throaty voice. Something you'd hear from your grandfather. The person on the other end of the line had been young and had that sharp tone prevalent in the military.

The device buzzed.

There was an incoming call from a secure line.

Maybe she should turn it off and try this again another time?

She answered.

"Hello?"

"Governor!" The relief in Desmond's voice was palpable.

A warm wave washed over her body, and her throat constricted to the point where she couldn't even respond. She just choked back sobs.

"Governor Chu, are you still there?" Desmond asked hurriedly.

"Yes," she managed to croak out.

"Well done on making contact! Are you safe? What's your situation?"

"I managed to obtain a datapad. I have it encrypted, I think." She hesitated. How much of her situation should she tell them?

"That is why we terminated the call and rang you back. Our electronics specialists have secured your line." There was some background talking, and Des paused briefly. "Ah, yes. They also tell me they've established a 'hard line' between these two devices to further mask the signal. Unfortunately for you, that means any address you enter will *only* communicate with the device I'm currently holding, regardless of what you enter."

"That's fine. As long as they cannot trace it back to you."

"No, no. They assure me that it is perfectly safe as it is now." Desmond had that pleasantly reassuring voice that most good attorneys deployed. It had always been something she had mocked in private. Now that she was the one scared shitless on the receiving end of that assurance, she had to admit it sure felt wonderful. Fake or not.

"We can catch up later. I have someone here who desperately wants to speak to you."

There were some muffled sounds as the datapad was transferred.

"Governor Chu," came a warm, confident, if somewhat younger-sounding voice. "I am Edward McAaron, and I sure am glad you pulled this off."

She smiled. The voice had that natural slick charisma that had once attracted her to Bruce. The my-shit-refuses-to-stink confidence coupled with a casual interest in the conversation. With Bruce, it had all been a sham. Hopefully, the same wasn't the same with Ed.

"Mr. McAaron, I was sorry to hear about your father. I must admit I had limited interaction with him, but he certainly cared about his community."

"Ed," came the prompt reply.

"Excuse me?" Maybe she had a bad connection?

"Call me Ed. Mr. McAaron was my father." There was still raw emotion in his voice, but it wasn't sadness. It was anger. "I'd love the opportunity to talk about it further with you, but in person. Right now, I think it's best if we use this time to gather as much information on your situation as possible."

He was right.

It just felt so *damned good* to talk to someone not pointing a gun in her general direction.

She started with the assassination because that's where it had all started.

It took over an hour, and her throat was hoarse and raspy by the end of it. She spared no detail in her retelling.

Ed whistled softly over the line when she finally finished speaking. "You've been through it, Governor."

"Helena."

A light chuckle. "Fine, fine. Helena. I have something to ask of you Helena, and you're not going to like it. I want you to consider it regardless. *Really* consider it before you make your decision. And know this, I will take steps to secure your escape regardless of your answer."

What was this? She just wanted out!

He continued into the silence, "You're in a rather unique position, which may prove to be overwhelmingly beneficial to our efforts out here. You're on the *inside*. Do you know what I mean? We have spotty intelligence out here, but with some of our help, you could access the internal networks. Possibly even grant us remote access. That kind of direct intelligence could save lives—*our lives!*"

Again, her throat constricted, and her stomach boiled with nerves.

He was asking her to *stay?*

How *dare* he!

Everything in her wanted to flee immediately. She wanted out right now. Fuck their needs! She couldn't see that bloodstain one more time, not while a possible rescue was on the table.

Except, she knew she'd help. Even as her mind railed against the idea of sleeping another night in the same building as Bruce, of bearing the burden of her captivity, not even being able to take a shit in privacy, she knew she would accept the role.

"Just tell me what you need me to do."

A long exhalation sounded on the other side. "I know what I'm asking of you now, Helena. I had no idea it was this bad... Does Brennan know this?"

"I doubt it. I'm not sure how he could. It's been kept intentionally need-to-know."

"Helena, it's not my place to speak about another man's feelings toward you," there was a kind hesitance in his voice as he continued, "but, you should know that where you are concerned, the good General completely loses his shit. Do you know what I mean?"

A smile fought its way onto her face. Twitching into existence tentatively, like a small rodent emerging from a rubbish pile after being chased there by the house cat. Although it was a small pathetic thing, the expression was mildly painful. What from the beating, the atrophy, the constant grinding of her teeth—she shouldn't be surprised it hurt. *Everything* hurt. Her world was a continual blur of physical and emotional pain.

Brennan was with McAaron! He wasn't dead like the Protectorate assumed, nor had he fled the planet. He was working with the rebellion. This was the best news she could've hoped for.

"I do," she managed to choke out around a threatening sob. "Were I you, Ed, I'd not share my story with him."

"That's what I was getting at. Helena, I *will* get you out of there, I promise. Just not yet. You could save a lot of lives from where you are now."

It was true, fuck, but she wished it wasn't.

"I'm going to put you on with our lead analyst now. Her name is Ninlil. She's amazing, worked as our main technician in the company for years."

Again, there were some scuffling sounds as the headset was passed around.

Then, a pleasantly thin voice came through, "Good evening Governor, are you ready?"

"Just tell me what I have to do, Ninlil."

"First, do you have an internal network connection? I'm assuming so as you can communicate with us from inside, despite the shielding."

"Yes." Helena felt her anxiety spike. If anyone detected this communication, she was finished. All hope of safety would be lost in an instant.

"Excellent. We need to penetrate their firewall, which should be only moderately difficult from the inside. How experienced are you with technology?"

"Not very," she admitted.

"That's quite all right. I will walk you through it slowly. At any time, say the word, and I can explain in as much detail as you can handle. Before he passed, my husband told me I was long-winded."

"Thank you, Ninlil."

"I'm happy to help Governor. If you're comfortable with it, I'd like to begin."

She was true to her word. It took the rest of the night, but as the first streaks of artificial light began peeking through the windows in the bedroom, they had finished the connection. The Martian resistance had access to the Protectorate central computer network.

"That just about does it, Governor," Ninlil said. "You were wonderful. You make an impressive Governor, but you may have missed your calling as a technician Ma'am."

She was too tired to laugh. The last few weeks had just drained her of energy, and the intense all-night crash course in programming had depleted her beyond her ability to put on a good face for the other woman's benefit. So, instead, she just grunted.

"One last thing," she said hesitantly, "you'll need to hide this device as best you can and leave it powered on for as long as possible."

"But the battery will...." She left the rest unsaid. It was obvious.

How will you rescue me if the battery runs out?

"I understand your concern, Governor. I truly do. We will pull what data we can on the entire operation in that amount of time and use what we have gathered to put together an extraction plan. We will not forget you."

The call terminated quietly, and she felt as if an all too familiar weight settled back onto her back. Wrapping herself up in her comforter, she began looking for a decent hiding place. She needed something that was accessible in a rush. There weren't many good options, and none of her previously used locations would do it.

Brennan would not forget about her. They would come for her.

She'd do what she could to help until that moment. Then she'd watch it all burn.

CHAPTER 12

MARS WAS BEAUTIFUL in its own way, Lisa decided, as she admired the planet below from her X17 CCF fighter. It was one of the newer models, and it flew like a dream compared to the older craft she was used to at the academy. They weren't intended to be atmospheric, but they could handle upper orbit, which was precisely what they were doing now.

The hazy thin layer of atmosphere that coated the newly terraformed planet was stretched much further out from the planet's surface and noticeably thinner than Earth's. While the agonizingly slow terraforming process on Mars had coated the planet in a considerable amount of liquid water, it hadn't yet achieved that *blue marble* look. The red and blue hues from the planet's surface scattered into that mist to form a warm white color, not quite yellow. Lisa liked to call it *vanilla white.*

"This fucking sucks!" Marconi's voice griped over the squad comms.

The comment was at least his hundredth on this patrol alone. Lisa sighed heavily before she replied, "Should I take a shot at one of these freight haulers to give you some excitement, Marconi?"

"At this point, I'd prefer it if you just shot me down. End my torment."

"You are so dramatic!"

Azarov opened his comm channel just to chuckle.

Marconi, thankfully, kept his comments to himself.

Lisa felt so weary. They had a pretty sweet deal, just running patrols in orbit around Mars as the Fleet prepared a long-term blockade of the planet. A peaceful end to the rampaging violence in Hellas and some of the outlying communities. How things had gotten so bad on the planet, she had no idea; that was over her pay grade. Get people a little hungry, and they'd usually calm down.

Maybe we should ration Marconi's food. She smiled at the thought. Her wingmate loved his food. He'd definitely murder them all in their sleep if denied even a single meal.

Hopefully, the same wasn't true for the Martian communities. That was a sobering thought.

As dramatic as Marconi was about it, she begrudgingly conceded that he had a point. Babysitting civilian aircraft coming and going and flying close-support for the Fleet as it arrived and arranged itself into a blockade formation was far and away *not* exciting duty. That was for sure. What she appreciated about their assignment was being out from under the shadow of her mother. That was an incredible feeling of freedom she hadn't been able to experience at the Academy. Nothing could tear her away from this assignment so long as her mother stayed away.

"Echo two-one, this is Mother." The comms activated with their squad-wide double-click.

Lisa flipped the comm control to reply, "Echo two-one, go ahead."

"Echo two-one, we're reporting some unregistered flight activity in grid alpha-six-three. Request flyover."

"Copy all, Mother. Echo two-one out."

With a smile, she flipped her comms back to squad-only. "Well, there you go, Marconi, you got your wish."

A loud snort sounded over the comms.

Command transmitted the new flight data, and she adjusted the flight plan with the aid of the onboard artificial intelligence. Several atmospheric drops had occurred in only a few minutes between them. That was quite odd. Not only was it unusual to fly in such a tight formation, for civilian ships at least, but to all be making unregistered orbital re-entry drops was somewhat irregular. Sure, it could happen for a variety of reasons. Guess they were about to find out.

The ships had slung through the atmosphere, dropping below sensor thresholds above the Arcadian Sea, heading southbound toward the Amazonis Cove and Terra Sirenum Lakes. Her eyebrows raised as she scanned the velocity records. For giant freighters, they sure were moving at a pretty hefty clip.

"Echo, sync with my FP, and hit the blowers."

Her squad monitor went green across the board as they all synchronized their flight data, adjusting for their respective crafts, and she initiated the maneuver. Lisa enjoyed flying in the high and tight formation groupings that the Undead Legion had favored. Most squadrons claimed they were too risky and provided no benefit. They were correct, but the tight formations looked terrific.

They banked through the high orbit atmosphere and streaked their way toward the anticipated region the freighters would have landed. With their current velocity, they would be there in under three minutes.

"I can't believe we're chasing some flat-hatting freight haulers."

That did it; Lisa had had just about enough of the complaining. "Are you seriously going to moan about everything today?"

Flat-hatting, unauthorized low-level flying was pretty commonplace. Not with such a large group, though. It was interesting enough to attract attention. She couldn't understand why he had to piss and whine about every little thing.

"Sorry, sir." The sarcasm dripped over the comms. "I'll stow it."

She sighed.

Marconi was like a shithead little brother. Instead of realizing how good he had it, being a part of her squad and the opportunities it presented, he only wanted to see the nepotism. She would always just be the Admiral's daughter. It wasn't fair, and she had just about had enough of it.

Lisa spent the remainder of the distance deciding whether or not she should bounce Marconi to another squadron altogether. The move would look terrible on his record, and he'd never forgive her for the insult. But she couldn't have him undermining her authority every time she hopped in the hot seat, either. There was too much she had to prove to have to worry about her own squad making her look bad. Plus, it was just bad for morale.

"Colt," Azarov broke in, "this data is several hours old. Are we planning to look on the ground? With this kind of velocity, they would've had a difficult time landing anywhere in this hemisphere."

It was an interesting observation. They had indeed been screaming toward the ground. Frankly, she wouldn't be the least bit surprised to find a dozen or more smoldering impact craters somewhere near the cove. Not with the data she was showing.

"We're going to do as instructed," she said, wishing she sounded more authoritative on the idea. "Do our flyover and report back. The data is for Mother to sort out."

This attitude shift was precisely what she was worried about. With Marconi questioning and complaining about everything, it was inevitable that the rest of the squad would doubt her leadership and decision-making.

A beep indicated they were approaching the target destination.

"All right, let's fan and scan."

The formation broke, and Lisa activated her sensor array. The data would transmit directly back to command. That didn't stop her from watching it as it streamed through her cockpit, though.

There was nothing at all.

There were no hotspots from any recent landings or takeoffs, obviously, no ships to be seen across the algae plains that stretched from the cove to the coastal plains to the south. Either command had insufficient data, or the vessels had not stopped.

What would make a ship drop altitude so quickly, only to turn around and burn back into orbit? The data made no sense at all.

"Mother, Echo two-one," she said into the comm.

"Go ahead two-one," came the reply.

"I'm sure you see what we are here," she said, continuing her scan of the data stream. "Do you want us to proceed or rejoin our patrol?"

"Hold two."

Lisa adjusted her bank angle slightly and initiated a loop to pass back over the area. With the synchronized flight computers, all the other craft adjusted to match. While she did so, she viewed the canopy screens, which simulated an exterior view. The russet and tangerine swirls of algae made intricate patterns in the watershed. However, there was absolutely nowhere viable as a landing location. This was a bust.

"Echo two-one, you are Romeo-tango-bravo."

Lisa's eyebrows drew together. "Say again, Mother?"

"R-T-B, Two-one," the reply said, dropping the phonetic.

"Copy that, Echo two-one out."

Well, what the fuck? She punched in the new flight plan for a rendezvous with the carrier still in zone-five orbit, the maximum allowable. Once the systems registered, she punched it for home port.

The carrier ship, UNIC *Hemera,* was a beautiful thing. Every approach took her breath away. The craft was absolutely massive. The air traffic around the carrier was always overly full. Between drones, perimeter defenses, and support vessels, the carrier resembled a spaceport in the busy commercial area of Luna. A thousand glimmering dots with pulsing colored targeting reticles tracking their trajectories across her screen.

She loved the larger craft!

She loved space!

And, most notably, she absolutely loved flying.

Just being in the seat was enough to banish the thoughts of Spalding, the Undead Legion, and all the bullshit that went along with it. Up here, she could just be herself. Be free of doubts, of troubling thoughts about inadequacies. Everything made sense up here.

They received their dock protocols and maneuvered to hard lock with the carrier. The CCF craft attached itself to the underbelly of the carrier, like a honeybee on the comb. Each dock could support an entire fighter wing which consisted of up to twenty ships.

Once clamped tightly, an umbilical extracted the entire cockpit and withdrew it from the armored hull of the craft and into the belly of the carrier. The cockpit was raised through an airlock in the floor and then crack open like a clamshell, exposing the pilot compartment.

Unlike other models of craft, the close-combat-fighters were not designed to land without the carrier. In an emergency situation, the ship would crack in half and release the entire armored cockpit. With an independent oxygen recycler, power, and shielding, the pilot could wait to be picked up by rescue personnel after ditching the craft. Better than blowing up, but only barely. Rumor was that if the two halves of the fighter were undamaged, they could be reassembled. She had never heard of it happening, though.

As Lisa disconnected her flight computer, atmospheric tethers, and waste management systems, the deck chief approached her berth. Chief Maris Ursella was ancient and a legend amongst the Protectorate. Approaching her mid-eighties, she had a close-cropped cap of fuzzy gray hair, and even her wrinkles had wrinkles. Anyone she caught breaking flight deck protocols would learn just how sharp her tongue was, though. Every time the woman looked at her, Lisa felt nervous as if she had somehow earned the woman's ire. With her walking directly toward her now, she considered reconnecting her waste hoses for fear of pissing herself.

"Colt!" For an elderly woman, she had an obnoxiously loud barking voice.

"Yes, Chief?"

"Admiral wants to see you," she said. When Lisa didn't immediately react, she clapped her hands loudly together. "Move!"

She complied. Promptly.

— — —

Harris Olumide sat across from Lisa, drumming his fingers on his desk as he considered her. After instructing her to sit down, he had gone eerily silent. The minutes had passed by, how many she had no idea; she wasn't about to look behind her to check the clock.

The aging Admiral was dour-faced; the years had not been kind. He claimed it was the stress of the job. She kind of thought the alcohol consumption may have had something to do with it. But what did she know? Still, he was a sweet older man. The closest thing she had to an actual parent. The only thing her biological parents cared about was how good she made them look. Her grandparents had long since passed away; she hardly recalled them at all.

Olumide had always looked after her, and she'd be forever grateful for that.

Still, there was no way she'd interrupt his silence. She had made that mistake one too many times. So, instead, she endured it. Maintained eye contact as much as she could stomach and weathered the silent storm.

Finally, after what felt like an eternity, he blew out a sigh through his long, tangled beard. Being the Admiral had its perks, and facial hair was one of those. He wore his like his favorite medal of honor.

"What am I going to do with you, girl?" he finally said, an edge of exasperation in his tone.

"I've told you before, don't call me 'girl,' Admiral," she said tightly.

He harumphed loudly.

"Fine, Lisa, but I refuse to call you by your rank."

This was usually where he mentioned changing her diapers or telling her to stop eating her snot or something equally demeaning.

He surprised her this time, and refrained.

Well, how about that? We're all growing as people today, it seems!

"Have you spoken to your mother?" Harris was always trying to play the go-between with her. Always trying to save face for her mother. If it hadn't been so hopeless, it might've been funny.

"No, sir." In fact, the last interaction she had had with her mother had been in her quarters after graduation. That memory still stung, she hated to admit.

He stroked the whiskers below his chin, a thoughtful expression on his face now.

"Damn, but I wish she'd follow through with something every once in a while instead of leaving it to me to sort out."

Wait, what?

Had she just heard jolly old Uncle Olumide talk disparagingly about her mother? In all her life, she couldn't recall a single instance of him saying the slightest bit negative about the woman, despite ample opportunity to do so.

Lisa decided to keep her mouth shut and see where his train

of thought ended up.

"That whole business with her pet pilot has just got my trousers in a tangle," he said, scratching at a gray eyebrow. "Now, she's having me bounce you all over the system. It's just not good for morale. Not good for the optics. Makes us look disorganized. Plus, blast it all; I actually need your squadron here for the bloody blockade she's forcing me to put in orbit. I'm going to have to pull the three-twenty-fifth from the Earth perimeter. It just makes us all look bad. Unreliable. That's not a good look on us right now."

Pet pilot? Spalding?

What the hell was he talking about?It was apparent she was being reassigned, *again*; that much was clear. Marconi was going to have a fucking field day over this! Her anxiety was already spiking about how *that* conversation was going to go. But what was everything else about?

The silence stretched on, and she was just about ready to prod him about Spalding when he exhaled and stood slowly. She could hear his hips crack loudly. Her stalwart friend was beginning to show more than a few signs of slowing down.

Lisa held her tongue as she watched him shuffle slowly over to the counter, where the bottles of liquor sat glistening in the bright overhead light.

"I just wish this all could have happened differently. I'm getting tired of all of this upheaval."

He obviously wasn't talking to her any longer. That much was at least crystal clear. Yet, he hadn't dismissed her. So, was this some kind of confession? If so, he was acting awfully damn cryptic about it.

"Such a waste of talent, I said. But that didn't matter. She needed a high-profile event." Olumide took a long draw off the bottle before pouring it into a glass. "I guess I am getting old and just miss the old way of doing things."

He turned and seemed to notice Lisa sitting there still. With a sigh, he waved his highball glass in the air between them, "Oh, don't mind me. Just feeling grumpy today."

"I'm here for you," she prompted quietly, "if you ever need to talk, Harris."

Using his first name was a tactical move. If he could just get a bit more comfortable, open up to her a bit more, she might be able to weasel out some additional information. What was he talking about with Spalding?

Admiral Olumide snorted as he fell heavily into his chair, which protested audibly against the sudden weight. "Thank you kindly." He tossed a datapad at her. "Your new assignment. I have not dispatched it to the squadron yet."

Lisa suppressed a groan of despair. She felt like she had been close to gleaning some critical bit of information there. Every instinct told her she should push, dig, discover what she could. That was a terrible idea, now that he had started discussing duty. She would have to create another opportunity later.

So far in her early career as an Academy graduate, every order had been worse than the previous one. It was as if her mother were punishing her for leaving. She'd believe that, if she thought for a moment, her mother ever spent an iota of energy thinking about her for *anything.*

As she scanned the document, she felt the icy pain in her stomach suddenly warm, then her face flushed with excitement.

"We're going to hunt pirates in the belt?" she asked shrilly—excitement overriding decorum.

"Well," Harris said blandly, "don't sound so bloody excited about it."

Lisa hopped to her feet, dropping the datapad back on his desk as she leaned across and planted a small kiss on his cheek. "Thank you!"

Then she whirled and bolted for the door. Behind her, Admiral Olumide said, "Fucking strange kid, that one."

— — —

Of course, Marconi wouldn't be around to share the good news with.

That would just be too easy.

After weeks of his bellyaching, she finally had an *actual* deployment for them! No more babysitting civies in controlled airspace. Instead, they would be stalking pirates through the shipping lanes of the primary asteroid belt, what some called the Barrier Belt since it separated the inner and outer planets within the solar system.

She absolutely could not wait. *Marconi is going to shit his pants!*

Undeniable combat missions. It was almost too good to be true.

Besides the great news about being reassigned, she also had that inadvertent admission by Olumide about the deal between Spalding and her mother. What had all that been about? Why had he called Spalding her "pet" pilot? That seemed like an odd way to phrase it, especially given the Admiral's Mast. "Victim" would have been a much more appropriate descriptor.

Plus all that other stuff about how things used to be? Was he just waxing nostalgic? She didn't think so. There had been something to it, an emotion behind it. Had that been guilt? What had her mother pulled him into?

Since her squad was evidently up to no good elsewhere, she decided she'd poke around and see what she could find out about Spalding's termination from the Fleet. The press had been unkind at best, slanderous at worst. Even going so far as to pin him as a sexual predator. Using his rank and influence to seduce his subordinates. Funny, Amanda Aldis had been his superior officer, so if anyone would've gotten a tongue-lashing for fraternization, it would've been her and not Jonathan Spalding.

As she perused the archived mediacasts, she rapidly uncovered a pattern. When it came to negative publicity, Spalding had received the whole nine yards full in the face. In every forum, on every avenue, he was mocked and ridiculed. Most of it was a largely unfair commentary on proceedings that the general public had no substantive knowledge of. Hell, she wasn't even an expert on the whole idea of summary judgment by a Captain's or Admiral's Mast. It was old-school and probably an outdated process. This was likely the first time most people had heard the term, yet here they were shouting their bile from the rooftops.

The whole thing made her sick, and she idly wondered where Spalding was now. Hiding somewhere in a bar on Luna, presumably drunk as ever. Or dead. The thought hurt her heart, but she had to consider the possibility. Jonathan Spalding was a freewheeling badass, who didn't give two good shits about public opinion of him. The only thing that mattered to him was the opinion of his squad. That had been taken from him. That left him alone and vulnerable. With his cavalier disposition that all combined into a recipe for disaster. He had lost everything he valued.

But *why*?

There were so many questions and none of the potential answers made any sense.

Data from the engagement provided the evidentiary basis for his termination from the Fleet. It was sparse at best, fabricated at worst. Even she could recognize that, and she made no claims about her legal prowess. Having flown in the *Purdue* simulation with Spalding and the Undead Legion, she could recognize the discrepancy in communication style. The simple fact that they claimed Spalding *fled* the scene and sent his squad in to die against overwhelming odds, having full knowledge of an armed nuclear device abord the freight hauler. Well, simply put, it was bullshit.

Every single drop of this was complete hogwash.

She knew Jonathan Spalding enough to know he was a fearless pilot with a slight hero complex. He would've flown headfirst into the nuclear device if it would've saved his squad from harm without so much as flinching.

This whole thing stank much more than she thought it had.

It made her want to dig deeper.

Obviously, she didn't have the clearance to dig into previous action reports.

But she knew of one aging Admiral who did.

And it just so happened that she also knew the passcode to his personal quarters.

CHAPTER 13

"THIS IS REALLY something." Des whistled softly.

Ed stood next to him on the catwalk overlooking warehouse fifteen. It was by far the largest of the clustered warehouses nestled tightly up against the cliff face on the northernmost side of the Vulcan Complex. There were twenty in total, but for some reason, fifteen was the biggest amongst them. Trucks, mech-lifts, and powered skids zipped around the growing number of stacks of crates. Some of which were vehicle-sized, likely because they actually contained vehicles.

"I just hope it's enough." Ed breathed out as he leaned down to rest his elbows on the cold-forged iron handrail.

Des barked out a raspy laugh and glanced at him.

Ed found he was increasingly tired. Just a year ago, he had the energy of a teenager. Now, all he wanted to do was sleep. The idea of a good day now was one where nobody brought him any bad news. Hell, he couldn't even remember the last day that had actually happened. Were things really as bad as they felt? God, he hoped not!

Being the observant people-person that he was, the aged attorney rested his hand lightly on Ed's shoulder. The gesture made him think of his father. It was funny how much he missed him. The man drove him halfway round to insanity most days, but now… Well, now he felt lost without him.

Part of it was a feeling of inadequacy. This was not where his strengths were. Although, he was relatively proud of leveraging the black market to equip his forces. It was a solid move. The Protectorate would still think them wholly outgunned. The story had changed, and they were the only ones who knew about it.

One of the giant crates cracked open under the persistence of at least a dozen tiny bodies crawling around on the outside of it. It swung apart to reveal some type of sizeable armored vehicle which vaguely resembled a *fucking tank*!

Ed gaped openly and shared a look of astonishment with Des.

"Do we even have anyone who knows how to operate this shit?" Ed asked, worry creeping into his voice.

Des just shrugged, grinning like an idiot.

The real worry, wiggling its way deep into the back of his spine every day, was whether or not he was going to get all these good people killed. And for what? Did they really have a chance at *fighting* for their independence? Was this completely insane to even attempt? The premature guilt kept him up at night, and they had not yet even truly begun to fight. This, *all of this*, was about to get much, *much*, worse!

Heavy footsteps on the metal catwalk approached from behind him. He knew it was Brennan before Des glanced over his shoulder and stepped away to give the two some privacy. There was just something intimidating about how the man walked. Was that something they taught at the military academy? How to walk in such a way as to scare people?

Brennan came to that relaxed attention he always did around him. It was not exactly the snap and pomp of one military officer to another, but enough to show the proper amount of respect. Who was Ed McAaron anyway? Just some rich brat with a chip on his shoulder and the possibly inadvertent cause of an assassination.

That last part always left a bitter taste in his mouth.

Time to distract myself.

He stood to his full height. Most people would consider him tall. Not around Brennan, however. When he turned to look at Brennan, his breath caught. The old dove-colored Protectorate combat uniform had been dyed to this deep blood red color from head to toe. It brought out the amber hue in the man's black skin and clung to his body in a way that made Ed think of apex predators.

Everyone had heard Brennan called by his nickname. It was whispered in the mess hall with the mixed fear, reverence, and disgust that people spoke of the boogeyman.

What the fuck were people going to say about *this*, then? He looked like something out of a horror story.

Ed decided it was probably best to not comment on the wardrobe change. Saying something like, "Hey, you know everyone calls you Red Brennan because you were coated in the blood of their families after you massacred them, right?" Nope, probably wouldn't be appropriate. Best to leave this one alone.

Damn, but he was curious about it, though!

"Well," Ed motioned out over the expanse, "what do we think?"

He purposefully used "we" instead of "you" to reinforce that he felt they were a team on equal footing in this little resistance group. Ed wasn't exactly sure who he was trying to convince more, the General or himself.

With two purposeful strides, Brennan grabbed the edge of the railing and peered down at the veritable sea of crates. For being their most expansive warehouse, it sure was filling up quickly.

Nodding slowly to himself, and after what felt like an eternally long pause, Brennan finally said, "It's a start."

Of course he'd say something like that.

Ed let his disappointment show on his face. "You're a tough

man to impress, General."

Brennan half-smiled and clasped his hands behind his back. "I've been accused of that many times before, Ed."

Brennan exuded an air of self-confidence that Ed was simultaneously envious and appreciative of. That contrast made for an unsettled kind of kinship between them.

"I'd be curious to learn how you made this happen?" Brennan posed the question in a way that made it apparent he did not expect an honest answer.

"I sold out my family fortune to a known sociopathic, probably psychotic, serial killer and criminal." That just about summed it up as best as could be done.

There was no immediate reaction, and after a prolonged moment, Ed thought maybe he hadn't heard his answer.

"Well," Brennan said finally, "at least now you know what it's like to work in politics."

Ed coughed around a laugh.

Was that a joke?

Unsure of exactly how to react, Ed glanced over at Brennan. He was smiling broadly, looking out over the activity taking place in the warehouse below.

"You better be careful with that," Ed said ruefully.

"With what?" Brennan asked.

"That sharp sense of humor. You might get us all killed."

Brennan chuckled.

That tiny amount of mirth on his face might as well have been planet-splitting levels of hysteric laughter for anyone else. Hopefully, this meant the dark moods were a thing of the past. There was shit that needed doing, and he required Brennan's help to get it done.

Hell, we may even be becoming friends!

The thought was interrupted by a commotion behind them.

A messenger was sprinting down the lower catwalks, dashing up the stairs three at a time. Some of the posted guards fingered their brand-new shiny weapons.

The girl was red-faced and practically panting from exertion when she came skidding to a stop facing Brennan and McAaron. Her cheeks puffed furiously as she tried to draw enough breath to deliver her message.

"There's been another bombing," she gasped out quickly, sucking air between words, "Ballor and Cole are claiming some of the weapons from the delivery to make another run."

Ed cursed viciously. The echoes of the words punctuated the air behind him.

The girl's eyes went wide. She looked no more than fourteen.

Brennan stood there, stoic as ever, jaw set.

"I think it's time we dealt with Ballor and Cole," Ed finally said, grinding his own teeth to resist another outburst.

"I'd be happy to deal with them, sir," Brennan said. The honorific back into effect because of the messenger's presence.

"How do you propose we do that, exactly?" Nothing would destroy a resistance movement faster than infighting. That was the downfall of any team that grew in fame, power, influence, or whatever too quickly. There were bound to be assholes like Jared Ballor and Octavian Cole. Those who were going to try to make it all about *them* instead of all about the *cause.*

Brennan considered the question, then asked the girl, "Where are these two now?"

The girl pointed to the southern wall, where a steady stream of haulers were driving in crates. A small group of figures clustered around several containers that had been pulled off early.

Brennan started walking down the catwalk, the girl squealing and all but leaping out of his way.

Ed had to take a couple hurried steps to keep pace.

"I think it's time I had a discussion with those two about the importance of strategy."

Strategy? He couldn't possibly think that was going to work, could he?

Rather than question him directly, he asked instead, "You haven't met either of these two yet, have you?"

A shake of his head was the only response.

"Ah, well." Ed sighed. "They only have a few brain cells to rub together between them. They were heavy haulers for the corp who were constantly getting into trouble. Their parents were some of the company's first employees back when Dad had first started. Promised he'd take care of them. Neither is worth a shit. They manage now. The only way Dad could keep them out of trouble."

Unfortunately, it was quite a distance to travel to get back to the front of the building from where they were. The two of them walked for a while in silence. Ballor and Cole were a pain in the ass, but they had the right idea. Stick it to the man. Their tactic, or lack thereof, left a lot to be desired. In trying to hurt the government, they were just blowing up businesses and infrastructure that Martians needed just as bad, if not worse, than the Protectorate. Even if they won this little dispute and their independence, they'd need as much as possible to be intact. This would make the eighth side operation they had pulled. By the last count, over two hundred civilians had been injured, four dead. The number of enemies killed? One. No Protectorate installations had been targeted. It was all Martian infrastructure. Access tunnels, network relay stations, the spaceport, shipping byways. All things they'd *eventually* need to use themselves.

You can't just go around blowing shit up in the name of the cause!

Ed had tired of trying to communicate this to the two. Neither was very accessible these days. They were cloistered with their "elite troops" that had been secretly recruited under Ed's nose. That was something else he was somewhat cranky about. It would be one thing to run some rogue operations on your own. It was quite another to be recruiting from within to expand the potential of your dirty work. Adding an interesting, if infuriating, layer of complexity to the whole thing was the fact that the complex seemed to be split on whether they were justified in their actions or not.

Brennan remained silent as they started down the switchback staircase leading them to within a stone's throw of where the group stood talking with the Ballor and Cole.

They were both large, blue-collar workers their entire lives. Standing to an equal height as Ed himself but at least twice as broad across the chest. Their arms looked more like Ed's thighs. Both men had red scarves tied around their left bicep. A few others in the crowd appeared to have the same thing going on. Some way to designate the *elite* then.

With an effort that bordered on heroic, Ed resisted the urge to roll his eyes.

As they approached, the crowd parted to allow them to pass. Many eyes turned wide with surprise, anger, or both when they saw Brennan's outfit. *Nobody* said a word, though. So, that was something at least.

Both Ballor and Cole crossed their meaty arms across their chests as the two of them approached. "It's one thing to be accused of something and process the shame," Cole said acidly. "Quite another to literally wear it with pride."

Oh good! So, this is getting off to a great start.

They came to a stop just inside the inner circle, confronting the two burly men. It smelled of iron-rich dirt mingled with sweaty bodies and the synthetic cloying smell of packing materials. The warehouses had very little ventilation. While the surface of Mars wasn't exactly known for scorching temperatures, lack of airflow coupled with exertion could still work up a mighty sweat. Ed felt perspiration sliding down his lower back even as he regarded the sweaty masked faces around him.

This was a confrontation he had not been looking forward to.

Not that he was scared of these two. Far from it, in fact. He was more worried he'd do something rash and break this party up before it ever truly got started. These two idiots represented the very worst in almost half of their number. For those that just wanted to fight, any flimsy justification would suffice. Likely they had grown up in the households that blamed the Protectorate and UNIC government as a whole for every late bill payment, every missed meal, and every hour of unwelcome overtime.

Sadly, it was murky water for him to really dive in and have a conversation about. What with his private education, tutors for every subject, personal chefs and drivers, and the resources to basically get out of any bad situation. Nope, not really a way he could be credible discussing their point of view.

In a lot of ways, he envied their grit. Growing up, Ed was ashamed to say that he started and stopped a lot of things. From school activities to organized sports, he'd get a wild hair up his ass and decide he was going to do something grand. Only to realize it was quite a lot more complex than the other kids made it look. Then, Dad would have to explain to the coach why Ed was dropping off the team, or out of the club, or what have you; and typically make a parting donation to keep the "door open for a second chance."

Ed was tired of second chances.

Nobody, *especially* not him, lived up to them.

Brennan just stood with his hands clasped tightly behind his back. His face was impassive, expressionless. Ed made a mental note to explain to Brennan just how fucking terrifying a blank expression was on his face. Especially considering the new outfit.

Smile once in a while, would you? It almost made Ed laugh before he remembered where he was and what he was doing. *Keep your head in the game here, Ed. This has the potential to get very bad, very quickly.* The thought was sobering.

Ballor and Cole both glanced at each other. Whatever reaction they had been expecting from Brennan, they did not receive it. Thrown off their game, they were scrambling for a plan B to fill the tense silence.

Finally, Brennan glanced down at his red uniform. "I decided

I needed a reminder," the words came out low and slow. Not defensive, not irritated, but measured and calm.

The tone made the hairs on Ed's arms stand at attention.

Something about the contrast of the softly spoken words, and… Well, *him!* Just didn't mix in any comfortable way.

"A reminder?" Ballor spat into the dust at their feet. "Lucky for us, we don't need any fancy red clothes to remember that day. All we have to do is look around and see the missing faces of all the people who ain't here!"

There were some angry murmurs from the crowd. It was hard to tell whether they were for or against the statement. Either way, the discontent was beginning to mount. Whatever the play was here, Brennan best pull the trigger quickly and be done with it, or they'd lose more ground than they gained.

Slowly, Brennan raised his head and met each man's eyes, and held them for several heartbeats.

Ed tensed, and he noticed quite a few physical shifts throughout the encircling crowd.

If this became violent, it would not be a great situation for them.

Brennan visibly relaxed. He was still imposing but no longer a coiled snake ready to strike. "I appreciate your motivations for these operations. I really do. They seem to be well-executed, and yield results."

He… *Wait, what?*

It took absolutely every ounce of willpower he had to not openly gape at General Brennan. This was not *at all* what he thought they were coming here to do! Was he *encouraging them?* What the hell was this?

A sudden thought occurred to him.

If Brennan wanted to make a play for his job, this would be the best way to go about it. Strengthening and supporting, publicly, dipshits like these two would polarize the rogue portion of the resistance behind Brennan. A classic move, really, and Ed should have seen it coming. The fact that it hadn't even factored into his planning until this precise moment was galling.

A faint ember of an old instinct suddenly sputtered to life, deep within his mind. *It would be effortless, just turn and walk out the door. Nobody would stop you. Nobody needed you anymore. They had your money; that's all they ever wanted anyway. You didn't really think that you could lead a rebellion, did you?*

His feet ached to be moving, to carry him through those doors and away from this madness. *No.*

If nothing else, his childhood had taught him that quitting was something he would regret forever. He couldn't quit. Not now. There would be no way he could look at himself in the mirror if he walked away now. He'd just have to figure out how to deal with a hostile takeover. Maybe Des could help?

Brennan had been speaking, but in his blind panic, Ed had missed the details.

Stupid! Can't go off on tangents when the tensions are so high! What the hell is wrong with you? Stay focused!

There he was, doing it again.

"It's the overall strategy that I'm talking about," Brennan was saying. "Not the tactics themselves. By all accounts, you run a tight ship; you just lack leadership and actionable data." Ed felt his jaw click loudly and suppressed a wince. He was grinding his teeth so much lately his jaws ached.

"And you think you can provide those for us, do ya now, Red?" Cole laughed.

Ballor just sneered.

Ed hated that sneer.

"I do," Brennan said calmly, professionally. "With some guidance, you could make a real difference. I'm putting together a squad, with Mr. McAaron's blessing, of course." Brennan gestured toward Ed with an open hand and locked eyes with him briefly. There was no betrayal in them. Just a genuine sense of duty.

Emotionally floundering somewhat, Ed chimed in, "We don't argue your methods; we argue your targets. General Brennan wants to focus those into something that hurts the enemy instead of ourselves."

Which is what I've been saying this whole fucking time; I'd like to remind everyone!"With this unit, we can...." Brennan trailed off as both Ballor and Cole began laughing uproariously.

Ballor pointed a meaty finger at Brennan and growled, spittle flying through the gaps in his teeth, "You think we'd follow you, mate?"

A long breath escaped Brennan, and he clasped his hands behind his back once again, drawing himself up to full height. "I do. Mr. McAaron believes I'm wasting my time with you, but I see two men who have a desire to do their people right and have the makings of proper soldiers in them."

Silence. It was so thick, so *real* he could have reached out and touched it.

Nobody moved. Nobody dared breathe for fear of breaking the moment.

Ballor stood stuck in his mocking pose, his face a mixture of rage and confusion.

Cole, the sharper of the two, it seemed, had his brows drawn together considering.

So, this was it. The moment of truth.

A battle of wills was waged between the two men, the emotional energy surging back and forth between them, like warring bolts of lightning.

Ballor broke the stare first with a sudden, mirthless flurry of laughter.

"I'd rather be dead, as follow Brennan the Red."

There was a definite murmur of agreement. And, quite frankly, it had a catchy kind of propaganda ring to it. For a slogan, it sure ran off the tongue nice. Catchy things had a way of spreading, whether or you wanted them to or not.

"I understand your reluctance…." Brennan began, but Cole just waved him off.

"Go fuck yourself, Red. This conversation is over."

That was it. The game was over. Brennan had lost them.

Ed took a step forward before he knew what he was doing.

"You two idiots have caused more damage to the city of Hellas than the Protectorate. Just the damage to the spaceport and docks alone is going to take a decade to repair. That impacts everyone, *least* of all the fucking Protectorate. So, as I see it, we have two options here. You can join up with Brennan's crew and start venting your small-dick energy into something productive, or—"

Both men shot dark looks at Ed as they squared off to face him, effectively dismissing Brennan.

"Or what?" Cole demanded, the threat of violence radiating off of him like steam.

"Or you get the fuck out of my family establishment. You know it, the one my father welcomed your worthless piece of shit father into to save your family?"

Cole roared, but Ballor grabbed his arm, restraining him from attacking Ed. Brennan stepped up, all pretense about diplomacy gone. Now, he radiated menace as well. It seemed the only one who *didn't* look as intimidating as a demon was Ed himself.

Oh, but he could talk shit with the best of them.

"So, make your choice. Put up or shut up time." Ed uncrossed his arms, expecting a fight.

Ballor chuckled.

Not the reaction Ed was expecting.

"See, I think there's a third option here," the big man said and pointed around at the encircling crowd. "What you two fail to realize is that these are *our* troops. Nobody here gives two shits about you, your family, or your father's memory."

Ed felt his body go suddenly cold as if he had been dunked into a vat of ice water.

Ballor continued on, "Right? I think you're missing the point here, mate. This is a democracy of *real* people. What? You think you're nobility because of who your Daddy was?" The mocking tone was grating, like nails on a chalkboard. The fact that it was the truth made it worse yet. "Wrong. So very wrong. See, I think option three is, we execute this red-coat-wearing-motherfucker for the murder of hundreds, and we have ourselves a little election. Setup our new government the right and proper way."

The first gunshot took Ballor in the knee. The second took half of his face off.

The third ripped into Cole's chest and sent him tumbling to the ground.

Shocked screams ripped through the crowd, and people stumbled backward as they hurriedly put distance between themselves and the gunfire. The massive building echoed with the unexpected shots.

Cole was dying poorly, blood gurgling through the wound in his chest and out of his mouth in giant geyser-like sprays.

It took a moment for Ed to realize that Brennan had ahold of his outstretched hand, gently and slowly claiming the fancy gun the Pirate King had gifted him. The recoil still burned in his hand, a dull ache. He knew he had fired the weapon, but he had no memory of actually *doing* it.

The crowd had surged away from them, naturally. Now it had stopped to see what would happen next.

Human behavior had the propensity to make Ed sick to his stomach.

Cole died how he had lived, fighting every step of the way. It took four minutes.

When he finally stilled, Ed looked at the stunned and silent crowd.

"I will not let you lose this chance." The words came out, thick with emotion. "I refuse to stand by and let you fight over the freedom that you haven't even earned yet!" He was yelling now, a full-throated, rasping, and raw torrent of words. "You think I want this? *This?!* You'd be crazy to think that. I want this all to *mean something!* I want this to be a story about redemption, not retaliation! But what I want doesn't matter. Because they're coming for us. General Brennan assures me, they will not stop until they hunt every single one of us down, murder our families and us, and rewrite the history of this moment to reflect how nobly they protected us against ourselves. I'm fighting for the *story*. Not myself. And if I have to shoot every single one of you myself to achieve that goal, I will."

He grabbed his gun as he stalked by Brennan, slung it into his holster, and strode toward the open doors of the warehouse. He didn't even look back as he shouted into the warehouse.

"Don't make me do that!"

CHAPTER 14

BRENNAN AND MCAARON sat in awkward silence. Brennan tried to not notice the other man's hands shaking as he sipped his coffee.

Killing people was hard. As a soldier for his entire life, Brennan knew this firsthand. It was extraordinarily challenging to kill people you knew. People you felt responsible for.

Even though they had been misguided, the two deceased men had the right idea. Just the wrong application. If there had been even an ounce of willingness to see reason, they could have been heroes. They had the mindset and gumption necessary to do what needed doing. If only they could've gotten out of the way of themselves and their egos.

McAaron sighed heavily and leaned back into his chair. It reclined until he was almost parallel with the ground. In that position, he rubbed the bridge of his nose.

"This is the part where you tell me I fucked up," McAaron said woefully.

Brennan considered. The two men hadn't really left them much choice. He had been considering his next actions, and options besides violence were few and far between. Still, it would've been better if he had pulled the trigger, not McAaron. People needed someone righteous to hang their lives on. His soul was already stained. What were two more Martian lives on his tally?

As they sat there, he considered how best to communicate that to the younger man. They weren't that far apart in age, but several lifetimes' worth of experience with this sort of thing.

"I think you did the best you could with the hand you were dealt," Brennan said, crossing his legs and scrubbing at his own face. Damn, but it was a sad thing, killing your own troops.

There was a chime from the door.

McAaron leaned forward in his chair. "Well, at least I know it's not an angry mob hellbent on my head." Then he smiled coyly. "They probably wouldn't knock first."

He called for whoever it was to enter, and Brennan regarded him sidelong.

Desmond entered, carrying a few datapads stacked together quite precariously. Brennan had noticed that the elderly man had lost a bit of the spring in his step in the last few weeks. They hadn't known each other very long, but the stress of all of this was taking its toll. He didn't think that McAaron had noticed.

Best to not get involved in family affairs. So, instead, he just sipped at his coffee.

Thankfully, McAaron had taken the cue from their previous meeting that he was done with intoxicants. No more alcohol. Ever. That was a weakness that shamed him to his very core. There had been days he had been drinking to kill himself. Admitting that to himself had been almost impossible and had taken far too long. There was no way he could utter those words to anyone.

"I have Operation Blockbuster ready for your review." The old man looked up and noticed Brennan seated at the desk, "Ah, General Brennan. Good to see you. I'm glad you're here as well."

Brennan raised a questioning eyebrow at McAaron, who flushed slightly and stood.

"Figured we'd start using operational names instead of 'hey remember that plan we had about dispersing all our troops to hidden locations throughout the hemisphere' type stuff."

The only thing to do was nod, so he did.

Blockbuster, eh?

He couldn't altogether hide the crooked grin that teased at the corners of his mouth.

"Okay, look you two," McAaron chided, "I've had a rough afternoon. Can we please just get on with this?"

"Of course, sir," Des said.

Brennan gave a crisp salute.

McAaron sighed heavily.

Des sat the stack of datapads atop the desk and took the top from the pile. An overview of Hellas was already visible. With a few swipes, Des began to outline the plan. He talked them through it, detail by detail. They had thought of everything, even gone so far as to divide them up into a rudimentary command structure. While not exactly up to spec, it was decent enough to get the job done. They could adapt as they needed. Besides, the Protectorate way of doing things wasn't the only way to run a military. He had to remind himself of that.

Especially not with the war they were planning to fight. Guerilla warfare was a tricky, scrappy type thing. Utilizing smaller units that could further fracture into cells and operate independently of a proper command structure was historically the best methodology to adopt. That overall strategy gave the behemoth Protectorate nothing to swing at. This was a reasonable and necessary strategy because it was liable to be a lethal blow if they connected even once.

The point was to use their size and substantial bureaucracy against them.

Nobody could take a shit in the Protectorate without permission from at least three levels of ranking COs.

Conversely, their decisions were almost always perfect. Troop deployments were clean, crisp, and beautifully efficient. On top of that, they had impeccable intelligence with some of the most brilliant military minds to have ever worn a uniform, all in a room determining how best to wield that data with brutal efficacy. A perfect storm of death and destruction. Best to avoid it altogether, if possible.

When Des had finished, Brennan listened as McAaron fired off a barrage of questions. Several times, Des asked Brennan to intervene with his thoughts on how best to answer the questions. Part of him wondered if they included him just to make him feel invested or valued or if they really needed his guidance. Not that it mattered to him. He just wanted to burn out the corruption and rot from within the organization to which he had dedicated his life.

"What about equipment dispersal?" McAaron asked.

Des looked to Brennan.

Brennan considered a moment, then nodded and said, "I think our ace-up-the-sleeve, if you will, is the fact that we have all this heavy armor. They won't be expecting that. Nobody will. I'd say we leave that tucked away here in the mines until we have momentum for an all-out offensive. Then, use the heavy artillery to deal the knockout blow." He paused, then added, "Or if we start to lose, it's our Hail Mary."

All three of the men exchanged meaningful looks.

Best not to think about that.

The group clustered around the desktop fell into silence again as everyone surveyed the plan. It was solid. Distributing their leadership, equipment, and resources throughout the sector was smart. No one attack could cripple them. However, being so dispersed, each group was on its own for the duration. Help would be slow in coming and ineffective anyway.

"Well, good." McAaron perked up. "Gives our people the opportunity to learn how to operate the damned things. Have you looked inside one of those?"

Brennan raised an eyebrow at him.

"Oh, well," McAaron cleared his throat, "I suppose you probably have a time or two."

The funny thing was, Brennan found he genuinely liked Ed McAaron. Not just as a potential leader of a free people, but as a person. More so as an individual than part of any cause. Not that he had much experience with this type of thing, but he felt like the two of them could actually be *friends.* Not just *friendly*, but honest-to-goodness friends.

That was a strange thought to consider. The only other people he had ever really considered even close to having some kind of friendship with would be Manu and Marak. One had betrayed him, and the other was actively hunting him.

Hopefully, his poor judgment in friends wasn't a trend.

As he studied the map, he realized McAaron was watching him with a thoughtful expression on his face. It looked like he was chewing on something that didn't taste quite as good as he thought it was going to. Never a good sign.

Without raising his head from the map, Brennan said, "Best just get it out. Better to say a thing than let it fester inside."

McAaron chuckled. "I've read that book, too."

Then he sighed and vigorously mussed up his hair as he took a seat and gestured for Brennan to do the same.

Never a good sign, either. His own thoughts had a sour taste to them now, and he briefly wondered if his face matched McAaron's.

Des quietly excused himself. "I'll begin plans to distribute our resources accordingly." He exited, pulling the door closed gently behind him.

That feeling of dread grew ever more profound in his gut.

"I don't know exactly how to say this without setting your hair on fire," McAaron finally said, twirling a heavy gold ring atop his desk. "So, I'm just going to say it with one blanket disclaimer presented at the beginning."

There was a pause, so Brennan nodded slowly.

McAaron held his gaze and said firmly, "We're not going to do anything about this intel quite yet. There are excellent reasons why we're holding off. After you… lose your mind for a bit, I want you to talk out the logistics of my plan with me. Do you understand?"

He didn't. "Of course," he heard himself say.

"Governor Chu has made contact," McAaron said in a slow monotone.

Brennan's mind exploded. So quick were his thoughts that they piled upon each other too rapidly to be made sense of. He found he was standing, with no memory of getting to his feet. McAaron had leaned back in his chair, his hand out in a placating gesture.

Helena is alive!

There had been doubts. Without being seen for over a month, her status had been questionable at best. While he had never lost hope, not really, the soldier in him had already compartmentalized her loss to deal with later. Or never. Whichever.

If they had made contact, they could get her out.

We're not doing anything about this intel quite yet, McAaron had said.

Like hell!

"I'm going for her," Brennan said, leaning down so heavily on his clenched fists that his knuckles creaked.

McAaron looked up at him, more than a bit of concern set in his eyes. "Look, I'm going to acknowledge the fact that you look scary as hell right now, okay? And, admittedly, I'd be thinking the same way you are were I in your shoes. But, it pains me to say, I cannot allow that at this moment, General."

Brennan felt his jaw creak under the intense pressure he was exerting on his own body, taut as he was. He leaned down, halving the distance between them. "And who's going to stop me, Ed?" There was danger in his voice, a tone he was unaccustomed to hearing from himself. Especially when addressing a superior officer. "You?"

Without hesitation, McAaron said, "Yes. But I'd rather you hear me out first."

That's when McAaron slowly withdrew his hand from under the desk, one of his fancy new pirate-gifted handguns cocked and pointed right between Brennan's eyes. He could see the faint glint of the unfired round down the barrel length.

So, not friends, after all.

Brennan stood tall, straight-backed, not quite at attention but near enough.

"I personally spoke to Helena, Keith."

The fact that first names were being used suddenly was not lost on Brennan. Nothing pissed him off more than being *handled.*

McAaron watched him closely, finger poised on the trigger of his firearm. "She wants to help, from the inside. She's already established a line to the internal network of the Administrative building."

There was a lengthy pause.

McAaron looked slightly confused. "Did you hear what I said?"

"I did," Brennan snapped back.

The other man sighed heavily, the gun swayed and the lined-up shot fell askew. Brennan's muscles tensed. That was his opening. When he sighed, he relaxed his arms and lost his shot. Before he sighed, he always drew in a deep breath so he could expel it dramatically. The next time he did so, he'd make a play for the gun across the desk. It was a high-risk move. No more than a meter separated them; he'd have to be quick. You didn't have to shoot someone in the head at this range to get a lethal hit.

"This is as much her decision as it was mine," McAaron said heavily. "I knew you wouldn't like it, but I was hoping you'd see the advantages."

"You're right. I don't like it," Brennan said sharply.

He said it more to incite a sigh from McAaron so that he could make his move. The other man didn't oblige, this time.

"I want to get her out as much as you do," he started.

"I sincerely doubt that."

Do it, you two-faced bastard!

No sigh this time either.

"Okay, that's fair, maybe not as much as you do. I'm not exactly privy to the nature of your relationship with our Governor," he said, a little bit of… something… had entered his voice. Was that an accusation? "I do know that I don't want *this* job. I'm keeping the seat warm until I can plant her ass firmly into it. I'm no good at this Keith, and never wanted it. I have used up my worth in upending the family coffers and empowering the violent transition of power. I don't provide any other value."

Something about what he had said penetrated the furious anger boiling within his mind. The humility of it, maybe? Or was it the candid nature of the admission? It tugged at the back of his mind hard enough that he realized, too late, that McAaron was halfway through another long sigh.

It was very unlike him to miss a martial opportunity.

That fact alone changed his mind on the course of action he had been planning to take.

"I'm listening," Brennan said, trying to let some calm into his tone. "But, I don't listen well at gunpoint. Old soldier habit."

McAaron looked at the gun in his hand as if surprised to see it there. Then looked back up at Brennan without so much as twitching the weapon. "If it's all the same to you, General, I'd prefer to keep this right where it is. You look like a cornered momma bear who hasn't eaten in a week and has a burr squarely up her ass. Frankly, I'm regretting my decision to drink so much coffee before this whole experience, if you catch my meaning."

Brennan blinked. *Did he just admit to almost pissing himself?*

Unexpectedly, Brennan barked out a laugh. It was only partially from the comedy of the comment, more from a need to expel his coiled energy in *some* way. Like a compound bow pulled to the limit, it needed to be released.

McAaron wasn't convinced, but a corner of his mouth tugged upward into a lopsided grin.

"Fine, but get on with it before I take that gun and shove it up *your* ass."

McAaron paled somewhat but barked out a half-hearted nervous laugh.

"Fair enough."

As Brennan reclaimed his chair from where it had been knocked to the ground, he decided he'd share with McAaron that it hadn't been a joke. Maybe he'd wait until after he heard what the plan was.

CHAPTER 15

A CHIME INDICATED the process had finished.

The monitor flashed a warning: *<FAILURE: INCORRECT CODEC.>*

"Well, that's not helpful." Frankie stretched in her seat.

She had been working on the massive signal she had intercepted for almost a week. Nothing she threw at it had any effect. Part of her was beginning to wonder if it was maybe just some kind of transient fast radio burst from deep space. That type of thing had occurred randomly throughout the modern observation of space. Some scientists theorized it was caused by black holes colliding or possibly from neutron stars. It was technically possible that the FRB signal would show up as data, just a giant block of noise from space.

If that was the case, she had wasted a week of intelligence gathering at a time when it was likely the most critical to the entire operation. Part of her considered deleting the file and be done with it.

What she needed was a break from it.

With a few commands, she deactivated the file and placed it in her encrypted cold file storage. It would be undetectable to anyone else on the system while it was dormant. One of the rare advantages of working with a bunch of amateurs. A fat lot of good it did to the overall effort, though.

Her eyes hurt. She felt somewhat at a loss about how best to apply her talents while maintaining her anonymity. A lot of what she was doing now was covering her own tracks. If she didn't have to do that, she'd immediately increase her productivity. Unfortunately, that was the sad state of her excommunicated existence.

At the very least, the command structure had decided to go with her deployment plan, albeit somewhat deviated from what she had submitted. Everyone had to put their stink on a plan as it worked up the chain of command. Not that she thought her plans were always the best course of action, but arguably this time, it was. The adjustments wouldn't hurt the overall execution, but some cells would be too far away to receive help. Just unlucky for them, she supposed.

Sure, she saw the advantages of capturing the air-defense installations. Control of orbit was vital to not just their war efforts but to their overall survival. Almost half of the food consumed on Mars was grown on orbital platforms and shuttled to the surface for processing and distribution. Losing access to that would be, well, *really* bad. If Mars had control of both ground and orbit, it could be completely self-sufficient. If it lacked either of those, in whole or in part, it would operate at a deficit.

Of course, that wasn't even taking into account the military advantages of controlling orbit.

Fine, she got it. Orbit was necessary, so too was control of the orbital defense systems. However, the installations were spread out, that reinforcing any one location from another would be time-consuming. Which did bode well for their seizing of them, but not in their *holding* of them.

Her plan consisted of seizing the ADA installations and leaving a skeleton crew at each while capturing three significant areas of the inner perimeter of the city. While being less defensible buildings, primarily residential with some commercial strips, the main transportation arteries were nearby. That made transporting large numbers of people in and out of the area a relatively easy proposition. The city's outer ring of the most undersized infrastructure, which would cause delays in deployments and make each one much more vulnerable to attack. Any movements were restricted to only a handful of options, whereas the inner city had dozens of routes by comparison.

Had she been informed of the ADA priorities, she would've included that in her initial assessment. Why the intel on the blockade wasn't made available to the analysts immediately was beyond her. When your intelligence team was getting tactical data from mediacasts, you were in deep shit.

Everything about this made her want to run, hide, and wait out whatever came next. She may have been a lot of things, but she definitely was not a quitter. No, sadly, she was an idiot. There was a sense of loyalty that she couldn't shake. On top of that, she truly believed what they were doing was righteous.

Enough musing. There's work to be done.

Frankie slid her knees back under her workstation and adjusted her peripheral devices the way she liked them arranged. Now, which issue to tackle first? The list was so long, and everything was a P1, the highest priority, so it effectively destroyed any benefit having a priority list would have granted. If everything was the highest priority, then nothing was a priority.

That did it. Now she had a headache.

Maybe I should just clock out for the day. Try again tomorrow?

To her, that felt too near to quitting. If even temporarily.

She sighed heavily and put her head in her hands.

What she needed was some clear direction on what would best benefit the resistance. *Everything* wasn't an achievable goal. They had to start somewhere.

A beep sounded from her workstation.

A decoding process had been completed on the massive Protectorate breach they had performed. That was the one ray of hope she clung to. Having Governor Chu establishing a backdoor directly into the Protectorate Operational Field Office was… *huge*! Word in the complex was Ed McAaron had offered to rescue her immediately or leave her in play to establish the link. She had chosen the latter of the two. The number of lives that single act of self-sacrifice had saved from sure death was incalculable. Solid data, direct from the source, with a very unlikely to be discovered backdoor connection. It was exciting.

Now all they had to do was spend the processing power and time to decrypt the files.

Unfortunately, the intel they gathered was going to be random.

The first thing she had managed to decode had been a rather extensive laundry list.

Not helpful at all.

Frankie brought up the file and perked up a bit. It was a collection of drone surveillance archives. Thousands upon thousands of compressed video files, cataloged by sector and date. The date range was not exactly helpful to their current efforts, being quite a bit older than… She stopped that train of thought dead.

Scrambling across the keys, she brought up a rough timeline of events she had been working on while trying to decode the FRB. It lined up. The surveillance data was of a particular sector of the city during the period following the assassination. It was labeled as high-priority and classified. Which, of course, had immediately piqued her interest. What made it equally fascinating was the region of interest, centered on the McAaron estate.

With a quick cross-reference of her timeline, she found the exact date and time of the explosion that had killed Martin McAaron and leveled the estate.

That data in hand, she searched the archive… and found a match!

Breathing heavily, she loaded the video.

She swore quietly.

The footage was Multi-Optic, or MO, an overlay consisting of heat source, x-ray, and LiDAR. AI filled in gaps with registered building data, historical footage, and all sorts of other fun connected technologies. It was insanely helpful for military operations, as it gave an increased level of detail and could deeply penetrate buildings. Being able to see troop counts and movements in real-time was helpful.

Rather than make up her mind about the usefulness of the video before watching it entirely, she sped up the playback.

Her eyebrows slowly began to raise up her forehead.

As she watched, a large-scale Protectorate presence collected in the area. She recognized the group in the front, consisting of a few Peace Officer troop transports and an official support vehicle. That much had been on the news. What was interesting were the three companies deployed to the rear of the house in unmarked vehicles.

She punched in on those soldiers. The unit information was available, and her breath caught when she activated that filter. SPECOPS-DU-B2. Special Operations Demo Unit, Bravo 2. The other two were supporting units or cover units of infantry.

What the hell had a demo unit been doing there?

Well, blowing the place up, obviously. But still!

Questions swirled around in her head.

Zooming back out, she watched as the leading force went in and corralled the occupants, including Martin—who was the only seated individual in the building, obviously at his desk working.

As the scene played out, Frankie ran a side search for the operational audio recordings. Unfortunately, they didn't seem to be included in this package, which was only drone footage.

As the Protectorate officers burst into the foyer of Martin's office, she could see him flinch and raise his head. He had definitely heard them crash through the door and the commotion with an assistant. Instead of getting up to check, he had just leaned back in his chair.

That was interesting. Frankie paused the playback.

Were she in her office and heard a commotion just outside with her assistant, there was a reasonable chance that her immediate reaction would be to get up and investigate. Unless she knew it was coming, of course. *Had* Martin known it was coming? If so, how? Did he have inside information? And, more importantly, had he been prepared for that eventuality?

Questions piled upon questions, and she found herself smiling. This dodgy old fart had somehow outplayed the Protectorate. She could tell by the smug posture he had assumed when the commotion outside started. Every instinct told her that somewhere, somehow, there was more to Martin McAaron than the mediacasts had portrayed. Much, *much,* more.

She made a mental note to dig into that when she had some free time.

Excitement bordering on delirium caused her face to edge closer to the monitor. She started the playback again, grinning and glancing around to make sure she wasn't being observed. For being a room full of "intelligence" analysts, they sure were a bunch of impercipient louts.

The room filled with armed soldiers, all guns trained on Martin, who sat calmly in his chair. A central figure emerged, tall, somewhat feminine, and she seemed to address Martin. Frankie zoomed in on the interaction. She couldn't quite tell who the person was, but she had taken a relative measurement of her and Martin with a few gestures. The exact height and weight of Martin would be a matter of public record. Using AI, she could compare the relative size of the images and get approximate measurements of the other individual.

Another thought occurred to her.

She might not even have to go to that much trouble.

Fingers a blur across her devices, she brought up a secure link to archived mediacasts and searched for the footage of the McAaron estate moments before it blew. The Protectorate had withdrawn from the building just mere moments before it blew. In fact, one officer had lost her life in the blast. Shrapnel from the building had struck her tragically in the spine.

There!

Standing on the front step of the estate was a tall, well-muscled intelligence officer. Laura Castor. The woman that weasel-faced dick-for-brains Brillian had put in charge of the ground investigation!

She could tell it was the same person talking to Martin, but diligence was part of the job. She ran a comparison between the mediacast footage and the drone footage. It was an exact match, zero deviations.

This was huge. Her mind raced with the implications.

A sudden flash on the screen shook her from her thoughts.

A hot spot had appeared on the wall behind Martin, who slumped backward in his chair at an odd angle.

Frankie rolled the footage back.

Laura Castor drew down on Martin and shot him through the forehead.

An explosion hadn't killed Edward McAaron's father. Laura Castor had shot him, unarmed, unprovoked, and seated in his own office.

Holy shit!

Heart thumping loudly in her chest, she watched as Laura bent to pick up the spent round-casing and motioned to the team to exit. She must have given an order over comms as shots rang out throughout the household. Every occupant was summarily executed on the spot.

The demo team exfiltrated from the back of the property and sped off, each vehicle taking a different route.

Moments later, the screen went white with the fireball.

Frankie leaned back, the breath coming out of her in a rush.

She hadn't even realized she had been holding it.

The implications from this video were staggering. Just releasing this video wouldn't be enough to condemn the Protectorate, but it was enough to show the media line they had taken was inaccurate at best and a complete fabrication at worst.

She had something to work on now.

Piecing it together would be her focus. If she could show that this had been a hit by the Protectorate and *not* a terrorist action taken by Martin McAaron as the media had claimed… It could be the undoing of the hold the UNIC had over the planet. There would be no way the public would stand for that kind of deliberate assassination of a civilian, least of all one so well-regarded as the elder McAaron!

Plus, there was that smug body language exhibited by Martin. What had that been about? The old man had done something, she was sure of it. He was too cunning by half to act that way without good reason. Unless he was using it as a way to throw Castor off the trail of something?

Again, she cursed softly under her breath. There just wasn't enough information to process. She would need to do some digging. There was more to be learned here, she could feel it.

Her mobile datapad buzzed in her pocket and she reached down and extracted it. The message was received through a routing service she was using to intercept calls that were intended for her personal device. Given her delicate situation as supposedly being obliterated in space, she decided it wasn't the wisest idea to continue using that device—and had pitched it into the hull of the freighter she had *allegedly* been aboard. Best to be thorough.

Being able to monitor incoming messages to the line was advantageous enough to do the extra work.

A message from her brother: *DEPLOYING TO MARS, WANT TO MEET UP?*

The message made her heart hurt.

Not only did she miss her brother, but he hadn't been notified of her death, evidently.

She couldn't respond, of course, but she really was curious as to why his unit was deploying to Mars.

The other thing to consider was that it could be a trap. If anyone had gone through her records, they would have found a lengthy history with her brother, and determined the nature of their relationship. Toss out a note in a bottle and see what comes back. Classic intelligence gathering. For the results it often yielded, it was a very low-cost investment.

In either case, the situation twisted her guts into a knot.

Could she act on intel that would lead to her brother being killed in action?

No.

That dual loyalty was going to cause her problems down the road, she knew that for certain.

A problem for another day, perhaps. She stuck the datapad back into her pocket. Not answering messages was not really her style, so it was likely to raise concern from her brother. Which would lead to his discovering her "death" in space.

Nothing to be done about that.

There were bigger things at stake.

Like a dog with a bone, she knuckled down and tuned everything else out. This thread with Martin needed following.

It wasn't long before she had it put together.

The drone footage had been the clue to know she needed to look deeper. What Martin had done was smart. The clues were subtle, but she had eventually managed to trace them back to the Vulcan Complex and his personal files. Whoever had set up the transfer had been devilishly clever about it. Only with the clues she had obtained from the Protectorate footage would she have even thought to look, and even then, she had almost missed it.

The whole interaction had been recorded on several hidden cameras. Frankie had the audio and video feeds, from multiple camera angles, unedited and unaltered.

He knew they were coming for him. He knew how it would end. And he knew it would damn the Protectorate and their effort on Mars.

It was one of those things you had to sit back and appreciate.

Martin McAaron was a martyr. His death was going to do more to polarize the planet against the oppression of the UNIC than anything else could ever. Did he realize that as he was about to be murdered in cold blood? And moreover, did he realize what it would do? Was that why he acted so smug despite his impending doom? It had to be.

How had he arranged all of that without anyone knowing? Not even the family lawyer, who knew *every* dirty little secret from the family seemed to be aware of it.

The question was now: What to do with it?

Frankie leaned back and considered, briefly glancing around the room. It must've been late at night, only a few workstations were occupied and the room smelled heavily of coffee. How long had she been at this? Hell, she wasn't even sure what day it was at this point. Rubbing her eyes, she pondered her next move.

The right thing to do, would be to immediately package it and run it directly to McAaron. Let leadership decide what to do with it. The final moments of his father, and the implications his murder entailed. That was what she *should* do! Yet, she hesitated. What if he buried it? What if he failed to grasp what it could be used to achieve? Something about Edward McAaron intrigued her on a deep level, but she had yet to figure out exactly what it was; or how it made her feel. Unknowns were something Frankie detested, and they were something she was unused to personally experiencing.

If she released the footage to the media, odds were high they would suppress it, or worse still somehow spin it to their advantage. Video editing techniques were so sophisticated these days that you could barely trust what was broadcast in normal circumstances.

Unfortunately for Frankie, this was a critical move in the epic chess match. No one else could make this decision for her, and everything was at stake. This moment—right here—could make or break their efforts.

No, she realized. This wasn't her decision. Not by a long shot. This was McAaron's sole decision. If the roles were reversed, she'd expect him to do the same for her. And, regardless of her misgivings, she knew deep down that McAaron was fighting for the right reasons. He *believed* in what he was doing.

Decision made, she flagged it as a P1. Priority one, which made her sigh and pause. That wouldn't get it seen any quicker, given the total lack of organization. Instead, she took a risk. Hands shaking, she hacked her way into the datapad being used by McAaron. She deposited the file as an anonymous new message. Then, she cleaned up her trail so it couldn't be traced back. The file would just be suddenly there, as if it always had been.

That roughly six-minute-long clip could, *should,* change the trajectory of everything.

If McAaron had the balls to make it happen.

Frankie stood and stretched her arms above her head, raising up onto her tiptoes. She winced as her spine cracked in several places. All in all, she felt pretty good about the work she had accomplished. This could be that "one thing" the history books attribute to the rise and fall of an empire. Not that anyone would know it, but it was something she had a hand in.

Being a part of such a pivotal part of history felt odd. She wasn't sure she liked it much.

The room was dimly lit, and her eyes were blurry from overuse. Still, she made her way to the doors which would lead her through the facility to her bunk room with only bumping against two workstations. One had a sleeping analyst underneath it, who barked at her unhappily.

A loud boom thundered from the opposite doors.

"You!" a voice yelled out across the room, causing Frankie to jump.

She spun to see Edward McAaron, bare chest heaving, glints of sweat reflecting in the dim light of the room. His arm was extended and pointed to the nearest seated analyst. A wispy-haired older man by the name of Bel. His thinning alabaster hair always stood out at odd angles and contrasted quite nicely with his wrinkled deep-sepia skin. It gave him the look of always being surprised, or shocked. Just so happened that this time, he truly was.

"Me, sir?" the man stuttered.

"I need you to authenticate something," McAaron demanded, as he strode down the steps into the sea of workstations. Anyone in the room was anxiously locked on the exchange. "Can you do that?"

Bel glanced around before responding, "I think so, sir, it depends what it is."

"It's a video file." McAaron came to rest in front of him and offered the datapad clutched in his white-knuckled grip. "Can you authenticate it?"

"Yes, sir," Bel said, and took the proffered device before sitting down and jacking it into the workstation.

Frankie should leave. She knew it. Every muscle in her body was taut with the intention of pushing through the doors and discreetly leaving.

What she saw standing in that room terrified her. And, for whatever strange reason, enthralled her. Edward McAaron stood there wearing only black loose-fitting pants that appeared to be some kind of light fabric, possibly a synthetic, or maybe actual linen. They accented his fair fawn-colored skin that was dusted lightly with walnut-colored hair.

Perhaps feeling her eyes on him, he turned and their eyes met.

Frankie felt hers go wide.

His were dangerous flashes of sapphire lightning.

She turned and fled through the doors. The ache in her

muscles releasing her like an arrow shot from an overtaught bow.

The hallways blurred by in a rush.

When she finally entered her bunk room, she slammed the door and leaned her head against it. Her breath came in ragged gasps, and only partially from the physical exertion.

Maybe she had screwed up?

Maybe she should have sent it to the media?

The look in his eyes was… Madness. Rage. Fury.

What had she unleashed upon the world?

CHAPTER 16

LISA WAS GETTING the distinct impression she was being bounced around and kept at a distance from any *actual* conflict. It certainly hadn't come from her mother, because that would be of no benefit to the great and powerful Admiral Colt. No, this had the stink of Olumide all over it.

128 Nemesis was a large Barrier Belt asteroid, measuring some one hundred eighty kilometers in diameter. With its slower than average rotation, clocking in at just over seventy-eight hours to complete a single rollover, it was the perfect place for an early military installation. And, later it made for a wonderful halfway point between the inner and outer planets in the system. Nemesis Station now, was practically a city unto itself. Hosting more dock platforms than the sum total of Martian surface installations, some two-hundred-sixty-odd individual hardpoints.

The air traffic in the area was heavy. Space was huge, there was no getting around that. But, park a veritable shitload of massive freight-haulers all fighting over the same dock, with inter-ship shuttles zipping around the tight quarters, and you had a recipe for disaster. Nemesis was big, but it wasn't *that* big.

Fortunately, the hundred-fifty years it had been operational had ironed out a few kinks. Well, that and the trillions of dollars corporations had invested in developing the infrastructure to accommodate their substantial needs.

As the *Hemera* entered the airspace surrounding Nemesis all other craft must have been ordered away, because the carrier went straight to the Protectorate sector of the station. The original foothold on the asteroid was now just a tiny circular dot amongst the cacophony of structures littering the surface.

Given the significance of the rock as a major trade hub, security was extremely high. Lisa counted no fewer than eight full CCF squadrons patrolling this side alone. Each quadrant of the station was outfitted with massive defense batteries capable of kinetic bursts so ferocious they operated suspended in craters with inertia-adjusting rockets to compensate for the force so the asteroid itself would not alter its slow tumble through space.

Lisa left the midship observation deck, her pack already in her hands.

Marconi had been an absolute shithead the entire trip, so she had spent the last few days of their journey to Nemesis away from the squad room. The rest of the squad gravitated to his hardass style of leadership, which was fine. Chain of command ran through her, so he could be the best buddy of everyone in the squad so long as he followed her orders.

That all suited her just fine right now, anyway, because she was preoccupied with her attempt to break into Olumide's quarters abord the *Hemera* and steal the information on Spalding. If, and it was a big *if*, there was any information *to* steal.

She had attempted, on three different occasions, to gain access to Olumide's private quarters. Each time she had been unsuccessful at even penetrating the command wing. The guards were extremely rigid in their hall monitor duties.

Her last chance before they disembarked would be during the docking protocol. During that time, the guards would be rotated over to a fresh crew while everything was made ready to go ashore and new provisions were brought on board for the next journey.

The Protectorate Fleet could change over an entire carrier in under an hour. The protocols in place were inflexible and brutally effective.

That would leave her with a very tight window of opportunity, but it was all she had.

Who knew when the next time she'd even be on ship with Harris Olumide.

A horn blasted over the loudspeakers, followed by an announcement that docking would commence. Everyone was to take precautions.

Not me this time! She sincerely hoped that whoever was docking was reasonably seasoned at it. By not strapping in, she was putting herself at significant bodily harm, maybe even death. It was rare, but it had happened occasionally. Lisa really, deeply, hoped she wouldn't be one of those statistics.

There was a flurry of activity in the corridors of the carrier as everyone made their way to jumpseats to strap in. Lisa did her best to hang at the back of the pack and veer off when no one was looking, then sprint to the next intersection and join another group and repeat the process.

When she was on her fourth such circuit, she spotted Azarov and Marconi jogging up to the back of a group. They were having what appeared to be a heated discussion. Azarov was pretty mellow, for him to be worked up meant that Marconi must be practically apoplectic. Even though there were still people streaming by her to join the group, she veered off early. Bumping into those two would interrupt her mission, if not outright foil it.

There were a few odd looks, but she just shrugged as she swam up current in the steady stream of crew.

Finally, she came to the edge of the command wing. Thankfully, no guards were posted.

A chime sounded, followed by the pilot's voice. "One hundred meters."

Lisa dashed into the corridor, headed straight to Olumide's door.

The moment of truth; if he was inside, she was going to get her little ass lit up. Had she not been so rushed, she may have come up with some kind of cover story as to why she was barging into his personal quarters unannounced in a restricted area, especially during docking.

"Fifty meters." The voice echoed through the empty halls.

Screw it! Lisa entered the pin code, and the door *whooshed* open.

The room was dark and empty.

As she stepped through, the door shut and lights sprang to life.

Sparing no time, she ran behind the desk and pulled down the jumpseat located against the back wall of the small space. Every room in the command deck had one. Unfortunately, it was going to show as deployed to anyone who was paying attention. There was little to be done about it now.

"Twenty meters."

The harness was all wired in a neat-looking tangle; evidently it had never been used. Lisa just pushed the gut-wrenching anxiety to the back of her mind. Mission first; the rest can wait.

"Ten meters."

The damn thing was knotted uptight, there was no way she was going to get it buckled in time.

"Five meters, prepare for docking."

Lisa jumped into the seat and braced her feet against the desk in front of her, which was bolted to the ground. Then she reached under the seat and clung tightly. Bent over double with her head between her knees she could hear her heavy breathing.

A boom shuddered through the ship, and with the exception of a little pop up from the seat of her pants, there was little else to report. The pilot had done his job and it had been as smooth as could be expected.

Lisa withdrew her hands, her wrists an angry crimson from the tight grip she had kept. Two red abrasions were also visible through tears in the interior elbow of both her sleeves. Upon further inspection, it looked like the edge of the chair had caught her in the elbows with that tiny bump and scraped the top layer of her skin clean off.

If such a tiny bump could do that, she was immensely grateful the docking procedure hadn't been rougher. They'd likely have found a greasy red splotch against the far wall instead of a corpse.

She watched as a drop of blood fell from her elbow and splattered across the floor. For trying to be sneaky, unfortunately she was leaving quite a bit of forensic evidence to be found. There was nothing to be done for that, really. She knew this plan was half-cocked at best. Her only hope was to leave no reason to even launch an investigation, then her DNA wouldn't matter.

The thought left her nauseated.

Fighting that down, she leaped from the jumpseat, stowed it, then second thought the decision. It was still all bundled up properly, no lines had been severed. Maybe if she left it they'd just think it malfunctioned and opened on its own? It was worth the risk, she decided. At least this way there was a chance the unauthorized deployment could be explained without her involvement.

For a split second another fear crept into her thoughts. What if Olumide was one of those paranoid types who kept cameras in his quarters? She thought it through. No. It was very unlikely. The use of recording devices in quarters, *especially* any in the command section was strictly prohibited. Olumide followed the rules to the letter. Even if he were paranoid enough, which she doubted, he would never break that protocol.

Feeling foolish she almost bolted. This was not her wheelhouse at all! Guilt over betraying the trust of Olumide and over breaking several Protectorate regulations were distracting her. She was better than this; smarter than this. It was very unlike

Lisa to do *anything* spontaneously. Willing herself to calm, she took a few deep breaths and mentally committed herself to what she was doing. The bridge was crossed, there was no going back. Might as well make the trip worthwhile.

Plus, she *had* figure out what was going on with Spalding. Nothing else mattered, as insane as it sounded. There was something bigger going on here, of that she was certain. What happened with him was important somehow. What happened with him was a loose thread that she could pull on.

With renewed confidence her fingers pecked across the desktop, and the monitor sprang to life. She'd bungle her way through this little covert mission, but the next one would be methodically thought out.

The system was a mess of files. Lacking even basic organization, everything was just dumped into the root directory. Lisa groaned and mussed her hair. Was it too much to ask to have an *Admiral* be more organized than a five-year-old? This mess would take weeks to sort through! An entire career's worth of personal files, mission files, protocol updates, and communications, all littered across the desktop in a random heap.

Any searches she ran would be logged and reviewable later. Lisa hesitated. With just minutes to utilize, she couldn't go about this in any kind of reasonable fashion. Copying everything wasn't an option either, as that too would be logged. Any file transfers would notify the owner of the file.

Think, damn it, think!

The real problem was, she wasn't tech-savvy. Sure, she knew how to operate computers, they were necessary to pilot, but she was far from an expert. Novice at best. Electronic espionage was not something she'd ever make any kind of bold claims over her skillset.

"Docking protocols complete," the voice boomed over the loudspeaker.

That sunk in; she was out of time.

There was only one thing she could try.

As fast as she was able, she created a new user on the system and granted them root-level access. Which, as it turned out, was easy to do. There was no root-level encryption. At least something had gone her way today!

She committed the username's random string of characters to memory and entered an easy password. Ideally, she'd destroy this user the moment she had the information she was after. So, no reason to be too fancy with anything. The random username was in an effort to mask who had illegally accessed the system. Maybe if it was just a bunch of random characters they'd think it was caused by some kind of error. Those types of things happened, at least she had heard that somewhere. Maybe?

With a few swipes she had logged out of her user, set the account to private, and put the system in hibernate mode. There was no way to tell how long Olumide had been out of the office, or how long it took for his console to drop into low-power mode. It didn't matter, she was out of time. The hall guards would be reposting to duty in seconds, if they weren't already there.

Dashing through the office she manually dimmed the lights, and the door opened. Immediately she could hear Olumide's voice coming down the hall.

Shit! Too late!

Lisa stepped back into the room; the door automatically closed.

Breathing heavily, she looked frantically around the small room. They were spacious for a ship's standard, but tiny and barren when you were looking for a place to hide. The only option was the wall closet. She opened the doors and stepped into a sea of Protectorate coats and trousers.

Just as the closet mechanism clicked shut, she heard the *whoosh* of the front door, followed by a heavy sigh.

"Damn pirates." She faintly heard Olumide, muffled through the metal door of the closet and heavy fabrics hanging in front of her. The space was small, but thankfully so was she.

Please don't undress and hang up your clothes!

The last thing she wanted to do was see her would-be grandfather in the buff. That would make for a very interesting conversation, for sure.

"This is Harris," she heard him say, accompanied by the groan of his desk chair. "We've docked at Nemesis."

Lisa held her breath, straining to overhear the conversation.

"Yes, I know that's what you said." The old man was speaking candidly, maybe even a touch angrily. After a pause, he sighed. "That doesn't change the fact that you took it too far!"

He *was* angry now, she realized somewhat shocked. Sure, she had been around Harris all of her life, she had seen him upset. Enraged though? Never. Calm, cool, collected. That's how she always described their long-time family friend.

Not today, evidently!

"Maureen, I hope you know what you're doing."

There was a thud as his finger slammed down on the desk, presumably terminating the call.

"That dumb bitch is going to get us all killed."

Lisa felt her mouth fall open, slack-jawed, and had to put a hand over her mouth to keep from gasping out loud. Never, in her entire life, had she ever heard anyone talk about her mother in that way.

Interestingly enough, she felt her connection to the old man grow. Maybe she could talk candidly with him about this whole issue?

Right after she explained how she was eavesdropping in his closet.

Maybe not.

There was movement on the other side of the closet door, and she tensed. Her mind raced with possible ways to explain her presence. They were obviously all laughable, but her survival instincts were too strong. The movement faded, and she heard the telltale sound of the door opening and closing.

Muscles burning from holding perfectly still despite the cramped space, she launched herself out of the closet to a, gratefully, empty room.

In a few strides she was out into the corridor and walking hastily down the way she had first entered. There was no sign of Admiral Olumide, and she couldn't be sure which way he had gone.

As she rounded the final corner, two guards stood with their backs to her. They were chatting quietly; she could tell by the way they tilted their heads ever so slightly toward each other in an alternating pattern.

Lisa squared her shoulders, stood tall, and put a look on her face like she was on her way to do something incredibly important, and was extremely unhappy about it.

The guards glanced at her and stood a bit straighter out of reflex as she passed between them. Neither said a word. They weren't there to prevent people from exiting the section of the ship, just to keep people out.

When she managed to get a few more sections removed from the command wing, she bolted into a run. Her pent-up nerves exploding with the need to move quickly.

Her strides carried her across the ship and to the gangway leading out into Nemesis Station. Several deck crews were zipping around doing their duty, surveying the ship, restocking, and refueling. It appeared the flight crews had already been dismissed. She'd be made to eat shit for missing muster, but it would be worth whatever penance they required of her.

All that mattered right now was she get into her quarters, lock the doors, and access the information on Olumide's system before the *Hemera* left the station. Once they had disconnected, that would be it, the access she had would be severed. Any kind of remote access was far beyond her ability to sort out. That was high-level analyst work.

The walk to her new quarters was somewhat daunting, having

missed the orientation and initial muster. She had to ask three different deck crew and a Protectorate Colonel that had just disembarked himself. The grim-faced man was kind enough to give her a preview of the ass-chewing she'd get later, to go alongside quarters assignments off his datapad.

As luck would have it, she didn't run into anyone else she knew despite the high level of activity across the station. A carrier landing was a big deal and took quite a lot of labor to get situated.

The door hissed open to her quarters for the foreseeable future. It was considerably more spacious than her previous few. There was a living area, kitchenette, separate bedroom, and full bathroom with her own sonic shower.

Heaven.

A quick sniff of herself revealed the stress sweat of the day most assuredly needed seeing to, but not first. With a longing look at the shower, she turned and went to the small corner desktop workstation on the far side of the living space. The Protectorate section of Nemesis was small, and somewhat outdated, so it took her a bit to get her profile downloaded from the Protectorate mainframe and everything situated to her liking.

When she attempted to log in to her mystery user, she was alarmed to find her access was denied. A giant pulsing red warning alerted her to the fact that she had two additional attempts before the cybersecurity teams were alerted to potential unauthorized access.

Lisa bit her lip so hard it hurt.

Concentrating she played the username back in her mind and compared it to what she had entered. It was identical. The password was one she had been using since she was a child, so there shouldn't have been any issues with that. Had it already been discovered? Was *all of that* for nothing, then?

A feeling like being punched in the gut suddenly pressed on her midsection.

What did that mean? Dare she try again?

Instead, she wiped her profile from the workstation and left her room untouched.

As she entered into the main corridor a security detail jogged by her, headed toward her room. They didn't so much as look her way, but that didn't mean anything. They'd only have a room number to check out.

A buzz came from the datapad she was carrying.

It was an anonymous message: <SLOPPY! CLEANED UP YOUR MESS. DON'T TRY THAT AGAIN!>

Lisa stumbled to a halt, her eyes wide as dinner plates.

Sweat blossomed across her forehead and back.

Fingers trembling, she keyed a response: <WHO IS THIS?>

The message errored, citing an unknown user.

Then the thread spontaneously deleted itself.

She blinked rapidly, looking around.

There was no indication she had received the message at all.

What the hell had she gotten herself into?

CHAPTER 17

"ARE YOU..." BRUCE let the question fade. Instead, he decided he'd throw his datapad across the length of the conference room.

It ricocheted off the wall and spiraled down to the floor with a gratifying clatter.

This was the absolute worst news he could possibly get.

Was he actually losing control of Mars, like Trent thought?

The Senior Analyst stood across from him, her emerald eyes focused on the prone datapad not far away from his feet. The freckles on her face made him quite literally gag; the girl looked like she had shit splattered across her face. Even if she hadn't brought him this news, he'd have struggled to look at her. With her long braided brunette hair and sparkling eyes, it wasn't that she was bad looking—far from it, in fact. Just, not his type. Too *girlish.* He did like the cut of her pants, though, and the shoes were a decent choice.

With a growl, he launched himself into the highbacked leather chair once occupied by Helena. It still smelled like her. A slightly acidic floral smell, not unpleasant but not overly cloying either. A natural odor that brought out all kinds of animalistic urges in him.

But, he was letting himself get distracted.

There was a steaming pile of filth that needed sorting.

This, stupid, imbecilic, conniving... He couldn't even summon a description befitting the situation. He *knew* that Helena was behind this! Of course he had no idea *how*, being locked up in the ivory tower as she was. The situation just reeked of her!

"Tell me *exactly* what happened." His tone was quiet and had a dangerous quality to it. It was his stalking lion voice. The one he used to instill fear in his enemies.

The woman shrugged and smiled crookedly. "Just what I said, sir. We logged a session of unauthorized access within our firewall."

Bruce gaped at her. She had literally just repeated what she had said mere moments ago. He'd wager it was practically verbatim.

"Well," he scoffed hotly, "are you going to fill me in on the details of that access, or should I go find someone with two firing brain cells to rub together?"

The woman frowned slightly.

There, she got that one, thankfully!

Nothing was more disappointing than an insult that didn't land well. He'd have to dumb it down a bit for this one.

"I'm the lead analyst on this event, *sir*." He thought she put a little too much emphasis on the title, but it came and went too quickly for him to know for sure. "And, to answer your question, there are no details. Any information or trail was cleared before we could pin it down. Whoever did it was a total professional. No trace, no backtrail, nothing. Technically we don't even know how long they had access to our system, we only know about the initial breach."

That was... alarming.

"Well, how do we know they even left?" Bruce flung his hands up in the air in exasperation.

The woman considered, brows knitting together slowly.

It felt like ages before she finally inhaled to start speaking. "We don't."

The admission staggered him.

Floored him!

He gaped openly at her now.

"You *don't?*" he slung at her.

All she did was shake her head. She didn't even have the good sense to look abashed.

"Well," he leaned toward her and practically hissed the words, "might be a good thing to go and find out, don't we think?"

Again, she considered before she spoke.

"Afraid not," she said finally, shrugging nonchalantly. "Our systems alert us in real-time of any unauthorized access. If they got in and masked their presence, there'd be no way to tell if they had remained connected or not. Not without tearing down the whole network and rebuilding it. Which would attract notice from the rest of the Protectorate and the UNIC."

Did she smile ever so slightly with that last bit?

He thought she had.

This bitch was enjoying watching him squirm!

"What is your name, Analyst?" Bruce said, regaining some composure while crossing his legs and leaning back in the chair.

"*Senior* Analyst Chara Szofi."

"Well, *Senior Analyst Chara Szofi.*" He couldn't help it, he emphasized her title and name heavily, tasting it as it sprang from his mouth. It had the desired effect, she squinted her eyes slightly, finally off-center somewhat. "Let's play a game of *this* or *that*, shall we? Are you familiar?"

She shook her head.

"Oh, it's an older game, one we played at the Academy. Probably not the speed of you and your friends." He clicked his tongue and smiled. "Anyway, the way the game works is I present you with a choice, thus the 'this or that' name. Not very creative, I dare say. At any rate, you have to choose one of the two options, here and now, and if you fail then you must fulfill a challenge set forth by," he indicated himself with a flourish, "yours truly."

This time, she nodded. "And if I succeed?"

Fat chance. The thought made him smile, his first genuine one of the day he thought!

"Well, then you get to do a round of your own and present me with the choice. Easy enough, yes?"

"Sounds like a dull game," she said and crossed her arms under her breasts.

Bruce frowned slightly confused. The way her arms were crossed made her rather pert breasts pop out toward him. He recoiled as if he had been struck.

"No," she said finally. "I don't think I'll play, Mr. Afolabi."

The sudden lack of his title did not go unnoticed.

She turned and stalked out the door of the conference room.

What the hell had just happened?

"Stupid, dumb, dense...." He stopped when he realized he was gripping the legs of his trousers so tightly the delicate fabric started to stretch.

Damn it!

This was all starting to fray at the edges. Everything had been going so well up until this point. Trent had claimed the high seat like he was supposed to, and covered all their bases. Helena was neutralized and of little more use to anyone, really. He had taken great pleasure in making sure of that. Brennan was free, yes, but either dead by his liberators or in the wind. Rumor was he wasn't even on-world any longer. Fitting end to the stoic General Keith Brennan, in his mind, to tuck tail and run like a coward.

A good antagonist was so hard to find these days. Everyone reveled in their mediocrity. The whole thing was really quite sad. No style. No pomp. No sense of pride in your efforts. Just get the bare minimum done, and go home and occupy space until you got to do it all again the next day. On and on, and on, and on. Until you didn't wake up one day. What was the point? Did no one want to leave *their mark* on the worlds anymore?

Bruce did.

He most certainly would, too.

Clutching that thought like a torch in the darkness, he stood and stomped valiantly toward the conference room door. He would show them what it was like to lead. What it meant to do your duty. Bruce Afolabi was the picture of refinement despite complications.

Everyone avoided him in the hallways. He could see them veer to the far sides, or stop dead in their tracks and turn back to disappear the way they had come. They feared him. The power he wielded. He reveled in it. If he could bottle up that reaction and fill a tub with it, he'd bathe in it. These people were meaningless apparitions, specters of his will alone. If he no longer had a need for them, they'd vanish in a wisp of smoke.

Each time it happened it bolstered his resolve. Empowered him to do what needed doing.

By the time he had reached the main council chamber, he had every detail of his brilliant plan worked out. If this collection of simpletons couldn't do their job, he'd have to do it for them. Simple as that.

As he passed through the doors at the top of the chamber, he clapped his hands together loudly. In the ensuing echo he commanded, "Okay, people, listen up."

The room, which had just moments before been buzzing with activity, came crashing to a total silent halt. People stood and stared at him as he made his way down the steps to the center of the massive room.

"We had a breach," he said, pointing at Chara, who it appeared had just pulled back up to her workstation. "Without knowing who it was, what they were after, or even whether or not they've gone, we are at a bit of a tight spot. Wouldn't you say? I mean, pardon me for saying so, but it doesn't really *feel* like we know *anything*. Am I wrong?"

The room stood mute.

Idiots!

"So, let's turn this particular obstacle to our advantage, shall we?" Still, no one moved. With a sigh he clapped his hands together once more. "Come on people, let's move. Put together a strategic team or whatever it is you do." The room slowly began to move again, the buzz now more of a rustle of fabric and whispers. Bruce pinched the bridge of his nose. Why did they have to make everything so difficult on him? Here he was trying to save their asses, for *their* shortcomings, and you'd think everyone was moving through tar.

At long last, Lead Analyst Patritsiya Merete stepped from a side room and motioned for him to join him. She was tall, broad-shouldered, and dour-faced. Bruce was often reminded of a Heffer whenever he looked at her. She wasn't chunky, but she was *meaty*. As he picked his way through the tangle of workstations he recalled his previous thoughts about a *genuine* leather chair, and whether or not Analyst Merete's hide would work as a substitute?

The room adjacent to the main council chamber was more of a ready room. Where smaller meetings could take place outside of the main body, or for visiting dignitaries to prepare for presentations. Not exactly a green room, but near enough.

Merete had commandeered it for her own office, it seemed. Like the woman herself, the room was just, *plain*. No style, no organization that he could detect, just a barren room with a single workstation and a single chair. Which, frustratingly, she currently occupied. Not that he'd expected her to have any sense of decorum.

So, Bruce stood in his elegant suit at the head of her desk and looked down his perfect nose at her. The empowering angle felt better, anyway.

"Well," she said without ceremony or preamble, "what's this plan of yours?"

No showmanship. That's what people lacked these days! The

art of presentation.

"We have to assume whoever breached our systems is still inside, yes?"

She nodded.

When she didn't interrupt, thankfully, he continued, "Assuming the worst-case scenario it was the terrorists, working with Brennan, and now they have full access of our systems, let's set a trap."

Everything in his body wanted him to squeal with joy. This was a genius move. One that would be spoken of in history books for years to come. When Bruce Afolabi outfoxed General Brennan at his own game.

"It could work," Merete finally said.

Truth be told, it was a somewhat lukewarm response. Bruce felt himself flounder with disappointment. Not at all the golden trumpets and swooning sycophants he had imagined.

"What's the one bit of intelligence we don't have currently, that would scare out the resistance?" Merete mused, almost to herself now.

"Their location?" He was off his game now, but he blurted it out anyway.

Fingers like sausages drummed on the desktop rhythmically. Something about the gesture made Bruce wildly uncomfortable, but he couldn't figure out why.

"I like it," Merete said, slapping her sweaty palm down on the table. "If they think we know where they are, and are gearing up to come after them, they will move locations quickly. If we watch for that movement, we'll have them."

Wasn't that what he had already said?

The large woman grunted as she stood. She was possibly in her mid-forties, but he wasn't sure. "We will keep the location coded, so they don't know where we'll be looking. Technically, we won't be looking anywhere specific, just *everywhere* at once. However, I'll be sure to flag everything as ninety-nine percent reliable. That would be enough to make anyone nervous enough to run for the hills."

She smiled at Bruce and clapped him on the shoulder.

"Thanks Bruce, this might get the job done. We'll take it from here."

Then she walked out.

After a moment to process what had just happened, Bruce found himself walking back toward the Governor's office. Whereas his trip to the council chamber had been purposeful and proud, his walk back was more subdued and bemused.

Ultimately, he would need to report this to Trent. It could wait a short bit. He couldn't shake the feeling of unease that had started with Chara. *Nobody* had treated him like that in his *entire life*. Not even when he was a child. Then Merete had been rather off-putting as well. The tenor of the building had shifted, and not in his favor.

There had to be a way to spin this to his advantage with Trent. Everyone here could eat shit for all he cared, he derived his power from the President. And only for so much longer, he just had to hold out a bit more. Then he'd be the master in his own right. Oh yes, he had plans of his own. Who wouldn't in his position?

What he needed was a way to position himself to gain from all of this. Brennan, Trent, McAaron, everything. All the pieces would come together in a way that left him standing tall. That much he knew. Just the small matter of figuring it all out.

Trent was beholden to several corporations. That's what this was all about for him, money. Dictating policy on Martian soil for the next hundred years so that these dynasty corporations could continue to bleed the markets dry. Money! Such a silly thing. Bruce thought it was rather pathetic that was their entire motivator. I mean, how much money did a person *really* need? When ten generations of your offspring could not even lift a finger and *still* be counted amongst the wealthiest individuals in the entire system, was that not enough?

No, money wasn't the objective for him. Power was. Sure, the two were reasonably entangled, but one was fleeting and one was forever.

An idea began to flirt with the back of his mind. If you knew what someone wanted, what their deepest desire was, you could turn that against them. There were several ways to poison the well with the corporations, that was the easy part. The trouble was making it all stick to Trent, *without* trickling down to him. Sure, he had been careful throughout, but gravity was a tricky thing—and nothing was heavier than guilt.

CHAPTER 18

FOR THE HUNDREDTH time that minute it felt like, Ed impatiently checked his watch.

Here they were, standing outside the door to a long-abandoned and hopefully forgotten research facility, and potential headquarters of the uprising. Only to find the damn front door inoperable.

Stuck was what the soldier had said. So they filled the hallway, three people shoulder to shoulder, as far back as his height allowed him to see. It was an impressive sight, he had to admit to himself. All the "soldiers" were wearing matching battle armor and combat uniforms that had been part of the purchase from the pirates. For possibly the first time since this all started, he felt like maybe they stood a fighting chance. They looked the part, at least.

The hallway smelled thick with sweat, equal parts chlorine, and charred meat odors. The press of bodies made the air heavy with humidity. Sounds of fidgeting people echoed up and down the hallway, but next to no conversation at all. They had been warned to not speak until they had gone into the lowest levels of their new home. Who knew what kind of sensor capabilities the Protectorate actually had. What they boasted about was frightening enough, and who knew what tricks they hadn't shared with the general public.

Two technicians were bent over the disassembled door control panel, perspiration streaming down their faces and dripping in a steady trickle off the tips of their noses. The building was extremely insulated, half-meter thick carbon fiber and concrete walls with steel studding. Their intelligence also said the entire facility had been built with an extra layer of EMP shielding, despite it being underground.

Ed decided the first order of business, if they lived through this mess, was to pin a medal on whoever had found this place. It felt strange to be back in Solas City. He had argued vehemently against returning to the very location the search for him would be hottest. The location was just too good.

As a decommissioned early settler agricultural facility, it had everything they needed to survive. Carbon-dioxide scrubbers and proper air circulation, atmospheric pressure, ultraviolet lighting, hydroponic field rooms, and was *deep* underground. Solas had been the sister city to Hellas. It had been born from the extensive mining operation for resources to build out Hellas, which had left a deep cavern. That was eventually capped over, and a new city had been born. The first on the red planet to not utilize natural geography to kickstart the shielding process.

This facility was archaic. None of the computer systems were even worth powering on they were so outdated. Which also meant the systems had not been pinged by the Protectorate security sweeps in almost a hundred years or more. The city management AI had certainly archived any data on it to save on memory. It was perfect. There was no way they would be caught down here.

"Well," a quiet grave voice said coming up to stand beside him, "what do we think about it?"

"It sure smells interesting." Ed scrunched up his face and Des smiled.

"I'm sure we can find somewhere else, let me just tell everyone to turn around...." he faded off as Ed chuckled.

"It's great, Des. You all did a great job."

The older man had lost a bit of the vigor that had always impressed Ed. His face was drawn, and he looked a bit more tired than he normally did.

Ed almost suggested he go rest. Then he thought better of it and closed his mouth with a smile. He certainly didn't feel like being chewed out as the first order of business in the new headquarters.

As people streamed in carrying equipment, Ed stepped out of the way.

Des indicated an upper doorway that emptied onto a catwalk above.

"That's yours."

Ed raised an eyebrow questioningly.

The older man started walking toward a switchback staircase that went up to the mezzanine level and the door. "Not your quarters, just your office. Or whatever the military calls it. Everyone seems to have abandoned normal words for things since putting on the uniforms."

This time Ed couldn't help it, he choked out a hoarse fit of laughter as he followed Des up the staircase. It was old and ricketier than he would prefer. He'd have to get someone to look at it. The rings in the concrete seemed to be loose.

The door was of the older swinging style, and as Ed pressed it in it groaned loudly as bits of debris hung up under the threshold. The debris dragging across the floor made a sound like boulders being ground by giant gears, and it echoed loudly throughout the darkened room.

Because it was empty. Completely, utterly, devoid of anything besides dust and bits of concrete that had decomposed and fallen to the floor from the ceiling above. Nothing but a concrete box, about eight meters square give or take. For some reason the initial feeling was that of a coffin.

Concrete, dark, cold, box, deep underground.

Ed really, *really*, didn't want to die here.

The two stood there, appraising the room. By the sour look on his face, Des must have been thinking something equally dark.

A boot scuffing the ground behind them caused them both to turn abruptly. A young man, maybe eighteen or nineteen years old, stood in the doorway. His combat uniform was ill-fitted to his lithe frame, the shoulders bulging out awkwardly. Ed thought he looked like a child wearing his parents' uniform. The nanotube armor plating was cinched down tightly, which made all the bulging of the loose uniform that much worse. A rifle slung across his back poked out over the tangled mass of material poofing out like a fat mushroom perched atop his shoulders.

"Sorry, sir," the boy said. He continued in a rush, "Intel wanted me to tell you that all locations are secured and being stocked. Vulcan Base will be emptied out within the hour."

"Very good, thank you." It felt good to have something go right.

The boy left in a rush.

Des pulled out his datapad and began making notes. As he typed, he said briskly, "I'll make sure to get this room provisioned with everything from your father's office as soon as possible."

There was something about disturbing his father's belongings from the shrine of his office back at the Vulcan Complex. It almost felt like graverobbing. Now that he considered it fully, it practically *was* exactly that.

As the door was pulled shut behind Des, it made the same loud grinding it had when being opened. It was an atrocious sound. Hopefully, that was something fixable.

Now alone, he looked at the floor. The room was dimly lit by a shaft of light filtering through the bottom of the door. Little sparkles of dust danced in the light, motes floating about on the wind. There was so much going on, so quickly, he hadn't had the opportunity to reflect. With the exception of sleeping, he wasn't exactly sure when the last time he had been alone for more than a handful of minutes had been.

Regretting there was no chair to sit in, he slid his back down the wall across from the door until he had to stretch his legs out in front of himself to maintain his balance. His ass hit the concrete floor with a gentle thud. A cloud of fine dust particles spun into the air, and he realized he must have a giant dust streak down his back. Funny, that would have driven him partially mad not long ago. Now, it was little more than a dull reminder to have his laundry done.

So much had changed, so quickly he hadn't really had the time to process it. One day he had been one of those "failure-to-launch" trust-fund kids. The ones that everyone whispered about being a disappointment. Suddenly he was responsible for an uprising. It didn't seem right. Didn't at all seem remotely plausible. Yet, here he was.

It almost felt like some kind of cruel joke.

The doorway burst open, with the same atrocious grinding as before. That was going to drive him mad. A sweaty-faced girl, barely more than a kid, stood panting in the painfully bright light from the command center.

"Sir, you're needed!"

Ed almost chuckled at the punch line to his internal joke.

Instead, he rose to his feet, his knees grinding and cracking embarrassingly loud in the echo chamber of a room.

As soon as he lurched toward the door, the girl spun and raced down the switchback steps. Ed had to break into a jog to keep pace. By the time he reached the bottom of the steps, he was already feeling a bit winded.

Guess I had better start working out.

It may have been the first time there was a need, well… Other than to look good.

The girl ripped through the crowded command center, and

out into the hallway.

Ed followed not far behind. Thankfully, she paused at every intersection to make sure he knew which way to turn. The labyrinth-like maze of corridors made the Vulcan Complex look almost boring in its complexity. Plus, there was this *weight* one felt with being so far underground. Even though there was no direct stimulus to inform you, it was a feeling you couldn't shake. The body *knew* it was dangerously far beneath the surface.

The hallway opened up into a loading bay, and Ed realized dully they must have been running up a gradual incline. His calves burned ferociously.

Inside the loading bay, which had a high arched ceiling overhead and several large roll-up style doors at the far end, there was an impressive amount of activity. Someone had fired up the archaic loaders, which was like a wearable forklift. Crates flew by in the air via tracked hoists, and were offloaded onto upper-level catwalks, and wheeled away on carts. It looked and felt like a proper military installation, he realized. Everyone was really stepping into the roles they had been assigned. It was impressive, to say the least.

The girl, also somewhat flagging at this point, jogged slowly up to a group of soldiers surrounding a suited man. Ed immediately recognized the cut and style of the garment; it was one he had often worn himself. High quality, and exceedingly high price tag. With the similarly stylish hairstyle and immaculate grooming, this was obviously some kind of aristocrat.

What the hell was he doing here? More importantly, how did he even find this place?

Ed felt suddenly less secure about their new home than he had just minutes before.

As he approached, the group turned and their quiet conversation died off.

"Our first visitor," Ed said more cheerfully than he felt. "Pardon our dust, we just moved in." If nothing else, he hoped his flippant and somewhat sarcastic delivery offset the deep pit that had suddenly opened up in his stomach. A million questions sprung to mind, and none of the answers were good.

For what it was worth, the man seemed unperturbed by the situation. Instead, he graced them all with a too-perfect smile and extended his hand in greeting.

"Mr. McAaron, how wonderful to see you again."

Again?

That pit opened up a bit wider. No one from his past could be a good thing.

"You'll have to forgive me, as I'm notoriously bad with names." He wasn't, but that was fine.

"No, you're not," the man said, that same self-satisfied smile on his face.

It was the kind of back-and-forth banter, the battle of wits, Ed would've definitely enjoyed previously. The past iteration of him loved the mental sparring. Not anymore.

"Now I just feel rude," Ed said, then quickly drew his fancy firearm and leveled it inches from the other man's nose. "Let me try this another way; who are you, and how did you know to find me here?"

That self-assured smile fell quick as a brick and was instantly replaced with a pallid complexion and the acrid smell of urine.

"Ed!" Des called from behind him. "Ed! Stop!"

Neither removing his weapon, nor the locked eyes he had with the stranger, Ed called back over his shoulder, "You know him?"

Des, moving quicker than Ed had seen in a long while, came puffing up to the group. "Yes," he rasped, "I sent for him. This is Rory Drest."

The name tickled at a memory, but not enough to lower his guard.

Sweat fell from the older man's nose as he continued, still winded, "Rory was a liaison from the Hydra Corporation on Triton. You may recall your father, and his father had many dealings over the course of their careers."

David Drest, as Ed recalled, was a man his father had often dealt with. He'd even wager the two had been more friends than colleagues. Hydra Corp was the largest purveyor of water in the solar system. Frankly put, if the Hydra Corp hadn't come to be, Earth would've long ago become inhospitable. One of the first corporations to break out beyond the Barrier Belt, Hydra was old. Almost as old as Hellas, in fact. Those had been hard days, living on the distant moon. Rory was the only son of that long legacy.

Feeling somewhat foolish, Ed withdrew his gun, uncocked it, and holstered it. Ever since that damned pirate had gifted him these guns, he was always finding a reason to draw and point them at people. It was an outrageous habit to fall into. Or maybe it was the exact thing he needed? The whole situation was more complex than he would've thought from the outside. Either way, probably not an ideal negotiating tactic to be waggling his penile extensions under the other party's noses.

Rory let out a sigh of relief, then glanced down at the extending trail of liquid trickling down his trousers to the floor below.

Although, it sure gave me an advantage here. Nothing upended the tables quite like pissing oneself at the negotiation.

Thinking he should apologize, but not really knowing how, Ed was surprised to hear the other man splutter into laughter. Rory looked up, eyes twinkling.

"Now *that* was terrifying! Who taught you how to do that?" Rory exclaimed, glancing around at the group as if perhaps wondering if it was one of them. "That was like something out of the ancient Old West tales!"

Rory mimicked a quick draw with an imaginary gun.

"Sorry about that," Ed said dumbly.

"No, no!" Rory said cheerfully. "Although I do find myself in need of a wardrobe change. Care to wait a moment while I go find something a touch more... *dry*?"

Ed shook his head, bewildered at the whole exchange.

Still laughing, the group all watched as Rory made his way back to a docking bay and presumably his shuttle.

"What were you thinking?" Des hissed quietly.

The rest of the group suddenly found other more interesting things to look at in the area.

"I was thinking that here was a stranger, who somehow found our super-secret-new-headquarters and no one had told me to expect company," Ed said heatedly, partially because, well, he was angry, but mostly because he was embarrassed at being talked down to in front of some of his followers.

The rebuke caught Des by surprise, and he glanced at the others. A small nod of acknowledgment preceded his next, much more respectfully delivered, comment. "I apologize, I should have informed you, but I only just found his message and time was of the essence. He's here to negotiate some financial assistance for the rebellion, in exchange for relaxed trading rights with Mars."

He… *What?!*

Before he could vocalize the question though, Des continued, "I think it's something we should consider. Hydra has always been a strong ally, and they practically own everything in the greater Neptune area. This one alliance could make all the difference for what we're doing here."

"I am not in a position to negotiate trade terms for *Mars*, Des." Ed glanced around at the faces surrounding them. All eyes were averted, but every ear was straining in his direction.

As delicately as he could, he grabbed Des's elbow and guided him away from the group.

As if noticing them for the first time, the normally sharp attorney stuttered out an apology under his breath.

Ed waved it off impatiently. "Are you okay?"

The question confused the other man, who stood there with his brows furrowed.

Disconcerted, Ed pressed, "Des, I need to know you're okay.

You're not yourself these last few days."

Anger flashed in those knowledgeable eyes. "I'm perfectly fine, Ed," he replied tightly. "Nothing to be concerned with. Just has been a lot of moving around this last month. I'm tired. Not sleeping well." His tone softened as he continued, the defensiveness fading to abashment.

Slowly, Ed reached out and grasped the other man's shoulder and gave it a firm squeeze. "I can't do this without you, Des," he said genuinely. "Just a little bit more and then I'll send you on vacation. That work?"

Des just smiled. "Never been a fan, sir."

Ed thumped him playfully in the chest. "Don't you start that 'sir' shit with me, old man!" Then he glanced at the group watching them askance a short distance away and thought better of it. "Actually, it might help to be not so familiar in the public eye, if you catch my drift."

At a nod from Ed, the two strode back to the group.

Fortunately, that was at least one issue he had been able to solve today. Lately it seemed like every day created new challenges. Always working at a deficit made it tough to see the value in going forward. He knew he couldn't look at it that way. It was all about the little victories, the baby steps. Move the ball forward, even if just a little bit.

The group regarded them somewhat anxiously. Nobody enjoyed discord among superiors. So, Ed made a good show of draping his arm around Des's shoulders and engaging in some small talk with everyone while they waited for Rory.

It sure was taking him a long time to change. The thought sent goosebumps scampering across his arms, and a tingle started at the back of his neck.

No sooner had he decided to take a team and board the shuttle, than Rory appeared, jogging toward them. Not only had he changed his pants, but he had changed his entire ensemble. His hair was even styled slightly differently.

That certainly explains the prolonged delay. For some reason, it felt too neat. Too tidy of an excuse. Ed found his guts were telling him not to trust this new person. This, potential savior of the cause.

Or maybe his ego couldn't handle another version of *him* in the mix?

"I'm truly, truly sorry about that," Rory exclaimed woefully as he pranced up to them. "I dare say that may be the first time I've had a firearm drawn on me! Rather thrilling, wouldn't you say?"

The group shared glances all around at each other, no one was really sure how to respond. Ed knew for certain that some of the people here had lost loved ones at the Red Massacre. A quip about shooting people wasn't going to be well received here.

"So, Rory, what is it you're doing here?" Ed thought a moment, and held up a hand to forestall an answer. "Actually, while we're at it, why don't you start with *how* you've found yourself here?"

There was that twinkle again, like he was in on a joke but knew nobody else was.

"I'm glad you asked that!" Rory said, rubbing his hands together and looking at the group surrounding him with his boyish grin. "This," he gestured to the enormous room around them, "belongs to me."

CHAPTER 19

BRENNAN PURSED HIS lips in thought.

The orbital readouts showed the blockade forming up. Unfortunately, it was as bad as everyone had expected it would be. The Protectorate had brought their flagship, the seat of Admiral Maureen Colt's power, the *PCS Galileo*. The heavyweight ship was as big as the next two carrier-class ships combined. Built to be a command ship, it boasted more technology and armaments than anything ever constructed.

That meant lightweight frigates, close-combat fighters, bombers, and an array of perimeter and orbital offensive and defensive batteries.

Not to mention the two other carrier ships that complimented the blockade.

Admiral Colt had gone all out. This was an impressive showing.

What resistance they expected out of a few thousand ground-based troops was beyond him. That wasn't the point, and he knew it. Being *impressive* was. Intimidation was a powerful weapon, especially when it came to civil wars. Remind everyone who had all the firepower, and they'd think twice about endangering the lives of their loved ones, and themselves.

Well, she had pulled out the biggest gun in the system and slapped them upside the face with it.

The other, less critical, assumed objective of the blockade was to starve them out. By controlling what entered Martian atmosphere, they could control who ate, and who didn't. The flow of materials, food, water, could be easily tracked if it was intercepted in orbit.

It was only a matter of time before starving troops drifted back to the city, realizing they actually *weren't* that upset about the happenings on their planet. So long as they could eat again. This strategy had won a lot of wars, and stopped a lot from even happening.

Brennan was going to make damned sure it didn't work here.

There was an idea brewing in the back of his mind about how to handle the blockade, and overall air superiority of the Protectorate forces. For now, though, he had to focus on the plan ahead.

While Edward McAaron was not military-minded at all, he was socially cunning. The plans he had brought to the table were masterworks of manipulation. He was also morally justified in his actions. That part felt rather strange to Brennan. There had only ever been one side to every conflict, the Protectorate he served. Never before had he really taken into consideration who they were fighting, or what had motivated them.

Now, there was a certain amount of forced empathy that entered into the discussion. Why had he joined the rebels? Was it only because he had no choice? There was always a choice. Hell, McAaron had told him initially that if he wanted to leave, he could. So then, why *had* he stayed?

"Well," said the mousey analyst sitting across from him. "Anything else you'd like to see?"

Was there? What he saw was more than bad enough for one day. Hell, one whole campaign. Best to see all of it and go into the strategy with all the intel available.

"Are any ports open anywhere on Mars?"

The analyst began collecting data.

Brennan sighed and sat back.

He hated intelligence gathering. That was one reason he had hated being regulated to a desk instead of being out in the field. That was the number one reason why he had jumped at every possible assignment that put him out with the troops.

"The Protectorate Military Port at Fort Elysium appears to be active. All other ports are heavily restricted." She considered some of the data on her monitor a moment later, then inhaled sharply before continuing, "There is considerable activity in and out of that port."

That didn't help any. Elysium was a major Protectorate Installation on Mars, overseen by Eastern Command. The same division that Sundara Manu belonged to. Unfortunately, it was on the other side of the damned planet. Likely why it was still active, military exclusivity and geographically unassailable from their current position.

The fact that Elysium was extraordinarily active meant that ETAC, Eastern Tactical Command, must be spearheading the ground effort while the WTAC, Western Tactical Command would be focusing on the blockade and air support. That was exactly the strategy Brennan would have expected.

Of course, that didn't make it any less frustrating.

The Protectorate had access to effectively unlimited military resources. While this fledgling rebellion had more than they had previously, it was laughable in comparison.

An instructor at the Officers Academy, years and years back, had once told Brennan, "When outgunned and outnumbered, don't waste brain-space on complaining about that, and use what you've got."

What Brennan had was exactly that: decades of experience.

There was no sector of the Protectorate nor UNIC military

that Brennan had not interacted with directly. He had been in the rooms with the sitting President and interplanetary councils. Often being called up to report on military deployments, or strategies, or to give options for the group to consider.

Never, not in a million years, would he consider himself a politician. That was a job for someone else. But, he would say that he had been exposed to enough of them over the years to know how they thought.

Most, if not all, would be angling for how to spin this conflict into a financial boon or consolidate power for themselves, or the people who held their credits ransom for advantageous policymaking. This was how governments in the "free world" had been run for centuries. If you could sniff out how the various players would be looking to benefit, you could run the game with their playbook in hand.

"Are there any commercial ships involved in transporting to and from orbit? Any patterns you can determine?" Brennan had an inkling as to who it might be, given his previous interactions.

"Yes, sir." She rotated the monitor so he could read the chart for himself. "AGM has conducted approximately seventy percent of all orbital transfers, not including military activity, obviously."

Exactly as he had suspected. From what he had experienced, it seemed that Richard Trent was deep into the pockets of AGM, one of the largest and most cutthroat of corporations in the system. As a company they had their hands in just about everything, but foremost was military-grade electronics defense contracts. If it beeped or booped on a military craft, it was made with AGM tech. Hell, most of the Jovian moons were owned by the corporation, at least provisionally. Their principal research facility at Jupiter, was the system's largest orbital platform, dwarfing even the Protectorate Luna Base Complex.

Brennan wasn't sure how this information helped him in the short term, but if they managed to dig in somehow, or gain momentum, it could definitely come in handy. He was always focused on the long game.

"Let me see the blockade positions again." Brennan leaned forward to examine the monitor more closely.

The UNIC had turned out most of their big warships. Everything from this side of the Barrier Belt. They were staring down what was potentially the first major Fleet action in human history. Pirates didn't have the firepower to match anything close to this, and that had been the largest skirmishes the Fleet had suffered since its formation.

Floating high above them was enough firepower to decimate entire cities.

The thought made him want to look up, despite the ceiling and an impressive amount of rock, sky, and atmosphere between them.

Nothing was worse than the feeling of death hanging, quite literally, over your head.

Besides being impressive in size and scope, the blockade was completely sealed. There was no way a ship could safely run it.

Which meant the clock truly had started clicking down.

For the Protectorate Brass, this just turned into a waiting game. The conflict, as far as they were concerned, was over. Eventually, the members of the rebel forces, or their families more like, would get hungry. Attrition would soar. And this war, such that it was, would be over.

The real problems were going to be food and water.

So, the strategic area of emphasis would have to be the blockade.

Without handling that, it was only a matter of time before they'd be forced to surrender. Or, alternatively, watch each other starve.

That didn't sound particularly pleasant.

Frustratingly, the blockade was in an upper orbit. It would be challenging to knock them out with the ADA guns. Once they took the installations, they'd have a limited window of time to deploy them and try to catch the blockade off-guard.

These were the types of situations where you couldn't blink first. So much of fighting, regardless of scale, was who screwed up first. In every situation he had ever been in during the course of his military career, every fight had crystallized in a single moment. Win or lose, it had been one decision, or missed opportunity, that had defined the outcome. The training was there, in part, to create the muscle memory and ability to process the information rapidly enough to turn it to your advantage. All while being punched repeatedly in the face.

This really was their only way to fight back. Without a Fleet of their own, they were just pissing into the wind. Brennan had every inkling that if the Protectorate lost a few of their big and expensive carriers, they'd run with their tail tucked tightly between their legs. Bloody their noses a bit, and they'd withdraw to reassess.

What they were really lacking was an overall strategy. McAaron had a plan, and that was great. How to execute that plan, from a military logistics standpoint, was going to be quite challenging.

"Thank you, that's enough for now." Brennan stood, stretching.

The analyst just shrugged, and launched into another system entirely. Digging and doing her work, he was all but forgotten within moments.

Analysts were a strange breed.

With that being done, Brennan set out to walk the corridors. The practice helped to get the blood flowing and the creative juices stirred up. Normally, he'd go for a run. That practice didn't seem prudent in the tight corridors, nor could he really go outside and risk being recognized or captured on surveillance systems. So, a walk would have to suffice.

He and the others that had joined from the Protectorate had done the best they could in the limited time, and with limited equipment, to train these troops. Most had never held firearms before. Now, they were running constant drills throughout the compound.

Brennan stopped, turned around, and began walking toward the training area. If he couldn't go for a run, he could watch the training. That might help focus his mind.

The corridors blurred by as he walked. People greeted him as he passed by. Not the same kind of proprietary show of respect he was used to in the Protectorate halls, but personal greetings. Slaps on the shoulder, raised fists, genuine smiles. Damn, but it felt good to be a part of something. Truly, one of the most rewarding experiences of his life.

Any time he had these types of *bigger picture* thoughts, Helena would come to mind. Inevitably, every time she came to mind, his mood soured. The fact that she was being held captive, and he was unable to do something about it really galled him. Obviously, she was being used as bait for him. More importantly, she was a stopgap solution for appeasing the Martian population. She was loved by the people here. As long as she was seen as in power, the population would play nice. The media was being used to perpetuate that misconception, with lethal efficiency.

Nothing upset him more than the feeling of being played. That's what this all boiled down to. He had dedicated his entire life to upholding the law, and protecting the citizens of the system. Moreover, he had *believed* in the unity of the UNIC. Only to find out now how deep the corruption went. He wasn't naïve, he knew this was nothing new. The realization was just how deep the putrescence ran.

Being used as a pawn in someone's self-serving schemes made his knuckles ache.

Part of him wanted to just go back to his room, fish out a bottle of spirits, and let someone else handle this mess. A very small part, but it was present enough to make him think that was a good option from time to time. Helena was what kept him from that course of action.

The training grounds were situated inside one of the older bore shafts. The initial chambers had housed the banks of drills and were massive caverns supported with steel girders. The thought was, with approximately fifty meters of solid rock and dirt above them, their heat signatures should be safe from the prying eyes of the satellites overhead, while still managing vehicle deployment training, and live-fire combat simulations.

As soon as Brennan stepped onto the roadway that ran the full diameter of the monstrous cavern, he was greeted with a barrage of weapon fire. Near to two hundred would-be soldiers were down there learning the trade with ten times that number in total taking shifts in other areas. It was no small resistance force, until you compared it to their enemy. Then, it hardly seemed worth it. Futile didn't even begin to cover it.

There was no telling these people that, however.

If passion could win a gunfight, they'd stand a chance.

Unfortunately, bullets won every time.

"Impressive, isn't it?" Des was leaning against the wall behind him, flanking the entrance as if waiting for someone to surprise.

Brennan grimaced. "Yes, until the dying starts. Then it'll just be depressing.

Des chuckled softly.

For some reason, that got under Brennan's skin a bit. He turned and asked, "If you think they stand a chance against a trained military unit, even equipped as they are now, you're an old fool."

Des sobered somewhat, but his eyes still had that twinkle. "You're not much younger than me, General. I'd be careful throwing around words like *old*."

Now it was Brennan's turn to laugh. The tension deflated perceptibly.

The *senior* man was a bit of an enigma to him. From everything he had been able to find out, Des had been entangled with the family affairs of the McAaron household for his entire life. Apart from that, nothing. Until he became the legal representative for all the McAaron holdings, he had effectively been a ghost. No school records, not even so much as a citation or credit spent nor earned. What that meant, Brennan wasn't sure. He knew it was never good, though. For that alone, he couldn't trust the man. He had the ear of Edward, though, and that counted for something.

"Seriously, though," Des continued, "what do you think our chances are in a skirmish?"

Brennan didn't hesitate. "Without the element of surprise, zero. With, fifty-fifty."

Des raised an eyebrow. "That good, eh?"

"Maybe forty-sixty, against."

That seemed to sober them both. They watched the training quietly for a time.

"They really are good kids," Des finally said quietly, breaking the silence.

"Yes." That was all there was to say. After getting to know them better, Brennan had found he genuinely liked most of these people. Which was going to make it that much harder to watch them die, he suspected.

"Ed has approved your plan to take the ADA facilities," Des said without further preamble. "You've got a green light to move as soon as you can. The blockade has everyone nervous. Seems rather excessive for restricting our flow of goods."

Brennan had thought the same thing.

So, they'd storm the ADA facilities in the region, stretching from Hellas City to Solas. A total of twelve batteries. That was a tall order, but the element of surprise would be with them.

What they really needed was the overall population to wake up and realize what was happening right under their noses.

Until then, they were outnumbered, outtrained, and outgunned.

"We will deploy tonight." Best to get on with it before the intel changed again.

CHAPTER 20

SWEAT DRIBBLED OFF her forehead as she scrutinized the micronized electronics board. Helena, as it turned out, wasn't as adept with engineering principles as she was in other scholarly pursuits.

She sighed and leaned back in her chair. Her back ached from being hunched over for several hours.The mobile datapad lay in pieces across the nightstand, along with remnants from half a dozen other electrical devices she had acquired from her room. She had hoped she might be able to hotwire another power source to the device and squeeze a bit more usefulness from it. Somewhere along the way she had damaged some component or other and had been troubleshooting ever since.

It had been a week since her last communication with McAaron and the resistance forces. She knew they were going to be moving, but not to where. Her last 'visit' from Bruce had demonstrated how unstable he was. He had entered raging at her for ruining everything, and just as rapidly he'd left in excitement and smiles. She had tried multiple times since then to speak with Quinn and plead for help. He wouldn't budge from saying he didn't agree with Bruce's treatment of her, but he was just a soldier doing a job. She had decided to be her own knight in shining armor. And so far, she was failing miserably.

Frustrated and tired, she slammed her fists down on the pile of components. Parts flew everywhere. This was a futile effort, who was she fooling? She was no engineer. Tears welled up in her eyes, partially from despair but mostly from rage. Nothing infuriated her more than the feeling of inadequacy. This whole experience, more than anything else was rubbing her face in her shortcomings.

A chime sounded from the outer room and she bolted to her feet. On instinct she opened the nightstand drawer and raked all the electrical bits into it and slammed it closed. Suddenly, she felt foolish for her little attempt. All it was likely to do now was get her caught.

As she closed the distance to the cracked door, she heard Bruce's voice call out, "Helena! City duties I'm afraid. Really, Helena, still sleeping?"

She slammed the door as the voice closed in, and engaged the lock.

The door tweeted dully indicating it was locked.

"I just showered. Give me a moment to get dressed," she called through the door.

In reality, she wasn't sure when the last time she had showered actually was.

Too late, there was no finding a better excuse now; the clock was ticking.

Scrambling to the bathroom, she quickly doused her hair in water and wrapped it up in a towel. Then, she flung off her clammy, sweat-soaked clothes and wrapped herself up in one of the luxurious robes meant for visiting dignitaries.

A pounding sounded from the outer room.

Time was up.

As casually as she could, she opened the door, still wiping at her damp face.

Bruce, clever as always, appraised her.

"Really, Helena, dear. You've really let yourself go during your… vacation."

An almost overwhelming urge to claw his eyes out rippled through the muscles of her arms. She'd have her revenge, no matter the cost. This man would suffer and die if it was the last thing she did.

"I've found a significant lack in worthy reasons to do myself up, I'm afraid."

That wiped the smug smile off his face.

Dick!

Sniffing his disdain, he spun and walked stiff-backed over to the small dining table. There he deposited a datapad at one seat, and took the opposite for himself. When Helena didn't immediately follow, he glanced over his shoulder at her and sighed dramatically. Then, gestured to the chair, frowning.

"Take a seat. There's much to do."

I bet there is.

Helena planned to make it as difficult as possible.

The door chimed, and two guards walked in. Quinn followed the other guard in. When their eyes met, he smiled slightly, his eyebrows raised at her apparent partially hidden nudity. As if to say, "Hey there, why are you always half-naked when we meet?"

The thought made her stomach boil.

As the two took up positions, one behind her and one at the door, Bruce started talking. The words passed through one ear and out the other, and she busied herself with going through the documents on the datapad that required her signature. There was no choice. Obviously, she was *only* brought legislation that required her signature. There had been several instances where she had refused to comply: the proposals being far too extreme, or outlandish. Nothing galled her more than knowing the threat of physical violence had driven her to sign them anyway. If she had only been stronger, she would have refused and made them kill her.

Bruce droned on, and she skimmed each document before she signed it. The act reminding her of simpler times. There was a certain amount of muscle memory to this. It almost felt like everything was back to normal. That the nightmare was over. Just a fleeting thought.

Then her jaw dropped.

"What is this?"

Bruce rolled his eyes and said, "Were you even listening to me?"

"Yes, of course I was. Now, what is this about sanctioning *supportive industries*?"

He shrugged; a smile twitched onto his lips.

"Bruce, what does that mean?" There was some heat to her voice, and she felt the guard tense behind her. The sounds of his muscled body twisting underneath his tight-fitting armor was dangerously close to the back of her head.

"That particular piece of memo comes straight from President Trent, I'm sad to say." He frowned dramatically. "I intended something much more severe, but was overruled."

"I didn't ask who came up with it," she blurted out, unthinking. "I asked what was the intention?"

The full-strength slap took a moment to register, then the searing pain on her cheek started. Silvery-purple specks of light flitted across her vision like iridescent flies. She tasted blood, the sweet-metallic tang she was becoming accustomed to.

Bruce examined his hand, as if inspecting it for damage while he spoke. "Let's be clear about a few things, shall we? Since I'm not in the mood for your usual games this morning. I know about Natasha."

The world reeled. She felt as if she would faint. A persistent numbing cold began to spread across her face and jaw.

How did he know?

There was no way! The body was hidden in the room with her. A room she was not allowed to leave! Could they have possibly found it while she was sleeping? That seemed unlikely. Maybe from some kind of drone or sensor sweep? That seemed plausible. If that were the case, then *how much* did he know?

As her mind raced, Bruce must have seen the fear in her eyes. He relished it. Basked in it. A slow smile spread across his face. There was no mirth or warmth to it; that smile was as cold as space, full of hatred and unfulfilled promises.

"You didn't really think I'd not connect you to that?" Bruce asked dryly.

There was… something. The way he delivered it didn't sync with what happened. Was he fishing? The one thing she knew about Bruce was he loved the sound of his own voice. He reveled in watching the fish squirm in the net, gasping, and thrashing about wildly.

Suddenly feeling keenly sorry for every fish she had ever caught, she leaned back and watched the man across the table from her. He dusted off an imaginary speck from his suit lapel, and leveled his gaze at her.

"Oh, yes," he drawled out. "I know all about the little inside job you two pulled. Had she been working for you from the beginning, or did you use what little powers of persuasion you have left to you?" The bawdy glance at her breasts and raised eyebrows indicated which of those options he thought most likely.

He doesn't know!

The relief came as a warm flush emanating from her chest. The frigid feeling in her face faded slowly. Taking care to not show her relief, she held his gaze.

Keep him talking.

He obliged her unspoken request, for once in their wretched relationship.

"What you fail to realize, Helena dear, is you've upset the delicate dance between us. With what you and Natasha have done, you've committed treason against the UNIC. You've aligned yourself with the insurgents, and doomed yourself to face the harshest of punishment. You probably don't even fear death anymore, do you?" he mused, the question more an internal one than external. "Probably hoping for it at this point, I'd assume. What you should fear is the public humiliation of it!"

He clipped the last few words, his volume rising noticeably, and punctuated the sentence by slapping an open palm down on the table. The datapad jumped slightly, as did Helena. Despite the rising fear, she held his gaze.

Not getting the reaction he had hoped, Bruce rose and buttoned the top two buttons of his blazer reflexively. Helena held her breath as he walked toward the bedroom door. It took everything in her power to not gasp out a sigh of relief when he finally stopped, glancing through the open doorway.

He turned; his nose wrinkled up in disgust.

"You should really ask to have new linens brought in, Helena. This room smells like something died in it."

Helena almost laughed.

Clasping his hands behind his back, Bruce casually paced around the room. Eyeing the sparse décor with a critic's eye.

"Where is Natasha?" he asked quietly.

"I don't know." Helena finally spoke.

Bruce stopped, then turned to face her. His frown deepening.

"Listen." His voice was dangerously quiet. She almost laughed. As if she had a choice in the matter. He continued, hissing the words, "I don't have time for your petty games. Tell me where she is, and I will make sure your public execution for treason is respectful, dignified." As he spoke, he continued his languid patrol of her quarters.

"I don't know," she started.

He spun on her, face stretched in a fury. "Fuck with me further and I'll make every effort to disgrace and humiliate you! I'll dress you in tight white underwear so the cameras can see you shit and piss yourself! I'll give the barracks a few turns with you while you wait for execution so the world can see how dead your eyes are! I'll find and murder every man, woman, and child you ever loved! Tell me where Natasha is and how she accessed our systems!"

Sweat beaded his forehead, spittle flung from his lips.

He's losing control. The thought refueled her resolve. If he was cracking this much, he must be being pressured from the top. That realization made her almost giddy.

"You've made this bed, Bruce," she said firmly, not averting her gaze against that penetrating glare. "Don't complain about the lumps now."

Shock crashed across his features like a breaking tide. Then he roared and threw the chair between them across the room where it crashed into the wall. Helena reeled backward as he clambered across the table, roaring like some primordial beast.

Bruce grabbed her by the collar and punched her square in the face. It was a powerful strike, and the edges of her vision darkened and blurred briefly. There were second, third, and fourth successive strikes. Each coming faster and harder than the previous.

There were other noises besides that of the fleshy impacts of fist against her face, troubled shouts, furniture moving. Helena realized she must have fallen, the carpeted ground pressed against the side of her face. The weight of Bruce straddling her chest felt distant, vague. Yells and screams filled the air, and underneath it was something else. Something that didn't sound quite right; didn't belong in this moment. Laughter.

With some amount of surprise, she realized the laughter was coming from her.

Rich, maniacal, belly laughs.

Damn but it hurt! Her head was back, mouth agape, howling with glee.

Three sets of feet stood around her. She could just make them out through the tears, either from the pain or hilarity, she wasn't sure.

Bruce had stopped yelling, and the guards had ceased their shouts of warning.

Everyone must've been staring at her. Laying on the floor, face already a bruising mess of tears, snot, and blood.

As she calmed her laughter to semi-controlled giggles, Bruce was led out the door bodily by the other guard.

Quinn remained and helped her into a seated position, her legs stretched out before her.

"Are you hurt much?" he asked after the door had shut behind the other two.

She shook her head, giggles still threatening to upend her mental wagon again.

A momentary panic rose in her. Was she going mad? She didn't feel insane. But, did insane people recognize they were breaking? Or did it just happen one day? Did it matter?

Gently, he pressed at her cheekbones and used a handkerchief he produced from somewhere to wipe away some of the congealing liquids on her face.

That's when she looked into his eyes.

The pain she saw there was more than duty. More than the normal care of one human to another. This man had feelings for her that went beyond responsibility and respect.

Their faces were close enough she could feel the heat of his breath on her face. It stirred her hair. The warmth of him pressed in on her.

"He's going to kill me," she whispered.

Quinn stiffened. "He can't. There's a process."

She chuckled dryly and raised a hand to her face. "Is this part of the process, Quinn?"

Shame filled his features, and he looked down. "No, it's not. I'm sorry I let that happen."

"You had better get used to it. He won't stop now," she pressed.

He bit his lip thoughtfully.

They sat there, he balanced on his toes squatting next to her, all sprawled out across the floor. She was breathing heavily, and her robe had spilled open at the top. She could feel the cool air on her exposed skin. Quinn avoided looking down so intensely he may as well have been staring directly at her body.

"Help me stand, will you, please?" she whispered.

He did so, gently.

When she reached her feet, she fell heavily toward him. He caught her easily, but that was the entire point for the fall in the first place. Her robe had opened fully, the loose knot having finally failed. Her naked body pressed into his armored one, and he held her tight.

The feeling of someone close to her in a way that *didn't* want to do her physical harm was damn near intoxicating. Her head swam with their proximity.

"Help me." The words were out of her mouth so quietly she almost thought she imagined herself saying it.

"I am," he responded.

She looked into his eyes and shook her head slightly. "No, *help me*!" This time, the whisper was urgent, full of breathy desperation and despair.

Doubt filled his eyes, and she knew she was losing him.

She leaned in and pressed her clammy lips against his. It was unwelcomed and awkward, neither person fully committing to the passionless effort. Reluctantly he pulled away a few centimeters and looked into her eyes.

"I wish you hadn't done that," he said sadly.

So much for my womanly wiles.

The flirtations must have been a pitiful sight. She could tell her face was swelling. One eye was almost completely shut now. Her lip was split in at least two places, and she thought she felt a loose tooth. Here she was, practically naked, bloodied, and broken. Likely the least attractive person to have ever existed. How did she expect to *seduce* her way out of this? It was laughable.

Tears of frustration welled in her eyes. Resolve breaking, she became acutely aware of how much her body *hurt!*

Quinn gripped her tightly by the shoulders and gave her a little jerk. "Hey, don't do that. Don't cry. It will be okay. Believe in the process. If you've done nothing wrong…."

She pulled away slightly. "How could I have done anything wrong, Quinn? I've been *trapped* in here."

"Well…" he started.

Damn it! The one time… He had been the one to catch her in her escape attempt. His was the evidence that could condemn her.

Nothing upset her more about this than to be completely under someone's power. Her fate was completely up to this other person. Nothing she could do could influence whether she lived or died. On the one hand, he obviously cared about her to some degree. On the other, he felt a sense of duty and was a good soldier, and most importantly, he *knew* she was lying.

Helena did cry then. The first sob racked her body in a violent spasm as it broke through her defenses like a levy breaking. The subsequent sobs came of their own accord. She gasped for breath between them. She was going to die. Just like Bruce had threatened. Everything she had worked for, gone.

Unable to quell the sobs, Quinn made quiet hushing sounds and pulled her in for a tighter hug. It was awkward, given their position, and she found she had to grip him lower than she would have if she were standing straight up.

That's when she felt it. The stun rod handle on his belt. It was nestled just beyond his sidearm, closer to his ass than his hip. Not much bigger than a hammer handle and was only attached by a single magnetic latch. Adrenaline ripped through her.

Her other hand maneuvered down to clasp lower, grabbing the edge of his hip.

She whispered nonsense into his ear, so focused on distracting him while she eased the clasp gently enough to avoid detection.

His breathing had become deep, his chest rising and falling rapidly beneath the press of her. Their entanglement finally wearing down his resolve.

In one fluid motion, she powered on the device, drew it, and stabbed it into his ribcage.

A sound like paper tearing violently filled the air.

Their physical connection caused some residual buzzing sensation to hit her body, but he caught the brunt of the attack.

His went rigid, frozen almost, and then he slumped forward, taking them both to the ground.

The stun rod clattered to the ground as she rolled the unconscious man off of her.

Once she had regained her feet. She began to strip him down. He was considerably larger than she was, but she wasn't about to make an escape attempt half-naked again.

Quinn groaned and rolled his head to the side.

Acting on animalistic instincts, Helena grabbed the stun rod and activated it on his chest. He flinched a couple times and then went motionless.

Suddenly guilty, she reached down to his neck to feel for a pulse. It was there, albeit slight. Quinn was a good man, if somewhat conflicted. She'd feel pretty shitty if she killed him too. But, she'd do what she had to do to escape. There was no turning back this time. If she stayed, her next visit from Bruce would be her death sentence.

Once she had stripped Quinn, she began to don his clothing. It fit terribly, but she did her best to tuck, roll, twist, and conceal that fact as best she could. She took everything except his undergarments. Weapons, tools, belts, armor, helmet, and uniform. Top to bottom, she looked like a Protectorate Peace Officer now. She even had his ID card, she realized. That would hopefully get her through all the locked doors.

Helena checked the time on the wristwatch she had boosted from the fallen guard. She wasn't exactly sure because she hadn't been able to time them herself, but she thought a shift change might be within the hour. Two at most.

Nothing would be worse than having a guard discover a fallen, mostly naked, Protectorate Peace Office on her sitting room floor.

Lacking a better idea, she clasped his hands in hers and begin to slowly pull him toward the bedroom door. The effort took an agonizingly long time, but soon she was trying to lean him up against the bed. Even though he was considerably larger than she was, that would be difficult to make out underneath the sea of covers she had.

None of the guards had ever roused her out of bed, that she could recall. It might buy her some time if nothing else.

How could a person be so fit and *so damned heavy* at the same time! She had to lean with all of her might to bodily shove Quinn up into bed, head first, and then swing his legs up under the covers. The angle was all wrong, but the timing was everything. If she got caught here with another body under her covers. Well, she wasn't feeling exactly adept at seduction these days, so that was a situation she'd like to avoid if at all possible.

She donned the helmet and pulled the balaclava up over her split lip and bloodied nose. All that was visible was a puffy, blackening eye and some forehead. This would have to be enough. It just had to. With a quick glance in the mirror to make sure she was passable for a soldier, she squared her shoulders and walked out the front door of her room. Thankfully, there were no guards, given that Quinn and the other man would've been on duty when Bruce arrived. Who knew where the other was or when he'd return?

The hallway blurred by on her way to the elevators.

Using Quinn's ID, she swiped the access. A green light indicator pulsed to life.

A hum could be heard as the elevator began to ascend.

Having gotten this far, she realized she had no more of a plan of escape than the last time. She drew in several deep breaths to stave off the panic. Where should she take this elevator? The Administrative Building was more a home to her than her own flat. She knew every nook and cranny of the place. Much to the annoyance of the engineering and maintenance crew, she had insisted on being present for every major repair, upgrade, or retrofit the building had undergone. Many had thought the practice silly at the time, shouldn't there be more important things for a Governor to spend their time on than watching some maintenance people crawling around in ductworks?

At the time, she had felt it was important to have knowledge of the intimate workings of the building, and the people who performed those duties. As a matter of respect and diligence. How could she ask someone to do something that she had no idea the risks, or details of? Now, she was glad for that knowledge, because it gave her a few ideas on how to discreetly exit the building.

The waste management system was not easily accessible in Hellas. Water being at an absolute premium when the first settlers had put down roots here, they had piped everything to a central processing plant. Subsequent city growth had spiderwebbed out from there. The Administrative Building was near the heart of that initial spiderweb. She just so happened to know where the access hatch was that could lead her into the maintenance network. Little more than a one-meter-wide tube of reinforced concrete.

The elevator finally chimed, and the doors opened.

It was thankfully empty.

With the Administrative Building mostly emptied out, there was little reason for anyone to leave the first floor. All the above offices had been closed, the employees furloughed or terminated.

Once inside the elevator, she keyed in the access for the maintenance level. The Governor, somewhat frustratingly, didn't have direct access to the maintenance and engineering levels. She had argued the stupidity of that refusal to the Chief Engineer, who had reluctantly shared his personal code with her. While her codes would have been revoked and flagged, *his* code worked perfectly and within a few seconds the elevator was dropping down the shaft to the base of the building.

The doors opened directly into the maintenance level. A cacophony of pipes, ducts, harnessed cabling, and support struts lined the walls. An array of monitoring equipment nestled against the west wall, a single pressure door to the east. The room narrowed to a single hallway lit with red lights to the north. That was it.

She exited the elevator and turned toward the pressure door. Beyond it would be the maze-like maintenance shaft, and freedom.

A chime behind her indicated the elevator had been called up.

If someone had noticed unauthorized access to the engineering levels, they might come to investigate. Her guts writhed with nervous nausea, and a giggle rose in her throat. Maybe she was going insane?

Chastising herself for standing around wasting invaluable time like an idiot, she raced to the door and broke the pressure seal. The maintenance shafts connected to the waste management facilities which were above the city, so the tunnels themselves were kept at surface pressure. It wouldn't kill her, so long as she limited her exposure.

Her ears popped as the pressure from the room was sucked into the shaft. It pulled on the door, making it difficult to open.

Helena wasted no more time and entered the shaft. Spinning, she heaved the door closed behind her.

The pressure differential swinging back the other way made her dizzy.

The helmet and uniform she wore would keep her protected. Long enough to see her through to where she was going. That was the hope, anyway.

Wherever that might be!

As she jogged clumsily into the dark tunnels, she wished she knew where Brennan was. Hopefully, McAaron wouldn't mind that his *inside man* had fled.

If she had stayed, she'd be dead before anyone came for her.

That wasn't an option. She wasn't done yet.

CHAPTER 21

AN ALARM BLARED in Frankie's room.

Her eyes flew open. A hand went under her pillow to the small pistol she now kept there at all times.

The door was still closed. She was alone in the small space.

As she sat up, she recalled that was a benefit of living in a single tiny room. If you had a large dwelling, it was much more difficult to clear it of any potential threats. She herself had taken advantage of that to make a getaway not that long ago.

Maybe she was okay with living a simpler life?

Rubbing the sleep from her eyes, she hopped to her feet and began to don the clothing piled on the floor at the foot of her bunk. She sniffed it briefly. It wasn't *too* bad, but she definitely needed to wash it after today.

The alarm siren had ceased, but an amber light pulsed above her door.

Frankie had no idea what that meant, but she knew it couldn't be good.

Pulling her shirt over her head, she opened the door and joined a stream of analysts racing to the freshly put together command center. Their numbers had grown to nearly fifty, but only a half-dozen were really worth anything. Those six were worked to the bone. She had just finished a twenty-hour shift, trying to compile data on the placement of Protectorate safehouses and hidden garrisons in and around the city. If they could knock over a few of those, they'd be well equipped and deny the enemy supplies they were counting on.

The ground assault would come shortly after the blockade failed. It would have to. To do anything else would be to admit defeat. There was no way the Protectorate would *ever* allow that. What little forces the resistance had would be swallowed up in a dove-gray tide of fire and death. Unless they could erode the operational readiness of the Protectorate on Mars.

She had made that her entire goal and thought it was the best way for her to utilize her skillsets to maximize the action plan of their burgeoning revolution. The new equipment helped considerably.

Luckily, her quarters were not far from the main hub, and she elbowed her way into the room alongside several others. There was a buzz of activity, a group of analysts huddled around a workstation, all looking pensive.

"What's going on?" Frankie asked another analyst, a gray-haired woman by the name of Evelynn. Of all the other analysts in the room, Frankie would only put her life on the line with the information from this calculating, sharp-eyed woman. The rest were hacks, at best. She'd seen this woman work, and while she was lightyears behind Frankie in training, she had the gumption to do the job halfway decently.

Evelynn leaned in close, conspiratorially. "Attack on Theta Base." The codenames left a lot on the table regarding creativity, but at least it helped to differentiate them.

"Already?" Frankie sounded more shocked than she actually felt. If she were being totally honest, she was surprised to find everyone still alive every single day. The whole operation was still in the most delicate infantile stages. A lot of growth would need to happen and quickly.

The crowd pressed in against them, and Evelynn nodded sadly.

"Well, why the hell are we just all standing around watching?" Their people were dying, and everyone was just pressed in to watch the show?

Anger building, she shoved her way back to her workstation and accessed the feed from the chief analyst's desk. Then, she put it up on the large screen suspended at the far end of the room from McAaron's office doors.

Where was McAaron?

Someone needed to take charge of this. It just couldn't be her.

As her shiny new workstation sprang to life, she deftly accessed several critical systems in the Solas infrastructure. The problem with having a vast and interconnected city was it made it near impossible to monitor everything at once. With everything talking to each other, accessing systems between systems was not hard at all. *If*, you knew where to start.

Frankie considered herself an expert at remote information gathering.

The data she had available to her from the city-systems wasn't great. Theta base was in a heavily industrial area of Solas, and with many of the buildings penetrating the canopy above, it clogged the view of the cameras considerably.

Swearing under her breath, she sent a request through to be approved by the highest-ranking Analyst on the floor. Whoever that happened to be must have been watching, because the approval was almost immediate. Her request was simple: drone swarm to AOR.

Thanking any divine being that happened to be listening for pirates and stolen goods, she activated the intelligence assets list, and scrolled through the menus to find a company of drones. They had eight companies of drone swarms, consisting of approximately thirty insect-sized intelligence-gathering machines. DS-BAKER-ONE, was selected and a LAUNCH activation code was sent to her workstation.

Without hesitation she initiated and launched the swarm to the Theta Base location.

Then, she integrated the streaming feed into the main screen, alongside some news footage that was live in the area and the hacked city feeds.

There was a rustle and commotion behind her, with a quick glance she could see McAaron and his entourage making their way up the switch-back stairs to the mezzanine balcony. Ed looked tired, but was still dressed to kill. A resplendent charcoal suit with an aquamarine dress shirt unbuttoned at the top. She had to admit, he looked presidential.

"Someone talk to me. What am I looking at?" McAaron said from above.

The room noise fell below a whisper. The subtle thumps of fingers on glass-paneled workpane keyboards filled the air.

Chief Aslan took the lead, as was her duty. Frankie set about chewing on a pen vigorously to keep her opinions to herself.

"There's been an attack at Theta Base, sir," Chief Aslan said briskly as she noticed the main screen.

"I've gathered that much," McAaron said. "Tell me what the hell you're doing about it."

Frankie smiled to herself. Leave it to Edward McAaron to not give two shits about how attractive a woman was, and get right to the point. She knew she liked him for a reason.

Aslan, for what it was worth, took the rebuke better than Frankie would have expected.

"A drone swarm has been deployed to the area; we should have some usable intelligence in a few moments." Then, she redirected her words to the crowded command center. "Let's clear the room, everyone. Clearance level three and above, only. Someone get me a flight time on that drone swarm."

The familiar feeling of running an operation was comforting

for Frankie. The minutes blurred by as the automated drones made their way through the subterranean cityscape toward their targeted area.

Thankfully, the room cleared to less than twenty total people. The doors closed, barred, and clearance-locked.

McAaron paced above, talking in hushed tones to his advisors.

"They've breached the outer perimeter and are inside," Bel said, his eyes wide with apprehension.

McAaron slammed his hands down on the railing above, causing a deep metallic *BOOM* to reverberate through the railing.

"I knew we couldn't trust that prick!" he raged.

Des swooped in quickly and whispered quietly in his ear. While she couldn't make out what was being said, she could plainly see that McAaron didn't like nor agree with whatever it was he was hearing.

The outboard speakers suddenly crackled to life.

"CENOPS, Vandal actual, SITREP."

The room hushed. Nobody moved. Nobody dared breathe.

Frankie looked around and found Chief Aslan reading over something on her datapad.

Whatever it was she was looking for, she approved. She opened the comm and said, "Vandal, OPS, line secured. The enemy has breached the outer defenses of Theta base, request immediate reinforcement from all action-ready units."

A pause. "Copy. Permission to act autonomously?"

Aslan glanced up at McAaron.

"Who is Vandal?" McAaron asked of the Chief.

"Vandal is the unit led by General Brennan." Frankie heard herself say.

McAaron laughed, though there was no mirth in it.

"Yes, please! He's probably the only one among us who knows what to actually *do* in this situation."

Not exactly true, but she respected his viewpoint on it.

Aslan, by the sour set to her face, did not appreciate the comment.

"Vandal, from OPS-Actual, proceed with extreme prejudice. Out."

The line beeped to indicate the connection had been closed.

Support units were en route, which was part of the strategy of having several small bases within striking distance of each other.

Feeling somewhat better about the situation, Frankie decided to start unearthing exactly *how* they had been found out. It seemed somewhat coincidental they get a surprise visit from the mysterious owner of a decommissioned and long-forgotten facility and within days a surprise attack at one of their brand-new locations? It felt too tidy, too neat. Something wasn't adding up. Life was messy and unpredictable.

The rest of the activity in the room faded into the back of her mind, just a distant humming that was barely acknowledged. She started digging deeper than she normally would have from this location. They needed information, and they needed it quickly. If one of the new operational bases was compromised, they all could be. That was need-to-know-yesterday kind of intel.

All of her backdoors into the Protectorate mainframe had been found or blocked. As frustrating as it was, she knew it had only been a matter of time.

Nothing good is ever easy.

Electronic Warfare and Countermeasures were her specialties. This is where she thrived.

Let everyone else worry about leadership and politics.

The Protectorate had never really given her an opportunity to shine. Not with the amount of ego in the room. Too many pig-headed shit-for-brains wanting to swing their dicks around and pound their chests. Joining up with McAaron had felt like a last resort. The only choice she had left. Until now.

Here she could make a substantial difference.

In this room, with these people, right now, she could have

everything she always wanted.

Involuntarily, the thought made her shoot a quick glance up at the prowling McAaron. He looked, moved, and acted more like a black-furred jungle cat with every passing day. That transformation was equal parts terrifying and thrilling to watch. Something about him just drew her attention.

There was no time to explore that train of thought. Best let it derail down the tracks without her direct involvement.

Here we go!

She broke through in a low-sec portion of the Protectorate mainframe. With the heightened level of alertness given their active operation, it made any direct route a bit obvious. Working her way through the system was much like navigating a debris-littered sector of space. Not that she had *any* experience whatsoever at piloting. Anyone who let her into a cockpit was a fool.

Still, the thought had a way of making all of this feel much more glamorous. After all, she was just sitting in a chair punching some keys and chewing on a pen.

The pen clattered wetly to the tabletop when she realized what she was doing.

Nasty habit, that.

Sounds of gunfire ripped through the outboard speakers, and her head jerked up along with the rest of the room. On the main screen, media news feeds, and their own drone feeds confirmed that shots were being exchanged within the industrial building thought to house the "terrorists." Funny how that word got used these days.

While everyone else wrung their hands and watched the screen with wide eyes, fearfully wondering if they could expect a similar thing at any moment, Frankie continued to work. Hers were the only eyes not glued to the screen.

"Brennan is arriving with his unit, as are teams from Romeo and Echo bases."

The words registered, but not who had spoken them. Frankie scrunched up her eyebrows at the information flowing across her screen. Something was off.

On a hunch, she redirected her efforts into another portion of the system. Exploring the thread.

Within minutes she stumbled across the data. It was from the Department of Health and Safety, a sub-branch of the Protectorate Peace Keepers. They had reported an anomalous amount of people moving to the area surrounding Theta base. Of course! Being in an industrial area, any kind of large group of people would be flagged for investigation. While not commonplace, it happened, and most of those alerts were ignored. But not if the Protectorate was on the lookout for large groups of people moving locations.

Damn it! She should have thought of that.

One of those good news and bad news type situations. Given they had remained in the tunnel systems, this base was likely safe. The bad news was there were several other bases that would also have a high likelihood of drawing attention.

As best she could, she wrapped everything up into an intelligence report, prioritized it, and sent it along to Aslan. That was the best she could do for now.

Or...

She was inside. The Protectorate would not be expecting an electronic attack. Maybe she could disrupt the attack on Theta and cover the tracks of the other bases? If she tried anything, she'd have to do it quickly.

Easing back in her chair, she ran through potential scenarios in her mind. There were a million different ways to cause chaos within the system. A subtle approach was always best. Let them think that their data was secure and useful. They'd chase their own tails with it.

Change too much too fast, and she'd trigger alerts that would surely get her shut out at best and tracked at worst. That was something she'd have to be cautious of.

On that thought, she decided she'd avoid having her own people track this complex operation back to her as well. If somehow, one of these other analysts could backtrack her efforts, it would surely raise some questions.

Smiling to herself, she circumvented the defensive measures in place within her own systems and cloned Chief Aslan's credentials. She wasn't logged in as the chief, but the system would flag any of her commands as if she were. Any deep digging would reveal the ruse, but hopefully it would buy her time.

Frankie realized her situation was peculiar. Here she was, on the run from her previous employer, and hiding in plain sight amongst her current one. Not for the first time, she wondered who she *actually* was; more importantly, where her real loyalties were? Was she helping because she needed a place to hide, or was she there because she believed in the cause?

More the former.

What kind of person did that make her?

She'd worry about that later, she decided.

Properly cloaked now, she launched her inside assault on the Protectorate systems. Delicate as a neurosurgeon, she weaved in and out of the various reports, adjusting the data ever so slightly. A changed coordinate here, a different timestamp there, a corrupted portion of the file in a few critical spots. No one thing would trigger any alarm bells, but all of it together painted a picture of tampering.

After several tense moments, she backed out of the system the way she had come in.

Nothing exploded. No warnings. A clean getaway!

A breath tore its way out of her chest, and she looked at the ceiling. Sweat was pouring down her face, armpits, and underneath her breasts. It made her underclothes itch with that aggravatingly soggy feeling.

The information had been altered or corrupted to the point

where it would be rendered useless. So long as they had no offline backups, which would take a special recommendation from her old boss, they would wind up chasing their tails for a while. Inevitably, someone would put it together that the intelligence had been tampered with; but for now, the protocol would be to chase it down.

There was much left to be done, so a shower and change of clothes would have to wait.

More help was needed at Theta Base. Brennan and the others had arrived. Someone had patched into their combat camera arrays and were streaming that alongside the drone feeds. Now that the shooting had begun, the city feeds had been terminated.

They were holding their own, it looked like. Brennan was a whirlwind of violence.

Frankie needed to distract the enemy somehow.

What would the Protectorate do in their situation?

They'd send something nasty through the pipes somewhere else.

Smiling to herself, she cobbled together a bit of nastiness that wouldn't take long to render harmless, unfortunately. However, while it was active, it'd really mess with their ability to coordinate. All she needed to do was…

"Oh my God!" someone gasped from behind Frankie.

The sudden exclamation made her realize the room had gone silent.

When she looked up, she saw several pale, wide-eyed looks of shock and horror directed at the main screen.

Displayed there was wholesale slaughter.

Heavy equipment had been deployed, lines of Protectorate soldiers marched behind armored personnel carriers and mobile gun platforms. Red-armed rebels were laying down their weapons and raising their hands, only to be riddled with bullets moments later. A sea of dove-gray-clad troops could be seen from the aerial drone view far overhead spilling into the industrial complex. The flashes of kinetic arms fire flashing across the screen with such frequency it almost appeared like static.

That's when Frankie realized at some point or other, she had risen to her feet to join the rest of the crowd. What they were witnessing wasn't a police action. This was brutal, relentless… murder.

Thinking the word shook her to her core.

To think, little more than a month ago she had been working for the very people that would have issued the order to kill anything that moved. It was insanity.

The sea of soldiers trampled through the growing river of blood as they penetrated deeper and deeper into the facility. From the aerial footage you could just make out the speckles of bloody boot prints.

This sealed it.

Frankie Zoya was a part of the revolution.

Her jaw clenched tightly, she swung back into her seat and pulled various clips from the feeds. Thankfully, she noted, Brennan and his unit had fallen back and had initiated a fighting withdrawal from the scene. He would know better than anyone that the day was lost.

As she gathered some of the most violent clips from the various feeds, she also brought up a map of the area and patched it directly to Brennan's tactical channel.

"Vandal, this is CENOPS operator eight. I am working on your exfil."

Brennan was running, stopping every so often to allow others to catch up and provide cover fire. His words were punctuated with steady rhythmic breathing. "Copy Op-Eight, appreciate someone knows what they're doing up there."

There was nothing to be done for it now, eventually someone would put together that she knew more than she should. She had known the second she dedicated herself to saving as many lives as she could that it would expose her.

"Up ahead is a metro entrance; take that down two levels and I'll bypass the security on the service door. That will get you below the city level. Confirm when you're through and I'll lock it behind you. It won't be a permanent solution, but it'll buy you a few more minutes."

"Affirmative." The tac-channel clicked off, as he was likely transmitting unit-channel orders.

Frankie was good on her word. The security door bypass went through mere seconds before Brennan rounded the corner to the metro entrance. From his bodycam feed, it appeared his unit was mostly intact. The occupants of Theta were probably a total loss by now.

On that note, she decided it would be best to recall the drone swarm. No sense in tipping the Protectorate off to their new toys. That would spoil the fun.

"I have confirmation," said a shaky voice. Bel sat at his station, headset clutched in his hands. Everyone turned to look at him. Tears were just beginning to leak from his eyes. "The Protectorate Open Comms are reporting in, reporting complete annihilation of Theta base. No survivors… They killed all of them."

A door slammed above them.

Frankie turned to look up at the mezzanine level. McAaron's coterie were all staring at the now shut door to his empty office room.

"Op-Eight, we are through."

Fingers blurring across the keypad, she sealed the door and scrambled the codes.

They'd bypass it easily, but it would take some time.

Right now, time was their friend.

A yawn ripped through her unexpectedly, and she checked the time. She had only been asleep for a couple hours at most when the alarm had sounded. It might be a good idea to try to sneak in a bit more. They were done here, for now at least.

As she stood, she stretched, extending her arms above her

head and rising onto the tips of her toes. Being able to *do* something, felt really good. Part of her, a very small part, was also glad to have finally picked a side other than her own.

With her thoughts wandering more than usual, which was saying something rather profound, she made her way to the exit. Stopping to make sure she had exited without much notice, she turned and watched the room. Everyone still buzzed with subdued anxiety. More than one face was tear-streaked.

They had survived, but only just, and now everyone knew just how tenuous their situation was.

CHAPTER 22

"VESTA STATION, PERSONAL shuttle Alpha-two-six-four-three, requesting docking."

The minor-planet Vesta was a pretty one, Spalding had to admit. Being the second-largest object in the Barrier Belt, it consisted of approximately nine percent of the overall mass of the asteroid belt. Researchers had long held the belief that it was a failed protoplanet with a layered interior much like that of Earth. It wasn't until the first colony was formed, Dawnport, named after the turn of the millennium orbital spacecraft *Dawn,* which spent a full year studying the floating rock.

Vesta Station was nestled into a crater called Calpurnia that was in turn nestled against another crater named Marcia, which was the site chosen for the building of the first major asteroid colony.

Dawnport was nothing special, but at least there was a town on this rock. It would definitely have a place to buy a drink. That was the only thing on his agenda.

Well, that and find a job.

The station chief here was reportedly formerly Protectorate Fleet herself. So, on the ride over, he had decided he'd use an alias.

The problem with having an ego was, your name actually meant something to you. As far as names went, his wasn't the most exciting, but damn, it was all he had ever really had! Now, he wasn't even supposed to use it? Horseshit!

Still, it was better to be safe. Maybe after things calmed down on Mars and all of this blew over, he could come clean. Maybe fly for a Martian outfit and be reasonably close to civilization? Was that too much to hope for? Just a year ago, he wouldn't have given one thought to living on the red planet. Now, it sounded like a paradise beyond his worth.

So, Jason Tyr would be his new name.

He was still working on his backstory, but what he had come up with so far sounded good. A failed Protectorate pilot drop-out, who flew for private security out in the Kuiper Belt for a while but came back to bury a sibling and was looking for work.

On second thought, everything except the name sounded dumb.

It would raise far too many eyebrows.

Feeling somewhat out of his depth, Spalding decided he'd just go with the strong silent type "with a past." Simple, easy to remember when drunk. He liked it.

"Alpha-two-six-four-three, you are clear for docking procedure at bay nineteen. Welcome to Vesta."

He blew out a long sigh and adjusted the incoming angles to account for the ridiculous spin this rock had. Why anyone had decided to make this the main hub was beyond him.

Docking went smooth and easy, despite the rotation, and soon he was disembarking the borrowed shuttle. Jorge had procured the use of it for the trip, and someone would be coming to take it back to Luna eventually. So, as he stomped down the gangway, he didn't give the craft another thought. Like so many other things lately, that was someone else's problem now.

The docks themselves were relatively calm. It was middle of the night cycle local time, so only a few maintenance crew folks were out and about. Everything had that slow, dream-like feeling things often got in the wee hours of the night.

A tall lanky man, slightly beyond his middle years it seemed, was striding directly toward him. Spalding dropped his duffle, wincing slightly as the bottles clanked together a little loudly, and waited.

"Dockmaster, I presume?" Spalding said cheerfully when the man was just a few strides away.

"Pruitt. Nobody calls me Dockmaster around here." For being in the wee hours as it was, Mr. Pruitt here sure reeked of coffee. Spalding damn near gagged on the smell wafting from the sweat-stained jumpsuit.

Charming place to spend the rest of my life!

Spalding smiled anyway, and handed over his datapad so he Dockmaster could read his faked credentials. Hopefully, Jorge's man was as good as he had claimed.

After a few tense moments spent scrutinizing the paperwork, Pruitt handed the datapad back and said, "Looks to be in order. Says you're looking for flight duty with the security team?"

Spalding nodded.

Oddly, the man walked a tight circle around Spalding, eyeing him critically.

"Excuse me," Spalding said, feeling a little awkward. "Can I help you with something?"

"Nope, she'll like you well enough. Good luck with that one."

No further conversation was possible as he strode off whistling with his hands tucked in his pockets.

"Thanks," he called after him a moment too late to be heard.

There was nothing left to be done but suck it up and check-in. Spalding had a bad feeling starting to creep into his gut. This was probably the worst idea he'd ever let himself be talked into. Even worse than the time that Amanda and...

Every time he thought of her, or any of the others, it felt as if he had been stabbed in the heart with a red-hot hunk of metal.

He quickened his step, ready to get to *any work* just as a way to take his mind off the pain. That or get drunk. Whichever came first. Both preferably.

The area of the spaceport he had been directed to dock the shuttle was more a bay than a major dock. This was an area for personal transports, not the huge freighters. From what he could tell from his approach, the control tower was actually offset of center, favoring this side of the wagon-wheel shape of the spaceport. That would be where he'd find the Station Chief.

Walking with a quick-paced, confident-looking stride, he navigated as best he could. It took a little doing, but eventually, he found his way and was standing outside a door that read: STATION CHIEF—Vidya Carson.

When he tried the door, a buzzer sounded in two short bursts.

It was locked.

An audio recording played over the door panel speaker, "Station Chief Vidya Carson, normal operating hours are EMT 0800 through 2000 hours. Thank you."

The female voice on the recording sounded pleasant. If that was the Station Chief, suddenly he was more interested in meeting her.

Footsteps approached from behind him, and he glanced back the way he had come. A woman with long, bone-straight blonde hair was walking in his direction, face down, examining a datapad. Spalding was no stranger to attractive women, but this one had something interesting. Her posture was absolutely perfect. Straight-backed, confident, and comfortable. Something about that natural poise had always been more attractive to him than the dramatic swaying some attractive woman did to accentuate their figure.

With the Station Chief not answering and a few hours to kill before 0800, he suddenly had a mind to have some company.

Like a ship on autopilot, the woman veered at the last moment to access the door and collided right with Spalding. Who, at that precise moment, had taken a breath to blurt out whichever random line came to mind first but instead said, "Hey, woah!"

The datapad went tumbling to the ground with a loud clatter that echoed down the empty concrete halls.

"Fuck!" came the woman's response.

The voice, although not nearly so sweet as in the recording, was the same from the door.

"Station Chief?" Spalding wished he hadn't sounded so choked up, but there was nothing for it now. That ship had sailed.

Station Chief Vidya Carson was the very definition of attractive. With the hair, and glacial-blue eyes, rosy high cheekbones, alabaster skin with a somewhat lavender undertone, and a lithe well-kept body. Despite the plain work outfit she wore, she could've been in an advertisement of her own.

For the first time in a *long* time, he found himself at a loss for words. Mouth open, catching flies.

"Sorry about that," she said, her voice was deep and velvety. "I am so used to not seeing a soul at this hour."

She noticed he was standing at the door then motioned for him to enter.

The door beeped and opened with a hiss.

Dumbly, he just mumbled something that sounded like a "thank you" and made his way inside.

The room was dimly lit, a cluttered mess of knickknacks stacked on shelf after shelf, which encircled the room from the left, around the back of the desk, and ending on the right near the door. A matched set of blue and white herringbone pincushion chairs that had seen better days flanked a glass-topped desk supported by a framework of hammered metal struts. There was even an old-style cigar ashtray propped up in one corner. Slightly rusted, and devoid of any ash, but still!

The room clashed with the woman so severely that Spalding found himself wondering if he had inadvertently become part of some intricate prank.

"Station Chief Carson?" he asked again.

The woman sat down heavily into her chair, and nodded as she reached underneath it to withdraw a coffee press.

"Vidya Carson?" Spalding asked again, before he could stop himself.

She smiled ruefully. "That's my name, but I must have missed yours, Mr…?"

Vesta was suddenly looking up.

"Jason Tyr," he said, and felt a surge of pride with how quick his response had been. *Didn't even have to think about it.*

Vidya laughed and set about the room gathering the necessary implements to make herself a cup of coffee.

What she found funny, he couldn't understand. His brows furrowed. Did she think his name was funny? What the hell? He had gone to *heroic* lengths to make sure there was no way to make fun of his name. No funny ways to misconstrue the letters, or rearrange them, or substitute letters or anything! What did she find so damned funny?

"Has that actually worked on anyone?" she finally said when her laughing quieted to a throaty chuckle.

"Has what worked?"

"That alias?"

Well, fuck!

Every response sounded somewhat childish in his mind. She knew. That was all that mattered. No denying it was going to change it.

"How?" was all he wound up saying.

As she sat, she eyed him thoughtfully. "Not even going to try to deny it, hmm?"

"Would it have helped?"

"Probably not," she winked, "but sometimes it's fun to banter anyway, don't you think?"

Against all reason, he found himself smiling at her. A full genuine smile. Not his fake flirtatious smile, but one that made the constricting feeling in his chest slacken somewhat.

"I do." Damn, but he found that he was beginning to genuinely *like* this lady!

"Have a seat, Jonathan," she said while she poured hot water from a heated container into her press. "You're going to make me spill this."

He did as instructed. And damn, but if the chair wasn't the most comfortable chair he had ever sat in. It accepted his weight like a childhood hug from his mother. If ever he was to regain some semblance of wealth, he'd have to ask where she had gotten these. He'd like to have a set himself.

The water mixed with the ground coffee beans, instantly filling the air with the bitter-earthy smell of freshly brewed coffee. There seemed to be a pattern forming here on Vesta—these people really enjoyed their coffee!

Unfortunately, it smelled incredible, and as Vidya took her first sip he found his mouth-watering.

"They sent me your file," she said, setting her mug down with a slight sigh of pleasure.

"Who did?" Nobody should know he was here!

"Your contact." She leaned forward and checked something on the glass desktop panel. "Jorge something or other? Sent it about the time I received your flight orders. Did you really expect people to not recognize you?"

Her laugh was light and breathy.

Spalding ground his teeth. Jorge had warned him against sending forged orders. *Unwanted attention*, was what he had called it. Foolish. He should have listened.

Vidya was studying him through long eyelashes.

"Well," he said slowly. That was that. "I'm just passing through, actually."

"No," she smiled, "you're not."

Totally off his game now, he felt his teeth click shut.

Standing, Vidya picked up her mug of coffee and walked over

to the back corner of the room. She pulled on one of the figurines on the shelf nearest the back wall. Suddenly, the whole back built-in unit of shelves sank into the floor on whisper-quiet tracks. Hidden behind the shelves was a floor-to-ceiling view overlooking the primary bays.

Huge freighters moved slowly around, with docking spires arrayed in an ever-widening circular pattern. The blackness of space stretching out above them was beautiful. Everything in sight was mostly black and dark gray, with stellar dust softening everything as if through a lens filter. Spalding thought it looked like a moving tenebrism painting.

"Like what you see?" Vidya said. There was… something… in her tone.

He raised his eyebrows at her slightly. "The view? Helps to have the corner office, or so I'm told."

A strategic sip of coffee hid what he thought was a sly smile.

Is she flirting with me?

Nothing about this encounter had been what he expected. Here he was, looking for a fresh start, for a place to hide. Instead, he was falling right back into the same patterns. The question wasn't *if* she was flirting, really. It was more *why* was she? There was probably no one more radioactive socially than he was.

When he didn't play along, she finally rolled her eyes and sighed heavily.

"All business," she drawled. "I get it. Let's talk shop."

"I'm just," he found himself defending himself, "in a weird place right now."

What am I doing?

Vidya gave him a look that was equal parts disappointment and sympathy.

"Anyway, about the view. I'd like you to run it."

Spalding's mouth fell open. "You *what?*"

"Not my job, obviously, but run the security wing here. There's a lot going on right now with everything on Mars and an uptick in pirate activity out here in the belt. Kuiper is evidently even worse. Though I find that hard to believe, they always say they have things worse." She rolled her eyes dramatically to express her feelings on that count.

That was not an offer he had anticipated. Hell, most of what he had expected was to be shown the door; that was doubly true given that his cover, such that it was, had been blown.

"What's the catch?" It was a fair question. He had no clout here.

She shrugged. "Ninety days probation, and you report directly to me."

The offer just kept getting better and better.

Something didn't feel right.

"I'll have to think on it," he said slowly.

"No," she said grinning the whole time, "you'll take it. And, at half the rate you quoted me."

With a chuckle, she tossed her datapad with his file displayed onto the tabletop.

"Half the—" he started.

"Less?" she retorted quickly, sounding hopeful.

"No," he said, raising his hands between them, "half is fine. More than fair, given my situation."

"Great, you fly with the team starting tomorrow. Get to know the crew and earn their trust. Until then, I've got quarters set up for you. You'll find the information has been added to your working dossier for the station. Don't worry, it's a local-only file."

Of course, that was exactly what had been on his mind.

He stood and extended his hand to her.

"Jonathan Spalding," he said, grinning. "it's a pleasure to be working with you, Vidya."

"That's Station Master Carson to you, scrub."

They laughed together.

Smiling broadly, Spalding turned to leave. When he reached the door, he heard a quick inhalation behind him.

He turned to find Vidya had turned to observe the working spaceport. "The crew knows who you are," she said over her shoulder. "I wouldn't embarrass yourself with that awful alias."

This time when he turned, the charming smile on his face slid almost instantly from his features. Replaced with a severe scowl. Holding up that act of being friendly or actually giving a shit about what happened to him had been exhausting.

It would have been so much better if he had been able to start over. Without an image to live up to, he could have just drifted through the rest of his life. Preferably drunk.

So, his dreams of interplanetary espionage and living life on the run had been dashed to bits in less than an hour. However, he'd get to keep flying. There was that.

In the end, that's all that really mattered.

Rather than go check out his quarters, which he assumed would be little more than a bunk in a closet-sized crew hold, he decided he'd go check out the security section of the port. If he was going to fly, he'd like to see what his ass would be in, especially with all this talk of pirate activity.

Spalding was no stranger to pirate combat.

Vesta Station was massive. Adverts flashing around the various terminals claimed it was the busiest port in the system. From the view he had experienced in Vidya's office, he'd wager the claims were not baseless boasts.

After following an almost indecipherable map, and then wandering around for another couple of hours, he finally found the security bay. The blast doors were sealed and locked tight. He almost decided to just walk on, maybe find something to eat and call it his first night home.

Then the door hissed open.

Captain William Hayes stepped out, tugging off the gloves from his flight suit.

Spalding almost threw up, right then and there.

"Well, well," Hayes said cheerfully, "look what that mess on

Mars washed up on our decks!"

The older man had deeply wrinkled ebony skin, buzzed and balding hair with a well-groomed silvery-gray full beard. His dark eyes twinkled kindly as he reached out to grasp Spalding by the shoulder.

Emotions warred within Spalding. Hayes had been the freighter captain who had rescued him after the Legion had met their fate.

He forced himself to smile. "Captain Hayes, what are you doing here?"

"Just wrapping up my workday."

Spalding took in the flight suit, security issue. "Security that tight they're calling up all the retirees?"

Hayes doubled over laughing and smacked Spalding a little heavier than was absolutely necessary on the shoulder. "You can say that again! I hear they're even taking washed-up would-be actors from the Protectorate these days."

That sliced pretty close to the bone.

Hayes sobered slightly. "You'll like it here. Good crew. Good equipment. The boss is fun, too."

Probably not a good way to start his new career by saying *that* was exactly what he was afraid of. Spalding had a dicey history when it came to mixing bosses and *fun.*

"Come on," Hayes said as he started walking away. "Come have a drink with us."

There was no way he could say no.

"Sure," he said.

Hopefully, they liked their liquor as much as they enjoyed their coffee. If he was going to hang out with the older captain, he'd need as much liquid resolve as he could stomach.

CHAPTER 23

THE SOUNDS OF gunfire echoed up and down the alleyway as Brennan sprinted down it.

"Go!" he shouted into the helmet comms.

The soldiers who had been protecting the mouth of the alleyway turned and sprinted toward him. It had been half an hour since they had last come under fire, but the fighting was thick all around them. A fire had broken out somewhere, the enormous cavern was full of a sinister dancing crimson and tangerine haze as smoke rapidly filled it. Embers danced like fireflies high into the air above.

As the soldiers passed him, he pulled up his rifle and joined them.

A chime sounded from his wrist-worn gauntlet datapad, the same kind he had worn in the Protectorate. The instincts had kicked back in, and he turned his wrist over to read while at a dead run.

His tactical map was updated with troop placements, potentially threatened zones, and extraction locations. He felt good knowing that their analysts were finally putting themselves to good use. This felt eerily similar to how his missions had felt with the Protectorate. That had been a *job* and this had been his *life*, though. The stakes were vastly different.

The energy level of his squad was flagging, he could tell. Every corner they took slower and slower.

"Keep up if you want to live," he growled into his squad channel.

There was no response. They likely didn't have the wind to spare.

The streets blurred by and visibility was being choked off.

According to this latest intelligence, they were less than a kilometer away from a potential extraction point, with ground carrier vehicles en route to scoop them up it looked like. That was good news.

Three different companies had been ordered to leave skeleton crews at the ADA installations they had captured to assist with the Protectorate push. It had been too little too late, unfortunately. There was good news, however, as the surprise pincer attack had worked as intended. The Protectorate had launched a full-court-press assault on the newly acquired base, with little regard for protecting their flanks. They must have assumed that was their single base of operations. Well, that trick wouldn't work again.

The strategy was still sound. Brennan was able to attack the flanks hard, inflicting massive losses on the unsuspecting rear units, and then fade back into the city and lose the tail in the streets.

From his tactical overview, he still had approximately five hundred troops in the area, a dozen squads all melting into the various extraction points in the city. Guerrilla tactics were not his strength, but he definitely saw the advantages easily enough. With a little elbow grease and proper intel, they could really cause a lot of damage.

For possibly the first time, he thought they might actually stand a chance against the mighty Protectorate Forces. Still slim, but it wasn't certain death.

"I can't see shit, sir!" The comms crackled in his ear.

They weren't kidding; the smoke was becoming increasingly difficult to navigate. For the tenth time in as many minutes, Brennan silently thanked whoever was feeding them their data from CENOPS. That was saving their asses right now.

"Two blocks up and one over," he huffed out as he ran. "Then we're home free."

No response was forthcoming, and that suited Brennan just fine. For many, this was the first military action they had ever seen. There were a few veterans among the McAaron employees, but not too many who had seen anything more than a few pirate riots.

Brennan himself had been mostly regulated to desk duty prior to the assassination of Motwani. Being as high up in the Protectorate as he had been, the only action he typically saw were tours around the training grounds. All that had changed with the investigation. Funny, at the time he was thrilled to be out from behind the bureaucracy and bullshit. Now, he was beginning to feel like he had been played for a patsy from the very beginning.

They reached the corner of the block they intended to turn, and Brennan shook the thoughts from his mind. This was neither the time nor the place to lose focus. A wandering mind could get him, or his soldiers, killed. Everything else could wait. Stay mission-focused—that was the rule.

At a signal from Brennan, they slammed against the wall at the corner, stacking up shoulder-to-shoulder, the rear soldiers covering their backs. It was sloppy, but they had only been training a few weeks. And most of that had been without proper gear, so it was going to feel different now. They showed initiative. He was certain they would improve.

A quick glance around the corner didn't reveal any immediate threats.

Something didn't feel right to him, though.

"Who's got the M-O-H?" The multi-optical helmet was a

specialty piece of equipment that would overlay several wavelengths of the electromagnetic spectrum together and create an amalgam virtual image. Creating a customizable type of x-ray vision. It penetrated smoke, concrete, darkness, and up to three inches of solid steel.

One of the soldiers in the middle scooted forward in the pack and leaned around the corner. Faint tinting of the visor was the only indication she had initiated the optical array.

"There's a couple squads of soldiers in positions covering this street." She pointed to three separate locations. "There, there, and there."

Brennan checked his gauntlet again. They were the only friendlies in the area.

Shit!

"Send me the data on their locations." In a Protectorate squad, they would have transmitted the information up the chain of command without being told. These rebels weren't there yet.

Within a few moments, Brennan had the images and general distances of the soldiers.

Six soldiers each, in loose formation.

He couldn't be sure, but it sure felt like SPECOPS units to him.

Which meant it was likely Manu and his units.

That meant they already knew they were here.

"Abort," Brennan said, turning. "They...."

A flash of white filled his vision.

Sound suddenly vanished.

Without knowing how he had gotten there, he was on the ground, looking at the canopy covering the city far overhead.

Brennan *hated* flashbangs.

All around him, his soldiers were sprawled out, stunned.

He shouted at them to shake it off, to get to their feet, to *move!* He couldn't even hear his own voice, just the faintest ringing noise beginning to be audible.

Instead of wasting more effort, he hauled himself dizzyingly to his feet where he swayed like a tree about to topple. Once he was somewhat stable, he began to pull those nearest him up. Some readily complied; others seemed too disoriented to know what was happening and resisted.

As he got them to their feet, he shoved them in the direction they had come.

He was proud to see some of those he had helped up, now helping others to their feet. It was that kind of mentality that would win the day, every time.

Someone shouted something over his shoulder, and he spun in time to see them take a knee and open fire down the street. The hidden units were advancing. Brennan immediately recognized the units, and the person leading the advanced unit. His old buddy Sundara Manu.

If they caught them, they'd be dead before they knew what hit them.

"Go!" He roared it with all the breath in his lungs, but it sounded faint, distorted like he was shouting through jelly.

Surprisingly, the advancing units did not return fire. Instead, they moved cover-to-cover, and pressed onward at a steady pace. Not the way *he* would have done it, but Manu had always approached things in an odd way. Favoring the *how* something was done over the *what* was done. Whatever the thought process was, he was grateful to not be riddled with bullets already.

Or, they were under orders to capture them alive.

That wasn't a great thought.

Most of his squad were stumbling down the street the way they had come now. With a little push of encouragement, the few stragglers joined him jogging back.

He was grateful the dense smoke was there. Within a few dozen meters they had lost sight of the street corner where the enemy would be in mere moments.

Thank God for small favors, or however that saying went.

Unfortunately, they were now backtracking toward the staccato report of vehicle-mounted high-caliber weapons and persistent small-arms fire. It echoed down the concrete corridors and reverberated through the soles of his boots.

"CENOPS, Vandal actual, we need a new RP, previous compromised." He had considered doubling back to the original rendezvous point. The risk was just too high. Plus, with the history between him and Manu, he couldn't trust his instincts. Everything he had been trained to do, Manu would be expecting.

Brennan needed to start thinking like an insurgent, not a soldier.

"Take the next left, and double-back into that commercial structure halfway down the block." It would trap them, but if they could blind his optics for a moment, they might be able to utilize the confusion to get to the extraction point they were already near.

As they rounded the corner, Brennan called back to headquarters, "OPS, Vandal, we need some EMVI centered on our position." He read back the grid code off his gauntlet, knowing they had the same information but redundancy made for accuracy.

"Copy, Vandal, deploying electronic visual interference to your AO. Two minutes."

He smiled. They might actually live through today!

Damn, but it felt good to be able to call in strategic packages. They had drone swarms, tactical equipment, ECM deployables. They even had a few ground-to-ground rocket packages. Not that he had any intention of bombing his own people, but it was a comfort to have. EMVI was not something he would normally call in, as it was more a SOCOM order, but knowing he had some toys to play with brightened his day a little.

"Vandal, delivering your package in, three, two, one."

A scream sounded high above the rooftops, skimming just below the canopy. A pair of drones moving so fast the air tore around them, leaving long swirling tubes of smoke.

Then their electronics went dead.

The gauntlet showed nothing but static.

Comms were down.

Optics were shot.

Brennan released the visor-lock and flipped up the clear barrier. Instantly his throat and eyes burned with the acrid smoke. The rest of his squad was doing the same. A few retched, either from the smoke inhalation or fatigue; he wasn't sure.

"Inside, move it!"

They had approximately ten minutes before the electronic countermeasures would wear off. Less if they were unlucky.

What he was hoping they could do would be to get inside the building and into the basement. MOH technology could only penetrate the ground about six meters, and with the angle it wouldn't be enough. Manu would know they had gone to ground, but not which building. They'd have to search door-to-door, and Brennan hoped they'd be long gone by that point.

The squad approached the front sets of doors at a dead run. The glass was already broken, likely from the nearby artillery fire, which was most unfortunate. Any signs of forced entry would prioritize higher in a search. There was nothing he could do now; their path was set.

Like most commercial-style buildings, this one had a foyer with elevator banks, a receptionist and waiting area, even a decorative fountain bubbling away peacefully in the center. Several unmarked doors dotted each wall.

"Spread out, find the stairs." Brennan ran to the far wall, the same that housed the elevators, and started opening doors. Whenever he encountered a locked one, he'd just move on. Stairwells shouldn't be locked, regardless of the building, according to fire codes. Given just how serious a fire was in the tightly packed Martian cities, every precaution was taken.

"Here!" someone shouted. It was so quiet compared to having everyone inside his helmet via the comms, he almost ignored it.

The squad ran over to the doorway, concrete and steel stairs circled downward.

Brennan cleared the landing area and peered up through the dim lighting above. The landings appeared to be sectioned off by fire-rated doors. That was good. Brennan preferred to not be someone's "lucky shot" down eighty floors of steps from a roof.

When the last of his squad had cleared, Brennan pulled the door mostly shut behind them, and withdrew a sealant-charge from his armored vest. The small charge was used to seal doors and windows as a defensive strategy. He wadded it up and jammed it into the latch mechanism in the door and shouldered it fully closed.

A moment later there was a hiss and pop, as the pressure-activated charge welded the latch mechanism to the door frame.

As he turned, Brennan pointed down then put a finger over his lips. From here on out, they'd have to be quiet. There were other ways to locate them that had nothing to do with the eyes.

Quietly as they could, the squad moved in a tight formation down the first landing.

As the first sub-floor door came up, they fanned out and opened it slowly, utilizing angles to peer onto the next landing.

The two soldiers clearing the room motioned onward.

They repeated this process three more times.

Then they ran out of stairs.

Brennan glanced around the room, trying to gauge their depth and the thickness of the walls. He wasn't certain it was deep enough to avoid detection by a MOH, but it was what they had to work with.

Suddenly a boom sounded from several floors above them.

Likely someone trying the door they had sealed.

The group spread out along the square room, with just two doors to cover it made the location a decent place to make a stand. There was the door that led up, and a door that led out into whatever rooms this sub-level held. The unit made for the door, but Brennan stopped them and pointed to his ear, waggling his finger in a "no" gesture.

Using hand signals, Brennan arranged his troops two-by-two at various points in the room and assigned shooting lanes. It wouldn't do to have them all shooting each other if it came to a firefight.

More distant sounds could be heard above now. Very faint, but definitely in the building. For a moment he had hoped perhaps it was just artillery fire. That had a very distinct sound, and he could tell the difference.

The room was dusty. Between the smoke and the dust, Brennan could feel his nose start to tickle. He hated not having a sealed helmet. It drove him completely nuts. There were so many advantages to the damned things!

Everyone was still breathing heavily from their city-level sprints. Despite that, everyone was stacked up tightly, kneeling down, angled to the doorways, rifles held at the ready. Brennan was proud of them. They looked like the real deal. If he had just walked onto the scene without knowing any better, he would have mistaken them for Protectorate trained troops.

Another boom sounded from above. It was probably his imagination, but it sounded closer this time.

Brennan checked his data feed; it was still out.

If they got their electronics back online before they left the building, they would do a MOH sweep, and they'd find them huddled a few floors beneath them.

There was nothing in the worlds he hated more than being a sitting duck. Far better to die with a chance of survival than in a self-made coffin.

Crouching low, and rolling his steps to quiet the movement, he made his way to the upper-level door. The soldiers adjacent to the door gave him a confused glare. He signaled they should stay where they were.

Then, using the muzzle of his rifle, he slowly and silently

eased the door open a crack. Silence. One heartbeat. Silence. Two heartbeats. Silence. He eased into the door swinging it further open. The dark stairwell was empty as near as he could tell.

Staying low and moving slowly, he leaned out to the center of the chamber and followed the muzzle of his rifle up into the stairwell. The next level door was still closed. If he had had the time, he would've tried to weld-seal every door, just to stall the enemy.

A crash came from above.

He didn't think it sounded much like a door, more like something falling to the floor. Maybe they were trashing the upstairs looking for them.

A chirp sounded inside his helmet, and he swore silently.

The gauntlet's datapad on his wrist illuminated dimly, as it reset.

Time was up.

He made his decision.

He turned and snuck back into the room with his squad. Everyone was looking at their wrist-worn gauntlet computers.

"Okay, we need to move. We have to put distance between us."

They took the only other door available to them.

Thankfully, it wasn't locked. Brennan eased the door open silently. He felt it catch on some debris along the ground a moment before it started to screech. One of his soldiers bent down and used his hand to dust the area and clear the tiny rock. They all stood quietly, hoping to not hear any sounds of chase from above.

After a few moments, Brennan nodded and eased the door open the rest of the way.

A long sub-building corridor ran into darkness. Only dim amber emergency lights illuminated the way. Evidently, the artillery in the area had knocked out partial power. He hoped that worked in their favor, and not in the Protectorates.

Two soldiers took up defensive positions at the door to cover the rest as they entered the corridor, Brennan at the lead.

When they had all gone through, the two followed slowly, watching their backs, after easing the door closed.

This was the delicate balance every soldier endeavored to avoid. Run or fight? Speed or force? Brennan was typically in the latter camp for both. His philosophy was a strong and overwhelming offense was the best defense.

He knew for certain Manu prescribed to the same philosophy.

So, he'd rather not find out exactly how that would turn out.

They moved in a low crouch as quickly as stealth would allow. He counted off the distance in his head. Ten meters. Twenty. Thirty. At fifty, he started to rise out of his crouch and increase his speed. At this distance sound carrying shouldn't be an issue.

Within the next twenty meters they were all-out running again.

What is this place?

It appeared to be some kind of loading tunnel, from what the markings on the walls and ground indicated at least. There were loader tracks everywhere, and after a distance from the stairwell they came across more doors. As they sped past, they stepped into the alcoves to check the door panels. All were locked up tight, just like he had estimated. These were surely business storage from the companies who occupied the building above.

When they had passed through the collection of doors, Brennan almost stumbled as the ground under his feet began to slope gradually upward. Probably leading to a surface-level freight dock.

He checked his tactical map.

They would likely still be in the immediate search area from the enemy units. Depending on how far away this loading dock was, they could technically squirt around back to their original EP. It was going to be a risk.

Going back was not an option, so he kept driving on.

His dad had a saying, "If you're going to do something you know is stupid, might as well do a knockout job at it."

Full speed ahead!

They didn't have long to run as they came upon a set of massive metal doors whose windows showed the warehouse and loading bay behind.

The bad news was it wasn't nearly far enough to feel safe.

However, there was some good news. The room was absolutely littered with stacked shipping crates the size of a small vehicle and lit by a single amber overhead that barely penetrated fifty meters in the center of the room. If they could get across the expansive building, that *should* give them a straight shot back to their previous rendezvous point and hopefully a personnel carrier waiting to scoop them up.

As usual, he led the way into the darkness.

He switched on his enhanced night-vision and scanned the room.

"M-O-H, give me a scan."

The same soldier was already moving up to scan the room. Once done, she shook her head, her voice came in solid, "Empty."

"Let's go."

They followed in a tight line, close enough to reach out and grab each other by the trailing shoulder, rifles ready. Staying low and moving from cover to cover, they waded into the dimly lit room.

That's when they heard the explosion behind them.

A hot violent puff of air ripped out of the corridor they had just been in.

The building groaned violently around them in protest.

They all stopped on instinct, dropping to their knees and training their rifles at their designated areas of responsibility.

"That was awfully big for a door," someone said through the comms.

"Could've been artillery, but I don't think so," Brennan said, "move, move."

They resumed their egress.

Brennan felt his guts tying up into knots. The timing was too good. If they recovered the use of their optics systems the same time he had, they would've found the sealed door and realized it was a stairwell down. If they had a demo specialist with them, that was just about the right amount of time to set up and blow a charge. It fit the timeline.

Odds were, they had at least a couple squads hot on their trail.

Scanning his surroundings, the crates and darkness provided decent initial cover. Obviously, with their advanced optics, the darkness wouldn't do much for long, but for that initial exchange, it would help. They could technically make a decent stand here.

He knew there were other units out there, and once they had blown the door, they would have deployed troops to cover all the sub-level exits. Which, to the best of his knowledge, was just this single one. Trapped between the two.

Run or fight?

The decision always came down to that.

Shit!

Brennan pulled up into a group of crates arranged in roughly a 'C' shape.

His troops were winded again, their conditioning nowhere near as good as his was. Which was to be expected, given these soldiers had been merely tradespeople at best, desk-clerks at worst just a matter of weeks ago.

"Set up a perimeter in this position." He indicated the semi-circle of crates. "Teams one and two will cover the door, they're going to try to flank us from the other exit, so the rest of the teams will provide cover on our flanks."

There were more nervous glances than he would've preferred, but that was also to be expected.

"Hey," he said, smacking his fist into the chest plate of the MOH-wearing woman, "this is what we trained for. We have the advantage in position. I could hold this all day long by myself, with all of you. It'll be a walk in the park."

Not one for fancy speeches, he smiled and leveled his rifle at the door they had entered from.

Everyone else followed orders.

"Nobody fire until I give the word. The element of surprise is our biggest advantage here. They're going to expect us to be high-tailing it out of here as fast as we can go. They won't be expecting a fight. Don't get excited and blow that chance."

The wait wasn't overly long.

A rifle muzzle peeked through the door, and as it swung open, Brennan felt the tension of the other soldiers around him.

At least two dozen heavily armed soldiers in dove-gray spread out from the door.

The last to come through was one that Brennan recognized, even at this distance.

"Keith!" Sundara Manu said, using his external speakers, the word boomed across the cavernous warehouse.

It took Brennan a minute to realize he was calling him by his first name. Nobody did that. Hell, not even Brennan referred to himself internally by his first name.

Brennan didn't engage his mic, but he swore a litany of curses that would've made the foulest mouthed sonofabitch wither and die. Colorful wouldn't have even begun to describe it.

A few loud concussions echoed across the vast expanse.

Smoke spilled from the canisters as they bounced amongst the boxes.

Within a few breaths, the room was a smear of orange-gray smoke.

Brennan switched to his advanced vision, but he knew it was pointless.

The smoke was not your usual garden variety. This was actually ionized carbon dust, specifically meant to block optics. Not even a MOH would penetrate this barrier. They had missed their chance. The enemy was now just as dug in and protected as they were. This would now be a brutal firefight.

"They know our positions," Brennan said over the internal comms. "Fireteams pair off and work your way toward the rear exit. More units will be closing in. Our only hope is to beat them to the way out. Once clear, run for the rendezvous and don't look back."

With that, he tapped his partner on the back. The freckle-faced Matviy Aubrey looked at him with wide, terrified eyes.

Brennan pushed a fist into his own chest, then into Matviys.

"You watch my back, and I've got yours," he said, switching to the direct channel.

Matviy just nodded and shouldered his rifle a little higher.

Crouching low, asses damn near pressed together, the two wandered out into the sea of smoke.

It didn't take long for the first shots to ring out.

Unfortunately, they came from behind them and their planned escape route, not from in front of them. They were pinned in.

CHAPTER 24

"WHAT THE HELL, Colt?" Marconi barked from across the room.

Lisa jerked her head up from her datapad.

Marconi and Azarov were both staring at her from the doorway.

Seeing her sitting at the table, feet curled up under her, datapad in her lap, and the blank expression on her face, both looked at her critically.

"What?" she asked, confused.

"The 1800 briefing on maneuvers?" Azarov said, with a little more accusation than she liked. Marconi just scoffed, rolled his eyes, and strode back out into the hallway. Going to his quarters, most likely.

That's when it hit her.

Shit!

She had completely forgotten about the briefing scheduled for today. How the hell had she let that slip? An ass-chewing was in her near future.

"Yeah," Azarov said with mock severity, "*that* one."

Missing the briefing frustrated Lisa, sure, but it was probably a good thing she had not gone. Her knee-jerk reaction to the situation would be to fake sick, cover her neglect up somewhat. It would also serve double-duty, and she'd say she had been confined to quarters for most of the last few days. That way, if anyone suspected her of anything, she at least had a preliminary alibi.

The stress of what she had done compounded with the guilt. One thing she was immensely grateful for was the full knowledge that she should *never* go into any kind of espionage. She was *terrible* at it!

Between the guilt, the worry, and the stress, she was near sick enough to fail a physical.

"Bring me up to speed," she asked of Azarov. "I haven't been feeling right since we arrived."

The squad room was relatively large here on Nemesis, cozy even. Azarov stood at a bank of lockers, fishing some of his personal items from them. He eyed her skeptically before he slammed the locker closed.

"Fine, but just this once. I'd hate for my CO to acquire the nasty habit of skipping mission briefings." He grinned.

Lisa frowned thoughtfully as he pulled up a chair and sat next to her. She hadn't been feeling herself lately. The whole business with Spalding had turned her world upside down. There had to be some kind of resolution to that. For the first time in her career, hell, *her life*, she was questioning if she was on the right path. All she had ever wanted was to be the best pilot in the Fleet. Now, suddenly, as far as stats went anyway, she was. That honor didn't feel earned. It felt scummy.

Plus, she felt a closeness to Spalding. What had happened to him didn't seem fair. That bothered her on a deeply emotional level. Enough that she was sneaking around, playing at being a spy, and ignoring her duties as a leader, on her first *real* assignment, no less.

He did what she asked and brought her up to speed on the briefing. For the most part, it was standard information for their new deployment. Being on a larger station meant things would operate mostly how she was used to, with the exception of water shortages. That was new. They evidently only received water shipments every other month, so everyone was rationed on their consumption, and usage was strictly monitored.

They discussed the rise in pirate activity in the area, the whole *alleged* reason for Lisa and her squad to be there in the first place. While the data did show an uptick, it was nothing dramatic. Probably just seizing the opportunity the unrest on Mars was creating. Likely it would die back down to normal levels once a proper show of force was experienced. Easy to prey on unarmed freight haulers, it was a whole different story when ships returned fire.

After he concluded his retelling of the briefing, which was wildly thorough, and he had answered a few of her questions, Azarov left her to her thoughts.

That was the *last* thing she wanted.

For some reason, spending time with just Azarov made her think of Spalding. She found her thoughts drifting back to him. What her mother had done wasn't fair. Not that she knew exactly what had happened *yet*, but she knew her mother well enough to know it would be diabolic. That fact pained her to admit. The blood of her mother ran in her own veins.

Not that Lisa, for even an instant, felt capable of betraying the trust of anyone, let alone a member of her team.

There had to be a way for her to figure out what had been done to Spalding. Even someone as brilliant and cunning as her mother was bound to leave a trail. Especially someone with her power and influence, as they were prone to get careless. Right?

What she needed was her guardian angel to just go ahead and give her the information she had been looking for.

A thought occurred to her, and she bolted upright.

There were places within the network you could go to post job duties, put items up for sale, or whatever. Maybe she'd advertise for a hacker.

Except, hacking was illegal.

She frowned and bit her lip, deep in thought.

If there was a way she could post that she was looking for something close, with some kind of code phrase or something…

How would she discover the code phrase?

The idea seemed riddled with pitfalls. Plus, the Protectorate didn't take too kindly to their own committing felony electronic theft from inside their own stations. Or anywhere else, for that matter.

Thinking it through, she decided it would be best to post something generic and plan a face-to-face. Leaving a paper trail seemed like a bad move.

The door burst open, and Azarov stepped in, wide-eyed.

"We're scrambling," he said, just as amber lights begin to pulse around the perimeter of the room, a pleasant-sounding voice activating squad numbers and which bays to report to. "Pirates are after a freighter convoy. It's big! Let's go!"

Lisa jumped to her feet, then glanced down at her screen.

"Let's go, Colt!" Azarov said and bounded away down the hall.

She zipped up her flight suit to her chin and bent over the keypad. As quick as she was able, she posted a query in the job-postings section: <CORRUPT FILES. NEED COMPUTER ASSISTANCE. PAYS WELL.>

Then she created an anonymous message account and used that as the contact information.

Dashing from the room, she felt instant regret. Had she just gotten herself into even more trouble? Nothing was more prone to failure and disaster than rushing through something half-baked.

As she neared the flight deck and the adjoining locker room, the foot traffic increased dramatically. There was a hum of hushed chatter among the pilots and support crew.

Lisa pushed her way to her locker and keyed the code to access the contents. Marconi was already mostly suited up, with Azarov halfway there. Neither spared her a moment's notice, although she could tell Marconi was holding back by the set of his jaw.

With her flight suit already on, over top of her second-skin pressure suit, it was just a matter of connecting the biometric monitors and flight harness. This particular exercise had been repeated with such regularity in her life that she could practically do it blindfolded and half-asleep.

Marconi and Azarov finished their prep, grabbed their helmets, and sped off toward the bay. If roles had been reversed, she would've waited for either or both of them. In fact, truth be told, the roles were *often* reversed, now that she thought about it! More times than she could count were spent waiting for those two knuckleheads to finish their bullshit and get onto the flight deck.

They were just pissy because she had more important things to do right now than them. Petty of them, sure, but she had to admit the behavior for her was probably alarming. A new station, a new mission, away from the supposed support of her family and Olumide. Maybe they thought she was breaking under all the strain? Nothing to be said over the fact they had *just* gotten there. God forbid one of them actually ask her how she was feeling!

Well, Azarov had, she recalled. So, there was that.

Lisa leaned down and shoved the reservoir to her CXD—combat-extender-device—into the calf pocket of her exterior pressure suit. The porous collection system was integrated into the crotch inside of the suit. The nifty unit would automatically detect the presence of urine and pump it into the bag she now wore at her calf, making it possible to sit in a cockpit for hours. Thus, the system was nicknamed "cockpot."

All that done and sorted, she scooped up her helmet and tucked it under her arm before dashing out the door and onto the flight deck. On Nemesis Station, each fighter was locked onto the side via the cockpit passthrough, the craft hanging like bats nestled into a dangling perch upside down. The cockpits were kept in a partially deployed state, with a small airlock between the station and the interior. This allowed for extremely rapid deployment versus the slower carrier method, which relayed on a conveyance.

Marconi and Azarov were already doing their pre-flight checks when she took the steps to her airlock two at a time. Using the momentum, she grabbed the circular ring around the top of the seal and swung in feet first. She hit the seat hard enough to bite her tongue a little, but she bet it looked dramatic as hell.

Now inside the cockpit of a spacecraft, she felt herself relax.

The rest of her life could be total chaos and half a heartbeat from turning to shit. But, get her in a cockpit, and the world was right again.

Her comms crackled to life in her helmet as she zipped through her own preflight protocols.

"We get any details on the engagement?" Lisa asked.

"Negative," Marconi responded.

"Anyone else think it's a bit coincidental we have this big briefing about pirate activity in our AOR," Azarov mused, "then suddenly, here we are? Exactly the thing we just discussed being a possibility?"

Lisa smiled but didn't respond. She knew what came next.

"Shut up, Azarov." Marconi's voice was thick with mock patience. He really was a master of the facetious responses.

"No?" Azarov whined. "I'm really the only one that thinks it's just a tad bit *strange*?"

"We never decided if we were keeping our Academy callsigns," she gasped dramatically, hoping to ease the tension in the group somewhat. "Hell, we can even apply for a squad name now that we're on active!"

There was no response.

Oh fine, be that way!

"Mother, this is CCF bravo flight leader, designation CCF-bravo-one," Lisa said, a bit disheartened to have not been able to use an *official* callsign on her first real deployment. "We are green across the board and ready for separation."

There was a slight pause.

"Bravo-one, you are go."

Two manual toggles, and she throttled up.

Marconi and Azarov were right on her tail, the two new pilots to their little flight group out wide as flankers.

Damn, it felt good to be flying again!

The computer began calculating the best attack vector to take to the engagement. Their area of responsibility was considerably larger than she had anticipated. The attack was well within reach of the CCF attack group.

On her sensor screen, flowing from the station like bees from a hive, were at least three full squads of close combat fighters. Each flight would have anywhere from three to six craft in it and have a flight leader. Each of those flight leaders would report up to the squadron leader, who then would report to the commanding officer of the station.

All that information would've been really handy. If only she had shown up to her briefing. Of all the times to miss something…

Azarov was right; it felt too coincidental.

Her flight computer chirped at her.

Data was coming in from the long-range scanners on the station and subsequently was being uploaded to their systems.

"Are you guys seeing this?" Marconi said over their flight-only comms.

On the screen was a massive swarm of heat signatures, tiny pin-pricks of orange-red globes of light, blurring around a central larger signature. There were dozens of craft besieging that freighter.

Lisa flipped to command-tactical-comms, "Bravo-one to Squad Leader."

"Go for Bricks," came the terse reply.

Bricks? Wonder what the story is with that callsign?

"Recommend we push the envelope on this, sir. Our package is heavily engaged."

There was a pause, and Lisa willed the man on the other side to see reason.

"Affirmative, have your flight push ahead; we'll swing out and come in hot. Out."

Smiling, Lisa switched back to flight-only. "Let's put the metal down, shall we?"

As she throttled up, Marconi and Azarov matching her, half of the squad broke off to swing around wide. They would be somewhat delayed, but it was a solid strategy. Lisa and her units would be the tip of the spear, then they'd come in and mop up.

"Finally getting that action you've been wanting, eh, Marconi?" She was hoping to cheer him up.

"Copy that," came his disappointing reply.

If he wanted to act like a petulant child who wasn't getting his way, so be it. She was dealing with enough distractions as it was. The last thing she needed was some asshole getting in her head too.

Sorry, this pattern is full.

The time had long since passed that she should have her head in the game. She wasn't in the mood to die without a freaking callsign, that was for certain!

The computer adjusted her attack vector options automatically to adjust for her increased velocity. They would slam into the back of the crowd and lead with their high-velocity kinetic rounds. Then, as it got nasty and up-close, they'd switch to their mini-missile compliments. Each tracking projectile utilized an armor-penetrating round that would fire on the enemy ship within a specified proximity. So, they were less missiles and more close-proximity self-propelled mini cannons. Lisa had never had the opportunity to play with them, she was excited to give them a test drive.

Sure, she had used them in simulations, but never the real thing.

Another chirp from her computer.

Updated time to engagement, three minutes.

This was it. If they were going to bug out, now would be the time.

"Everyone see the plan? Go in hard and strong," she said to Marconi and Azarov, hoping they would follow orders despite their irritation with her. "We'll pound them with the forward guns, swing around, and lay into them with the MM payload. Copy?"

"Copy," Azarov said immediately.

Lisa waited.

"Copy," Marconi was *still* acting all disgruntled! Was he twelve?

Two minutes.

"Weapons hot!"

Lisa activated her main weapon systems. Several augmented reality controls hovered over her flight control sticks and system panels. The guidance display was also different; an overlay of target data, tracking reticles, and hit-probability danced and flickered across her screen. She recalled how dizzying the first few combat simulations had been when all this data cascaded across her canopy screens. Now, it was like chocolate. Something she yearned for, hungrily. The more data, the better.

This close, her systems had much more accurate data than the long-range scanners from the station. There was thirty-two craft in total, minus the one beleaguered freighter.

The scene that played out on her scanners had an eerie reminiscence to the *Purdue* simulation she had run alongside the Undead Legion and Spalding.

Except, in this scenario, real lives were at stake.

And, there was no doubt who the bad guys were. Gases were venting in an iridescent plume from the massive freighter. Little speckles appeared all over the hull with little bursts of light flickering like stars. Plasma torches. They were cutting into the armor plating, trying to breach the hull. The dark specks were mobile airlocks. Kind of like inflatable life-rafts that would seal on the side of the hull and allow boarding parties to enter then seal up airtight. Once they cut through into the pressurized portion of the ship, it would fill the cylindrical tube and allow an equalization.

It was something Lisa had studied at the Academy but never actually seen in action. One had to be pretty damn ballsy to trust a thin film of nanopolymer to the vacuum of space. Not her cup of tea, that was for sure.

Thirty seconds!

Lisa engaged the optical tracker and began to prioritize her targets for the forward guns. The kinetic rounds were brutal, impacting with incredible force at this speed. It helped that the carbon-nanotube-coated osmium rounds were *dense*!

Several of the enemy craft were pulling away from their perimeter to engage the new threat. Their movements were sloppy and uncoordinated.

"Engage!" Lisa roared into her comms.

A vibration filled the cockpit, a slight hum the only real noise. She had heard these things test fire in the atmosphere once. Even several hundred meters away, the sheer decibel level had left her mostly without hearing for three days. Now, even seated no more than a couple meters from the gun, most of the sound was lost to the relative void of space.

The white-hot rounds streaked across the projected view inside her canopy. Each hit registered within the HUD, the barrage from the three fighters tore through the sluggishly moving enemy craft. Four confirmed targets vaporized within a matter of seconds.

Then, they streaked by, initiating their return arc in perfect unison.

Like most battles, training and discipline could override numbers if appropriately used.

On their second pass, the pirate force had mostly recovered from that initial engagement and returned fire.

A *damned lot* of fire!

Lisa had to slide-roll out of harm's way and almost clipped Azarov in the process. They were flying "tight" even though they were hundreds of kilometers away from each other. The speeds in space boggled the mind. Still, flying synchronized as they did came with some risks.

Thankfully, technology had worked out how to control the g-forces and reduce the risk of being jellified by such extreme speeds and maneuvering in space. Even with that, the sudden change of trajectory pulled at her body and face. It always made her teeth throb for some reason.

"Bravo-one, this is Bricks, we are thirty seconds out, coming in one twenty mark, sixty-two, mark forty-four."

Lisa confirmed the three-dimensional trajectory matched what she had with her systems.

"Confirmed, all. Welcome to the party."

As she used her momentum to circle around on top of and behind the enemy, Marconi and Azarov pummeled the center of the enemy flight group. The rest of their units would be slamming into the trailing edge of that assault and hopefully mop up what was left.

Quick, easy, textbook.

Red lights erupted across her control panel, painting the entirety of her cockpit in the crimson glow. One of the enemy craft had locked on with a guided missile.

Alarms sounded.

She had incoming.

Whenever anyone asked her if she was ever scared of being shot down, or of death, she always shrugged. Just part of the job. What impressed her most was that her training kicked in. There was no panic, no frantic fumbling about. She knew what needed to be done, and if she executed the procedure well, she *could* live through this attack.

She rotated her craft ninety degrees, pointing straight "up" relative to the trajectory of the streaking missile, then she waited. When she felt the missile had reached top speed and was a little less than halfway to her, she slammed the throttle to full, altering her momentum into a steep collapsing arc. Then, she deployed several decoys, which were fist-sized white-hot burning short-living drones that would replicate her sensor data and hopefully confuse the tracking systems on the missile.

Thankfully, the missile took the bait and streaked off to explode a distance away from her.

Warnings flashed again.

Incoming kinetic fire ripped at her ship.

The impacts sounded like they were underwater, all bass.

So powerful were the hits that it altered the trajectory of her ship enough that she started an uncontrolled spin. The gyroscopic nature of the craft made it survivable, albeit incredibly nauseating and difficult to get out of.

More alarms sounded as the enemy fired at her tumbling craft.

Lisa wrestled with the flight sticks in an effort to reduce the spin and bring the craft back under control.

Meanwhile, the computer was giving her a line-by-line report on the damaged systems.

Mostly ancillary systems, but she'd hear about it back on the flight deck from the Chief, that was for sure.

"Need some help over here!" Marconi yelled.

Where were Brick and his flankers?

The CCF fighter finally came into a controllable alignment, although she was listing to one side. Likely venting something from the port-side, with how it felt. Not critical yet.

She flipped her nose over in a tight roll and began a retro burn to reverse direction. Marconi and Azarov both had no fewer than four enemy pilots on their tails. Worse still, the boarding procedures appeared to be mostly completed as most of the attached inflatable airlocks had been pressurized all around the freighter. Which meant the boarding parties were, even now, slaughtering the civilians inside.

That's when Brick and the flankers streaked in from her left. A glittering barrage of kinetic fire sprang to life like a line of iridescent flames between them and several of the craft harassing her wingmen. Now the fight was incredibly lopsided.

Not what was happening inside.

"Brick, Bravo-one, are there marines en route?" Lisa had only seen CCF and close-support craft launching, but there could have been another bay launching marine shuttles.

"Negative Bravo-one," Brick replied solemnly.

Then they were too late. The freighter would be a loss, and they'd have to shoot it down. That was the protocol. Protect it, but do not let them get away with the property. Protect or destroy.

The situation just went from bad to worse. Thinking on her feet, Lisa thumbed the comm control over to the designated freighter channel. "This is Protectorate CFF Bravo-one, is there anyone on comms?"

The channel crackled to life. The sound of screams, gunfire, and chaos mingled with a frantic voice. "We need help in here!"

Her gut clenched. There was no help coming.

"What's the situation in there? How many of them are there? Are you in a secure position?" She felt like an asshole asking someone who was under threat so many questions, but she needed more information in order to make an informed decision.

"There's a dozen or so," a potent scream ripped through the comms, the speaker breathing heavily as if running, "we're trying to hold the bridge now."

A dozen. Three verses twelve were long odds. Reports on the pirates said they were only loosely organized, lacking proper training. Could their primary combat training trump the four-to-one odds?

Something had to be done, or they'd lose the freighter and the people on board.

Lisa couldn't let that happen and live with it.

"I'm going in." She rolled hard into an approach to the freighter's exterior dock. Switching to the TACCOM channel. "Mother, I need the freighter dock codes!"

"Hold two, Bravo," the reply was tense. There was only one reason she would need dock codes.

A chime indicated a private squad communication. "Are you out of your fucking mind?" Marconi yelled into the comms.

"We're not marines, Colt!" Azarov echoed.

"No," she kept the line to TACCOM open but muted her mic on that channel to address her two rattled pilots, "we are not marines, but we are soldiers. I'm not going to fly around and watch that crew get murdered or murder them myself. I'm going in but won't order you to do so. If I lose control in there, follow the protocols."

Silence.

"You're crazy!" Marconi said, but a lot of the edge was out of his voice.

"Maybe so, but I'd do the same if it were you in there, Marconi. This is what soldiers do."

And she believed it. She realized that *this* was why she could never believe the things that were spread about Spalding. This is how he would react in this situation. She had witnessed it during the *Purdue* simulation. He was willing to risk life and limb to save those he had sworn to protect. That was what he felt he had lived for. Lisa felt the same. Maybe that's why she had always felt such a connection to Spalding?

Lisa altered her course and began prepping for an approach. Bricks appeared to have most of the enemy fighters destroyed, disabled, or disengaging.

Then she switched back to the squad-wide channel. Bricks and his units would need to know what was happening. She'd hate for someone to decide to blow the freighter early.

"Bricks, Bravo-one, I'm going in to engage the boarding party."

"Say again, Bravo?" Bricks asked.

"I'm going in."

"Do not advise that course of action, Bravo, recommend securing the perimeter and awaiting ground units."

That would have been the smart thing to do. Unfortunately, it would also be too late to save anyone.

"Appreciate the recommendation," she said and began reducing her speed. "Keep the area secure, and I'll see you in a bit."

"Coming in behind," she heard Marconi say.

"Me too," chimed in Azarov.

"Ah, hell," said Bricks, "guess that means we're all going."

Pilots in a ground battle. What could go wrong?

Lisa couldn't help but smile. If more of them went, she felt better about the odds.

"You three take the cargo bay. The rest of us will penetrate at the various hard locks. Good thing I remembered to bring my sidearm this time."

That caused a bubble of laughter to cut through the tension. Everyone knew it was against regulation to fly without a sidearm, but the joke wasn't lost on her. She was having a seriously difficult time trying to remember when the last time she fired her sidearm even was. Would she even be able to use it?

When her mother heard about this little stunt, she was going to get an earful. So much of her life had been spent trying to be *different* from her parents. There were a lot of positive traits they had instilled in her, some bad too, naturally. The decision she had made to embrace those qualities previously was reinforced here. While her mother only cared obsessively about herself, Lisa cared deeply for her people. Enough that she was willing to risk her life to save total strangers aboard this freighter. Enough that she was willing to risk her career to right the wrongdoings leveled against her hero. Doing the right thing meant more to her than anything.

"Bravo Team, stand by for code authentication."

Lisa engaged her computer to handle that process while she lined up to approach the cargo hold. Unfortunately, there was no such thing as shielding, contrary to the hopes and dreams of science-fiction. Nothing strong enough to hold back atmosphere, at least. Which meant she had two options. Find an exterior airlock and go through the docking protocols, or land in the cargo bay and rely on her pressure suit to see her safely to the airlock.

It was a riskier proposition by far to go in through the cargo bay. But it would save her an incredible amount of time. Upwards of ten minutes to get through the entire docking procedure, all of which would be spent clamped onto the exterior hull of the freighter and a sitting duck for the remaining pirates circling the area.

Speaking of which, Bricks and his team were in a pitched battle now. Lines of kinetic fire and bursts of mini-missiles exploding flashed and fizzled across her canopy screen. Without the enhanced optics and computer tracking, she would have never seen it, everything *felt* close, but in reality, it was really freaking far away!

As long as the other pilots could keep the enemy off of them, they could sneak into the cargo bay and provide some much-needed military might in defending the citizens aboard that freighter. If they didn't, odds were the pirates would kill them all and detonate the ship with a satchel-nuke, denying recovery of the goods. Steal and disrupt, the motto of the pirate.

Could three pilots turn the tide of an all-out assault on a ship, though? That was the bigger question. Truth be told, it was a terrible idea.

The three of them swung in wide, doing a quick circuit of the freighter. The cargo bay doors were closed, obviously, but intelligence was working the issue and would open it soon. Or, she'd splatter across them and be the laughing stock of the Fleet for years to come.

That was a lovely thought.

"What's plan B?" Azarov said over the comms.

Lisa bit her lip. Was there a plan B? Ground assault crafts were considerably slower than their fighters. Plus, with the pirate's reluctance to be taken alive, they couldn't guarantee the safety of either the cargo or the crew. They just frankly didn't have any time.

"We'll cross that bridge if we get to it," she replied. "Stay mission-focused."

Red lights, tiny spinning specks of light, begin to illuminate around the main cargo bay doors. Seconds later, the doors slowly began to spread apart.

"That's our opportunity, punch it!" Lisa said and jerked her sticks in that direction.

The computer complained immediately.

<COLLISION IMMINENT>

<PROXIMITY WARNING>

On and on, the warnings went. The persistence of the warnings was annoying. This wasn't the first time that Lisa wished there was an override. Evidently, Spalding was notorious for somehow disabling his computer guidance systems. Which was utterly insane. The amount of delicate mathematical computation required to navigate space at the speeds they did had to be physically impossible for the human brain to execute. Hell, it was challenging enough doing the work the computer *didn't* handle for her.

"*SHIT!*" Marconi shouted over the comms, and a moment later, another warning blossomed on her screen.

<BRAVO-TWO HULL INTEGRITY WARNING>

She jerked her head around to look at the projection of the

space behind her. The eye-tracking system assisted her and panned the camera to give her a rear-view angle just over her shoulder instead of wholly turned around.

Marconi was knocked off course, completely out of control, venting vast plumes of gases, spontaneously igniting and extinguishing in the vacuum of space. Each puff of flame further spun his vehicle.

The craft responsible was sliding in a tight arc around to line up a kill shot.

Lisa reacted without much thought other than a desire to save Marconi.

Again, her screen filled with warnings as the gravitational forces pressed slightly on her. She executed a horizontal rotation of the entire craft, pitching the nose as she did so to line up the enemy craft. There were only seconds before the other pilot would fire the killing blow.

Lisa knew she was too far away for her main kinetic guns, and she was going too fast to reverse course, her craft effectively flying at incredible speeds *backward* directly at the looming freighter.

There just wasn't *time* to properly engage!

Don't overthink; act!

She fired *everything*!

Mini-missiles, kinetic fire, and even her single long-range rocket.

As she unleashed hell, her compensating engines fired, causing her to jerk around violently inside the cockpit.

"LISA!" Azarov shouted over the comms.

Without enough time to see if her desperate gambit paid off and saved Marconi, Lisa rolled her ship back around. Just in time to see the gaping maw of the cargo bay filling her screen. Unloading all of her payloads at once behind her had added to her velocity and altered the approach calculation she had done.

She did the only thing she could think of.

She continued her flip, so she was again facing behind her,

slammed her engines into a retro burn, maxed out the engine power. Then she ejected.

The canopy suddenly went blank, exposing the dark gray woven medium that created the rich three-dimensional view of the surrounding space and heads-up-display elements.

A snap sounded as the cockpit hull locked around her.

Then her head snapped back, and the gravitational force on her body increased *significantly!*

She had never executed an actual ejection before, although she had done it half a hundred times in the simulators. Her vision blurred and darkened at the edges, slowly encroaching on the center. Speckles of light danced across the darkness in the dark interior of the cockpit.

So intense was the gravity being exerted on her, she couldn't even raise her hands to the controls. She knew from the simulators that once clear of the now pilotless fighter, her controls would activate, and she'd be able to navigate.

That happened on her third breath from hitting the eject button.

With a quick flash, her canopy was back to showing the space around her.

A half-a-heartbeat later, her HUD was blinking back into existence.

Just in time to see the cargo bay doors flash by.

She fired the engines to slow down and try to soften her landing.

On her fifth breath, she struck the cargo bay floor of the freighter.

The world upended itself.

She vomited into her helmet.

The canopy screen errored, half the screen suddenly black and white flashing bars. The cockpit struck something else, and her direction altered again.

She screamed as she felt a sudden pain in her chest. Likely a broken rib or four, right where the harnessed pinned her tightly to the seat.

Several more minor bumps jostled her around, then the cockpit stopped.

She hung limply from the seat, the pressure of the harness causing her midsection to scream in protest.

As she hung, she counted to thirty, then reached down to undo the strap.

With her systems utterly useless, she could be anywhere. She could have ricocheted out of the cargo bay and even now be floating off into the depths of space. Or, if she were lucky, she would've come to rest inside the bay itself.

When the harness gave way, she fell face-first against the canopy and control board. The flight stick smacked painfully into her thigh.

Falling was a good sign. That meant there was gravity, and she was likely safe in the hold.

She inspected her flight suit for damage and thankfully found none. She unlatched her air source from under her seat and clipped it to her belt. It was only about 20 minutes of emergency oxygen, but that should be plenty to get her out of the cargo bay and into the pressurized portion of the ship.

A dull roar sounded outside.

Engines.

Hopefully, that was Marconi and Azarov landing safely.

Please don't let Marconi be dead!

The man was a complete asshole on his best days, but he was *her* wingman. The guilt of not being able to do enough to save him from trouble would be a death sentence for her.

Every breath hurt her ribs as she grasped the manual pressure release on her cockpit.

The cockpits were kept at very minimum pressure to avoid a blowout. Early ships had pressurized the entire cockpit, but even a tiny hole would cause catastrophic damage as the air was rent from inside the ship, from causing a pressure explosion to sucking the pilots out through holes no bigger around than the tip of their little finger. It was the latter accident that made them decide to just pressurize the helmets of the pilot and leave the cockpits mostly pressure-free.

Regardless, that little bit of pressure hissed out, the gasses becoming visible in the seams as it condensed in a rush to escape.

Then the hatch fell away.

Lisa rolled out, tears streaming down her face from the beating she took.

The cargo bay was a wreck. She had smashed through thousands of armored crates. The wreckage had flown around with such force that a considerable amount had been ejected into space. She could just make out the glittering bits of debris twinkling out into space.

The vomit in her helmet was beginning to sting her eyes.

Just the fact that she had vomit *in her eyes* made her want to vomit again.

Which would be incredibly counterproductive to the whole vomit-in-the-eyes thing.

There were stories of pilots who had vomited into their helmets. It was a common enough occurrence. But, damn if she wasn't completely embarrassed.

Two craft were settling down onto piles of crates, further crushing their contents and sending a spray of debris up around them. Lisa backed up into the relative protection of her cockpit to avoid being shredded by the flying shards and bits.

At least Marconi was alive. The entire starboard side of his craft was a blackened, mangled mess. Part of his cockpit had been exposed even. He was lucky to be alive.

A sudden thought made Lisa giggle.

They hadn't even started the *hard* part of this mission yet!

Her giggle turned into a full-throated laugh.

Which sent shocks of pain ripping through her ribs.

That just made her laugh harder.

When Marconi and Azarov approached her at a run, she had fallen to the ground, holding her midsection tightly with both arms against the pain, howling uncontrollably with laughter.

The worried look of the two faces that came running up to her only made her laugh that much harder.

"This is fucking batshit!" Marconi said, cursing a steady stream into the air between them.

Azarov just shook his head at them both.

This was a terrible idea, of that, she had no doubt.

Most importantly, though, it was the right thing to do.

In the end, that was all that mattered.

"Help me up," she wheezed into her helmet. "We've got some pirates to kill!"

CHAPTER 25

MAYBE I SHOULD have just stayed?

Helena couldn't shake that particular thought as she surveyed the *literal* sea of wastewater stretching out below her little perch.

The low-level indicator inside the helmet beeped at her again. The Protectorate helmet she was wearing indicated she was down to twelve percent remaining on the emergency oxygen tank. After that was exhausted, she'd be down to the residual oxygen in the suit, which wasn't a whole hell of a lot. Surface levels were enough to survive for a time, but it wasn't comfortable and definitely not a long-term solution. She *had* to find a safe shelter, and soon.

Skirting the half-meter-wide catwalk along the edge of the bubbling bog of stench that stretched out as far as the eye could see off to her left, she was extra sure-footed. Not only would it be terrible to fall into a sea of shit, but she had no idea if there was even a way back up onto the catwalk. The sidewalls were smooth metal riveted into the stone beneath, without a ladder or anything climbable she could see in any direction. Drowning in filth was not how she wanted to go out.

Helena cursed herself relentlessly for going off on a half-formed plan again. It was unlike her. She was a thinker, ponderously planning and plotting to guarantee success.

Ultimately, it didn't matter. If she had stayed, she would be dead soon at Bruce's orders. So, what was the difference if this little adventure killed her instead?

Dead was dead.

A rather large bubble of what she assumed was methane gas boiling up from the bowels of the holding tank popped loud enough to cause an echo.

Maybe *how* one died was rather important, on second thought.

A faint *something* flickered ahead. Some kind of light. It was very far away and quite vague, but it was the first indicator that something was changing up ahead.

Another beep, followed by an AI warning, "Warning: Atmospheric levels dangerously low."

She abandoned her careful pace and sprinted toward the light flickering like a faint star in the distance guiding her home. Hopefully.

As luck would have it, it was, in fact, a door.

Par for the course for how her day was shaping up, it was naturally locked.

Panic was just beginning to really set in now. Sure, she had been nursing a healthy dose of concern since leaving her plush prison cell, but that had matured into something a bit more frantic.

Biting her lip, Helena half turned around. There was no going back. Not enough time, even at a full sprint, she'd have to ditch the helmet long before she made it back to the pressure door.

Her hand grazed the handle of the sidearm tucked into the belt.

Could she *blast* her way through?

She withdrew the pistol and examined it. While she had technically never fired a weapon like this particular model, she had seen enough briefings to know a little about them. The EP-

517 fired a caseless kinetic charge, with a rapid rate of fire and impressive damage profile at short range. There was no way to know whether or not it would penetrate the pressure door, not without testing it.

What if it sparked?

This room was probably full of methane.

Thinking better of the plan, she holstered the weapon and instead examined the door.

There was a keypad, which required two-factor authentication like most city-service system areas, a pin, and an ident card. Even though she knew it wouldn't work, she tried the Protectorate ident card. The indicator flashed red.

Damn it!

The door itself was thick, devoid of handles, and sealed tightly. That was, she realized ruefully, the entire job of a pressure door.

Helena sighed and bent over, hands on her hips.

The indicator in her helmet flashed again.

Four percent!

This one fucking door was the only thing between her and freedom!

Another chime.

Three!

Standing, she drew the pistol in one fluid motion and fired it at the door.

The gun vibrating slightly in her hand, but that was it as far as recoil was concerned. She had expected it to buck violently in her grip. A stream of projectiles slammed into the door, puncturing it in a dozen places before it stopped. An indicator read "00" on the side, and whenever she pulled the trigger, the gun just clicked impotently.

It didn't matter; it had worked!

There were no sparks.

No explosions.

Not even any smoke.

Wind hissed violently as the pressurized side pushed atmospheric gases into the chamber.

Helena holstered the pistol again and shouldered the door. It resisted, but she felt it budge. She slammed into it again. It gave a little, the small bent fragments of attached metal groaning in protest.

"OPEN!" she bellowed into her helmet.

Her helmet buzzed at her.

"Oxygen levels depleted," the AI voice pleasantly reiterated.

Gasping from exertion, she leaned as far as she dared out over the expanse of waste and used the two-stride distance to put as much force into her next shove as she could.

Her head rebounded off the wall so hard she saw stars. Or maybe that was the lack of oxygen?

She backed up and repeated the process.

Once more.

Twice more.

On the third time, she careened off the side and fell to the metal catwalk in a heap. She just wasn't strong enough to physically force it open. If she had a bit more room for a direct running start, maybe. But she didn't.

Helena coughed a little.

The air was becoming thick, hard to choke down.

A chime sounded, and she wanted to curse at the helmet. She *knew* she was in danger! Nobody in their right mind would need a damned computer to tell them that in this situation! They would be as painfully aware of their imminent demise as she was!

The door panel above her went green suddenly. Then, oddly enough, the door swung in with a sudden puff of air and dust.

A Protectorate soldier stepped out and immediately went down on his knees next to her.

Helena went entirely still.

"Hey," the soldier said. "Are you alright?"

With her eyes closed, all Helena could do was feel him moving her around, checking her ident card, maybe?

The man cursed quietly to himself, then began to scoop her up.

She got her feet discreetly under her as he tried to bring her up into a shoulder-carry. Then, she *shoved* for everything she was worth.

The man's eyes went wide as he flew over the railing, catching it with his hips and tumbling head over heels down into the filth below.

The thick liquid made a *plop* sound, and he was gone. She waited for a moment, breathing heavily.

He did not resurface.

She ripped the helmet from her head and threw it into the water, along with the ident card and anything else she thought might contain a tracking unit.

Then she ran, gagging on the stench and lack of breathable air.

Warning lights were flickering up and down the tunnel as she ran, creating this tangerine-strobing nightmare. The walls were streaked with rust from decades of moisture build-up, which added to the hellish aesthetic. It all blurred by, her eyes watering as sobs shook her body. Simultaneous elation at being alive and abject horror over what she had done.

Little doubt existed in her mind that if she had been captured and found out, she would have been marched right back to the looming public execution as a scapegoat for Bruce and his coup.

Still, she had now murdered two of her people to save herself.

When would enough be enough?

Was she willing to sacrifice anyone for her own life? Everyone?

The hallway became her own version of purgatory. Emotion drained her every step as she half-ran, half-stumbled her way ever upward to the supposed exit.

Helena had no idea how long she had spent running when she finally burst through a door and into a large maintenance bay. The Martian landscape stretched out in its muted rust-red glory through thick glass windows. There was the sound of something breaking, and she turned her head to see a maintenance woman with her hand in the air where it had been holding the coffee mug just moments before. The mug itself, bits and pieces still spinning and clattering across the concrete floor, the liquid creating a crater-like wet splotch on the ground.

Several other occupants were now taking notice, standing and gawking.

"Governor Chu?" the woman asked, obviously rattled.

"I need your help," she rasped out, her breath raw from emotion and physical strain. "The government of Mars has been overthrown by an enemy faction through a coup. We must act quickly. They know I'm here!"

There were a dozen or so in the room, and she could hear quiet conversation floating through the open doors to her left and right. The controls which ran the city's waste reclamation facilities hummed and beeped occasionally, but otherwise, the room was quiet. Odor and heat wafted up to her nose through the seal of the suit she wore, the iron smells of blood, pungent aroma of ammonia, and foul-earthy smells of moldering lettuce. Between that and the dried blood and disheveled appearance, they probably thought she was one of the rat-people. Sewer system dwelling people, hiding for whatever personal reasons; drug addictions, on the run from crimes, homeless, or mental health challenges.

The woman exchanged a few glances with her colleagues.

"What do you need us to do, Governor?"

With heroic effort, Helena managed to hold back the violent sob that threatened to choke its way out of her guts. She did feel her lip begin to quiver as she said, "Thank you."

"Okay, folks," a man said from a chair at the controls, "we

have work to do, best to get it done."

The room suddenly burst into activity.

A blanket was brought from someplace and draped around her shoulders.

The woman, who had produced another steaming cup of rich black tea, led her by the hand over to a chair and coaxed her into sitting.

Everyone was talking at once, and the whole scene was stimulation overload for Helena. This was quite a bit more activity than she had become accustomed to over her time in captivity. The lights were overly bright, and she found herself squinting painfully at the windows and overheads.

All the noise blended together into a cacophony almost unbearable to track.

Tears welled up in her eyes again and threatened to spill out onto the floor with the rapidly evaporating tea that had been spilled.

"Governor, are you well?" a deep male voice asked.

"No," she whispered.

The man shooed everyone away and offered his hand.

When she looked at his hand, somewhat confused, he told her quietly, "When was the last time you slept?"

Not knowing what day of the week it was, she just shrugged.

"You can use my office as long as you need. There is a sink and a small private restroom where you can get cleaned up. It's nothing extravagant, mind you, but I've taken a birdbath in it a time or two myself. It'll get the job done in a pinch."

She took his hand and stood on shaky legs.

As promised, he escorted her through a hallway and into a modest office space. The restroom was little more than a converted closet, with a sink-toilet combo unit that folded out from the wall. It may as well have been Heaven.

"There's a little food in the top drawer of my desk. You're welcome to it and anything else you need."

With that, he pulled the door shut.

Helena felt a moment of panic and bolted to the door. She fully expected the door to be locked when she yanked on it. The door flung open, so strongly it slammed against the inside wall, causing a loud boom.

The man was only a few strides down the hall, and he turned. Worry blossoming on his face.

"Sorry!" Helena said in a rush, feeling the fool. "I'd prefer if the door stays unlocked. Actually, open… If that's okay?"

He furrowed his brows at her, considering.

"Whatever you need, Governor Chu, my station is yours."

He turned to leave, and Helena inhaled sharply, causing him to turn back.

"What is your name?" It felt like such a dumb unimportant question at this point, but it mattered to her.

He smiled. "DeForest."

Helena returned the smile. "Thank you, DeForest."

Chuckling, he turned and called back over his shoulder, "My pleasure, Governor. You do pay my salary, after all."

"I have one more favor to ask," she said hurriedly.

He waited patiently for her to gather the courage to voice the request.

"I need you to reach out to the resistance fighters. General Brennan or Edward McAaron, specifically. Can you do that?"

Please! She pleaded with him internally, with the Universe. Please, grant her this one thing.

"Of course," he said, shrugging slightly.

Just like that. Helena almost felt weak from the headrush of relief she experienced.

DeForest must have noticed her swaying. He added quickly, "It won't be easy, mind you. They're dug in somewhere, allegedly, and no one is even sure if McAaron is still on-world. And, as I'm sure you're aware, we are a government facility. But, we will be delicate."

Despite his assurances, she felt her guts twist into knots. Trust was in relatively short supply these days.

"Can you get me some recording equipment?" she thought out loud. "It doesn't need to be overly sophisticated, just a way I can send something out to the media?"

He pursed his lips in thought. "I am sure we have something that would work." He hesitated, drawing in a long breath. "But... Governor, please forgive me for asking this. Do you think that is wise? They will almost assuredly trace that message back to this facility and you."

"I don't plan on being here long and will not deliver it from here. I would not risk your people in this effort." She meant it, too.

"Ah, but in that, you are wrong, I'm afraid." The words were spoken pleasantly, which clashed somewhat with the subject matter. "We have already committed treason by providing aid. Our only safe course of action would have been to restrain you and call the authorities to come to pick you up. Anything else aligns us with the resistance, I'm sad to say."

That thought hadn't occurred to her. Had it really progressed to that level in the short amount of time she had been held captive? Were they *really* so far along as to be drawing definitive lines in the sand? That meant they were considering this a civil war, no longer just riots or social unrest.

"Once I'm cleaned up, I'd appreciate it greatly if you could bring me up to speed on everything that's been going on out here. My information has been somewhat limited."

"I'd imagine so." He turned to leave.

Helena left the door cracked open, going so far even as to place one of the trinkets from a nearby shelf between the door and the gap it would slide into once closed. The little barricade would do little to protect her from being locked in the room while she cleaned up, but doing something felt better than nothing.

When she entered the bathroom, she was stunned at her appearance in the mirror. She had lost an impressive amount of weight, her cheekbones were prominently visible, her eyes sunken. Her usually vibrant skin was waxen, still splotched with yellow and green bruises from her neck down. The more recent slap and punches from Bruce were livid purples and mottled red.

As she stripped down, she examined her body.

What she found horrified her.

A tapestry of discoloration and neglect.

Nothing about her body was familiar to her. Grimacing, her teeth gritted against the cold and pain as she used a washcloth to scrape off the built-up dirt, dead skin, and filth. The exposed ribs, sunken chest, and bony hips felt like a stranger under her hands.

A soft sound came from the room behind her.

Stripped to the waist, she spun and raised the washcloth over her head as if it were a bludgeon.

The woman from the control room stood there, eyes wide.

"What *happened* to you?" she breathed out the words softly, privately, glancing at the still-open door.

In her hands, she clutched a change of mismatched clothing. Old service worker uniforms from various eras or crews, it seemed, along with a change of underclothes and a beat-up-looking second-skin suit.

Lowering the washcloth, Helena could see her heart pounding in her chest in her peripheral vision. The flight or fight instinct surging adrenaline into her system out of habit now.

Thinking it best to ignore that question instead, Helena said, "What's your name?"

The woman blinked, caught off-guard by the sudden change of topic. "Lindsey."

"Thank you for your help, Lindsey." She nodded toward the clothing. "And for the clothes. You can leave them on the desk."

Helena was no prude, and the fact she was bare-chested around the other woman would typically not bother her. Except now, in her frail state, she felt incredibly self-conscious. She found she had wrapped her arms protectively around her midsection without even realizing it, an effort to retain what little pride she had left.

"Is there anything else I can do, Governor Chu?" The older woman sounded genuinely distraught. Concerned etched onto her face, causing crisscrossed wrinkles over her, much deeper smile lines. She nodded toward the mirror and the reflection of Helena in it. "Your back is filthy, dear. If you'd allow me, I can help you get cleaned up properly?"

The thought of someone touching her was like ants patrolling her flesh. She cringed in disgust and trepidation with the mere thought of it. Yet, how else was she supposed to scrape the caked-on filth from her back? She glanced over her shoulder at the reflection of her back, only to find dried blood streaked through with lines of sweat and dirt. It created a khaki, ochre, and crimson marbling over her sandstone skin.

Absolutely not!

Inside her own head, she screamed it, howled it like a caged animal, clawing and raging.

"That would be helpful, thank you." The words came from her mouth; she felt the air passing over her lips and her tongue forming the sounds. Still, her mind rebelled against it.

Lindsey set the clothes on the edge of the desk and moved forward slowly, hands raised to her chest with her palms out. Much like one might approach a wild horse.

With as much dignity as she could, Helena turned and watched the other woman in the mirror. Her touch was light, delicate, grandmotherly. This was something she had done before, evidenced by the methodical and practiced way she scrubbed first across, then down. Even going so far as to cupping the wet cloth and wringing it out occasionally in the sink so as to not spread the filth further.

"Relax, you're safe now," Lindsey said.

"No, we're not," Helena replied with a bit more force than she had intended.

Lindsey paused, scrubbing her back, brows furrowing again.

"I'm not exactly sure what the endgame is here, but they're coming after us. The UNIC is behind all of this. I'm not sure who all, or how, but they won't stop." She choked up a bit, emotion thickening her voice. "Our independence scares them. They never intended for it to happen."

The cool air stirred against her wet bare skin, and she shivered slightly. Lindsey noticed and continued her cleaning, a contemplative look on her face.

Helena looked down. "You should leave Mars." She looked at the woman's reflection square in the eyes and punctuated each word, "Get your family and get *out!*"

"No," Lindsey replied, not even pausing her work.

Helena cocked an eyebrow, bewildered.

After a moment, Lindsey continued, "I come from a family of fighters. Even if I wanted to get my family to safety, they'd refuse. I haven't even heard from my daughters in a month. I half expect they've already joined in with the resistance."

"But they'll die!" Helena protested.

"They might." Lindsey considered her following words carefully. "Running from a fight, especially one they believe in, would be worse than dying. Do you know what I mean?"

She did. Damn it all to hell, but she did!

Slowly, Helena nodded. "We will make sure it is all worth it."

"That's all we can ask of you," the old woman winked, "Governor."

CHAPTER 26

YAWNING SO FEROCIOUSLY his jaw popped, Ed swiped at the control panel to turn off the lights to his quarters.

Had it been two days ago he had last slept, or three?

Time was beginning to fuzz together.

The meeting with Rory was keeping him up at night. The rich puffed-up twat seemed reasonable enough, but Ed knew that type of person. Hell, he'd reluctantly admit to having *been* that exact person not so long ago. It was odd that he considered himself different now. When the hell had that happened, exactly?

Unfortunately, the bed in his quarters was about as soft and smooth as a bed of stacked rocks. Des promised him they would prioritize getting him some more suitable sleeping arrangements. At this point, Ed felt like that would be a waste of critically low resources. He would hardly use the damned thing at this rate, anyway.

Groaning against the uncomfortable mattress, he stretched out. Getting horizontal felt lovely, and he draped his elbow over his eyes and did his best to get comfortable.

There was a rapid pounding on the door, then it sprang open.

Ed sighed quietly.

"Sir," said a young voice, "you're going to want to come and see this."

Did he, though?

"Fine," he said, bending at the waist, quickly sitting straight up in bed. "Give me a moment to, I don't know, splash water on my face and suck some more coffee down or something."

The young man smirked, then dodged out the door.

He didn't even bother shutting it.

Well, the laying down part was nice enough. At least there was that.

True to his word, after a shot of coffee and a splash of cool water on his face plus a rub through his hair, he made his way into the corridor.

His quarters weren't terribly far from the control room.

Now that he thought about it, maybe he should just put a comfortable couch in his office there above the control room. Since he never fucking left the place anyway.

With the forces split up, there was far less traffic in the hallways. Given this was what they considered CENOPS, it was mostly intelligence agents, anyway. He wasn't entirely sure how he felt about that. The whole electronic-warfare thing was lightyears beyond him. At least shooting a gun at someone, he understood. Everything that took place in the room below his little balcony was a mystery.

When he entered the room, he knew something was up. Everyone was standing, eyes glued to the main screen. Front and center on that screen was a paused video message from a middle-aged-looking woman wearing a city-services department jumpsuit. She had a smudge of what looked like grease along her hairline. It suited her weathered face. The background was of a windowed room, and the salmon-colored steppes which surrounded the Solas Planum, the triple-shield volcano peaks of Tharsis Montes overshadowed by the massive Olympus Mons in the distance.

"Okay, everyone's so tense, might as well get on with it," he said, taking an offered chair from someone and sitting.

The video began.

"Mr. McAaron, I hope this message finds you well. We have a package for you, it was misdelivered to us by mistake. I'm sure you'll be looking for it. Mind reaching out and letting us know how to resend it? Much obliged."

The screen flickered and returned to the general intelligence overview screen, consisting of maps with various color-coded regions to signify God only knew what.

Stifling another yawn, Ed looked around the room, hoping to prompt the looming question.

When nothing was forthcoming, he rubbed the bridge of his nose with his thumb and index finger, pinching slightly. He definitely had a migraine coming on, probably from lack of sleep and overuse of stimulants. Odd, a few months back, that would have meant he had gone on a bender for a few days. Now, apparently, it was just part of being a rebellion leader. "Okay, people anyone have any idea what they're talking about? Did they get an errant delivery of goods from Gregório, maybe?"

Heads rotated, shoulders raised, eyes studied the floor.

But no mouths uttered a sound.

Ed was just about ready to lose his cool, frail though it was, when an analyst stood up. She was the one who had joined them at Vulcan, and brought some handy information along with her. Something was off with her. He had known it from the start. He could spot acting, even *good* acting. Living a life in the criminal underworld gave a person a particular instinct to sniff out acting. Most of the time. This girl knew more than she was letting on.

Which raised some pretty serious alarm bells for Ed.

"Sir, I think I found something here," she said, eyes still glued to her workstation monitor. "Listen to this," she began quoting what was written on the screen, "package missing, please return to sender, condition irrelevant, for a full refund."

Ed waited for more, hands in his lap.

The girl, Frankie, he recalled her name from looking up her file back then, hesitated and looked suddenly uncomfortable. Her gaze flickered around the room at the other analysts. Definitely someone who had been in some kind of trouble previously. She had that look of knowing something but not wanting to incriminate herself with *how* she knew that something. Ed knew that look all too well. He had to get to the bottom of this and fast. There wasn't time to screw around.

The chair groaned slightly, or maybe that was his body, as he stood. "Frankie," he paused, considering, "it is Frankie, right?"

Reluctantly, the girl nodded.

"Why don't you come with me up to my office. I am afraid I need another cup of coffee, and I'd like to hear more about these postal concerns that are keeping me from my nap."

The girl flinched subtly, blinking rapidly as she watched him turn to walk away. Maybe he had said that a bit too harshly? He had meant it as a joke, but in hindsight, it probably was in poor taste.

Making a mental note to apologize for that, he climbed the steps up to the mezzanine and entered his office space. Des, as promised, had made every effort to redecorate it exactly as Martin's office had been back on Vulcan. Which wasn't hard, as it turned out they had brought over everything from that office, it looked like.

The one notable addition he had insisted on was the old-style coffee press. Sure, modern drink appliances were incredible. Able to recreate just about anything from a database stretching back to historic drinks from ancient Rome, based on collected scientific data and references from literature. Ed had once watched as one of these machines had been serviced in his youth. The molecular "soup" used as a basis for all the generated beverages was disgusting. It appeared like a khaki-gray opaque, almost chalk-like liquid and smelled atrocious. He'd have his drinks the old-fashioned way, thank you very much.

Plus, the drinks were generally restricted from producing alcoholic beverages. Which, up until recently, had provided him with approximately eighty percent of his daily fluid intake.

As he set to work measuring out the ground coffee into the glass press, he heard light footsteps behind him.

"Go ahead and shut the door." He thought it sounded like an order. He was getting too used to talking like that these days. That simple tone of voice reminded him so much of his dad. To soften it, he quickly added, "Would you like a cup of coffee?"

"No, thank you, sir," she said, all proper military decorum.

Ed turned and looked at her, his eyebrows cocked.

He hadn't heard her talk like that before. Everything had been quiet, contemplative maybe, and reluctant. This had the practiced ease of training.

More to this one than meets the eye, that's for sure.

"Okay, well, have a seat."

The chair and clothing rustled behind him as he heard her comply. After a few minutes more, the room began to fill with the earthy aroma of freshly brewed coffee.

Taking a careful sip of the piping hot liquid, he made his way over to the desk and sat down.

Frankie sat straight-backed and confident. There was no hint of nervousness.

"Why don't we start with who you are?" Ed said, taking another careful sip.

"I'm Frankie. I went to the Kepler Academy on Luna, received my degree in Computer Technology...."

Ed waved her off, and she complied immediately.

"I've looked at your file," he said, "but nothing in that file tells me *who* you are, Frankie. It's not lost on me that you never use your last name. So, I'm assuming the one in your file is a fake?"

The last part was half question, half accusation. He wondered how she'd take it.

She sat there, contemplatively, before sighing slightly.

"Zoya."

The single word, he assumed her actual last name, was as much an admission of the lie as if she had fallen on her knees and begged to be spared. Better, actually. He would not have responded well to that show of weakness.

"Look, I get it. You know my background, I'm sure," he said and leaned back, crossing his legs, comfortably in his chair. "I want to be able to trust you, but that's hard to do when I know I'm being lied to."

The only response was a slight reddening of her cheeks.

When she didn't provide any further information, he said, "Is it that you don't trust me? Or you've done something previously? Look, we've all done things that we're not proud of. Me, probably, most of all."

"I'm Homeland."

The word hit him like a slug in the face. He rocked back as if she had struck him a physical blow.

"Not currently," she said hurriedly. Seeing his reaction, she laughed nervously. "Sorry old habits. I used to work for Homeland. Not anymore. They attempted to terminate me the hard way."

Homeland had tried to *kill* her? Was that what she was saying?

Ed suddenly felt very much out of his depths and wished Des was in the room.

What was that favorite saying of his dads? *When they have you on the ropes, smile so they know you're not scared.*

So, he did. Even going so far as to chuckle a bit.

"I came here because I had nowhere else to go," she said, "and while I was in Homeland I witnessed some things that made me believe in what you are doing here. I think this was orchestrated from the top down. Further intel acquired since joining you at Vulcan has reinforced that."

"Unless those were plants by you, to cement you as a mole in the ranks. None of it is damning information, just provocative."

"Correct, but I never claimed credit for any of those discoveries. If my motives were to gain trust or demonstrate loyalty, I did a piss-poor job of it, sir."

That much was true, he had to admit. In fact, the chief analyst had taken all the credit, even claimed to be working "round-the-clock" in an effort to get him something usable. He filed that info for a later follow up.

"Let's say I believe you for a minute," the words came out slowly, measured, calculating. "I'm not saying I am, yet. I'm saying it's possible. Do you follow so far?"

"Yes."

"What is that whole package business about?"

Frankie looked down at the hands in her lap for a moment, brows knitting together. When she looked up, there was determination in her eyes. "I believe, but have no supporting evidence to back up this claim, that Helena Chu has escaped captivity."

Ed's mind reeled with the implications. Still smiling he didn't betray his inner turmoil and asked simply, "Why?"

"That was the kind of language Homeland used when I was there. Essential people or I guess even goods, were often referred to as 'packages' and would use delivery language when there were issues. It's standard espionage to mask communications, especially if you are aware you are being monitored or suspect as much. Most people in the other room would dismiss this as a routine communication about something mundane. I can read this for what it is. Effectively, an all-points-bulletin that their VIP has escaped them."

Ed released a breath that he had held during that delivery. Could it be? Could she have escaped on her own? Trying to orchestrate a rescue mission to the very heart of Protectorate control in the capital city had felt an awful lot like a suicide mission. Sure, Brennan was pushing for it, but his motivations were suspect at best. Ed couldn't risk the lives of hundreds of his people to rescue one person. He strongly felt like that would be a tactical blunder. Every person there was a potential liability, should they be captured alive and tortured for information.

If she had escaped on her own, that was one less thing he had to worry about.

What did that mean for him and the leadership of the uprising?

What about the revenge he owed his father?

Too many questions for this moment, he realized.

"Say that was true," he leaned forward onto the desk, "how did you find that message if it was meant for the Protectorate Intelligence division?"

"Honestly, sir, one of the first things I did with Helena's hack job into the administration building was to install several unmonitored backdoors with tripwires for exactly this. They're not activated unless there are keywords used. Things like attack, deploy, location, McAaron, Brennan, VIP, and of course, package. By not being an active stream, they are more difficult to trace."

Ed stood, and Frankie followed him to his feet.

"What's the next move, then?" Ed could feel his heart thudding in his chest.

"Confirm, and make contact. We should try to get Governor Chu here as quickly as possible. There's something else, sir."

Ed gulped down the hot coffee in a rush and motioned for her to continue.

"They've made it clear in the communication that there is no capture-and-return order. Which may as well be a kill order."

Walking to the door, he set the mug down on the back shelf to see to later. "Best not waste any time." He paused before opening the door. "Your secret is safe with me, but no more bullshit between us. I want you to report directly to me. I'll tell Aslan I'm assigning you to some task force or something."

Without hesitation, she nodded.

"There's one other thing," he said. "I want you to find Laura Castor."

This may have been the best scenario for him. Having an ace-up-the-sleeve that was beholden to, and reporting exclusively to him, could be the only way he was able to get retribution for the murder of his father, especially with Governor Chu making her way back. Odds were, this would soon be her office. A part of him felt bad that everyone had taken so much time in setting it up for him just to have him be evicted.

That was a silly thought. Everyone would be grateful that the leadership was back in capable hands.

Frankie was studying him with her large, intensely calculating eyes.

"What?" he asked and gave her a mischievous grin. "You weren't expecting me to rise above my petty revenge, were you?"

"I'd not considered that eventuality at all, sir."

He decided he liked her. Quite a lot, in fact.

The two exited the room, and he started barking orders. They were maybe his last.

Better make them good!

"Someone get me a secure connection to," he realized he didn't know who that woman had been, "them!" He pointed at the paused video of the older woman on screen.

The room began buzzing with activity. Frankie glanced at him and nodded slightly when their eyes met. Then she strapped on her headset and got to work.

There was really no reason for him to be here, looming like some dark overlord, but he couldn't bring himself to leave. He had no real idea how long it would take to communicate with this other person.

"Where are they? With that background, they could be on the surface in Solas, right?"

He thought the angle was right but couldn't be sure.

Several analysts in the gaggle down below put their heads together and appeared to be doing some triangulation. Finally, one turned around.

"They're on the surface of Hellas City."

"Dispatch a personal vehicle to the approximate location," he ordered. "Tell them not to go fast, or do anything to attract attention. Just someone going to work, or something." Vehicles on the surface were fairly uncommon, with the mass transit systems between the major cities. Unlike Earth, there weren't very many "suburbs" on Mars. Everything belonged to one of the major metro areas. They'd have to risk it.

Down below the door opened, and Des walked in carrying a datapad in front of him. Ed watched as the elderly man glanced around, noting the paused video and hum of activity, then made his way to the staircase.

"Afternoon," Ed said cheerfully.

"I hope this is good news?" Des said, indicating the screen.

"I'd say so," he replied. "Proof positive I'll be out of the job soon."

It stung to say out loud, but that was the truth of it. Best be flippant about it.

Des furrowed his bushy eyebrows, glancing at the screen in confusion.

Ed leaned over to whisper quietly, "They think Helena has escaped and has been acquired by these nice folks over in Hellas."

There was a choked inhalation as Des leaned back, a shocked look on his face.

"We will know here, soon enough, if that's the case." Ed leaned against the railing, crossing his arms casually.

All of this was probably for the best. The orbital blockade was in place above them in an upper orbit, frustratingly out of reach of the ADA installations they had captured. Sure, they were safe from landing parties, but supplies were going to run out awfully quick in the major cities. Without the full support of the population, that effectively meant they'd be up shit creek without a paddle in as little as a month.

If he wasn't meant for this job, why did leaving it feel so wrong?

"Sir," Aslan said, looking up from her workstation, "we have made contact. Want me to patch them through?"

"Is that wise? Won't they be able to see where we are?"

There was some commotion down below.

"We will scramble the return feed. They will be able to hear you but not see you."

He nodded.

Within a few moments, the woman's face appeared on the screen.

"Thank you for contacting us," she said solemnly. "My name is Lindsey; I'm one of the engineers of WMS Station number two-forty-two. I'm afraid I have good news and bad news."

Isn't that always the damn case?

Ed grimaced. "Better start with the bad, then."

"Our previous communication was intercepted, and we anticipate Protectorate soldiers at any moment."

"Well, I hope the good news is excellent?" Ed swore internally. Even having discerned their location and deploying the craft before contact had been made, odds were not good they would beat the Protectorate to the site.

"I'd like to think so," she said, then she nodded off to the side of the camera and stepped away.

An emaciated face filled the screen a moment later. There was a fresh red-purple bruise forming on one sunken cheek; the eyes were hollow and red-rimmed. The woman looked terrible, all things aside. Ed found himself staring at the image in equal parts disgust, and bewilderment. Who was this shell of a person, and what good news did they have?

"Hello, Mr. McAaron. It's good to see your face again."

Ed, along with most of the occupants of the room, gasped in shocked unison.

The high cheekbones, the penetrating eyes, the voice. He knew this person. They all knew this person.

Governor Helena Chu.

"Holy fucking hell, Governor!" Ed blurted out.

Smiling sadly, Helena chuckled. "I'm sure the feeling isn't mutual, given my current state."

Something distracted her momentarily, and she nodded solemnly.

"They're telling me I don't have much time; the Protectorate is coming. I have recorded a message for you, which I hope can help in your efforts. I believe in what you're doing and have supported you as best I could from the beginning. I'll be the first to admit, given what little I knew of your character before all this started, I'm pleasantly surprised by who you've become."

Emotion rose in his throat. He felt like he should say something, some quip to alleviate the heaviness of the discussion. His brain wouldn't cooperate.

"I do not anticipate having the opportunity to say what I have to say in person, so do what you want with the message we are uploading to you now."

While her voice was strong, confident, self-assured, a tear leaked out of her left eye and quickly slid down the steep angles of her face.

"Helena," he said, "we are coming! We will get you out safely."

A warm smile spread across her features. "I appreciate that, Ed, very much." Hesitating, she bit her lip, almost looking bashful suddenly. "Keith doesn't happen to be with you, does he?"

"I'm afraid he's doing what he does best and has been out of radio contact for several hours. When we heard you were free, we broke radio silence to try to contact him. I was hoping to send him in to rescue you."

Finally, a smile actually touched her eyes. "That would have been lovely. Ah well, next time."

For one, Ed sincerely hoped there'd never be a "next time" for all of this.

"I must go. The transfer is complete." Her shoulders rolled back as she straightened and nodded so deeply it was almost a bow, "give 'em hell, President McAaron."

The feed terminated.

Hands shaking, knees weak, and feeling rubbery, Ed exhaled sharply.

Everyone in the room was looking at him, including Frankie.

"Do we know where that came from?" Ed barked.

There were some scrambling noises.

"Yes, the exact location was received during transmission."

"Do they know where we are?"

There was a crossroads before him, and the answer to this next question would determine which path he would take. Resolute in that decision, he waited.

The delay was agonizing.

"No, we were scrambled."

"Good," he said. "Scramble the fast-moving troop transports at whichever base is nearest to us."

The room exploded into activity.

"And someone get me equipment. I want wheels up in three minutes."

He wasn't exactly sure he had used the phrase correctly, but it had been said in a lot of the war movies he had seen, and liked the way it sounded. This had felt like an appropriate moment.

Des grabbed his arm as he turned toward the staircase.

"What are you doing?"

A bit more forcibly than he had intended, Ed, ripped his arm free of the grip.

"I'm going to go rescue our President." He walked away and called over his shoulder, "You coming?"

CHAPTER 27

"GET DOWN!" BRENNAN roared through the comms.

A bright flash and he found he was suddenly weightless.

Then he smashed into a stand of crates.

Something crunched in his back. It was difficult to tell if it was his spine or part of the crate. As he struck the ground and flipped end-over-end a few times, he hoped it had been the crate.

Groaning, he got to his feet.

The world lurched dizzyingly.

Several fires had been started from the battle raging inside the massive warehouse. Entire pillars of stacked crates were now writhing columns of fire. The vision was terrible in every spectrum. Smoke clogged up everything, painting everything in gray, black, and orange tones. The moving light had him jumping at every shadow. The constant barrage of EM Scatter charges made all their equipment useless.

All things considered; they were in a really tight spot.

The gunfire had come from behind them, initially.

The support unit had gotten to their planned exit route much quicker than he had anticipated. Manu and his forces were moving stealthily from the tunnel entrances, like soft-footed jungle cats, closing in on their prey.

All his attempts to call for support had been scrambled by the enemy. They were on their own, and the odds were not looking favorable.

Gunfire ripped through the crates ahead of him, angled from left to right across his vision. Screams sounded mutely from the swirling smoke.

Cursing quietly, Brennan braced against the side of a crate, trying to get his bearings. Between being spun around half a dozen times, and this cursed smoke, he couldn't tell which direction he needed to go.

Orange light flared ahead, two dark smudges in the smoke resolved into the silhouettes of soldiers. Of course, there was no telling whether the shadow-shapes were friend or foe, not with all their systems on the fritz.

"Take your team and secure the far wall in that direction. Nobody gets out, you get me?"

Brennan recognized that voice.

Marak.

One of the soldiers vanished into the smoke.

From what he could see, Marak was alone. There was no way he was without a guard detail nearby. That meant he'd have to do this as quietly as possible.

Brennan slung the rifle around to his back and drew his belt knife.

Staying in a slow-moving crouch, he kept the light between him and the backlit figure.

As he drew nearer, he increased his speed slightly, as much as was possible, with his weight transferring from heel-to-toe, rolling each foot silently on the ground.

"Hey!" Someone shouted no more than a meter from him.

Pain ripped into his shoulder a split second before the retort from a rifle sounded dully inside his helmet.

Rolling his body as it fell to the ground, Brennan launched the knife end-over-end at the figure that had fired at him. His aim was true, and it struck the man solidly in the throat, sinking to the crossguard.

Brennan smacked the ground hard. He watched as the other soldier fell backward, kicking wildly, trying to hold the blood back that was spilling from his throat.

Several dark shapes crowded around above him.

After a moment, he heard the click of a visor opening.

Then a booted foot slammed down hard onto his face.

He felt his jaw crack, sending spikes of pain radiating down his neck.

Another blow took him in the ribs.

Then an absolute fusillade of strikes rained down on him. Kicks to the head, body, groin, legs. His jaw and shoulder screamed in agony. Every time he attempted to curl up to protect his face and vital organs, hands would pull them apart.

A particular savage strike to the side of his head forced his first uttered sound, a groan.

Dots sparkled across his vision.

He needed to vomit.

That's when he heard Marak's laughter.

The man leaned down close to Brennan's face and reached up under his helmet to disengage his visor. Brennan gagged on the acrid smoke, the stench of burning plastic overwhelming the smell of blood and sweat.

Marak hacked deeply, then spit full-on Brennan's exposed face.

"Not so mighty now," Marak hissed, "are we?"

Brennan smiled.

Then slammed the boot knife he had drawn in his failed attempts to assume the fetal position, squarely through Marak's left eye. The scream that tore from him was forceful enough the heat of it wafted over him like a warm summer breeze.

That was one of the most satisfying experiences of Brennan's life.

As Marak flailed backward, the small handled knife protruding from his face, blood spraying out from a clipped artery, several soldiers disengaged with Brennan to attend their commanding officer.

One, unfortunately, had the presence of mind to pull a sidearm and draw it down on Brennan.

The first round took him directly in the breastbone. Just like he had instructed his soldiers to do half a million times. There was no pain, well, at least not any recognizable over the sheer volume of injuries he had sustained in the last few moments. They all blurred together into a numbness, his body unable to properly communicate how endangered it felt through the pain had just shut down. Shock was an odd sensation.

The next shot sounded. He couldn't even tell where he had been hit.

A third, fourth, fifth.

Gunfire exploded all around him.

Brennan closed his eyes and accepted death.

Something heavy landed on him, across his knees.

His eyes snapped open to find the soldier who had shot him in the chest, lying motionless across his legs, the back of his helmet and head a smoldering ruin. All around him, soldiers were taking fire from somewhere in the crates.

Brennan laughed. Which turned into more of a gurgle of blood. He coughed, blood filling his lungs from the injury at a rapid pace. As absurd as it was, he couldn't help laughing. Marak was on the ground, blood already slowing in a pool around his head. A wet trail of urine leaking slowly out of his pants where he had pissed himself. The treacherous coward. Good!

Everyone lost control of their bowels after they had been dead for a while. Not everyone was so scared to die they'd piss themselves, though. Brennan wasn't afraid of death. He had made a career of not looking for it terribly hard, but he had dodged his fair share of it.

A pair of hands grabbed him by the head and hauled him up.

That suppressed pain flared back to life.

He screamed, blood splattering out of his lungs like some macabre sprinkler from hell.

"Easy, friend," a familiar voice said.

Brennan turned to see Manu, helmetless, kneeling next to him.

"Come to finish the job?" Brennan asked. "Must feel good to be number one, finally."

Manu frowned, brows furrowing. "What do you mean? I always was!"

Brennan laughed again. This time it ended in painful coughing. A weight was stuck in his chest. It danced around with each cough but refused to dislodge.

Manu examined Brennan's body and the variety of injuries, spending an exceptionally long time on the chest wound.

"This is fatal without immediate surgery." A clinician's triage response, completely devoid of emotion.

"I'll just walk it off, sir," Brennan said, an old inside joke between them from their Academy days.

Another soldier ran up beside Manu, one of his special forces soldiers. He dropped a bag down next to Brennan, a field surgeon's kit.

Manu removed his body armor and began rolling up his sleeves.

"Lucky for you," he said. "I was a surgeon before I was ever a soldier."

"Bull," he coughed, gagged, laughed, choked out, "…shit!"

Then the needle slammed into his arm vein, a bit more forcibly than was absolutely necessary.

As the drugs burned into his system, Brennan said, "If you were ever a friend, please don't let them take me alive."

Manu nodded solemnly. "I will not."

Darkness fuzzed from the edges of his vision until the world was nothing more than a pinprick of orange and gray light.

Then the darkness consumed even that.

CHAPTER 28

THE ROOM WAS so quiet Bruce could hear the exhalations of those around him. He gaped openly at the screen.

Bruce was no military commander, but he knew enough to have an inkling as to how bad this actually was.

Red globs appeared on the map at various points, relatively evenly distributed throughout the Western hemisphere. Each of those represented an Air-Defense-Battery and military supply depot. All of them, within a matter of hours, had fallen to the enemy.

Then, as if it couldn't get any worse, like a coordinated orchestra of destruction, they had opened fire on the orbital blockade.

Two of the carriers had been destroyed, and countless cruisers and patrol craft.

Their satellites had been wiped from the area.

It had all gone to shit so quickly, no one had any idea what to do. Everyone had just frozen and watched the screens, too stricken to move.

Of course, Bruce had yelled himself hoarse. He had threatened, berated, degraded, and bullied anyone who would stand still long enough to listen to the tirade.

None of it helped.

All the yelling in the world couldn't stop the loss of equipment. The loss of life. And, most importantly, his personal loss of face.

So it was no surprise when Laura Castor, the brutish bitch, strolled into the General Assembly room. The swagger in her step told him everything he needed to know. She was here for his job. Maybe his life?

The thought that he should run screamed in his ears, but his pride wouldn't allow it. Not even facing death and disgrace. He wouldn't give her the satisfaction of watching him tuck tail and run.

If she lived up to her reputation of ineptitude, he'd have ample opportunity to flee. Of that simple fact, he had no doubt. She had failed miserably with the McAaron operation. Not confirming that the son had also been present. Just assuming that he was a non-issue. Look where that had landed them all!

"Good evening, Ms. Castor," he rewarded her with his most charming grin. "It is, Miss, yes?"

The glower that spilled from the ugly woman's face was priceless. Only through sheer force of will, was he able to resist laughing. Still, he felt the edges of his mouth twitch up slightly.

Like a single-minded bull, she strode right by him. Coming to a stop, much like a boulder coming to rest, at the operations desk. After looming over the analyst's shoulder for a moment, she bent over and whispered something into his ear.

Bruce didn't much care for how rigid the man suddenly became.

That kind of reaction never boded well.

"As of right now," she said, raising her voice to project over the ambient noise of the room. "I am assuming command of the Martian Colony."

Bruce smiled and crossed his arms across his chest.

Nobody referred to Mars as a Colony these days; it was offensive.

Grumbles and rumblings sounded all around the room. Laura had been in charge no more than five seconds before she had stepped in shit. This wasn't going to last long at all.

"I want field reports every fifteen minutes," she continued, meeting the gaze of anyone looking at her. "We have ground units from the Eastern Command as well, so coordinate channels and report directly to me."

Then, she turned and glared directly at him.

"Mr. Afolabi, if you'd join me in my office?"

I'd prefer not. The thought threatened his calm disposition. He couldn't help but notice the slight emphasis she put on the "*my,*" though.

"I'd be delighted!"

In actuality, he was second-guessing his options. He was much too smart to be caught without half a dozen actionable plans. Finding the most advantageous one was always the trick.

He followed her as instructed. The room was somewhat more somber than the last few hours had been. Which wasn't at all surprising, given that they had just had their collective asses beat bloody. Not to mention an unexpected shift in the power dynamic. Everyone knew what Laura Castor was; little more than a trumped-up sociopath. How she had ever been trusted by Trent and his goons, he would never understand, even if given a million years to contemplate it.

Laura waited off to the side as he walked through the open door. The lights came up as she hit the privacy switch on the windows.

"Listen, Laura, I know we," he gasped the last.

A sharp pain stung at his neck about halfway down. Followed by a deep burning sensation that blossomed from that tiny point, spreading rapidly through the rest of his body.

He clutched at his neck and stumbled a few steps further into the room. His body went deathly cold then flashed to brutally hot within a few heartbeats. He felt sweat suddenly bead on his skin.

Laura stood motionless by the now closed door, her eyes intently fastened on him. Her silence was more terrifying than threats would have been. Bruce attempted to ask a question, but he suddenly found his tongue felt three times its usual size. Like a shoe had been shoved into his mouth. So, rather than a proper question, he croaked and garbled spit onto his chin.

A new wave of cold sensation was rapidly spreading from his heart, through his chest, down his limbs, and up to his neck.

The world spun as he collapsed to the ground. Odd, he thought he had struck it somewhat hard, but he didn't feel anything at all.

Dizzyingly, he was rolled over to face up. Laura loomed over him, holding a syringe. The plunger of which was fully depressed.

"Didyoudruggggmeeee?" The words came out slurred together; his face was growing number by the moment.

She looked at him curiously. For a moment, he thought she almost looked… Sad.

"Mr. Afolabi," she said quietly. "I haven't drugged you. I've killed you."

Panic shot through him like a hot knife.

Not like this! Not in some backroom. Not poison. This was not the way he had thought he would die. This felt cheap, laughable.

He wanted to stand up, flee! Every instinct was telling him to do whatever he had to in order to get out of there. Survive another day!

Like some kind of slow-motion horror movie, Laura straddled his chest, the heat from her groin contrasting sharply with the ice-cold feeling in his chest. The look in her eyes was part madness, part desire.

Bruce tried to fight, but his body wouldn't respond.

When she placed her thumbs over his windpipe and leaned

down gently, applying pressure until his airflow was cut off, he screamed in his head. No sound came out.

He looked at her eyes; the intensity he found there was terrifying. She was absorbing every second of detail, pupils darting around examining the nuance of his fear.

A dull *CRACK* sounded in his throat as something gave way.

Laura leaned down harder.

The world began to darken around the edges.

This can't be happening!

Only it was.

When the darkness closed in, and only a pinprick of light remained, all he could see was her eyes, so close their noses must have been touching.

He felt his bladder and bowels release into the trousers of his designer suit.

Then, he felt nothing at all.

CHAPTER 29

AS SOON AS she opened the door, the impact of small-arms fire slammed right next to her head, denting the bulkhead. Lisa recoiled, breathing heavily.

The thing about boarding a ship by force was, they were generally enormous but rarely had large crews. Some ships, like the Protectorate Carriers, for instance, were like small cities. They had hundreds of military and support personnel. Freighters, on the other hand, were almost entirely automated and required very little in the way of a crew.

So, a dozen pirates could easily overwhelm a freighter crew. Some corporates deployed security forces to escort their gear. The outer belts were notorious for it, in fact. Not this one, it seemed.

Lisa and her small strike force of lightly armed pilots numbered just short of two dozen. Hopefully, that put the numerical odds in their favor in addition to the training and equipment. The not-so-lucky part was that the pirates had the proverbial "high ground" and were waiting for them at every choke point.

They had fought what felt like half a hundred minor skirmishes, slowly gaining ground on their way to the bridge.

Gunfire echoed down the halls, growing steadily closer. The battle up ahead was furious.

Marconi raised his eyebrows at her, she waved him off. She was fine.

One of Bricks pilots, she wasn't familiar with her name, unfastened a flash grenade and slung it around the corner. It clattered down the hall.

A moment later, a loud POP sounded with a light that illuminated the hallway.

All the pilots swung around the bulkheads and into the hallway, advancing at a quick but controlled pace.

They found the pirates writhing on the ground, blinded and stunned.

Marconi dispatched one, Bricks the other. Two rapid shots, one to the chest and one to the head. Expedient and efficient—the pilot way.

Another door was sealed ahead.

Lisa wanted to sigh. This process had been repeated so many times now she had lost count. At first, it had been thrilling to be *boots on the ground* fighting, for once, now it had become somewhat repetitive. Was she an idiot for wishing it was a bit more exciting?

"I'm going to pop the door," said another of the other flight team.

"Ready," Marconi and Azarov both said in unison, guns at the read.

The door popped open a few centimeters.

Gunfire slammed into it.

Marconi winced and fell back, clutching at his abdomen.

Lisa was there an instant later.

Sucking air through his teeth, Marconi gritted out, "Shrapnel from the fucking door!"

He was right; little sharp bits of twisted hot metal stuck out from his flight suit, which provided little armor. Black seeped slowly underneath. Not enough blood to be concerned with. At most, it might leave a scar or two.

As gingerly as she could, Lisa extracted all the bits she could easily access.

"You'll need to get those cleaned out when we get back, but you should be good to go."

Wincing, he took her hand and stood up.

The gunfight behind them appeared to have ended.

Two more bodies lay still at the end of the hallway.

"How many is that now?" Azarov asked.

"I was just thinking there seems to be too many of them," Bricks said, panting and sweating profusely, "that's got to already have been a dozen or more. And it seems there are quite a few up ahead. Was the crew armed?"

"Not usually," Lisa muttered. The practice was stupid, in her opinion. Just knowing you were up against an armed crew might make pirates second guess coming aboard in the first place.

Then again, maybe they'd just come with more firepower.

The group advanced to the next junction. They could go left or right.

Lisa checked her gauntlet. "Schematic says left."

"Good, everyone always goes right," Bricks puffed out. "I like being rebellious."

As a team, they rounded the corner, moving tightly, covering every angle they could.

Up ahead, the corridor split again.

"The bridge should be up ahead."

"Wait for a second," Marconi said. "Listen."

The hallway was silent.

"I don't hear anything," Bricks said.

"Exactly, the firing has stopped," Lisa said apprehensively.

Were they too late?

"Double time, then!" Bricks said, and the group moved forward at a faster pace than before.

They stacked up on the bulkhead just before making the corner.

Azarov was in the lead. He flicked his head around the corner.

When he came back around he held up two fingers, then made a gun signal.

Two armed combatants ahead, covering this approach.

From the rear came another of Bricks men. He passed them a flash grenade and hung back with the rear guard.

Azarov took it, charged it, and tossed it down the hallway.

A shout of alarm preceded the now-familiar popping sound.

As before, they swung around and charged the hall.

This time, though, gunfire ripped into them.

She heard the slugs penetrate Bricks' chest. The faintest sound of fabric tearing, followed by a hollow *THUMP*. He went down silently, not even a grunt escaping his lips. Just suddenly unable to bear his own weight.

Two others were hit, shouts of pain and alarm rang out.

The pirates had claimed the bridge and its occupants.

The group pressed on, weapons firing. The Academy trained that the best defense was an overwhelming offense.

The two who had been guarding the open door went down, taking multiple gunshot wounds.

As Lisa approached the door, she noticed one was clutching something.

She spun, grabbing Marconi, and throwing them both to the ground.

A flash of heat and light slammed her in the back.

The two went down in a heap.

Her vision blurred; she couldn't hear anything except a thumping ringing in her ears. Rough hands grabbed at her and rolled her off Marconi. He had his mouth open wide and his finger buried to the first knuckle in his ear.

The other pilots had pulled them to the side of the door, hidden from whatever remained of the enemy inside.

Sounds began to return to her, slowly. Everything sounded like she was underwater.

"Are you okay?" Someone was asking her. The face was still blurry from the tears in her eyes.

She nodded and almost vomited again. The world was set to spinning. Not unlike that night she had gotten drunk with Spalding at the bar on Luna. A night she'd rather not remember. Hopefully, the effects were not as long-lasting from a grenade.

Marconi appeared to be okay and was shoving away hands trying to help him. The dark stain on his chest had stopped expanding, she noted. That was good. She'd feel like a total asshole if she failed to assess his injuries properly.

Someone shoved an ammonia tab under her nose.

It burned her nostrils and made her recoil.

"What the hell?" she bellowed.

The pilot leaned back on his heels, looking somewhat confused.

"I wasn't unconscious dipshit, just stunned."

I mean, really, where do they find these new recruits? The thought made her sound like a cantankerous old vet, not the fresh-faced Academy grad she actually was. *Damn, I sound like my mother.*

That was a sobering thought.

Someone was yelling, she realized.

Standing, she found Marconi and several others positioned in the open door. Marconi was yelling and pointing at the ground in the room.

"Throw your weapons to the side and get on the ground!"

Whoever he was yelling at was yelling back, but she couldn't make out the words.

Stumbling a bit, she leveled her pistol and edged around the corner slowly.

Inside she found three more pirates and eight hostages kneeling with their hands behind their heads between them and the enemy.

Much like those that had come before, the pirates were dressed simply. One was in a dark navy jumpsuit, the other was in some kind of old-style combat uniform. The third was dressed casually, a dark red vest over a white second-skin and utility pants. Walking down the street, you'd not look at them twice.

Lisa had to admit she was disappointed. All the movies always made pirates out to be flamboyant characters, harkening back to the days on the Earth's oceans. These just looked like ordinary people.

Ordinary people didn't hold innocent freighter crews hostage.

Then she noticed one had a rather large bag slung over his shoulder. The way it pulled at the fabric indicated it was significantly heavy. Likely a nuclear device. The man was sweating profusely, much like Bricks had been, and kept glancing at his fellows nervously.

The one in the red vest was yelling at Marconi and pointing at the ground."Put down your guns, or we kill all of these fine people!"

He had a thick accent, one she couldn't immediately place. It made it difficult to understand. Well, that and Marconi was obnoxiously loud.

"Put down your weapons and back away!" he was shouting.

This was going to go on forever.

Lisa pulled the trigger.

The man's head rocked back sharply as the rounds took him in the face.

The other two gasped and watched the body falling backward.

That gave the others time to fire.

Their chests exploded in a spray of blood.

The crisis was suddenly over.

"Secure that bag and make sure they didn't arm whatever nastiness is waiting for us in there," she said and holstered her weapon.

Marconi was staring at her mutely, rubbing his chest wound lightly.

"What?" she asked.

He shook his head and holstered his weapon, moving over to help secure the freighter crew.

"They hadn't armed it yet, satchel-nuke. A nasty bit of work too." said one of the others, showing it to one of his wingmates, who just whistled appreciatively.

Something warm spilled from her nose. She reached up to wipe whatever it was away, only to pull her fingers back red-stained with blood. She wasn't surprised, considering her crash landing followed by some gunfire, scrambling, and grenades.

In an effort to hide it, she scrubbed her nose with the back of her gloved hand.

"I'm going to go see about radioing in a ride home."

Marconi waved his acknowledgment over his shoulder in a "shooing" motion.

Dick.

She approached the control board for the freighter, which was really just a more substantial version of her own controls, and tracked down the comms. When she reached out to flip to the Protectorate frequency, she realized her hand was shaking violently. Furrowing her brows, she raised her other hand up. It, too, was shivering.

Lisa shook her head to clear the fuzzy feeling threatening to overtake her and punched the comms button.

"Mother, Bravo-one, the freighter is secure. Requesting medical and transport services. Three KIA, several wounded. Out."

Not even waiting for a reply, she turned the comms off and braced herself against the workstation, hanging her head.

She had a pounding headache.

Footsteps approached behind her.

When she spun she found Marconi coming up the few steps

to the control section of the bridge. Behind him, the rest of the pilots were escorting the shaken crew out into the hallway.

"What was all that?" Marconi asked after turning around to see they were alone. For once, his voice was soft. He almost sounded… Concerned? Could it be? She wasn't sure she had ever heard that tone in his voice before.

"What was what?" Lisa asked back, hoping the blood wouldn't drip from her nose.

"The swooping into a ground fight? Counter-attacking a seasoned pirate boarding party? Saving me not once, not twice, but *three* damn times on one operation? There something I need to know here?" Marconi put his hands on his hips, but his tone was still reasonably civil. For him, at least.

Was there? She wasn't sure.

"Look, we're a team. I *always* got your back. No matter what. I just wish you felt the same." Lisa heard herself say, an edge of fatigue emerging. If he wanted to do this here, now, then why not. "If you're so fucking unhappy, request a transfer. I'll approve it since I'm your CO now. I've earned everything I've ever gotten. Nobody does me any favors, alright? So stow your shit!"

She was yelling at him by the end.

Marconi actually took a step back from her tirade, eyes widening in surprise.

"Damn," he said after a pause, "you just sounded a lot like your mom."

"Go to hell!" The effect was ruined because she couldn't stop the grin from twitching at her lips.

They stood there in uncomfortable silence for a minute or two.

Then Marconi nodded. "I got your back."

With that, he turned and stomped his way down the stairs and out of the bridge.

"Huh." Lisa grunted. "Well, that was easier than I thought it'd be."

Something told her getting his ass pulled out of the fire a couple times in the last hour had softened his disposition enough to be receptive to her rant. On any typical day, he'd just dismiss her and treat her like shit for trying to be upfront.

Little victories were necessary, she decided.

Azarov came skidding into the room, a worried look on his face. "You need to come and see this."

Lisa didn't like the sound of that. She jogged up to him and followed him down the corridors. The bodies of the fallen pilots were being tended to. The pirates would stay where they had dropped until a cleanup crew came aboard back at the station. Part of her felt wrong about that. They likely had families too. It was considered bad luck to handle enemy combatants. She wasn't sure when that philosophy had begun, but she didn't appreciate it. When she died, she'd like to be treated as a respected enemy.

That was the difference here, she thought. She had very little respect for pirates.

Azarov took her into a room that was obviously a mess hall and rec room. A glass pool table sat off in one corner, with a few tables bolted to the floor. It appeared like the most recent meal had been interrupted. Plates were on the floor, greasy trails of food streaking behind them like comet tails.

Lisa was just about to ask what this was all about when she saw the reason he had brought her here.

Sitting at the table, bound and gagged, head back eyes open wide and staring blankly, was Amanda Aldis. Her throat had been slit, recently by the color of her skin, just now starting to turn waxy. With the exception of being in plainclothes, much like the rest of the freight crew had been, and maybe a touch skinnier than their last encounter, she looked awfully healthy considering she was allegedly months-old worm-food.

"What the fuck?" she whispered.

"Right? That's what I said," Azarov said quietly.

Lisa circled the body wearily, almost as if it might animate spontaneously and attack them.

This made no sense at all. Amanda Aldis had died in the attack that had been the cause for Spalding's Admiral's Mast and the subsequent dishonorable discharge. But, if she had been alive at the time…

The implications were mind-boggling. What did this mean? If Aldis was alive, were there others? Why had she not come forward?

Questions piled upon questions.

Azarov watched her carefully.

"Seal this room. Don't include it in your report. We were never in here."

"But…" She held up her hand, and he trailed off, teeth clicking shut.

"Seriously, Mikhale, we don't talk about this again. I don't know what's going on here, but she was executed. I don't want to wind up like this." Or like Spalding, for that matter.

Azarov grunted, looking perplexed. "I think that's the first time you've called me by my first name."

"What?" That couldn't be true, could it? They had gone to Academy together.

He shrugged and motioned toward the door.

It was definitely time to go.

Something sinister was at work here. Now, more than ever, she felt like Spalding had been framed. Why was the question? She didn't want to ask by who. She had a sick pit in her stomach that told her she already knew that answer.

They sealed up the mess hall, leaving Amanda to be discovered by whoever, she couldn't help but get lost in her thoughts.

She had utterly botched her little experiment in espionage and still had worries her indiscretion would get found out. And yet, here she was again, going down the same rabbit hole as before. Smelling fire in the woods.

The problem was, that corpse had been proof of foul play; on multiple levels, in fact. Nothing was adding up the way it should've.

More than anything else, she was suddenly worried about Spalding's safety. Reports were he had withdrawn from public view and was somewhere on Luna if the media could be trusted. Seeing how Aldis had been dealt with, she couldn't but think that someone was cleaning up a mess. Tying up loose ends. Spalding had a way of complicating things, he was far too bright by half. That wit had painted a giant target on his forehead.

When they arrived at the airlock, the marine landing party was just breaching the airlock. Once aboard, the Captain removed his helmet and spoke briskly.

"We've removed all the portables from the exterior of the craft. Additionally, we scanned for any stowaways, and finding none, believe the ship to be secure."

"There was a satchel nuke aboard, we have disabled it, but still," she nodded meaningfully, "thought you should know."

He thumped her on the shoulder as he walked past.

Lisa found she was exhausted. Her head was still pounding, the room still threatening to topple off to the side at any moment. More than anything, she wanted some rack time.

If only she could quiet all the thoughts tumbling around inside her head.

"You and Marconi good?" Azarov asked quietly.

"Yeah, why?" she said, rubbing her temples gently.

For being a quiet guy typically, he sure wasn't acting like it today. "I saw you two getting after it lately." The words came out slowly, reluctantly. "If you two didn't figure it out soon, I was going to request a transfer. "

The words hurt, but she understood. Nobody wanted to be in a unit that had any internal conflict. You had to know that everyone had your back, without reservation.

That was one way she differed significantly from her mother,

her squad meant everything to her. Oddly, that was part of why she couldn't let go of the Spalding thing. He was the last of the Legion, officially. Arguably the greatest figher squadron in human history. And it was beginning to look more and more like they had been betrayed from the inside.

She fully intended to get to the bottom of it. Up until this point, she had dabbled at the idea. What had just happened had galvanized her resolve. Squadmates would do anything for each other. You certainly wouldn't trust suspect information. So much of what was going on with Spalding left too many question marks.

Nothing was going to stop her.

For now, she was going to wait around to see who handled the bodies.

Then she was going to hitch a ride back to the asteroid station she called home, try out her shower, and sleep for a few days.

Hell, she might even try getting drunk again.

After that, she intended to right the injustices leveled against Spalding. Regardless of the costs. There were even a few ideas she had bubbling in the back of her mind.

Lisa was engrossed in thought; she almost missed when the representatives from AGM arrived to collect the corpses.

Lisa smiled.

Her squad didn't know it yet, but they were going to make a detour on the way back.

CHAPTER 30

FRANKIE JOSTLED THE soldier next to her as she typed furiously on her datapad.

He gave her a dirty look.

Her instinct was to stick her tongue out at him. She kept that in check, albeit barely.

She could say that she had used every trick in the book. Except, half of what she was doing wasn't even in *the book*. So it felt like a poor description. She'd have to work on that at some point. Or maybe she'd rewrite the book?

Her situational overview showed two dozen fast-moving troop carriers, their entire complement of the vehicles as it turned out, streaking across the Martian landscape. They had lost contact with Station two-forty-two almost fifteen minutes ago. On their last report, Protectorate air support had surrounded the buildings. They were flying low to avoid the ADA battery in the area. That was unfortunate, with the big guns under rebel control they could blow them out of the sky, if they'd just gain a little altitude. She knew they wouldn't, that would make things far too easy.

"Aren't you an analyst?" a soldier across from her asked.

He was cute, if somewhat boyish.

"Yep," she said, only glancing up briefly to make certain he was talking to her. Not that there were any other analysts on this mission.

"What the hell are you doing out here? Do you even have a gun?" Several others exchanged incredulous looks.

She didn't, as it turned out. That was what she had forgotten in her hurry to join McAaron on this suicide rescue mission; she knew there was something. The sidearm was still on her bed back in her quarters where she had set it down.

Well, shit.

"I'm here to make sure you don't all die," she said blandly. "Now. Can you shut the fuck up for a minute so I can hear myself think?"

The young man choked out an incredulous laugh, glancing around him to see what to make of it. Had she been joking? Was she insulting him?

Neither, but she had no time to explain it.

With a few final keystrokes, she executed the program, then leaned back in her seat with a soft exhalation of breath she hadn't realized she was holding.

She wasn't shy about claiming to be bright. She could objectively say she was one of the most intelligent people she knew. Weird-smart, her family had called her. During those first few years at the Academy she had occupied her time while others attended parties or slept around in drunken stupors, with practicing hacking into the Protectorate mainframe and playing pranks on superiors.

While a bit rusty, that bit of youthful fun was shaping up to be incredibly useful at this very moment.

The program punctured a hole into the firewall of the Protectorate network. It wasn't subtle. It wasn't secretive. The attack was a bludgeon on the nose. She smirked as she thought of the apocalyptic fit Brillian would be having. Everyone at

Homeland would be losing their minds right now, trying to trace the attack.

When they attempted that, they'd find they were being attacked by almost every connected electronic device in Hellas City. At least that's what it would look like. No, she hadn't compromised every network all at once, but the attack would appear like she had. Utilizing a clever bit of ghosting scripts she had been toying with, there would be so much data to sort through by the time they had figured it all out; hopefully, this little strike team would be long gone.

Or dead.

That was a highly likely outcome as well.

Best not to think about that.

Once through the firewall, she had immediate access to everything the Protectorate had with basic security clearance. Nothing in their special operations catalog would show up, but most black-bag operations were of no interest to her, anyway.

The details of the "extraction" operation underway at WMS Station two-forty-two were visible as the active operation. Two companies of soldiers, a flight of attack drones, and a support flight of urban-assault gyrocopters. A standard threat response unit.

That told Frankie one very important thing; they were not expecting heavy resistance.

Good! Let's keep it that way.

The familiarity of the systems used by Homeland made her feel somewhat nostalgic. The clean, minimalist, efficient framework was lightyears better than the cobbled-together crap the resistance forces were using. You couldn't really purchase military intelligence software, though. She supposed she should be thankful they had programmers capable of at least cobbling together what they had. Still, it was refreshing to be back in the old systems.

Unfortunately for them, that meant she could quickly

navigate the systems.

"Hey," she shouted up to the driver, "I need you to connect me to Aslan."

The soldier seated next to the driver exchanged some quiet words with the driver, then leaned back over his shoulder. "Sorry, no can do."

"I outrank you," she shouted back. "Make that fucking call."

He turned to look at her, the ill-fitted armor bunching up comically around his fat neck.

"Fine, but it's your ass if she gives me any shit."

A moment later, Aslan was heard over the speaker. "What is it?"

"Chief, Frankie, I need you to get the ADA installation Charlie-six in grid twenty-one-sixteen, to fire at these coordinates when I say."

"Under whose authority…."

"McAaron's, shut up and do it." Frankie was quickly losing her patience. There 'was no time for this shit. A moment of silence.

The soldiers around her were all staring at her as they jostled around, armor and weapons clattering against each other.

"Okay, they're ready for the coordinates."

She gave them.

Aslan repated them back and then confirmed they were ready to fire.

Frankie watched the screen.

"Be ready," she said. "Three, two… Fire!"

A thunderous boom sounded through the armor-plated vehicle. The massive cannon firing up into the atmosphere would be heard over the entire region. Even with them being several hundred kilometers away, the sound was so loud you could feel it in your chest.

"Woah," one of the soldiers down the bench said, "that's a big ass gun!"

A moment later, the satellite feed that the Protectorate had been monitoring of the area surrounding the WMS Station glitched and terminated. *No signal.*

Frankie pumped a fist in the air silently.

Now they'd have no idea what they were up against.

The gyros and drones presented a problem. They would be able to communicate directly.

But only if the relays were working in the area.

"Frankie, what just happened?" Aslan asked.

"We disrupted their feed from the satellite. I'd recommend we take them all down, now, before they realize what we're doing." Then she addressed the passenger, "terminate the call, please."

The soldier shook his head and mumbled something inaudible but did as he was instructed.

The screen showed a flurry of activity by the Protectorate, trying to ascertain what had happened to their satellite. They'd put it together with the ADA firing soon enough, but there was nothing they could do about it. Perhaps divert another satellite to the area, but that could potentially take hours. They'd be long gone, one way or the other, by then.

"Two minutes out!" the driver shouted.

Everyone started readying their equipment.

The soldier that was across from her rolled his eyes, drew his pistol, and leaned across the aisle to hand it to her.

She took it reluctantly.

"It's hot and ready to go," he cautioned.

"Thanks," she said.

He just nodded and went back to checking his gear, then turned to the soldier on his right and started checking her gear. The same process was repeated up and down the bench seat.

For not being soldiers, they sure looked and acted the part.

This felt like a real operation! Not some half-assed rebellion full of schoolteachers and industrial machine operators.

She had never really thought this rebellion stood a snowball's chance in hell of panning out until this moment. There was an overwhelming sense of pride as she watched the men and women preparing to go do battle. Even the pudgy passenger emanated confidence. Frankie smiled.

At that moment, she decided she would give it her all.

All across the region, ADA batteries fired. Some were audible, but none with the force of the first that had fired. The analysts at Homeland had caught on and were desperately trying to evade the assaults against their satellite network. It was far too little, much too late. Within a few moments, the entire satellite grid over the western Martian hemisphere went dark.

Hoping to still have the element of surprise, Frankie started work on trying to disrupt the communications between the units on the ground and Homeland.

Unfortunately, these systems were airtight, and she quickly realized it was a no-go. Rather than waste time butting up against something impassable, she moved on to the next objective.

"Thirty seconds!"

With the pressure of time on her mind, she crashed through the systems in her way. She knew it was sloppy, but she would deal with that later. Accessing the Waste Management stations mainframe, she killed the power. That would hopefully slow the enemy down.

The vehicle lurched to a stop.

A moment of quiet fell over everyone like a cold blanket.

Then bright light spilled in from the rear doors opening.

They must've switched to in-helmet comms because without any cue she could determine, everyone suddenly started moving in an organized way toward the rear.

She was swept up in the tide.

Her datapad was jostled from her hand, clattering to the floorboard of the vehicle.

Of course, she'd prefer to have it, but it wasn't the weapon that would be most useful at this moment, so she left it where it fell.

Once out of the vehicle, she took in the building before them.

Several gyros hovered overhead, drones screaming around in a tight circle.

The WMS Station was a squat building with severely sloping edges and a flat top. Almost like a pyramid that had been sliced cleanly three or four stories up. The ground level was windowless, while the uppermost level was almost entirely windowed. Other than those features, it was a boring metal box.

Dove-gray figures swarmed around the sides of the building.

That's when the shooting started.

Heat flashed across her bare cheek as a round ripped the air near her head.

She inhaled sharply, only then realizing she had neglected to put her mask on. The cold, thin atmosphere burned in her lungs.

Frankie had neither body armor nor helmet. She was exposed to the weak atmosphere more than most. Her second-skin suit would protect her from most of the exposure, low pressure, and trace radiation.

Cursing herself for not thinking this all the way through and being distracted by waging electronic warfare and neglecting the *actual physical* violence aspects of this mission, she ducked behind the carrier she had just exited.

She looked overhead, counting gyros. There was one missing from the number she had seen on the deployment notes from Homeland.

Which meant it was on the ground.

They had Helena.

She banged the shoulder of a nearby soldier who stopped firing long enough to glance back at her. He tapped the ear plate of his helmet, indicating he could hear.

Yelling anyway, she said, "Follow me, they have Helena in custody!"

Wide-eyed, he nodded and spoke silently into his helmet.

A dozen soldiers pulled their rifles up and fell back behind the vehicle.

Trying to recall the map of the area and wishing she had her datapad, she motioned to the building. "On the backside, there is a landing pad, it's very small, but a gyro could easily navigate it. Mostly used for maintenance drones. They'll be loading her in from the rear entrance. We need to move, gyro is already on the ground!"

An older woman, maybe in her early forties, nodded gravely.

Then she made several quick motions with her hands, indicating which fireteams should go in which direction.

They dispersed.

Frankie stood there. Not sure if she should follow or stay put.

Decision made, she darted back around the corner of the transport and dove in headfirst. Her datapad was cracked from being dropped, trampled, or both. But it still functioned.

She shoved it into her chest pocket, vowing to get one of those neat wrist-worn gauntlet systems when she got back. Then she ducked out of the vehicle and ran to the next vehicle down the line, taking cover at the wheel.

Her ass hit the ground hard. She'd likely bruise.

Already her breath was coming in deep gasps. While she wasn't exactly out of shape, she certainly wasn't used to running around in low-atmo.

The firefight was a pitched battle now. Gunfire ripped across the ground all around her. This had been a terrible idea. She was no soldier. She struggled to recall if she had ever been in a fistfight, let alone a gun battle! Sure, she had training, every analyst had. But her battles were fought at desks with lattes in hand. Not like this!

McAaron was racing across the open expanse, pistols flashing with rapid-fire.

His protective detail surrounding him and laying down suppressing fire.

Frankie dashed out of her cover to join the rear of the troop.

A soldier recognized her and shoved her into the protective ring with McAaron.

They ran across to the building opposite where the bulk of the enemy soldiers had gathered, a low concrete barricade-like fence.

While they all caught their breath for a second, Frankie studied McAaron. With his fancy matched pistols, hair blowing in the Martian breeze, eyes alight with fear and exhilaration, he looked every bit the hero from storybooks.

She really hoped he lived through this.

But she kind of expected he wouldn't.

This moment had that certain gravity that she suspected "final moments" would.

As one, the team stood, and she followed just a split second delayed. They rounded the corner, two of their forward guard dropped, armor sizzling from the heat of the rounds that punctured their chest cavity.

They were dead before they hit the ground.

Gunfire exploded all around her as the rebel team returned fire.

She could tell McAaron was shouting by his body language, but she couldn't hear anything, especially not with the concussions of gunfire all around her. The rapid-fire magnetically fired rifles causing mini sonic-booms as the air popped out of their muzzles. It sounded like really loud metallic zippers being zipped continuously. *VVVVWHAAAP! VVVVWHAAAAAP!* Sounded over and over again all around her in short and long bursts.

Whenever the gunfire stopped, her ears rang tinnily.

As they turned the corner to the rear of the building, she heard a gyro fire up.

Helena was being dragged by the hair, kicking and screaming and biting, toward the gyro. The sight of that fighting spirit was inspiring, and without knowing exactly when she had raised it, she fired her pistol into the Protectorate soldier, shoving her along the landing pad.

Her shot was true; it took half the man's head off, blood splattering the withered body of Helena.

Then all hell broke loose.

Someone shoved her to the ground and lay across her protectively.

She watched McAaron run toward Helena, cowering on the ground, her hands over her ears. The rest of his unit followed, exchanging fire with the suddenly outnumbered Protectorate. When had that happened?

More Rebel soldiers spilled around the opposite side of the building. Now, stuck in a crossfire, the other soldiers were quickly struck down.

Then a sound like some prehistoric beast tore the air above them.

One of the assault gyros had fired the forward cannon.

A cloud of dust, debris, and heat filled the air where the flanking force of Rebels had been just moments before.

When everything settled, nothing but a debris-riddled patch of soil remained. Not even the concrete of the landing pad had withstood that firepower. Of the troops that had been there, not even a greasy spot remained.

After a stunned second, the troops around her pointed their rifles skyward and opened up. Tracers streaked across the sky toward the low-flying gyros. Several scored hits, but the damage was absorbed by the rugged hulls of the craft.

McAaron had reached Helena, and along with a few other soldiers, was scooping her gingerly off the ground. The image seared itself into Frankie's mind. All she could do was watch, open-mouthed, while a soldier effectively sat on her to keep her safe.

The gyro above would vaporize the small team standing out in the open.

Frankie could feel it coming.

Her guts clenched as McAaron looked skyward, directly at the hovering gyro.

Then it exploded as a missile streaked into it from the opposite side of the building.

Everyone turned.

There was no other craft in the sky to be seen. The trail of the missile arced from the ground on the other side of the building.

Someone had fired a surface-to-air missile!

To the best of her knowledge, they hadn't received anything quite like that from the pirates!

Who the hell?

Suddenly, more missiles fired into the sky.

Gyros banked hard to try to avoid being hit. Some were successful, most were not.

Fires blossomed in the sky as they exploded. Debris rained down, impacting the ground all around them. A bit of hot metal landed on her arm, searing the skin before she could peel the hot bit from herself.

Then she was being hauled to her feet again.

McAaron had rejoined the main unit, with Helena in tow.

They ran.

As they rounded the corner, Frankie felt the wind go out of her as if she had been punched in the diaphragm.

Pinning their escape vehicles from the opposite side were probably fifty Protectorate vehicles. Troops were arrayed in a defensive perimeter between them and their escape.

It was over.

They had been played.

They had known they were coming. She hadn't been that sloppy, had she?

All of this had been for nothing.

The designations on the foremost troops showed they were SPECOPS units. Not even your average soldier. They were all dead, just waiting for the bullets to fire.

The group stumbled to a breathless stop.

Their backs to the building behind them, and the troops arrayed in front of them, they were stuck between a rock and a wall of guns. The soldiers around her glanced around, desperate to find a route to escape.

McAaron looked at Helena, and Frankie felt the intent behind it despite not being the subject.

The look seemed to say, "I'm sorry it wasn't enough."

Some motion behind the two-deep line of rifles pointed at them caught her attention. Someone was striding forward. Two people, it turned out. One was a straight-backed soldier wearing the same SPECOPS gear, the other was wearing the bloodied remnants of a second-skin suit which appeared to have been cut away, the white-pink of wound-sealant contrasted with his dark, heavily muscled skin.

Red Brennan held a still-smoking but empty rocket launcher in one hand.

It fell to the ground when he saw Helena.

McAaron dropped to his knees, guns clattering noisily to the ground.

Frankie gaped.

Helena ran toward the line of Protectorate soldiers arrayed behind Brennan.

What the hell is happening?

Brennan ran to meet Helena.

They embraced, Helena practically climbing Brennan like a tree.

McAaron's shoulders shook violently, and she thought he might be sobbing. Disgust flashed through her. How *dare he* show that kind of weakness at this moment! What type of leader did that? Then, she watched as he reached up and disengaged his helmet, letting it roll off the top of his head, down his back, and onto the ground.

He was laughing. Bellowing mighty guffaws, sucking vast gulps of the thin air in between the bouts of laughter. Tears streaked down the red dust on his face making rust-colored trails like war paint. His eyes twinkled with mirth.

The laughter was infectious, and she found herself chuckling.

Everything felt suddenly surreal.

They should be dead.

Everyone knew that. It was an immutable fact. The remaining dozen or so soldiers could not escape. They'd be cut to ribbons in a matter of seconds.

Yet, here they were. Watching Helena and Brennan cling to each other like long-lost lovers. Laughing hysterically, while the straight-backed SPECOPS commander stood stoically next to them.

That was it; that was all she could take. Frankie yelled across the expanse and over the clamor, "What's going on? Who are they?"

The group of soldiers was utterly still, arrayed in an aggressive formation. They looked like some kind of sculptor's rendition of a battle scene. The fine powdery dust swirled, giving the whole scene a dreamlike look.

Brennan gently held Helena at arm's length and found Frankie in the group. There was no smile on his face, but he glanced at the SPECOPS commander at the front of his troops before saying, "An old friend."

What?

Brennan turned and went back to the embrace. That was evidently the only answer she was going to get for now.

One day, someone was going to have to explain to her what happened.

Right now, she just wanted to get the hell out of there.

That's when her datapad chirped. An insistent high-pitched repeating chirp.

She broke off her laughter instantly, bringing the pad out of her pocket, instantly focusing on the new information at hand.

<WARNO: ORBITAL THREAT IMMINENT>

She looked skyward.

Streaks of light blossomed in the air above them, from horizon to horizon.

McAaron had also broken off his laughter and was now watching the streaks.

A flash of light blossomed on the horizon, a glowing white streak racing up into the sky. A deep resounding boom sounded, the dust jumping in ripples across the ground.

The ADA battery fired again. Then again. Several muted *BOOMS* sounded from the other batteries far in the distance.

This time it hit something high in the atmosphere. An explosion blossomed like a tiny rose opening up.

McAaron scooped up his helmet and strapped it back on.

Everyone started moving and shouting over exterior speakers at once.

"WE'VE GOT TO GO," someone roared. "NOW!"

She heard them then.

Bombers.

The orbital blockade had deployed bombers.

They were going to bomb their own city!

Chaos reigned for a number of heartbeats, then she was pulling herself up onto a bench seat in a carrier opposite McAaron.

As the vehicle punched it, he ripped off his helmet, grinning wildly.

"That was fun as hell," he said and winked at her. "Can we go again?"

Laughing at him, she'd never wanted to punch someone so bad in all her life.

CHAPTER 31

THERE WERE SOME things you did, despite being bat-shit crazy, that just felt *good!* Ed thought today was going to be one of those things. Everything about their little rescue mission had been half-baked at best, relying on luck more than any kind of strategy.

The ride back had been full of adrenaline-induced whooping and hollering. Frankie had been a good sport but not quite as enthusiastic as he had been. At one point, she had even looked more likely to hit him than laugh with him. She was an odd one; that much was certain.

Once they had driven around for an extra hour, exchanging vehicles at various drop points—Frankie's idea, not his—they found themselves back at their headquarters.

They had been met by a frantic analyst, who all but bodily dragged the two of them to the control room.

The bombers had indeed dropped their payloads on Hellas City, as well as Solas and the connective tunnels between the two. The media was reporting the "terrorist" threat had been caught out in the open and eliminated by "precision orbital bombardments."

"Precision, my ass!" Ed roared.

The loss of civilian life was going to be astronomical. Entire swaths of the city were little more than smoldering rubble. The death tolls would be in the thousands at least.

There was a stir among the people in the room. Ed turned to find Helena Chu entering the room. Brennan at her side, helping hold her upright. She was a shell of her former self. Just looking at her made Ed's face hurt.

A look of abject horror had painted itself on her face as she walked in, her eyes never leaving the screen in front of her.

"Someone get the Governor a chair," Ed barked.

"Thank you, Mr. McAaron," she said smoothly, "but I much prefer to stand at this moment."

Somewhat abashed, he just nodded his head.

Ed suddenly felt like a third wheel. What could he offer over the ultimate power couple that he suddenly found in their midst? Not much.

"Do we have any numbers yet?" Helena asked.

The silence that followed was all the answer they needed.

Ed decided it would be best if he made his way out. He turned toward the stairs, only to realize he probably shouldn't go to the office in case Helena needed it. Maybe he'd go for a jog?

This feeling, more than any other, was one that Ed disliked. It reminded him too much of his childhood, always in his father's shadow. The Great Martin McAaron! Who, with bowing reverence, people would upend their pocketbooks for at a moment's notice. Ed missed his dad, but he didn't miss that feeling of never measuring up.

There definitely was no room in his life to feel that from the Governor and the General.

When Ed got to the door leading out, he paused. If anyone were to stop him from leaving, now would be the moment. He even coughed into his fist quietly, drawing a confused look from the nearby analysts. Nobody else so much as glanced in his direction.

Ah well, he tried.

He slung his sportcoat on and pushed open the doors.

The truly ironic thing: he had *liked* leading people.

Damn, if he wasn't passably good at it, too!

His had never really been an existence that had asked the big questions. The "Why am I here?" Or the "What am I meant to do?"

Now, after all this, he found he was feeling lost. Obviously he wanted to help the rebellion. He *believed* in it wholeheartedly. Not just because of his revenge, admittedly that was a huge part of it, but not the only one. People had believed in him. Followed *him!* For possibly the first time in his life, he had felt like maybe, just maybe, his father would have looked at him with pride instead of disappointment.

Ed almost stumbled as he suddenly stopped walking.

Realization dawned on him. Not only was he without a course of action, but he was also completely and fantastically destitute. Broke as a joke. Every cent had been spent toward the war effort.

A laugh bubbled up, or maybe it was a sob, and he started walking again.

Maybe he'd be able to… What? Get a *real job?*

Not likely, with his resume, not to mention being on the Protectorate's all mighty shit list.

Plus, that wouldn't solve the issue of needing to be involved with liberating Mars. And righting the wrongs done against his family.

Perhaps Brennan could make him something that didn't carry much responsibility or require much in the way of military prowess? Janitor, perhaps?

That thought didn't sit quite right.

"McAaron!" A voice shouted down the hallway at him.

Ed turned. "Ah, speak of the Devil!"

Brennan, resplendent in his blood-red armor, with his powerful strides and build. He looked like something out of ancient mythology. The thing of nightmares.

As he caught up, Ed turned, and the two walked in silence for a while.

"I dig the red," Ed finally said, unable to withstand the silence any longer. "Don't let anyone talk you out of it."

Brennan eyed him sidelong as they walked, but that was the only acknowledgment.

Inside his head, Ed sighed dramatically. More a groan than a proper sigh. He had thought they had grown somewhat close in the recent month spent together. Not friends, not really. Could someone like Keith Brennan actually have friends? What, would they cruise bars together? Play Pinochle at each other's houses? That thought almost made him laugh.

"Where are you going?" Brennan asked.

Good question. The thought was a somewhat bitter one.

"Oh, I don't know. I thought maybe I'd go into hiding somewhere. I might try to see Earth for a bit, see what opportunities there are there. Who knows?"

Brennan looked at him fully then, his brows drawn down so far they almost touched above his nose.

"No," he said. "What? You're leaving?"

"Keith, follow along! I've suddenly become redundant. Let's not let things get awkward, eh?"

Brennan reached out and grabbed him by the bicep.

DAMN, but the man was stronger than anyone had any right to be. Ed winced.

"You cannot leave," Brennan stated it plain, simple, devoid of any emotional attachment.

"That's sweet, really." Ed started to continue, but Brennan squeezed his bicep.

"No, you misunderstand me. I don't want you here for sentimental reasons. Helena cannot lead this war. Not anymore. Maybe not ever. She's too close to the people, how would she divide her loyalties? It must be you." Finally, thankfully, he released the vice-like grip on his arm. "Not even I can do the job that you have done. You've done well here. The people respect you, even fear you somewhat."

Ed did laugh then. *Fear me? More like, fear my decision-making abilities!*

"Let's go. You're needed." Brennan turned to walk back the way they had come.

Suddenly confused, Ed just stood there and watched the red figure walk, all full of purpose and self-confidence, down the hallway back to the command room.

Somewhat reluctantly, his feet began moving in the same direction as Brennan. Within a few strides, he was moving more purposefully. This is what he wanted, wasn't it? Just moments ago, he was pouting that he was no longer needed. What Brennan said made perfect sense. Helena was beaten, quite literally and figuratively. Nobody would follow her at this point, not into a fight. Brennan was still hated by many, especially those outside of the freedom fighters. All they knew was that he was the face of the Red Massacre.

The real problem with all of this was the Protectorate controlled the media. Thus, they controlled the flow of information. Whatever they said was by virtue of being the *only* information, the truth. That had to change if they had any hope of winning this conflict.

When Ed stepped back into the room, Brennan was standing behind a seated Helena. She looked exhausted, like the very thought of standing was too big of a burden to bear. She was still dressed in the dirty ill-fitting maintenance uniforms she had been rescued in.

Helena waved him over to her.

"I'm sorry if my entrance made you feel uncomfortable, Ed." Her voice matched her posture, tired and reluctant. "It was not my intention to make you feel pushed out. I meant what I said before. This is your conflict now. I am nothing more than a resource for you to call upon."

She smiled sadly. Not so long ago, she had stood at a podium expecting to be the first Martian President. How things have changed. None of it seemed fair.

"I have something that may help," she said and extended a datapad over to him. He took it gingerly, noticing the UNIC Maintenance Department stamp on the back.

Ed raised an eyebrow at her.

Helena shrugged an emaciated shoulder. "We use what resources we have available to us."

On the screen was a paused video of Helena.

He looked over to see Helena and Brennan whispering quietly to each other. Helena playfully slapped at Brennan's chest, and the big man smiled. The expression looked awkward on his chiseled features. Neither were paying any attention at all to the screen.

The rest of the room, however, watched Ed curiously.

Frowning, he hit the play button.

— — —

Helena gathered herself and spoke directly to the camera lens, tiny as it was.

"When I tell you that I've been through hell," she said confidently. "I'm not talking in metaphor. When I tell you that more of you will join me on that journey, I'm not saying it, hopefully."

She drew a deep breath, tears already threatening to spill out of her eyes.

"Up until this point, what you have heard from me has been at the behest of the UNIC and its Protectorate goons. Sent here, by President Trent, to further *personal* ambitions by him and his friends. The sadness and despair we have felt over the loss of our loved ones can only be attributed to those corrupt, backroom dealings. In an effort to forestall our *much deserved* independence, a conspiracy the likes of which the system has never seen has unfolded before our very eyes."

She paused, glancing to the side at the live audience of a few maintenance workers.

"I was forced to say things to you I did not believe, under threat of torture and worse. I was bullied into the signing of documentation and executive orders the details of which I was not made aware. It shames me to say, I was beaten for it all anyway. Tortured, starved, and beaten. Because I would not back down from what I believe to be *fair!*"

As she continued, her voice grew stronger. The quaver in it fading.

"But I escaped my captivity. And I have joined with the forces that are here, even now, fighting and bleeding for all of you. The Protectorate will stop at nothing—*nothing*—to see the colonial chains placed back on the people of Mars. Because we make them wealthy with our sweat, or blood, and our tears. Well, no more. Rise up with me. Join me in the fight. A united Mars is the one thing that scares them the most. And for a very good reason." The smile on her face was a wicked one. "We will never back down from a fight."

The feed went black.

Ed sat back and exhaled deeply.

That was likely the fiftieth time he had watched it.

He still got chills.

Through the door to his office, he could hear the buzz of activity outside in the command room. When Frankie had hacked the media server and played that video to the entire system, Ed had hoped it might give them a little breathing room.

Instead, the people had responded in a way he hadn't thought possible.

They took to the streets.

They fought.

Thousands at a time stormed Protectorate strongholds. Many

died. But eventually, they overwhelmed and overtook the few guards left to protect these stations. Some even tore off their Protectorate badges and tossed them to the ground in protest themselves! Not many, but enough to give Ed a warm fuzzy feeling.

With that one recording from former Governor Chu, the entire tide of the battle had shifted. Even while rescue crews dug through the bombed-out rubble of Hellas and Solas, battles raged across the surface of the planet. Syrtis, Alba, Elysium, all the major cities were rioting. Not just social disobedience, but a coordinated revolution.

A knock sounded at the door a moment before it was pushed open.

A red-clad figure stood looming like some ancient God of War in the threshold.

"Are you ready?" Brennan asked.

Ed stood, placing his father's heavy gold ring on his finger and buttoned his sport jacket.

There was much work to be done.

EPILOGUE

SERGEANT HEATHER UMANI watched out the dropship window as the bombers made their second pass. The Air-Defense-Artillery guns were firing down below, a steady stream of incredible firepower launching up into orbit. A particularly close explosion rocked the cabin.

It was easy to tell who was on their first deployment. Every shake or rattle would send their eyes rolling wide and wild, like a spooked horse. You could almost see their thoughts, "Is this it? Am I going to die now?"

Only they didn't.

The dropship kept flying.

She didn't worry too much about dying. Hell, it was just a daily hazard of the job to her. Nothing to get worked up about. Death was one of those things that would happen when it was meant to happen. A force of nature. Nothing you did would slow it down or stop it. Just embrace that it would come for you, eventually. And enjoy every moment between now and then.

"Alright, listen up!" Came the call from the rear of the ship.

First Lieutenant Randall James was all business, all the time. With his close-cropped hair, and boyish good lucks, it was a little disappointing. Not that she'd fraternize with a commanding officer. His attitude just made *thinking* about it disappointing. Which was somehow worse.

Private Michael Lee fidgeted with his rifle in his lap on her right. He took getting rattled to a whole new level. Why he had enlisted was beyond her comprehension. Sure, every fresh-faced recruit left a lot to be desired when it came to performance, but Lee was probably the worst soldier she had ever met.

To his right sat Specialist Pio Skanda. The mouth of her fireteam. For being lighter than her and ugly as hell, he sure did have a foul mouth on him. What he lacked in physique, he more than made up for in attitude. She had been in more bar fights to save his bony ass from a pounding than she cared to think of.

The last member of her team sat on her left, Corporal Marlon Pavel. Where Skanda was a needle-dicked-shit-for-brains, Pavel was a hulking brute of a man. A full two meters tall and easily weighing in over one hundred kilos, none of it fat. He was scary-looking. Nice as pie, though. Funny how that works out, most of the time.

The three boys were her responsibility. And she took that to heart.

Which was why she took it upon herself to lean over and yell to Stavlos.

"You need to make sure your battle buddy here maintains muzzle-awareness, or when the guns go live he's likely to shoot himself. Or you."

Stavlos, never stopping his nail-chewing, used his other hand to smack Lee upside the head. No other action was necessary.

Lt. James was walking down the aisle, making sure he had everyone's attention.

One of the soldiers down the line was drooling out the side of his mouth, helmet limply hanging by his fingers, sound asleep.

James kicked his foot and leaned down.

The soldier startled awake, looking around groggily.

"You enjoy your nap, cookie?" James roared in the boy's face.

Umani half expected the smell of urine to waft up from the back of the ship.

Everyone noticeably more attentive, James stalked back toward the flight compartment. There, two screens were activated, displaying maps of Hellas City.

"The one-two-two has been dropping payloads on Hellas for the past hour, targeting known rebel operational bases. They've done their job softening them up for us, but now we need boots on the ground to see this thing done."

A cheer went up from the more eager of the bunch. With a glare from James, it was regulated to a quick outburst.

"We'll be dropping in at four major points over the city surface structures. The mission is to retake the ADA batteries, fortify and await further instructions. If we cannot take the installations, we are to scuttle them. Each company has been provided with a DEMO SPEC and proper ordinance. Take it, or blow it."

Then he got into the nitty-gritty details, and Heather mostly tuned out.

Those details would be transmitted to her gauntlet data unit.

She got the mission.

Go in, get the big guns back, reclaim air superiority.

Copy that, L-T.

"You think we'll see Red Brennan down there?" Pavel whispered the question.

Skanda, on the other hand, didn't know how to be quiet on the best of days. "Fuck that traitor! I hope we run into him! I really do! I'll shove my muzzle so far up his ass he'll beg me to pull the trigger!"

Then he demonstrated the action in intimate detail.

Several soldiers around them laughed. Not Umani, though.

Another woman across from them leaned forward, "You had better hope you don't come across him. He doesn't take prisoners." Then she drew her thumb across her throat.

Pavel looked concerned. "He's not in Hellas, right? Word was he had left the planet?"

Umani sighed heavily. For someone so big and scary, he sure was timid. If Pavel and Skanda could swap personalities, she thought she might prefer it. The contrast was just too much sometimes.

A light flashed amber in three steady pulses.

Get suited up.

Their training kicked in, and they began readying their gear for the drop.

All their electrical locks were removed, and all up and down the benches, rifles, and helmets were activated. Gauntlet systems booted up and received relevant mission data.

Once she was prepped, she turned to Pavel and gave his systems a once over. When she was done, he checked hers. All up and down the line, a second look was given. Orbital drops were no joke. You wouldn't want your systems to be on the fritz and find out halfway down.

They checked the air seals on their suits and helmets.

Everything went green. They were sealed up.

"Alright, see you on the ground!" James barked. Then, he and his team began checking their own drop equipment. That was one of the things she respected most about James. He wasn't about to take a separate shuttle with the soft seats and cushy landings. If his troops were dropping in the hard way, so was he.

The amber light flashed two long pulses.

Everyone stood and turned to face the gangway.

A bright line of light appeared at the roof edge, toward the back of the ship.

The wind whistled and screamed out the seam, forming little eddying wisps like smoke.

Then, the compartment went silent. Not the silent like a library, but the type of silent you only got when in space. *Absolute* silence. Sure, she could hear her own breathing, even so far as the air traveling in and out of her chest. There was also the repetitive thump-thump-thump of her heart beating in her ears. But other than those internal noises, there was nothing.

It made the blood boil.

Humankind was never meant to experience the void of space.

The body recoiled at the alien nature of it.

The amber light came on solid.

"Comm check, Echo Team," Umani said into her comm.

"Echo Two, check," came Skanda's immediate reply.

"Echo Three, check," said Pavel.

"Echo Four, check," answered Lee, although he sounded out of breath.

"Lee, you check your gas mix?" Heather couldn't turn around, not now.

"I got him, Sarge," said Skanda. "Yeah, he's green down the line. Just getting ready to shit his pants on the way down."

Pavel snickered in an open mic.

Even Umani smiled.

The rampway continued lowering, intermittent flashes of yellow and blue light danced around on the interior ceiling. When the ramp was fully lowered, Mars stretched out in all its red-sanded glory below. The pops and flashes of light dancing around were other dropships and their escorts being destroyed by ADA fire.

As if to punctuate that point, the ship suddenly rocked to one side, a bright flash filling all the port-side windows.

The solid amber light turned green.

"GO, GO, GO!" the jumpmaster shouted through their headset.

Soldiers began to jump into the dark expanse of space.

Being in a line like they were, there was no choice but to go forward.

When her time came, she didn't hesitate. She welcomed the jump.

The view was incredible.

Mars had a weaker atmosphere than Earth, so orbital drops could be done without the extra layers of protection. There was just something special about being in space without a ship blocking your view.

As she plummeted down toward the planet, she was amazed at the size of this operation. All around her were dropships streaming troops into the atmosphere.

An explosion below her blinded her. Everything went black.

She flailed around for a brief moment, worried she might be permanently blinded when she realized she could still see the underlighting from her helmet. Something was on her visor. As she continued her descent, she scrubbed the thick dark liquid away. Blood, she realized. Someone had been in that ADA blast.

Hell of a way to go.

A warning beeped in her helmet.

She looked at the gauntlet system on her wrist.

<WARNO: SYSTEM FILES CORRUPT>

"Anyone else seeing this?" she said over her comms.

There was no response. Not even static.

Her systems weren't transmitting.

What the fuck? Were we hit with an EMP?

This wasn't good. Without her systems, she had no idea where to land. Even if she had paid attention to that particular part of the briefing, it would be almost impossible to know *exactly* where to land without guidance. Not only that, she'd be unable to track her relative altitude and velocity for timing her retrojets.

She had simulated drops without systems before, but it had been a while. And, frankly, she hadn't been that good at it anyway. There was nothing to be done for it except to prepare herself for a rough landing.

The atmosphere began to thicken, and sounds began to come back. The constant whine of the wind racing over her body, broken with the staccato booms and thunder of enemy fire.

Thankfully, these rebels didn't have an air force. Or they'd be sitting ducks for any combat jets.

The structures below began to glimmer as she approached. The ADA installations were easy to pick up, with giant cannons pointing at various points toward orbit. Each time they fired, it was like a ball of sunlight spontaneously burning into existence over the giant cannon's mouth before it arced far above her into the upper orbit.

A dark shape flew past her.

Followed by another.

She glanced up to see debris from a dropship twirling above her as it spun away from the explosion that had separated it from its craft.

Another bit of debris whistled past.

A sound like paper tearing filled the air below her, screams audible over the incredible noise.

A soldier had been struck by the debris, a slice clean through his shoulder, and partway through his abdomen had almost cut him cleanly into three pieces. Blood splattered everywhere as it caught the turbulent winds. The screams quickly quieted, and the body fell limply flailing with what remained of its momentum.

Umani thought she might be sick, but fought it down, thankfully. She'd never vomited into her helmet, and she wasn't about to start now.

The ground was closing in fast now. It looked as though she might be below the minimum fire line for the big guns, which was nice. Anytime the gun fired nearest her, she could feel the air pressure from it impact her chest with enough force to make her heart skip a beat or two.

No wonder they wanted those damn things back! They were brutal!

The tops of the tallest towers sped past.

She started a count.

When she hit ten, she fired her retrojets, forward-facing jets jerking her back and slowing her descent. The powerful little jets were great, except they could only carry so much fuel. They sputtered and burned out, with three or four meters left to fall.

Umani hit the ground hard, tucking at the last minute into as much of a roll as her momentum would allow. She felt a crack in her hip and knew that would hurt like a bitch later.

She had landed on a main broad avenue on the surface, situated between two large industrial complexes. When she came to a stop, she looked skyward. Troops were still dropping, but they were all over the place.

If this had gone according to plan, people would be concentrating in four areas to then spread out in force to their objectives. This looked like people were spread out all over the city, some even beyond the city limits.

Everyone must have suffered the same cat-fail as her systems had.

For all she knew, she could be alone in her immediate area.

Gunfire sounded up the street.

She fingered the safety of her rifle off and pressed up against the nearest wall.

Again gunfire echoed up the street.

She set off in that direction.

"Echo Team, Echo-one, anyone read me?"

The ground war of the Martian Revolution had just begun.

THE STORY CONTINUES…

The complete Sol Saga:
Book 1: Revolution
Book 2: Retaliation
Book 3: Revelation

AUTHORS' NOTES

The thing that has been most exciting about this journey so far is the interaction with all of you readers! I've had so many thrilling discussions with some of you. So, please, if you have enjoyed The Sol Saga thus far, reach out and say hello! I would love to hear your thoughts.

So, to you the reader, a heartfelt "thank you!" I got a smile out of writing certain sections, recalling conversations with some of you, and thinking to myself, *soandso is going to LOVE this chapter/scene/dialogue/character!* I've always been a fan of team sports, played them quite a bit when I was younger, and the feeling of having a "team" participating in this story with me has been incredibly satisfying.

My main intention with *Retaliation* was to get right into the action. While *Revolution* was a lot of setup and intrigue, this was meant to really force the situation on Mars beyond the tipping point. There's no spin that could undo the damage done. After this, there's no hope of the inevitable conflict. It's here.

Character growth is important to me, and so some of my inner-dialogues can become a bit rambling and tangential. We are getting to know characters while they're undergoing some intense changes. There are bound to be some thoughts and feelings that coincide with those changes. The Sol Saga is not just an exploration about a civil war in space—but what that does to the people who participate in such a conflict. Hopefully with some thrilling action and political intrigue that is somewhat engaging!

The other part to this whole effort that has been quite fun, has been the research. Being able to talk with current and former soldiers about their experiences, both good and bad, has been a particular highlight. I have so much respect for those who serve. I endeavor to represent proper protocols and procedures as closely as I am able, and aim for authenticity wherever possible. Obviously, I am writing about an organization that doesn't exist, in a future that hasn't happened yet. So, I'm going to stray and modify somewhat. But, the effort is there!

All the research professionals, educators, and scientists I've had the pleasure of speaking with about "the human potential" in space; you all have been incredible to spend time in chats with! In particular, I'd like to thank SFFCon (The Science Fiction & Fantasy Convention), of which I'm a part of (full disclosure). The two years I've attend this convention has been wildly beneficial to not only the world I've been building, but to my writing in general. If you're unfamiliar with SFFCon, go check it out! It's worth a look if you're into genre stories! (sffcon.com)

Finally, I'm excited to be on track to finish The Sol Saga Trilogy on target. When I set out to write this series as a debut, I was advised to start with a one-off and not something spanning multiple books. As a new author it was important to establish myself, so readers would trust me to invest their time in a series. While I recognized the wisdom of that, I was hell-bent on writing this series. So, I made a solemn promise to myself; I would finish the entire first trilogy in a calendar year. *Revolution* published on Jan 5th, 2021. I plan to publish the final book in the trilogy on Jan 5th, 2022.

So far, I'm on track to do that.

Book 2 was slightly delayed because I snuck a book I co-authored with A.K. DuBoff in between. The Cadicle Universe is SO exciting to work in, so I could not pass up the amazing opportunity to collaborate. Especially with the concept I was handed. If you haven't checked it out yet, I highly recommend it.

As usual, an extremely heartfelt thank you to my beta-readers, who keep me from going off on insanely long tangents. Trust me, there would be more without their heroic efforts. To my editors, Kaitlin and Crystal—you're both amazing! Thank you for putting up with my rampant misuse of commas. And of course, to Amy and everyone at Dawnrunner Press for the unending support and diligence you all provide. None of this would be possible without all of you, and for that I'm eternally grateful.

Buckle-up, because Book 3 is already underway, and when I say it's going to be epic, I'm not messing around! Even the outline is exciting!

With that, I'll get back to writing! Reach out, connect, and read on!

ABOUT THE AUTHOR

Native American and Californian, James Fox is a natural storyteller. After graduating from the Academy of Art in San Francisco, with a BFA in Directing, he became the Founder of Dawnrunner Inc. and has championed the company through numerous award-winning projects over fifteen years. As a writer, Fox devotes his energies to the careful crafting of compelling characters and diverse worlds.

www.thejamesfox.com

Printed in Great Britain
by Amazon

25679918R00219